The Fenwick Notes of William Wordsworth

edited by Jared Curtis

Humanities-Ebooks, Tirril, 2007

© Jared Curtis, 1993, 2007, 2008

First published in 1993 by Bristol Classical Press, a division of Gerald Duckworth & Co. Ltd.

Revised electronic edition published in 2007 by *Humanities-Ebooks.LLP,* Tirril Hall, Tirril, Penrith CA10 2JE.

Paperback editiuon published in 2008 by Humanities-Ebooks on Lulu.com.

The electronic edition is searchable and the pages of editorial commentary are hyperlinked to the pages of Wordsworth's notes. It is available only from http://www.humanities-ebooks.co.uk

ISBN 978-1-84760-004-2 Ebook from Humanities-Ebooks.co.uk
ISBN 978-1-84760-075-2 Paperback from Lulu.com

Contents

Acknowledgements	4
Abbreviations	7
Introduction	12
About the Text	29
THE FENWICK NOTES	37
Illustration [Notebook 57]:	93
Manuscript Notes	[foot of each page]
Editor's Notes	217
Glossary of Selected Persons and Places	384
Index and Recommended Search Terms	395
Index of Wordsworth's Writings	413

Acknowledgements

To Stephen Gill I owe the idea for this book and the encouragement to proceed with it. He suggested to me the notion, as he put it later in his biography (*William Wordsworth: A Life* [Oxford, 1989]), that we are unfortunate in lacking access to the Fenwick Notes except in piecemeal fashion 'amongst the mass of other notes that accompany scholarly texts on the poems'. The notes, he urged, 'are best read entire, not as a source of information merely, but as a document in Wordsworth's autobiography' (pp. 407–8). The 'real value' of the Fenwick Notes is not the details and opinions Wordsworth associated with single poems but 'the insight provided by the whole body of the notes into Wordsworth's preoccupation and fundamental concern as a poet with specific places, with the lives of lowly people, with history, and with the relation between politics, individual morality, and religion, and into his struggle to integrate his desire to celebrate the local and actual with his reluctance "to submit the poetic spirit to the chains of fact and real circumstance" (note to *An Evening Walk)*'. 'They matter', Gill argued persuasively, 'because they are a great poet's last attempt at what had been his lifelong endeavour—to record, interpret, and harmonize disparate experience' (pp. 408–9). For the first time since the appearance of the third volume of Alexander Grosart's edition of the prose in 1876 we have the opportunity in this edition to see the Fenwick Notes whole.

It is a pleasure to acknowledge the many others who lent their minds and hands to this project. Student assistants at Simon Fraser University who worked on several phases of it are Janet Bergunder, Idamay Curtis, Simi Desor, Manuela Myers-Fedorak, Sukeshi Kamra, Cam Martin,

Daniel Reid, and Nellie Villegas. For knowledge generously shared I owe a debt of gratitude to Alan G. Hill, editor of the Wordsworth correspondence, and to those scholars who have published or are preparing volumes in the Cornell Wordsworth series, but especially Paul F. Betz, James A. Butler, Karen Green, Geoffrey Jackson, Michael C. Jaye, the late Carl H. Ketcham, Carol Landon, Stephen M. Parrish, and Mark L. Reed, both for their published work and for contributions beyond the scholarship presented in their own volumes. I owe thanks as well to those who have assisted me with the volume of 'Late Poems' in this series, Jeffrey C. Robinson, Jill Heydt-Stevenson, and Apryl Denny.

I have received financial support for this project from the Social Sciences and Humanities Research Council of Canada and from the National Endowment for the Humanities, an independent U.S. federal agency. I am especially pleased to acknowledge the award of a Visiting Fellowship by the Huntington Library, San Marino, California, which made it possible for me to work in that splendid library with the assistance of its helpful staff for a period of two months. To the late Robert Woof, the late Jonathan Wordsworth, and acting members of the Wordsworth Trust I owe the opportunity to work in the Wordsworth Library and Museum in Grasmere and the permission of the Trust to publish my transcription of the Fenwick Notes manuscript. I am grateful to the editors of *Texte: Revue de Critique et de Theorie Litteraire* for permission to reprint material from my article cited in the Introduction, note 28.

Completing this project without the love, support, and encouragement of my wife Ida is unimaginable.

Jared Curtis
Simon Fraser University, 1992

In revising the text I have benefitted from suggestions made by helpful readers of the first edition. Some changes in the index and in styling were dictated by the requirements of electronic publication. The illustration of page 160 and the facing page of the Fenwick Notes manuscript has been included in this edition courtesy of Dove Cottage, The Wordsworth Trust.

Seattle, Washington, 2007

Abbreviations

A Life	Stephen Gill, *William Wordsworth, A Life* (Oxford: Clarendon Press, 1989)
Chronology: EY	Mark L. Reed, *Wordsworth: The Chronology of The Early Years, 1770–1799* (Cambridge: Harvard University Press, 1967)
Chronology: MY	Mark L. Reed, *Wordsworth: The Chronology of The Middle Years, 1800–1815* (Cambridge: Harvard University Press, 1975)
CWjr	Christopher Wordsworth, Jr, Wordsworth's nephew and author of *Memoirs* (q.v.)
DQ	Dora (Wordsworth) Quillinan
Dora W	Dora Wordsworth
DW	Dorothy Wordsworth
EQ	Edward Quillinan
EY	*The Letters of William and Dorothy Wordsworth: The Early Years, 1787–1805*, ed. Ernest de Selincourt (2nd edn, rev. Chester L. Shaver; Oxford, 1967)
Exc	William Wordsworth, *The Excursion*, ed. Sally Bushell, James A. Butler, and Michael C. Jaye, with the assistance of David García (Ithaca: Cornell University Press, 2007)
Grasmere Journals	Dorothy Wordsworth, *The Grasmere Journals*, ed. Pamela Woof (Oxford: Clarendon Press, 1991)

H at G	*Home at Grasmere, Part First, Book First, of 'The Recluse' by William Wordsworth*, ed. Beth Darlington (Ithaca: Cornell University Press, 1977)
Hayden, *Europe I*	Donald E. Hayden, *Wordsworth's Travels in Europe I* (Tulsa, Oklahoma: The University of Tulsa Monograph Series, no. 22, 1988)
Hayden, *Europe II*	Donald E. Hayden, *Wordsworth's Travels in Europe II* (Tulsa: The University of Tulsa Monograph Series, no. 23, 1988)
Hayden, *Scotland*	Donald E. Hayden, *Wordsworth's Travels in Scotland* (Tulsa: The University of Tulsa Monograph Series, no. 21, 1985)
Hayden, *Tour*	Donald E. Hayden, *Wordsworth's Walking Tour of 1790* (Tulsa: The University of Tulsa Monograph Series, no. 19, 1983)
Hayden, *Wales*	Donald E. Hayden, *Wordsworth's Travels in Wales and Ireland and Ireland* (Tulsa: The University of Tulsa Monograph Series, no. 20, 1985)
HCR	Henry Crabb Robinson
HCR Correspondence	*The Correspondence of Henry Crabb Robinson with the Wordsworth Circle*, ed. Edith J. Morley (2 vols; Oxford, 1927)
HCR Books	*Henry Crabb Robinson on Books and their Writers*, ed. Edith J. Morley (3 vols; London, 1838; rpt. New York, 1967)
HCR Diary	*Diary, Reminiscences, and Correspondence of Henry Crabb Robinson, Barrister-at-Law, F.SA.,*

	ed. Thomas Sadler (2 vols, 3rd edn; London and New York, 1872)
IF	Isabella Fenwick
JC	John Carter, Wordsworth's secretary
Journals, I, II	*Journals of Dorothy Wordsworth*, ed. Ernest de Selincourt (2 vols; London, 1959)
LB, 1797–1800	*'The Lyrical Ballads,' and Other Poems, 1797–1800, by William Wordsworth and Samuel Taylor Coleridge*, ed. James Butler and Karen Green (Ithaca: Cornell University Press, 1992)
Levin	Susan Levin, *Dorothy Wordsworth and Romanticism* (New Brunswick and London: Rutgers, The State University, 1987)
LY, I–IV	*The Letters of William and Dorothy Wordsworth: The Later Years, 1821–1853*, ed. Ernest de Selincourt (2nd edn; rev., arranged, and ed. Alan G. Hill, Oxford, 1978, 1979, 1982, 1988)
Memoirs	Christopher Wordsworth, Jr, *The Memoirs of William Wordsworth* (2 vols; London: Moxon, 1850)
Moorman	Mary Moorman, *William Wordsworth: A Biography*, 2 vols. (London: Oxford University ress, 1968)
MW	Mary Wordsworth
MWL	*The Letters of Mary Wordsworth 1800–1855*, ed. Mary E. Burton (Oxford, 1958)
MY, I, II	*The Letters of William and Dorothy Wordsworth: The Middle Years, 1806–1820,*

	ed. Ernest de Selincourt (2 vols, 2nd edn; Part I, 1806–11, rev. Mary Moorman, Oxford, 1969; Part II, 1812–20, rev. Mary Moorman and Alan G. Hill, Oxford, 1970)
Notebook	The Fenwick Note notebook, DC MS. 153
N&Q	*Notes and Queries* (London)
OED	Oxford English Dictionary
Poems, 1785–1797	William Wordsworth, *Early Poems and Fragments, 1785–1797*, ed. Carol Landon and Jared Curtis (Ithaca: Cornell University Press, 1997)
Poems, 1800–1807	William Wordsworth, *'Poems, in Two Volumes,' and Other Poems, 1800–1807*, ed. Jared Curtis (Ithaca: Cornell University Press, 1983)
Poems, 1807–1820	William Wordsworth, *Shorter Poems, 1807–1820*, ed. Carl Ketcham (Ithaca: Cornell University Press, 1989)
Poems, 1821–1850	William Wordsworth, *Last Poems, 1821–1850*, ed. Jared Curtis, with April Denny-Ferris and Jill Heydt-Stevenson (Ithaca: Cornell University Press, 1999)
Prose	*The Prose Works of William Wordsworth*, ed. W. J. B. Owen and Jane Smyser (3 vols; Oxford: Clarendon Press, 1974)
PW	*The Poetical Works of William Wordsworth*, ed. E. de Selincourt and Helen Darbishire (5 vols; Oxford, 1940–9)
PW (1841)	William Wordsworth, *The Poetical Works* (6 vols; London, 1841)

PW (1850)	William Wordsworth, *The Poetical Works* (6 vols; London, 1849–50)
PW (1857)	William Wordsworth, *The Poetical Works* (7 vols; London, 1857)
PW (1857P)	William Wordsworth, Proof pages of *The Poetical Works* (7 vols; London, 1857). Simon Fraser University Library
Recollections	Dorothy Wordsworth, *Recollections of a Tour Made in Scotland, A.D. 1803* (in *Journals* I, above)
SHL	*The Letters of Sara Hutchinson*, ed. Kathleen Coburn (London 1954).
Sonn	William Wordsworth, *Sonnet Series and Itinerary Poems, 1820–1845*, ed. Geoffrey Jackson (Ithaca: Cornell University Press, 2004)
STC	Samuel Taylor Coleridge
STCL	*Collected Letters of Samuel Taylor Coleridge*, ed. Earl Leslie Griggs (6 vols; Oxford, 1956–71)
STCN	*The Notebooks of Samuel Taylor Coleridge*, ed. Kathleen Coburn (3 vols.; New York, 1957–)
WC	*The Wordsworth Circle* (Philadelphia)
WW	William Wordsworth
Wordsworth's Hawkshead	T. W. Thompson, *Wordsworth's Hawkshead*, ed. Robert Woof (Oxford, 1970)

Introduction

1

Most readers of Wordsworth are familiar with the Fenwick Notes to his best known poems. We all recall the account Wordsworth gave in his note to *We are Seven* of the walking tour he took with his sister Dorothy and Samuel Taylor Coleridge, when *The Rime of the Ancient Mariner* was conceived and composed—'the most remarkable fact in my own poetic history and that of Mr. Coleridge'. But this and the few other familiar notes make up only a part of a much larger enterprise. The handwritten notes fill 180 leaves of a bound notebook, a labour of several months in the first half of 1843 when Wordsworth reviewed his life's work by turning over the pages of the most recent six-volume edition of his *Poetical Works* (that of 1841) and the one-volume collection called *Poems, Chiefly of Early and Late Years* (1842). For each of approximately 350 poems in these volumes Wordsworth dictated to his friend Isabella Fenwick[1] what came to mind as relevant to the reader's understanding of the circumstances of composition, the historical context, and the poet's intention.

Two recent tours with family and friends provided impetus for his composing the notes at this time. The first was in the summer of 1840 when Wordsworth, his wife Mary, their daughter Dora, Isabella Fenwick and her niece, and Edward Quillinan and his elder daughter Jemima,

---

1 Isabella Fenwick (1783–1856) was the daughter of Nicholas Fenwick, of Lemmington Hall, Edlingham, near Alnwick in Northumberland, and his wife Dorothy Forster, who was the first cousin of Henry Taylor's step-mother. Taylor's tribute to his cousin's mind and character and his account of her relations with the Wordsworths are found in his *Autobiography of Henry Taylor* (2 vols; London: Longmans, Green and Co., 1885) I, 52–8, 333–9, and II, 55–9.

travelled through the Duddon valley, visiting scenes Wordsworth had known from his days at Hawkshead School and written of in *The Prelude, The Excursion, The River Duddon,* and in a number of descriptive poems centered on Black Combe, the mountain rising west of the Duddon Sands. The second tour included his visits to Tintern Abbey in the Wye valley, and to Alfoxden and the Quantocks just before and after his daughter Dora's marriage to Edward Quillinan in the spring of 1841. This latter *'pilgrimage'* as Mary Wordsworth called it, seems especially to have renewed his sense of the immediacy of the past.[2] A few days after the second leg of this tour with Wordsworth and his family, Isabella Fenwick wrote to Henry Taylor of their visit to 'Wells, Alfoxden, &c.':

> He was delighted to see again those scenes (and they were beautiful in their kind) where he had been so happy—where he had felt and thought so much. He pointed out the spots where he had written many of his early poems, and told us how they had been suggested.

His recollection, she reported, of 'what his sister, who had been his companion here, was then and now is, seemed the only painful feeling that moved in his mind'.[3]

But there were other motives prompting his decision to compse the notes. From the first appearance of various 'memoirs' soon after the deaths of his friends Charles Lamb and Coleridge in 1834 and 1835, Wordsworth was increasingly dismayed by the inaccuracies and unfairness of publications by Thomas De Quincey, Thomas Allsop, Henry Nelson Coleridge, Joseph Cottle, James Gillman, and Thomas

---

2 In *William Wordsworth: A Life* (Oxford: Oxford University Press, 1989) Stephen Gill has given a concise and moving account of WW's last decade, taking particular notice of these origins of the Fenwick Notes (pp. 400–23). MW commented on the pilgrimage to Alfoxden in a letter to Susan Wordsworth, 15 May 1841 *(MWL,* p. 245).

3 20 May 1841; quoted in *Autobiography of Henry Taylor,* I, 338.

Noon Talfourd, to name the chief offenders.

Wordsworth wrote to Joseph Henry Green, the executor of Coleridge's estate, in mid-September 1834 to complain of De Quincey's first (of four) articles on Coleridge in *Tait's Magazine*,[4] urging Green to take steps to 'put a check upon communications so injurious, unfeeling, and untrue'.[5] In a letter to Edward Moxon, 10 December 1835, Wordsworth reluctantly acknowledged the appropriateness of Moxon's publishing Lamb's lively and colourful letters, though he had himself selected and severely edited those he contributed, and complained with some bitterness about the 'speedy' publication of Coleridge's letters in Thomas Allsop's *Letters, Conversations, and Recollections of S. T. Coleridge* (1836) and of the indiscretion of Henry Nelson Coleridge in publishing *Specimens of the Table Talk of the Late Samuel Taylor Coleridge* (1836) while the persons Coleridge 'talked' of were still living.[6] In a letter to Henry Crabb Robinson, 1 November 1836, Wordsworth expressed his misgivings about Joseph Cottle's 'disingenuous[ness]' in preparing his *Early Recollections; Chiefly Relating to the Late Samuel Taylor Coleridge* for the press (1837), and in the same letter he reacted to Robinson's warning that Coleridge's *Literary Remains* (the first volume, edited by Henry Nelson Coleridge, appeared in 1836) would inevitably contain references to Wordsworth's 'tragedy' by telling him, partly in jest, to 'say nothing about it, lest destruction [of the manuscript of *The Borderers*] should follow'.[7] On 17 May 1838 Wordsworth wrote to Daniel Stuart, publisher of the *Morning Post*, correcting the statement made by James Gillman in his *Life of Samuel Coleridge* (1838) that Wordsworth was employed by the *Morning Post*, with Coleridge and

---

4 September, October and November 1834 and January 1835 issues.
5 *LY*, II, 740.
6 *LY*, III, 134–5; *HCR Correspondence*, I, 315; 20 December 1835.
7 *LY*, III, 312–14.

others, as a contributor to its 'Literary department': for his own part, he wrote, stretching the truth to emphasise the point, 'not a word of mine ever appeared…in any Newspaper, Review, Magazine, or Public Journal whatsoever', and he added that the book is 'full of all kinds of mistakes'.[8]

In 1840 Barron Field completed his 'Memoirs of the Life and Poetry of William Wordsworth, with Extracts from his Letters to the Author', in which he hoped to defend the great poet's work from its detractors. Though Wordsworth wrote to Field to thank him for his efforts, in the same letter he dismissed them as 'either superfluous or injurious' and objected to Field's inclusion of 'notices of me by many others' that were 'full of gross mistakes, both as to facts and opinions'. Wordsworth went to considerable pains to talk Field out of publishing the 'Life', elaborately correcting and commenting on his manuscript and eventually dissuading him and his publisher, Edward Moxon, from going to press.[9] While he was successful in this instance, he must have realised he could not always be so and that any 'memoirs' of him would be certain to be rife with error. In fact, Field continued to revise his manuscript with the intention of publishing it after the poet's death

8 *LY,* III, 589–90.

9 Barron Field (b 1786), whom Wordsworth had met in 1815, began writing his 'Life' of Wordsworth in Gibraltar in 1836, but when he presented it to Moxon for publication, Moxon sent it on to Wordsworth and it was left in manuscript at Wordsworth's request. The manuscript is in the British Library; it is edited and introduced by Geoffrey Little as *Barron Field's 'Memoirs of Wordsworth'* (Sydney, Australia: Sydney University Press, 1975); see William Hazlitt's essay on WW in *Spirit of the Age* (1825), WW's letter to Field, 16 January 1840 (*The Letters of William Wordsworth: A New Selection,* ed. Alan G. Hill, Oxford: Oxford University Press, 1984, p. 299); see also E. Moxon to WW, 14 January 1840 (Wordsworth Library), WW to E. Moxon, 10 January 1840 (*LY,* II, 996–7), H. G. Merriam, *Edward Moxon, Publisher of Poets* (New York. 1939; rpt. 1966; p. 148), and William S. Ward, 'Laying Bricks and Squaring a Circle: Wordsworth and Two of His Literary Friends' *WC,* XII, 1981: 15.

but Field predeceased Wordsworth by four years and his manuscript remained unpublished until 1975.

Perhaps one such 'injury' in Wordsworth's eyes was Field's repetition of Hazlitt's earlier published notice of Wordsworth's *The Borderers,* written, Field said, 'when he was young'. In correspondence, published within months of their deaths, both Lamb and Coleridge had also referred to some of Wordsworth's early work that was still in manuscript. As early as 1838 Wordsworth considered making an arrangement to publish this poetry among his 'juvenilia' after his death, and, feeling perhaps that there was some risk it might find its way into print without his authorisation, or, more important, without any opportunity for him to revise it for publication, he prepared it for the press himself. *The Borderers* and *Guilt and Sorrow* appeared in 1842, a half-century after they were composed. In his Advertisement to *Guilt and Sorrow,* standing first in the 1842 volume, and in the end-notes to *The Borderers* and several other poems, Wordsworth invited his readers to consider biographical and historical matters affecting the poems. But he remained circumspect nevertheless, failing to explain, for example, that as they stood in 1842 the two long poems were markedly different from the ones he wrote in the 1790s.[10] While the pilgrimage to the Quantocks and to the still isolated and peaceful Alfoxden in 1841 stirred the poet's recollections, those very memories may have prompted him to tell the true story for himself, especially with regard to his narrative of the Alfoxden years,

---

10 Gill comments on the misleading nature of WW's encouragement of 'historical, even biographical interpretation, of these poems' in *A Life* (pp. 404–5). In a letter to John Kenyon in the summer of 1838 WW mentioned the existence of the 'Salisbury Plain' poem and speculated on posthumous publication (*LY,* III, 616). For full accounts of WW's revision of his early manuscript poems before their publication see the editions of *The Borderers* and *The Salisbury Plain Poems,* both in the Cornell Wordsworth series, edited respectively by Robert Osborn (Ithaca: Cornell University Press, 1982) and Stephen Gill (Ithaca: Cornell University Press, 1975).

an account so badly bungled by Cottle in his *Early Recollections Chiefly Relating to the Late S. T. Coleridge, During His Long Residence in Bristol (1837).*

2

Though inspired by revisiting the Wye and Alfoxden, and impelled as always by his own motivation to shape the reception of his work by readers, he was actively encouraged to compose the notes by the circle around him, principally by his daughter Dora and Isabella Fenwick. From Dora's childhood Wordsworth enjoyed his daughter's playfulness and accepted her mischievous chiding, continuing in this pattern as she grew into a confident young woman who adored her father but who was not in the least in awe of him.[11] Even after her marriage, while transcribing the Fenwick Notes, she seized the opportunity to correct his misstatements (about the date of his gift of Applethwaite to her) and to scold him for his severity (with the poet George Crabbe). Dora had long been involved in her father's verse-making as listener, subject, copyist, critic, and transmitter (through her letters to friends and relations). Wordsworth tells us that she appropriated one of his sonnets as a valentine to send to her cousin Christopher Wordsworth.[12] Indeed, her name figures almost as prominently in the dictated notes as those of her aunt Dorothy, her mother Mary, and her father's friend Coleridge.

---

11 R. P. Graves in his *Recollections of Wordsworth* (in *The Afternoon Lectures on English Literature* [Dublin, 1869]) said of Dora as a young woman that 'in a bright mood, she would playfully contend with him [slightly misquoting WW's *The Triad*, ll. 123–4], "happy as a bird / That rifles blossoms on a tree, / Turning them inside out with arch audacity"' (p. 308). Frederika Beatty gives brief biographies of Dora and Isabella Fenwick in her *William Wordsworth of Rydal Mount, An Account of the Poet and his Friends in the Last Decade* (London: J. M. Dent & Sons Ltd, 1939; pp. 58–72, and 89–100).

12 'Why art thou silent! Is thy love a plant'; see WW's note to 'Sonnet 53', notebook p. 50.

In adult life Dora accompanied her father on several tours, the incidents and scenes of which were the inspiration for his poetry making. She was herself keenly interested in the historical and particularly the domestic origins of her father's poems, as evidenced by her many letters enclosing her father's poems and containing accounts of the circumstances under which they were composed. She had a profound effect on the scope and tone of the notes through her role as audience for her father's poetry—in the past as a much loved daughter and touring companion, in the present in her newly married state and living away from Rydal Mount, and in an imagined future clouded by her uncertain health.

Without the presence and encouragement of Isabella Fenwick, however, it is unlikely that the notes would have been composed at all. She first signed the visitors' book at Rydal Mount in June 1831, though she probably met the poet a year or two earlier through her cousin Henry Taylor. She spent months at a time there as guest of the Wordsworths in subsequent years, and came to live in Ambleside in 1838 in order to be close to her friends at Rydal Mount. In August of that year she wrote to Henry Taylor that Wordsworth often visited her cottage, Gale House in Ambleside, as a 'refuge' from the crush of up to thirty visitors a day at Rydal Mount, and for a month he and Mary Wordsworth were her guests there in February 1839. They conversed for hours at a time but Wordsworth also read or recited to her portions of the *Prelude,* which he was then revising. And he included her in the small circle of 'familiar friends' who were permitted to read the manuscript of this still private autobiographical poem.[13]

Isabella Fenwick often walked with Wordsworth among the nearby

---

[13] WW uses the phrase 'familiar friends' in the Fenwick Notes. IF read other manuscripts as well, including DW's record of the tour of Scotland (1803) and MW's journal of the continental tour (1820). See *Correspondence of Henry Taylor*, ed. Edward Dowden (London, 1888) pp. 93–8.

valleys and fells surrounding lakes Windermere, Rydal Water, and Grasmere, places that held so many associations with his poetic life. This woman of intelligence, imagination, and strong affections in some sense filled the gap left by Wordsworth's sister Dorothy in her debilitating illness, and his letters to her in her absences from Ambleside and Rydal Mount vividly attest to his deep affection for her.[14] Trusted and loved as much by Mary and Dora as by Wordsworth himself, she was the mediating force which made possible Dora's marriage to Edward Quillinan in April 1841, a union to which Dora's parents, especially her doting father, were initially very strongly opposed.[15] Later when work proceeded with the publication of *Poems, Chiefly of Early and Late Years,* Isabella Fenwick undertook to copy large portions of the text for the printer. A few months after, probably late in 1842, Wordsworth accepted her offer to take dictation of the notes to his poems, and they commenced work in January 1843. In March Isabella Fenwick reported working hard on the notes and they completed their work six months later at 'Rydal Mount June 24th. 1843. St. John Baptist Day', as she noted at the close of her transcript. Among those outside the immediate family, and many within it, there was no one better qualified for such a task, no one so in tune with its aims and its spirit.[16]

---

14 See *A Life,* p. 402. Gill suggests that IF also compensated WW for the loss of his friend and sister-in-law, Sara Hutchinson, in 1835.

15 From the spring of 1839, when she was living in Bath, Isabella Fenwick took an active part as adviser to Dora Wordsworth and Edward Quillinan, and intercessor with her father and mother. See IF to Dora W, 18 April 1839, Wordsworth Library manuscript (WL MS A Fenwick).

16 WW mentions IF's direct influence on the creation of the notes several times in the text, the final time as he began the long note to the *Excursion:* 'Something must now be said of this Poem but chiefly, as has been done through the whole of these notes, with reference to my personal friends, & especially to Her who has perseveringly taken them down from my dictation' (notebook p. 158).

In his comments on *The Cuckoo-Clock* Wordsworth remarked that the notes were 'chiefly undertaken' for her.[17]

Although Dora and Isabella are quintessentially the audience for Wordsworth's dictated notes, his wife Mary and his sister Dorothy are often in his thoughts as he reviews his life's work. Mary must have been present for much of the dictation and on at least one occasion redirected the course of his reflections from the solitude of composition to the claims of social duty.[18] And he often pays her tribute by singling out the poems addressed to her—for example, the fine series of love poems written in 1824, 'Let other Bards of angels sing', 'How rich that forehead's calm expanse', and 'Oh dearer far than life and light are dear'. In other notes he acknowledged both her presence to his mind and her contributions during the composing process. After noting that *Liberty* and *Humanity* were originally composed as one piece, WW admitted that Mary 'complained of [the poem] as unwieldy & ill proportioned; & accordingly it was divided into two on her judicious recommendation'. He also acknowledged her contribution of the 'two best lines' in 'I wandered lonely as a cloud'.[19] As for Dorothy, although she could take no part in the process of creating her brother's notes, she is a continuing force in these pages, both in the clarity of his remembered past and in a present darkened by her mental illness.

The two different editions Wordsworth used while dictating the notes, as mentioned above, were *Poetical Works* (London: Moxon, 1841) and *Poems, Chiefly of Early and Late Years* (London: Moxon, 1842). In 1845, when he published the one-volume, double-column *Poems,* he integrated the pieces published in the 1842 edition into the various

---

17 Notebook p. 153.

18 See the opening paragraph of the note to *The White Doe of Rylstone,* notebook p. 65.

19 Notebook pp. 91–2, and 26.

classes of the *Poetical Works,* but meanwhile *Poems* (1842) was sold as a seventh volume in the 1841 set. It should be kept in mind that, while he mentioned most of the poems in these volumes, he did not annotate every one. The reader can determine whether Wordsworth declined to comment on a particular poem found to be missing from the Fenwick Notes by noting if it appeared in the 1841 or 1842 editions. A brief account here of Wordsworth's choices and omissions will give a sense of his general practice.

He made only indirect reference to the several Prefaces and other prose sections of these volumes. For the most part he did not draw attention to the class of poems he was discussing except where its classification bore directly on a particular poem, or, in the case of sonnets, when he felt obliged to explain the origin of his interest in the form. He made some comment, if only to note the date of composition, on each of the poems in the first two volumes of the 1841 edition, proceeding from Poems Referring to the Period of Childhood through Poems of Imagination. But when he came to the third volume he selected poems from each of the groups—Miscellaneous Sonnets, the several Tours, Sonnets Dedicated to Liberty, and Inscriptions—for particular annotation. He followed this pattern with the fourth volume, choosing poems for comment from *The River Duddon, The White Doe of Rylstone,* the Itinerary Sonnets, and *Ecclesiastical Sonnets.* In volume five most of the Poems of Sentiment and Reflection and those in *Yarrow Revisited* drew a response, but Wordsworth was less thorough with the remaining pieces, those from the 1833 Tour, Evening Voluntaries, Poems Referring to Old Age, and Epitaphs. At this point, turning to *Poems, Chiefly of Early and Late Years,* he commented at some length on *Guilt and Sorrow* and *The Borderers* and on the miscellaneous pieces found in this volume, but he omitted reference to *Sonnets on the Punishment of Death,* the only titled group of poems totally overlooked. Finally, he turned his attention to the poem for which he composed the most detailed annotations, *The Excursion,* in the sixth volume of the 1841 edition.

3

Once she had completed her task, Isabella Fenwick, in her diplomatic way, may have invited Mr and Mrs Quillinan to perform the service of copying her original notes into a leather-bound folio notebook for use by family and friends. In any event Edward Quillinan, who had assisted with some of the dictation earlier in the year, undertook to re-transcribe the first eighty-six pages soon after Isabella Fenwick's departure in June. Dora Quillinan took up the pen, mid-sentence, and finished her share of the copying on 25 August 1843, as she noted at the foot of the last page of the notebook.

Wordsworth's aims in the Fenwick Notes were broadly interpreted by those who inherited the notebook, and his notes were put to various uses that he might not have countenanced were he alive at the time. Indeed, the history of the notes after his death is of interest in understanding the part they have come to play in the image of the poet we now receive. Isabella Fenwick seems to have had possession of the Quillinans' copy of the notes from sometime after August 1843 until several months after Dora's death in July 1847. She may have held them with the intention of keeping them out of Wordsworth's hands, for in a letter to Edward Quillinan of 11 February 1848 she forewarned him of the arrival of the notebook he and Dora had transcribed:

> By the post this day I have forwarded "The Notes["] it will be a satisfaction to hear you received them safe—I put *private* on the letter that should you receive it in Mr or Mrs W's presence you

should not begin to read it—and that on account of these *notes*—for on Mr W's being reminded of them—he would immediately wish to see them and you might have some difficulty of getting them again[,] not that there would be any design of keeping them from you but because he would *intend* to *add* to them—At any rate it is well to be prepared to deal with the case[;] it would be very desirable that he should add to these Notes in which case you could offer your assistance to him.—dear Mrs W. said something in one of her letters about the papers I had[;] I then made no answer[,] now I can say they are *yours*[.] I always said that what I did was for Dora—and now they fall to your course—[20]

Isabella Fenwick's unstated motive for withholding the notes from Wordsworth may have been her reluctance to deepen his continuing grief over the loss of Dora, a subject she would have avoided raising with Quillinan, who was himself in mourning for his wife's death and felt excluded by her father's sorrow.[21] By placing the notes in Quillinan's hands, she may have meant to provide him with an opportunity to overcome the barrier that had developed between grieving father and husband; she seemed to think he might approach the poet on ground they both shared—their interest in presenting Wordsworth's poems to readers in the best light. But Wordsworth did not add to them, though Quillinan himself made a number of annotations and at some point, probably after Wordsworth's death, Mary Wordsworth read them through, or had them read to her—for by this time her eyesight was very poor—and made a few pencil revisions and comments.

Mary Wordsworth's interest in Isabella Fenwick's 'papers', mentioned in the letter of 11 February 1848 quoted above, no doubt stemmed from Wordsworth's decision about this time to commission

---

20 Notebook pp. 91–2, and 26.
21 See Beatty, pp. 69–70, and Gill, *A Life,* p. 420.

Christopher Wordsworth, Jr, his brother's son, to write a brief memoir to be published with his autobiographical poem (*The Prelude*) after his death. This choice of biographer, whether made by Wordsworth alone or participated in by the family, was a great disappointment to Quillinan, for it is clear from his correspondence with Isabella Fenwick that he believed that 'the task of writing [Wordsworth's] Life' would 'be confided' to him and that he had been unceremoniously 'set aside' by the Wordsworths 'in their pecuniary arrangements' in general, and in particular in their choice of the poet's biographer.[22] In the summer of 1849 Christopher wrote to Isabella Fenwick to request the loan of her original manuscript of the notes, but she in turn wrote to Quillinan, asking him to respond, if he wished, by loaning to Christopher what was now the only copy of the notes.[23]

Nearly a year later, shortly after the poet's death, Quillinan formally agreed to turn them over, indicating in a letter to Henry Crabb Robinson

---

22 EQ to IF, 25 July [1849] (Wordsworth Library manuscript). The choice of CWjr seems to have been in the minds of MW and DW well before the formal agreement was made, for, according to CWjr in a letter to Mary of 13 September 1850, 'many years earlier' his two aunts invited him 'from time to time ... to come and stay at Rydal, to write his life' (WL 1/11/51). And indeed some sheets of his notes of WW's conversation, probably dating back to 1834–5, survive among papers in the Wordsworth Library.

23 IF to EQ, 21 July 1849, and EQ to IF, 25 July 1849 (Wordsworth Library manuscripts). The phrasing in IF's letter suggests she retained no copy of her own of the notes: 'being with him (Dr W)—I thought it well to tell him that the notes I had taken from Mr W's dictation and which had been mentioned to him—I had given to you as what I was sure the beloved Dora for whom I had taken them would have wished I should—that they had been transcribed by *her* and *you* in the book which now contains them—but that should he (Dr W) ever want to see them with reference to the notice of his Uncle[']s life which it was understood he was to write I was sure you would allow him to see them'. None of her original transcription of the dictated notes survives (for discussion of a fragmentary copy she made from the Quillinan copy see the section 'About the Text' below).

on 11 May 1850 that he still intended to use them himself, if not for a 'Life' then for an edition of Wordsworth's poems:

> I have given [Dr Christopher Wordsworth] those precious Notes; to be dealt with at his discretion, and then returned to me. But what if he uses them all up? Patience! It would have been as well perhaps to have left him to write the Life, and me to edit the unpublished Poem [the *Prelude*], and to use my treasure of Notes as I might think proper with you for a check. But you and I wd probably have agreed to print those Notes entire. Perhaps he will do so; for I have not told him not[.]²⁴

But not until October 1850, six months later still, did Quillinan send Christopher the notes for use in the *Memoirs*, and even then only under the stringent condition that Christopher return the original and any copies he made, so that no 'complete copy' should 'exist in any other hands than my own'.²⁵ He also specified, on behalf of Mary Wordsworth, that Christopher was 'to give anything, or everything, that may illustrate the Poet in the Man—but to exclude all that is not

---

24 *HCR Correspondence*, II, 731, EQ to HCR, 11 May 1850. By 20 May 1850 he had made the best of his loss by claiming to HCR that there were 'many reasons ... why I am content not to be saddled with the responsibilities attached to the office of a faithful chronicler' (*HCR Correspondence*, II, 739).

25 EQ to CWjr, 29 October 1850 (Wordsworth Library manuscript). In May EQ signed a formal statement describing his understanding of the arrangements the family was now making for 'an ample biography' to be written by CWjr to supersede the latter's earlier approved plan to produce a 'short sketch' to preface the poem on 'the Growth of My Mind', the *Prelude,* now being put in readiness for publication by John Carter (Wordsworth Library manuscript, dated 16 May 1850). The understanding between WW and CWjr dates from 1847 when WW signed, and MW witnessed, a statement authorising CWjr to 'prepare for publication any notice of my life' and to be furnished by 'family executors and Friends' with any needed information. Two copies of this agreement survive among family papers in the Wordsworth Library; see also *MWL*, pp. 324–5, and *HCR Correspondence*, II, 728.

necessary to that object'.²⁶ Though Quillinan was acknowledged for his contribution to *Memoirs* by its author in his Preface, he died before any of his own plans to make use of his 'treasure of Notes' were fulfilled.²⁷

In the two volume *Memoirs,* published late in 1850, Christopher Wordsworth did reproduce most of the Fenwick Notes, though he rearranged and edited them to suit his purposes in his account of his uncle's life. The notebook was returned to Quillinan, however, as promised, and was used again by John Carter when, acting as one of the executors of Wordsworth's estate, he included the Fenwick Notes as headnotes to individual poems in the collected edition published by Edward Moxon in 1857. In 1876, the notebook was owned by Quillinan's daughters, Jemima and Rotha Quillinan, who loaned it to Alexander Grosart for his edition of Wordsworth's *Prose,* where he published it entire, but with his own alterations and some rearrangement.²⁸ The Fenwick Notes have been available to readers of modern editions only in the narrow confines of page notes and end notes to each poem. They are here presented whole in a form as close to the original manuscript as print will allow.

4

In his note to the second poem to *Lycoris* Wordsworth apologised for his 'egotism' by saying he was writing these notes 'for my familiar

---

26 So EQ reported to HCR on 21 May 1850 *(HCR Correspondence, II,* 740).

27 In CWjr's complicated negotiations over the profits from *Memoirs* with MW and her two sons, John and William, CWjr offered EQ a 6th of the proceeds from the volume (an equal third with John and William of MW's half; CWjr to EQ, 2 September and 9 September 1850, WL 1/11(29).

28 In this Introduction I have made use of revised portions of my article, 'The Making of a Reputation: John Carter's Corrections to the Proofs of Wordsworth's *Poetical Works* (1857)' *Texte* 7 (1988) pp. 61–80. For a full account of later treatments of the Fenwick Notes by Carter and others see my article.

friends & at their earnest request' (notebook p. 88).²⁹ In another note he called the notes his 'minutiae' (*Personal Talk,* notebook p. 41). But as he began the task he referred more generally and confidently to 'thoughtful readers into whose hands these notes may fall' (*Lucy Gray,* notebook pp. 2–3), and, though he strays into gossip (as his scribes are prone to notice), and quarrels with prevailing political opinion, his underlying purpose is to link place and time and incident with the workings of his own mind, to bind the days 'each to each'—one of his sustaining interests in a long career of poem-making. Another interest of equal duration and intensity was to apply in these notes the same discursive pressure that he brought to bear in 'Advertisement', 'Preface', 'Prelude', and 'Essay Supplementary', all of these explanatory statements attached to the several collections of his poems, to prepare the mind of the sympathetic reader to receive them in a true spirit.³⁰ Finally, though less a purpose than a consequence of this reflective exercise, he brought his thoughts and feelings to bear on current and recurrent issues of social, religious and political urgency—the meaning

---

29 Stephen Gill continues the story of the Fenwick notes through the nineteenth century in his study of the rise and flowering of Wordsworth's significance to the Victorians. The young Matthew Arnold, for example, was among the 'friends' permitted by the Wordsworth family to read the manuscript notebook after the poet's death (*Wordsworth and the Victorians,* Clarendon Press: Oxford, 1998; p. 177).

30 Scott Simpkins, in 'Telling the Reader What to Do: Wordsworth and the Fenwick Notes' *(Reader: Essays in Reader-Oriented Theory, Criticism. and Pedagogy* 26 [1991] pp. 39–64), criticises WW's propensity to manipulate the reader's response to his poems through the Fenwick notes, though a significant part of Simpkins' argument rests on his misunderstanding of both the immediate context of the creation of the notes and the history of their use. It is not true, for example, that WW intended to give the notes a prominence calculated to 'manipulate' his readers by positioning them 'as prefatory indexes to the poems' (p. 59); it is true that after his death his nineteenth-century editors, notably John Carter, his personal secretary and literary executor, and William Knight, did give them that prominence.

and use of the past, the place of ordinary people in a rapidly changing society, the growth of the towns in industrial England, the dwindling of ancient customs and knowledge, the onslaught upon the imagination by utilitarian manufacturing practices, as well as by similarly single-minded educators, politicians, and religious leaders, and much more. Yet, in all this, he maintained a unified voice and an equanimity that make accessible this important document in the record of a poet's life-work.

About the Text

The text of the notes is transcribed from the manuscript of the Fenwick Notes in the Wordsworth Library, Grasmere. This leather-bound notebook (DC MS. 153) was copied from Isabella Fenwick's notes by Dora Wordsworth Quillinan and Edward Quillinan in July and August 1843. For an account of the occasion for composing the notes and their intended use see the Introduction.

My purpose in this edition is to present a reading text of the notebook that retains as much of its informal appearance as is possible in print. Accordingly I have kept indigenous linguistic features like spelling, punctuation, abbreviations, and visual features like paragraphing and superscripts, and have emended the text only where clarity or consistency break down and where scribal errors occur. For example, local spellings have been preserved while what appear to be misspellings have been corrected. As they provide some of the informal character of the manuscript notes, ampersands have not been expanded. However, for clarity of presentation, underlined characters have been converted to italics throughout. The copyists' habitual abbreviations ('w^h.' for 'which', for example) have been retained, though any that might not be obvious are expanded in the editorial notes. Double quotation marks ("…") in the manuscript have been retained.

Occasionally the copyist used initials to represent personal names, a practice Wordsworth himself often followed in his letters and published works. Where the context does not make the reference clear, the full name is given in the editorial notes.

As explained in the introduction, it is not clear that any of the corrections and additions to the notebook, by the Quillinans and in a few instances by Mary Wordsworth, were initiated by, approved of, or even seen by Wordsworth. However, from its inception the document was a socially generated one: Wordsworth formed his thoughts in the presence of and dictated his words to Isabella Fenwick, whose notes, almost immediately after she had departed from Rydal Mount, were then transcribed by Edward and Dora Quillinan, whose transcript was later corrected and supplemented by the Quillinans and by Mary Wordsworth (Dora died in July 1847, Edward in July 1851 and Mary in January 1859). I have therefore seen fit to include all of the corrections and additions to the notebook in some form, if not in the text itself then in editorial or manuscript notes to the text.

In general I have accepted corrections and additions into the reading text proper if (a) they seem to emanate from Wordsworth, the principal clue being that they appear in ink, or (b) they seem to provide a reasonable solution to a crux. In most cases ink corrections seem to have occurred almost immediately upon transcription of the document and can be presumed to result from the copyist consulting either Isabella Fenwick's notes or Wordsworth himself. Some of the pencil corrections supplied by Edward Quillinan were vetted by Mary Wordsworth after her husband's death and are used where appropriate, as are those entered by Mary herself, probably after 1850. Additions to the notebook that can be determined not to have been dictated by Wordsworth are given only in the editorial notes, including the one instance in which Dora incorporated her own supplementary anecdote into the note she was transcribing. Scribal revisions and words and phrases deleted by the copyists are recorded in Manuscript Notes at the foot of each Notebook page: 'Written at Alfoxden' on notebook p. 3, for example, is recorded in the Manuscript Notes as 'Written at Alfoxden *revised from* Written at Allfoxden', indicating a correction in ink on this page of the notebook (the phrase *in pencil* is added where appropriate). The editor's emendations are also listed here.

Edward Quillinan copied the text from notebook p. 1 to mid-way down 86; Dora Quillinan carried on from mid-sentence on p. 86 to the end, where she added a testimonial to her completion of this copy and the date, 'this Twenty fifth day of Augst 1843'. Unless otherwise stated, the hand in each section is assumed to be that of the primary copyist. Wherever possible the hand of any other annotator is given in the editorial notes. Isabella Fenwick's original notes do not survive, but in the Wordsworth Library there are three leaves of notes in her hand (WL MS A Fenwick) that correspond approximately to the contents of notebook pp. 16–17. Comparison with the text of the notebook (DC MS. 153) suggests that the leaves were probably recopied by Isabella Fenwick not from her original notes taken from dictation but from the Quillinans' copy in the notebook.

To preserve the scale of the notebook and to allow ease of reference to notebook pages, one page of this book is devoted to each page of the notebook. Pages of notebook begin with the [bracketed] page number of the note-book and are hyperlinked to the editor's explanatory notes, which elucidate any terms printed blue. The symbol ↜ indicates the presence of such notes, which are Bookmarked using the notebook page number for identification (for PC users the symbol is hyperlinked). The 'previous view' button will return the reader to the anchor page of the Fenwick Notes). Terms treated in the Glossary are printed orange, and Glossary pages are bookmarked.

At the time of transcription, only the leaves transcribed by Edward Quillinan were numbered, in ink. When Dora took over on p. 86, she broke the pattern he had established of using (and numbering) only the left-hand page for copy, leaving the right free for later annotation.

Instead she filled both sides of the leaf for the next two leaves. When she reinstated the versos-only pattern, however, she continued to omit the numbers. Subsequently Edward Quillinan's pagination was continued, with some correction, with penciled numbers added perhaps by Edward himself, to the pages on which text appears through the end of the notebook. This existing pagination has been adopted in the text that follows.

Three further layers of 'insider' contribution to the Fenwick notes are supplied by (1) the selected transcriptions printed in *Memoirs of William Wordsworth* (London: Moxon, 1851) published by the poet's nephew, Christopher Wordsworth, Jr; (2) the surviving proofs of *Poetical Works* (1857; Special Collections, W. A. C. Bennett Library, Simon Fraser University) that were corrected by John Carter, the poet's life-long secretary and one of the executors of his estate; and (3) an occasionally censored version of all the notes prepared by Carter and issued by Moxon with Wordsworth's *Poetical Works* in 1857. These sources, where used, are acknowledged in the editorial notes.

Some unusual editorial problems bear further comment. Punctuation, like spelling, may be thought to be wholly scribal; yet these marks are probably the best effort the scribes could make in representing the poet's oral pauses and emphases as recorded first by Isabella Fenwick. I have emended, then, only where confusion could arise. Where there is no end punctuation at the close of an entry, or at the end of a paragraph, the closure is apparent and no punctuation has been added. Where Dora Quillinan's habit of completing a date with a full stop makes a sentence seem to end in mid-course, I have suppressed the stop. I have added or emended a closing quotation mark to match an opening mark but have not regularised the scribal practice of using mainly double quotation marks while occasionally entering single ones.

For the most part, however, punctuation in the notebook is adequate though not always consistent. For example, at the outset of her stint of copying Dora Quillinan tended to run sentences on or simply omit any end punctuation and initial capitals in a fashion very like her letter-writing style. It seems quite likely that Isabella Fenwick's notes from dictation provided insufficient or ambiguous information about where one sentence ended and another began since her epistolary style is not unlike Dora's in this respect. While Edward Quillinan would have imposed a more standard usage upon his source, Dora probably began by copying the notes as she found them but without any sense of possible confusion, since her own informal practice was similar. At any rate, as she progressed with her task she adopted a more 'public' style that accords with that used by Edward Quillinan throughout his portion. Occasionally, therefore, and chiefly in this context, the punctuation has been supplemented or emended for clarity's sake. All emendations are indicated in the Manuscript Notes.

Titles and first lines used in the Fenwick Notes present unusual problems. Occasionally a local and familiar title is used for a poem untitled in print, or the title is omitted and only a fragment of the first line used. In one instance Wordsworth recovered an earlier version of a poem's title, a change he adopted in print in 1845. Further, since Wordsworth was using the 1841 *Poetical Works* as his guide (along with *Poems, Chiefly of Early and Late Years,* 1842), designations like *'Sonnet'* in the manuscript notes are useless without these specific editions at hand. Accordingly I have supplied full titles in the editorial notes (and first lines if needed) when the poem discussed is not fully identified. For this purpose I have used the titles and first lines as they appear in the editions Wordsworth was using, noting any changes through the last edition of his *Poetical Works* of 1849–50 in editorial notes. The index includes titles and first lines in the versions published in 1850 where they differ from those found in the manuscript notes and in the edition of 1841.

Wordsworth's dating of poems and events is not always accurate, although his statements are not to be dismissed out of hand. From the time of his collected edition of 1815, when he introduced composition and publication dates of some of the poems listed in the table of contents, Wordsworth was concerned to report this information to his readers. In 1836 he began the practice of printing the composition date below the text of most poems in his collections and occasionally altered these in subsequent editions. Notice is made of such dates when the date assigned in print differs from the one Wordsworth gives in his note, and so far as is possible the correct date is supplied in the editor's notes when evidence suggests that a more precise date can be assigned or that Wordsworth has erred.

A great many names of persons and places appear in the Fenwick Notes. Where the context does not sufficiently explain the reference made, an explanation, if available, appears in the editorial notes. Names appearing frequently in the text are annotated the first time with a direction to see the Glossary, found at the end of the book. Entries in the Glossary give the notebook spelling followed by the accepted spelling, if it differs.

Especially helpful information about the Wordsworth circle and the community of Grasmere in the Wordsworths' Dove Cottage years is to be found in Pamela Woof's edition of *The Grasmere Journals* by Dorothy Wordsworth (Oxford: Clarendon Press, 1991); included with the editor's annotations are detailed maps of the central Lakes area and of Grasmere (pp. 138–9) that are keyed to the people and places mentioned by Dorothy Wordsworth in the journals. Other useful guides to the names and places mentioned in the Fenwick Notes are

Berta Lawrence, *Coleridge and Wordsworth in Somerset* (Newton Abbot: David and Charles, 1970) and David McCracken, *Wordsworth and the Lake District, A Guide to the Poems and their Places* (Oxford and New York: Oxford University Press, 1984). I have also consulted the guides published by Donald E. Hayden in The University of Tulsa Monograph Series (nos 19–23), *Wordsworth's Walking Tour of 1790* (1983), *Wordsworth's Travels in Wales and Ireland* (1985), *Wordsworth's Travels in Scotland* (1985), *Wordsworth's Travels in Europe I* (1988), and *Wordsworth's Travels in Europe II* (1988), all published in Tulsa, Oklahoma. Though Hayden's guides are not indexed, they do provide maps and details of the itineraries followed during Wordsworth's various tours.

Besides those mentioned above, editions of the Fenwick Notes consulted and occasionally cited in the editorial notes are:

William Wordsworth, *Prose Works*, ed. Alexander B. Grosart, (3 vols; London: Edward Moxon, Son, and Co., 1876)

William Wordsworth, *The Poetical Works of William Wordsworth*, Ernest de Selincourt and Helen Darbishire (5 vols; Oxford, 1940–9, rev. 1952–9).

Wordsworth and Coleridge, Lyrical Ballads, 1798, ed. W. J. B. Owen, (2nd edn, Oxford, 1969; corr. 1971)

and the Cornell Wordsworth editions listed in Abbreviations on pp. vii–xi above.

Additional information on dating is drawn from these same Cornell Wordsworth editions; the letters of William and Dorothy Wordsworth as listed on pp. vii, ix–x; and the following sources:

Mark L. Reed, *Wordsworth, The Chronology of the Early Years, 1770–1799* (Cambridge: Harvard University Press, 1967)

Mark L. Reed, *Wordsworth, The Chronology of the Middle Years, 1800–1815* (Cambridge: Harvard University Press, 1975);

F. B. Pinion, *A Wordsworth Chronology* (London: Macmillan, 1988)

Stephen Gill, *William Wordsworth, A Life* (Oxford: Clarendon Press, 1989).

The Fenwick Notes

My Heart leaps up— This was written at Grasmere Town-End 1804.

To a Butterfly. Grasmere Town-End. Written in the Orchard 1801.—My Sister and I were parted immediately after the death of our Mother who died in 1778, both being very young.

Foresight. Also composed in the orchard Grasmere Town-End.

Characteristics of a Child 3 years old. Picture of my Daughter Catherine, who died the year after. Written at Allan-Bank, Grasmere 1811.

Address to a Child. Town-End Grasmere. 1806.

The Mother's Return D°. by Miss Wordsworth. 1807

Alice Fell. 1801. Written to gratify M[r]. Graham of Glasgow, brother of the Author of the Sabbath. He was a zealous coadjutor of M[r]. Clarkson, and a man of ardent humanity. The incident had ↯

Manuscript Notes

1778 *MW revised in pencil from* 1777 *and EQ noted opposite,* March 1778.

MW inserted dates 1806…1807…1801 *in pencil*

[2]
happened to himself, and he urged me to put it into verse, for humanity's sake. The humbleness, meanness if you like, of the subject, together with the homely mode of treating it, brought upon me a world of ridicule by the small critics, so that in policy I excluded it from many editions of my poems, till it was restored at the request of some of my friends, in particular my son inlaw Edward Quillinan.

Lucy Gray.   Written at Goslar in Germany in 1799. It was founded on a circumstance told me by my Sister, of a little girl, who not far from Halifax in Yorkshire was bewildered in a snow-storm. Her footsteps were traced by her parents to the middle of the lock of a canal, and no other vestige of her, backward or forward, could be traced. The body however was found in the canal. The way in which the incident was treated & the spiritualising of the character might furnish hints for contrasting the imaginative influences which I have endeavoured to throw over common life with Crabbe's matter of fact style of treating subjects of the same kind. This is not spoken to his disparagement; far from it; but

---

Edward *revised by erasure from* [?Col] Edward

[3]
to direct the attention of thoughtful readers into whose hands these notes may fall to a comparison that may both enlarge the circle of their sensibilities and tend to produce in them a catholic judgement.

We are Seven.   Written at Alfoxden in the Spring of 1798, under circumstances somewhat remarkable. The little Girl who is the heroine I met within the area of Goodrich Castle in the year 1793. Having left the Isle of Wight & crost Salisbury Plain as mentioned in the preface to Guilt and Sorrow, I proceeded by Bristol up the Wye, and so on to N. Wales to the Vale of Clwydd, where I spent my summer under the roof of the father of my friend Robert Jones. In reference to this Poem, I will here mention one of the most remarkable facts in my own poetic history and that of M^r. Coleridge. In the Spring of the year 1798, he, my sister, & myself started from Alfoxden, pretty late in the afternoon, with a view to visit Linton & the Valley of Stones near it, and as our united funds were very small we agreed to defray the expence of the tour by writing a Poem

---

Written at Alfoxden *revised from* Written at Allfoxden

1793. Having *revised from* 1793 having

Guilt and Sorrow *revised from* guilt and sorrow

[4]
to be sent to the New Monthly Magazine set up by Phillips the Bookseller and edited by D^r. Aikin. Accordingly we set off and proceeded along the Quantock Hills, towards Watchet, and in the course of this walk was planned the Poem of The Ancient Mariner, founded on a dream, as M^r. Coleridge said, of his friend M^r. Cruikshank. Much the greatest part of the story was M^r. Coleridge's invention; but certain parts I myself suggested, for example, some crime was to be committed which should bring upon the Old Navigator, as Coleridge afterwards delighted to call him, the spectral persecution, as a consequence of that crime and his own wanderings. I had been reading in Shelvocke's Voyages a day or two before that while doubling Cape Horn they frequently saw albatrosses, in that latitude the largest sort of seafowl, some extending their wings 12 or 13 feet. "Suppose," said I, "you represent him as having killed one of these birds on entering the South Sea, and that the tutelary Spirits of these regions take upon them to avenge the crime." The incident was thought fit for the purpose and adopted accordingly. I also suggested the navigation of the ship by the dead men, but do not recollect that I had anything more to do with the scheme of the poem. The gloss

---

along *revised from* towards
dream, *revised from* dream of
myself *deleted in pencil*
as a *revised from* [?from] a

in *inserted*
Shelvocke's *ed. emended from* Shelvock's
in that latitude *inserted*
crime." *ed. emended from* crime.

[5]
with which it was subsequently accompanied was not thought of by either of us at the time, at least not a hint of it was given to me, & I have no doubt it was a gratuitous afterthought. We began the composition together on that to me memorable evening: I furnished two or three lines at the beginning of the poem, in particular

> And listened like a three years' child;
> The Mariner had his will.

These trifling contributions all but one (which M^r. C. has with unnecessary scrupulosity recorded) slipt out of his mind as they well might. As we endeavoured to proceed conjointly (I speak of the same evening) our respective manners proved so widely different that it would have been quite presumptuous in me to do anything but separate from an undertaking upon which I could only have been a clog. We returned after a few days from a delightful tour of which I have many pleasant and some of them droll enough recollections. We returned by Dulverton to Alfoxden. The Ancient Mariner grew & grew till it became too important for our first object which was limited to our expectation of five pounds, and we began to

---

child; *punctuation added in pencil*

[6]

talk of a volume, which was to consist as M^r. Coleridge has told the world, of Poems chiefly on supernatural subjects taken from common life but looked at, as much as might be, through an imaginative medium. Accordingly I wrote The Idiot Boy, Her Eyes are wild &c, We are Seven, The Thorn & some others.— To return to We are Seven, the piece that called forth this note, I composed it while walking in the grove of Alfoxden. My friends will not deem it too trifling to relate that while walking to and fro I composed the last stanza first, having begun with the last line. When it was all but finished, I came in and recited it to M^r. Coleridge and my Sister, and said, 'A prefatory Stanza must be added, and I should sit down to our little tea-meal with greater pleasure if my task was finished.' I mentioned in substance what I wished to be expressed, and Coleridge immediately threw off the stanza thus:

  A little Child, dear brother Jem,—

I objected to the rhyme, dear brother Jem as being ludicrous, but we all enjoyed the joke of hitching in our friend James Tobin's name who was familiarly called Jem. He was brother of

---

which *revised from* as
The Idiot *revised from* the Idiot
We *revised from* and We
to and fro *revised from* back and

finished.' *ed. emended from* finished."
Jem,— *revised from* Jem,— / That
He was brother *revised from* He was the brother

[7]
the dramatist, and this reminds me of an anecdote, which it may be worth while here to notice. The said Jim got a sight of the Lyrical Ballads as it was going through the press at Bristol, during which time I was residing in that city. One evening he came to me with a grave face and said, 'Wordsworth I have seen the volume that Coleridge & you are about to publish, There is one poem in it which I earnestly entreat you will cancel, for, if published, it will make you everlastingly ridiculous.' I answered that I felt much obliged by the interest he took in my good name as a writer, and begged to know what was the unfortunate piece he alluded to. He said, 'It is called We Are Seven!' 'Nay,' said I, 'that shall take its chance however,' and he left me in despair.—I have only to add that in the spring of 1841 I revisited Goodrich Castle, not having seen that part of the Wye since I met the little girl there in 1793. It would have given me greater pleasure to have found in the neighbouring hamlet traces of one who had interested me so much;

---

ridiculous.'…Seven! '…however,' *ed. added closing quotation marks*

[8] but that was impossible, as, unfortunately, I did not even know her name. The ruin, from its position and features, is a most impressive object. I could not but deeply regret that its solemnity was impaired by a fantastic new castle set up on a projection of the same ridge, as if to shew how far modern art can go in surpassing all that could be done by antiquity & nature with their united graces remembrances and associations. I could have almost wished for power, so much the contrast vexed me, to blow away Sir — Meyrick's impertinent structure and all the fopperies it contains.

Anecdote for Fathers. This was suggested in front of Alfoxden. The Boy was a son of my friend Basil Montagu, who had been two or three years under our care. The name of Kilve is from a village on the Bristol Channel, about a mile from Alfoxden; and the name of Liswin Farm was taken from a beautiful spot on the Wye. When M^r. Coleridge, my Sister and I had been visiting the famous John Thelwall who had taken refuge from politics, after a trial for high treason, with a view to bring up his family by the profits of agriculture,

---

unfortunately *revised from* I   agricult-ure *runs over to p. 9*

[9]
which proved as unfortunate a speculation as that he had fled from, Coleridge and he had both been public lecturers: Coleridge mingling with his politics theology; from which the other elocutionist abstained, unless it were for the sake of a sneer. This quondam community of public employment induced Thelwall to visit Coleridge at Nether Stowey where he fell in my way. He really was a man of extraordinary talent, an affectionate husband and a good father. Though brought up in the city on a tailor's board he was truly sensible of the beauty of natural objects, I remember, once when Coleridge, he, and I were seated together upon the turf on the brink of a stream in the most beautiful part of the most beautiful glen of Alfoxden, Coleridge exclaimed, 'This is a place to reconcile one to all the jarrings and conflicts of the wide world,— 'Nay' said Thelwall 'to make one forget them altogether.' The visit of this man to Coleridge was, as I believe Coleridge has related, the occasion of a spy being sent by government to watch our proceedings, which were, I can say with truth, such as the world at large would have thought ludicrously harmless.

Rural Architecture. These structures, as every one knows, are common among our hills, being built by shepherds as conspicuous marks, and occasionally by boys in sport. It was written at Town-End, in 1801.

This is a place to *revised from* To altogether.' *ed. emended from* altogether."

to Coleridge *revised from* to Coleridge, being built by shepherds *inserted*

[10]

The Pet Lamb.   Town End. 1800. Barbara Lewthwaite, now living at Ambleside (1843) though much changed as to beauty, was one of two most lovely Sisters. Almost the first words my poor Brother John said, when he visited us for the first time at Grasmere, were, 'Were these, two angels that I have just seen?' and, from his description, I have no doubt they were those two Sisters. The mother died in childbed; and one of our neighbours at Grasmere told me that the loveliest sight she had ever seen, was that mother as she lay in her coffin with her babe in her arm. I mention this to notice what I cannot but think a salutary custom, once universal in these vales. Every attendant on a funeral made it a duty to look at the corpse in the coffin before the lid was closed, which was never done (nor I believe is now) till a minute or two before the corpse was removed. Barbara Lewthwaite was not in fact the child whom I had seen and overheard as engaged in the poem. I chose the name for reasons implied in the above; and will here add a caution against the use of names of living persons. Within a few months after the publication of this poem, I was much surprised and more hurt to find it in a child's School-book, which, having been compiled by Lindley Murray, had come into use at Grasmere School where Barbara was a pupil. And, alas, I had the mortification of hearing that she was very vain of being thus distinguished; and, in after-life,

---

one of our neighbours *revised from* a neighbour of our's

done *revised from* done,

[11]
she used to say that she remembered the incident and what I said to her upon the occasion.

Idle Shepherd Boys. Grasmere—Town End. 1800. I will only add a little monitory anecdote concerning this subject. When Coleridge & Southey were walking together upon the Fells, Southey observed that, if I wished to be considered a faithful painter of rural manners, I ought not to have said that my Shepherd-Boys trimmed their rushen hats as described in the poem. Just as the words had past his lips two boys appeared with the very plant entwined round their hats. I have often wondered that Southey, who rambled so much about the mountains, should have fallen into this mistake, & I record it as a warning for others who with far less opportunity than my dear friend had of knowing what things are, and far less sagacity, give way to presumptuous criticism, from which he was free, though in this matter mistaken. In describing a tarn under Helvellyn, I say,

> There, sometimes, doth a leaping fish
> Send through the tarn a lonely cheer.

This was branded by a critic of these days, in a review ascribed to M^{rs}. Barbauld, as unnatural & absurd. I admire the genius of M^{rs}. Barbauld, & am certain that, had her education been favorable,

---

rushen *EQ revised in pencil to* rustic with *revised from* who far *EQ revised in pencil to* with far There *written first on line above.*

then deleted sometimes, *revised from* something through *revised from* from

[12] to imaginative influences, no female of her day would have been more likely to sympathise with that image and to acknowledge the truth of the sentiment

 Influence of Natural Objects. Written in Germany 1799.

 The Longest day. 1817. Suggested by the sight of my Daughter (Dora) playing in front of Rydal Mount, and composed in a great measure the same afternoon. I have often wished to pair this poem upon the *longest* with one upon the *shortest* day, and regret even now that it has not been done.

 Dear Native Regions. 1786. Hawkshead.—The beautiful image with which this poem concludes suggested itself to me while I was resting in a boat along with my companions under the shade of a magnificent row of Sycamores, which then extended their branches from the shore of the promontory upon which stands the ancient, and at that time the more picturesque, Hall of Coniston the Seat of the Le Flemings from very early times. The Poem of which it was the conclusion was of many hundred lines and contained thoughts & images most of which have been dispersed through my other writings,

---

EQ repeated Dora *in pencil*
Hawkshead *revised from* Haws-head

suggested itself *revised from* was suggested

[13]

An Evening Walk. The young lady to whom this was addressed was my Sister. It was composed at School, & during the first two college vacations after I left. There is not an image in it which I have not observed; and now, in my seventy third year, I recollect the time & place where most of them were noticed. I will confine myself to one instance—.

> Waving his hat, the Shepherd from the vale
> Directs his winding dog the cliffs to scale.
> The dog bounds barking mid the glittering rocks
> Hunts where his master points the intercepted flocks.

I was an eye-witness of this for the first time while crossing the pass of Dunmail Raise.—Upon second thought, I will mention another image:

> And fronting the bright west yon oak entwines
> Its darkening boughs and leaves in stronger lines.

This is feebly & imperfectly exprest; but I recollect distinctly the very spot where this first struck me. It was in the way between Hawkshead and Ambleside, and gave me extreme pleasure. The moment was important in my poetical history; for I date from it my consciousness of the infinite variety of natural appearances which had been unnoticed by the poets of any age or country, so far as I was acquainted with them: and I made a resolution to supply in

---

during the first two college vacations after I left *revised to* after my first two college vacations
time & *inserted*
where most *revised from* of most

Waving *revised from* Moving
winding *revised from* wandering
but *revised from* but the image when I first observed it
distinctly *inserted*

[14]
some degree the deficiency. I could not have been at that time above 14 years of age. The description of the swans, that follows, was taken from the daily opportunities I had of observing their habits, not as confined to the gentleman's park, but in a state of nature. There were two pairs of them that divided the lake of Esthwaite & its in-and-out flowing streams between them, never trespassing a single yard upon each other's separate domain. They were of the old magnificent species, bearing in beauty & majesty about the same relation to the Thames swan which that does to the goose. It was from the remembrance of these noble creatures I took, 30 years after, the picture of the Swan which I have discarded from the poem of Dion. While I was a School-boy the late M^r. Curwen introduced a little fleet of these birds, but of the inferior species, to the Lake of Windermere. Their principal home was about his own islands; but they sailed about into remote parts of the lake, and, either from real or imagined injury done to the adjoining fields, they were got rid of at the request of the farmers & proprietors, but to the great regret of all who had become attached to them from noticing their beauty & quiet habits. I will conclude my notice of this poem

---

I had of *revised from* of

but in *revised from* but comparatively in

[15]
by observing that the plan of it has not been confined to a particular walk or an individual place; a proof (of which I was unconscious at the time) of my unwillingness to submit the poetic spirit to the chains of fact & real circumstance. The country is idealized, rather than described in anyone of its local aspects.

Descriptive Sketches. 1791–2, Much the greatest part of this poem was composed during my walks upon the banks of the Loire in the years 1791, 1792. I will only notice that the description of the valley filled with mist beginning "In solemn shapes" &c was taken from that beautiful region of which the principal features are Lungarne & Sarnen. Nothing that I ever saw in nature left a more delightful impression on my mind than that which I have attempted, alas, how feebly to convey to others in these lines. Those two lakes have always interested me especially, from bearing, in their size and other features, a resemblance to those of the North of England. It is much to be deplored that a district so beautiful should be so unhealthy as it is.

The Female Vagrant. I find the date of this is placed in 1792 in contradiction, by mistake, to what I have asserted in "Guilt and Sorrow." The correct date is 1793–4. The chief incident of it, more particularly her description of her feelings on the Atlantic

---

1791-2. *inserted*
beginning *revised from* beginning the
shapes" &c *revised from* shapes &c"

features *written twice with second entry deleted*
in their *revised from* [?] their
1793-4 *inserted in pencil*

[16] are taken from life.

Poems founded on the Affections. The Brothers. 1800. This poem was composed in a grove at the north-eastern end of Grasmere Lake, which grove was in a great measure destroyed by turning the high road along the side of the water. The few trees that are left were spared at my intercession, The poem arose out of the fact mentioned to me at Ennerdale that a shepherd had fallen asleep upon the top of the rock called The Pillar, and perished as here described, his staff being left midway on the rock.

Artegal and Elidure. Rydal Mount—This was written in the year 1815, as a token of affectionate respect for the memory of Milton. "I have determined," says he in his preface to his History of England, "to bestow the telling over even of these reputed tales, be it for nothing else but in favor of our English Poets and Rhetoricians, who by their wit will know how to use them judiciously."

The Sparrow's Nest. The Orchard, Grasmere Town-End 1801. At the end of the garden of my Father's house at Cockermouth was a high terrace that commanded a fine view of the River Derwent and Cockermouth Castle. This was our favourite play-ground. The terrace wall, a low one, was covered with closely-clipt privet, and roses, which gave an almost impervious shelter to birds, that built their nests there. The latter of these Stanzas alludes to one of these nests.

The Butterfly. 1801. Written at the same time & place.

A Farewell. 1802. Composed just before my Sister and I went to fetch Mary from Gallowhill near Scarborough.

Written in my copy of Thomson's Castle of Indolence. 1802. Composed in the Orchard Grasmere Town-End

---

water *revised from* lake
The few *revised from* The few th *revised from* They
Rydal Mount— *inserted*

1801 *inserted*
at *revised from* in
This…play-ground. *sentence inserted*
(notes for p. 16 continue on p. 17)

[17]
Coleridge living with us much at the time, his son Hartley has said that his father's character & habits are here preserved in a livelier way than in anything that has been written about him.

I met Louisa in the Shade.   Town-End. 1805.

Strange fits of passion have I known, **She dwelt among the untrodden ways, I travelled among unknown men.**   These three poems were written in Germany, 1799.

Ere with cold beads of midnight dew.   Rydal Mount 1826. Suggested by the condition of a friend.

Look at the fate of summer flowers.   Rydal Mount 1824. Prompted by the undue importance attached to personal beauty by some dear friends of mine.

'Tis said that some have died for love.   1800.

There is a change, and I am poor.   Suggested by a change in the manners of a friend. Town-End 1806.

Let other Bards &c.   Rydal Mount, 1824. Written on Mary Wordsworth.

How rich that forehead's calm expanse.   Rydal Mount, 1824. Also on M.W.

Oh dearer far than light and life are dear.   Rydal Mount 1824. To M.W.— Rydal Mount

Lament of Mary Queen of Scots.   This arose out of a flash of moonlight that struck the ground when I was approaching the steps that lead from the garden at Rydal Mount to the front of the house. "From her sunk eye a stagnant tear stole forth" is taken, with

---

16 closely-clipt *inserted*
   which *revised from* and
   birds, that *revised from* birds who
   The *revised from* This
   Composed...Town-End. *revised from* Written...Town-End. *revised from* Coleridge

17 among the untrodden ways *revised from* beside the banks of Dove *revised from* beside the Springs of Dove
   travelled *revised from* have wandered
   Rydal Mount *inserted*
   light and life *so PW (1841)* life and light *notebook*

[18]
some loss, from a discarded poem "The Convict," in which occurred, when he was discovered lying in the cell, these lines.

> But now he upraises the deep-sunken eye,
>   The motion unsettles a tear,
> The silence of sorrow it seems to supply
>   And asks of me, why I am here.

The Complaint of a Forsaken Indian Woman.   Written at Alfoxden, in 1798, when I read Hearne's Journey with deep interest. It was composed for the volume of Lyrical Ballads.

The Last of the Flock.   Produced at the same time, & for the same purpose. The incident occurred in the village of Holford, close by Alfoxden.

Repentance.   Town-End, 1804. Suggested by the conversation of our next neighbour, Margaret Ashburner.

The Affliction of Margaret.   Town-End 1804. This was taken from the case of a poor widow who lived in the town of Penrith. Her sorrow was well known to Mary, to my Sister, &, I believe, to the whole town. She kept a shop, and when she saw a stranger passing by she was in the habit of going out into the Street to inquire of him after her son.

The Cottager to her Infant.   By my Sister. Suggested to her while beside my sleeping children.

The Sailor's Mother.   Town-End 1800. I met this woman near the Wishing Gate, on the high-road that then led from Grasmere to Ambleside. Her appearance was exactly as here described, & such was her account,

---

it *written over illegible erasure*
why *revised from* Why
Hearne's *revised from* with
poor *deleted in pencil*

Suggested *deleted and reinstated*
beside…children *revised from* [sleeping *deleted*] watching my children asleep
from *revised from* to

[19]
nearly to the letter.

The Childless Father. Town-End, 1800.   When I was a child at Cockermouth, no funeral took place without a basin filled with sprigs of boxwood being placed upon a table covered with a white cloth in front of the house. The huntings (on foot) in which the Old Man is supposed to join as here described were of common, almost habitual, occurrence in our vales when I was a boy; & the people took much delight in them. They are now less frequent.

The Emigrant Mother.   1802. Suggested by what I have noticed in more than one French fugitive during the time of the French Revolution. If I am not mistaken, the lines were composed at Sockburn when I was on a visit to Mary and her brother.

Vaudracour & Julia.   Town End 1805. Faithfully narrated, though with the omission of many pathetic circumstances, from the mouth of a French Lady, who had been an eye and ear-witness of all that was done & said. Many long years after, I was told that Dupligne was then a monk in the Convent of La Trappe.

The Idiot Boy.   Alfoxden, 1798. The last stanza, "The cocks did crow & the sun did shine so cold" was the foundation of the whole. The words were reported to me by my dear friend Thomas Poole; but I have since heard the same repeated of other Idiots. Let me add that this long poem was composed in the Groves of Alfoxden almost extempore; not a word, I believe, being corrected, though one stanza was omitted. I

(on foot) *inserted*
less frequent *revised from* dwindling away
had been *inserted*
long *inserted*
Dupligne *revised from* Duplique *(EQ queried*

the name in pencil; perhaps then correcting it in ink.*)*
& the sun . [sun *revised from* moon]...cold *inserted*

[20] mention this in gratitude to those happy moments, for, in truth, I never wrote anything with so much glee.

Michael.   Town-End, 1801. Written about the same time as 'The Brothers.' The Sheepfold, on which so much of the poem turns, remains, or rather the ruins of it. The character & circumstances of Luke were taken from a family to whom had belonged, many years before, the house we lived in at Town-End, along with some fields and woodlands on the eastern shore of Grasmere. The name of the Evening Star was not in fact given to this house but to another on the same side of the valley more to the north.

The Armenian Lady's Love.   Rydal Mount, 1830.

Loving & Liking, by my Sister. Rydal Mount, 1832.   It arose, I believe, out of a casual expression of one of M\[r]. Swinburne's children.

The Redbreast, Rydal Mount, 1834.   Our cats having been banished the house, it was soon frequented by Red-breasts. Two or three of them, when the window was open, would come in, particularly when Mary was breakfasting alone, & hop about the table picking up the crumbs. My Sister being then confined to her room by sickness, as, dear creature, she still is, had one that, without being caged, took up its abode with her, & at night used to perch upon a nail from which a picture had hung. It used to sing and fan her face with its wings in a manner that was very touching.

---

those *inserted*
to whom *revised from* to whom
it the house *and* in *inserted*

Our *revised from* All our *revised from* Our
been banished *revised from* disappeared

[21]

Her eyes are wild.   Alfoxden, 1798. The subject was reported to me by a Lady of Bristol who had seen the poor creature.

The Waggoner.   Town-End, 1805. The character & story from fact.

A Morning Exercise.   Rydal Mount, 1825. I could wish the last five stanzas of this to be read with the poem addressed to the Skylark.

The Flower-Garden.   Planned by my friend Lady Beaumont in connexion with the garden at Coleorton.

A whirl-blast from behind the hill.   Observed in the holly grove at Alfoxden, where these verses were written in the Spring of 1799. I had the pleasure of again seeing, with dear friends, this Grove in unimpaired beauty, 41 years after.

The Oak & the Broom.   1800. Suggested upon the mountain pathway that leads from Upper Rydal to Grasmere, The ponderous block of stone, which is mentioned in the poem, remains I believe to this day, a good way up Nab-Scar. Broom grows under it and in many places on the side of the precipice.

The Waterfall & the Eglantine.   Suggested nearer to Grasmere on the same mountain track. The Eglantine remained many years afterwards, but is now gone.

To a Sexton.   Written in Germany 1799.

To the Daisy. *To the same flower*—and *The Green Linnet*—all composed in Town End Orchard where the Bird was often seen as here described.   ☙

Waggoner *altered in ink to* Wagoner *(but Waggoner is correct)*
A Morning *revised from* The Morning
holly grove *revised from* groves
I had…after. *revised from* I had the pleasure of again seeing this Grove with dear friends, 41 years after.

Upper *revised from* upper
Eglantine remained *revised from* shrub remained
The Green Linnet *revised from* to the Green linnet
all *inserted*
in *revised from* at

[22]

To the Small Celandine. Grasmere Town-End, 1805. It is remarkable that this flower, coming out so early in the Spring as it does, and so bright & beautiful, & in such profusion should not have been noticed earlier in English verse. What adds much to the interest that attends it is its habit of shutting itself up & opening out according to the degree of light & temperature of the air.

The Redbreast chasing the Butterfly. Observed as described in the then beautiful Orchard at Town-End.

Song for the Spinning Wheel. 1806. The belief on which this is founded I have often heard expressed by an old neighbour of Grasmere.

Hint from the Mountains. Bunches of fern may often be seen, wheeling about in the wind as here described. The particular bunch that suggested these verses was noticed in the Pass of Dunmail-Raise. The verses were composed in 1817, but the application is for all times and places.

Needle-Case. 1827.

The Parrot and the Wren. The Parrot belonged to M^{rs}. Luff while living at Fox-Ghyll. The Wren was one that haunted for many years the Summerhouse between the two terraces at Rydal-Mount.

The Danish Boy. Written in Germany, 1799. It was entirely a fancy; but intended as a prelude to a ballad poem never written.

Song of the Wandering Jew. 1800.

Small *revised from* small
Hint from *revised from* Hint to
wheeling about *revised from* about

Fox-Ghyll *revised from* Fox-ghyll at
Rydal-Mount *revised from* of Rydal-Mount

[23]

Stray Pleasures. Suggested on the Thames by the sight of one of those floating mills that used to be seen there. This I noticed on the Surrey-side between Somerset-House & Blackfriars' Bridge. Charles Lamb was with me at the time; and I thought it remarkable that I should have to point out to *him,* an idolatrous Londoner, a sight so interesting as the happy group dancing on the platform. Mills of this kind used to be, and perhaps still are, not uncommon on the Continent. I noticed several upon the River Saone in the year 1790; particularly near the town of Chalons where my friend Jones and I halted a day when we crossed France, so far on foot. There we embarked & floated down to Lyons.

The Pilgrim's Dream, or the Star & Glow-worm. I distinctly recollect the evening when these verses were suggested in 1818. It was on the road between Rydal & Grasmere where glow-worms abound. A star was shining above the ridge of Loughrigg Fell just opposite. I remember a blockhead of a critic, in some Review or other, crying out against this piece. "What so monstrous, said he, as to make a star talk to a glowworm!" Poor fellow, we know well from this sage observation what the "primrose on the river's brim was to him."

The Poet & the Caged Turtle-Dove. Rydal Mount, 1830. This Dove was one of a pair that had been given to my daughter by our excellent friend Miss Jewsbury, who went to India with her husband, M^r.

1790 *ed. emended from* 1799
Rydal & *inserted*
above *revised from* just above

star talk *ed. emended from* star-talk
one of a *revised from* one of the
husband *revised from* friend

[24]
Fletcher, where she died of cholera. The Dove survived its mate many years, & was killed to our great sorrow by a neighbour's cat that got in at the window and dragged it partly out of the cage. These verses were composed ex tempore, to the letter, in the Terrace Summer House before spoken of. It was the habit of the bird to begin cooing & murmuring whenever it heard me making my verses.

A Wren's Nest. 1833. Rydal Mount This nest was built, as described, in a tree that grows near the pool in Dora's field next the Rydal Mount Garden.—

Rural Illusions. Rydal Mount. 1832. Observed a hundred times in the grounds at Rydal Mount.

The Kitten & Falling Leaves. 1805, Seen at Town-End, Grasmere. The Elder-bush has long since disappeared: it hung over the wall near the cottage; & the Kitten continued to leap up catching the leaves as here described. The infant was Dora.

There was a Boy. Written in Germany, 1799. This is an extract from the Poem on my own poetical education. This practise of making an instrument of their own fingers is known to most boys, though some are more skilful at it than others. William Raincock of Rayrigg, a fine spirited lad, took the lead of all my schoolfellows in this art.

---

after A Wren's Nest. *EQ added* in Dora's Field in pencil

Rayrigg, *revised from* Rayrigg to *with to anticipating* took

[25]

The Cuckoo. Composed in the Orchard at Town-End 1804.

A Night-piece. Composed on the road between Nether Stowey & Alfoxden, extempore. I distinctly recollect the very moment when I was struck, as described "He looks up at the clouds &c."

The Yew-trees. Grasmere, 1803. These Yew-trees are still standing, but the spread of that at Lorton is much diminished by mutilation. I will here mention that a little way up the hill on the road leading from Rossthwaite to Stonethwaite lay the trunk of a yewtree which appeared, as you approached, so vast was it its diameter, like the entrance of a cave & not a small one. Calculating upon what I have observed of the slow growth of this tree in rocky situations, & of its durability, I have often thought that the one I am describing must have been as old as the Christian era. The tree lay in the line of a fence. Great masses of its ruins were strown about, & some had been rolled down the hillside & lay near the road at the bottom. As you approached the tree, you were struck with the number of shrubs & young plants, ashes &c. which had found a bed upon the decayed trunk & grew to no inconsiderable height, forming, as it were, a part of the hedgerow. In no part of England, or of Europe, have I ever seen a yewtree at all approaching this in magnitude,

---

leading *revised in pencil from* leaving   appeared, *revised from* appeared so vast

[26] as it must have stood. By the bye, Hutton the Old Guide of Keswick had been so imprest with the remains of this tree that he used gravely to tell strangers that there could be no doubt of its having been in existence before the flood.

Nutting. Written in Germany, intended as part of a poem on my own life, but struck out as not being wanted there. Like most of my schoolfellows I was an impassioned nutter. For this pleasure the Vale of Esthwaite abounding in coppice-wood, furnished a very wide range. These verses arose out of the remembrance of feelings I had often had when a boy, and particularly in the extensive woods that still stretch from the side of Esthwaite Lake towards Graythwaite, the seat of the ancient family of Sandys.

She was a phantom of delight. 1804 Town End. The germ of this poem was four lines composed as a part of the verses on the Highland Girl. Though beginning in this way, it was written from my heart as is sufficiently obvious.

The Nightingale. "O Nightingale thou surely art &c" Town-End. 1806.

Three Years she grew in sun & shower. 1799. Composed in the Hartz Forest.

A slumber did my spirit seal. 1799. Germany.

I wandered lonely as a cloud. Town-End, 1804.

The Daffodils. The two best lines in it are by Mary.

---

nutter *revised from* lover
range *revised from* range

for this pleasure from my heart *revised from* in my heart

[27]
The daffodils grew & still grow on the margin of Ulswater & probably may be seen to this day as beautiful in the month of March nodding their golden heads beside the dancing & foaming waves.

Poor Susan.   Written 1801 or 2. This arose out of my observation of the affecting music of these birds hanging in this way in the London Streets during the freshness & stillness of the Spring Morning.

The Power of Music.   Taken from life—1806.

Star-gazers.   Observed by me in Leicester Square as here described, 1806.

The cock is crowing.   Extempore. 1801. This little poem was a favourite with Joanna Baillie.

The Beggars.   Town-End. 1802. Met & described by me to my Sister near the Quarry at the head of Rydal Lake—a place still a chosen resort of vagrants travelling with their families.

Gipsies.   Composed at Coleorton, 1807. I had observed them as here described near Castle Donnington on my way to & from Derby.

Ruth.   Written in Germany 1799. Suggested by an account I had of a wanderer in Somersetshire.

Resolution & Independence.   Town-End. 1807. This Old Man I met a few hundred yards from my cottage at Town-End, Grasmere; & the account of him is taken from his own mouth.

Taken *revised from* The [?]   This little *revised from* The

[28]

I was in the state of feeling described in the beginning of the poem, while crossing over Barton Fell from Mr. Clarkson's at the foot of Ulswater, towards Askam. The image of the hare I then observed on a ridge of the fell.

The Thorn.   Alfoxden. 1798. Arose out of my observing, on the ridge of Quantock Hill, on a stormy day a thorn which I had often past in calm and bright weather without noticing it. I said to myself, 'Cannot I by some invention do as much to make this thorn permanently an impressive object as the storm has made it to my eyes at this moment.' I began the poem accordingly and composed it with great rapidity. Sir George Beaumont painted a picture from it which Wilkie thought his best. He gave it to me; though, when he saw it several times at Rydal Mount afterwards he said, "I could make a better & would like to paint the same subject over again." The sky in this picture is nobly done, but it reminds one too much of Wilson. The only fault however of any consequence is the

---

Arose *revised from* It arose
on the *revised from* on a

permanently *MW revised in pencil from* prominently
moment' *ed. emended from* moment.

[29]

female figure which is too old & decrepid for one likely to frequent an eminence on such a call.

Goody Blake & Harry Gill.   Written at Alfoxden 1798. The incident from D#. Darwin's Zoonomia.

Hart-Leap-Well.   Town-End. 1800. The first eight stanzas were composed extempore one winter evening in the cottage; when, after having tired and disgusted myself with labouring at an awkward passage in "The Brothers," I started with a sudden impulse to this to get rid of the other, and finished it in a day or two. My Sister and I had past the place a few weeks before in our wild winter journey from Sockburn on the banks of the Tees to Grasmere. A peasant whom we met near the spot told us the story so far as concerned the name of the well, and the hart; and pointed out the stones. Both the stones and the well are objects that may easily be missed: the tradition by this time may be extinct in the neighbourhood: the man who related it to us was very old.

The Horn of Egremont Castle.   1806. A tradition transferred from the ancient mansion of Hutton John, the Seat of the Huddlestons to Egremont Castle.

The Feast of Brougham Castle.   See the note attached. This poem was composed at Coleorton while I was walking to and fro along the path that led from Sir George Beaumont's Farm-House, where we resided, to the Hall which was building at that time.

---

decrepid *a 19th century spelling of* decrepit OED

that led *revised from* which led

Sir *revised from* M#

Farm-House *revised from* to the Ha

[30]

Tintern Abbey. July 1798. No poem of mine was composed under circumstances more pleasant for me to remember than this: I began it upon leaving Tintern, after crossing the Wye, and concluded it just as I was entering Bristol in the evening, after a ramble of 4 or 5 days, with my sister. Not a line of it was altered, and not any part of it written down till I reached Bristol. It was published almost immediately after in the little volume of which so much has been said in these notes (The Lyrical Ballads, as first published at Bristol by Cottle).

It is no spirit who from heaven &c. 1803. Town-End. I remember the instant my Sister Sara Hutchinson called me to the window of our cottage saying, "Look, how beautiful is yon Star! It has the sky all to itself." I composed the verses immediately.

French Revolution. An extract from the long poem on my own poetical education. It was first published by Coleridge in his Friend, which is the reason of its having had a place in every edition of my poems since.

Yes, it was the mountain echo. Town-End 1806. The echo came from Nab-scar, when I was walking on the opposite side of Rydal Mere. I will here mention, for my dear Sister's sake, that, while she was sitting alone one day high up on this part of Loughrigg Fell, she was so affected by the voice of the Cuckoo heard from the crags at some distance, that she could not suppress a wish to have a stone inscribed

---

Nab-scar *hyphen added in ink*
I will here mention…proceeded. *lightly crossed out in ink*

suppress *revised from* repress

[31]
with her name among the rocks from which the sound proceeded. On my return from my walk I recited these verses to Mary, who was then confined with her Son Thomas, who died in his 7th. year as recorded on his headstone in Grasmere Church-Yard.

To a Skylark. }   Rydal Mount—1825.
  Ethereal Minstrel!

Laodamia. Rydal Mount—1814. Written at the same time as Dion and Artegal and Elidure. The incident of the trees growing & withering put the subject into my thoughts, and I wrote with the hope of giving it a loftier tone than, so far as I know, has been given to it by any of the Ancients who have treated of it. It cost me more trouble than almost anything of equal length I have ever written.

Dear Child of Nature. Composed at the same time, and on the same view as "I met Louisa in the shade." Indeed they were designed to make one piece.

The Pass of Kirkstone. Rydal Mount, 1817. Thoughts and feelings of many walks in all weathers by day and night over this pass, alone and with beloved friends.

To —— on her first ascent of Helvellyn. Rydal Mount, 1816. The Lady was Miss Blackett, then residing with Mr. Montague Burgoyne at Fox Ghyll. We were tempted to remain too long upon the mountain; and I imprudently, with the hope of shortening the way, led her among the crags and down a steep slope which entangled us in difficulties that were met by her with much spirit and courage.

---

sound *revised from* rocks
On…walk *inserted*
these verses *revised from* them
who *revised from illegible words*
Ethereal Minstrel. *revised from* Up with me!

has [*revised from* than has]…by *inserted*
any *revised from* the an
anything of *revised from* anything I have ever written of
shade *revised from* Shade *revised from* Vale

[32]

Water-Fowl. 1812. Observed frequently over the lakes of Rydal and Grasmere.

View from the top of Black-Comb. 1813. Mary & I, as mentioned in the Epistle to Sir G. Beaumont, lived some time under its shadow.

The Haunted Tree. 1819. This tree grew in the park of Rydal, and I have often listened to its creaking as described.

The Triad. Rydal Mount. 1828. The girls Edith May Southey, my daughter Dora & Sara Coleridge.

Wishing-gate. Rydal Mount 1828. See also "Wishing-Gate Destroyed."

The Primrose of the Rock. Rydal Mount, 1831. It stands on the right hand a little way leading up the vale from Grasmere to Rydal, We have been in the habit of calling it the glow-worm rock from the number of glow-worms we have often seen hanging on it as described. The tuft of primrose has, I fear, been washed away by heavy rains.

Presentiments. Rydal Mount, 1830.

Vernal Ode. D°. 1817. Composed to place in view the immortality of succession where immortality is denied, as far as we know, to the individual creature.

Devotional Incitements. Rydal Mount. 1832.

Jewish Family. Coleridge and my daughter and I, in 1828, passed a fortnight upon the banks of the Rhine, principally under the hospitable

---

my daughter...Coleridge *revised from* Sara Coleridge and my daugher Dora
1831 *ed. emended from* 1821
Coleridge and *revised from* When Coleridge and

principally...Gotesburg, *revised from* (principally...Gotesburg)
hospi-table *runs over to p. 33*

[33]
roof of M^r. Aders at Gotesburg, but two days of the time were spent at S^t. Goa or in rambles among the neighbouring vallies. It was at S^t. Goa that I saw the Jewish family here described. Though exceedingly poor, and in rags, they were not less beautiful than I have endeavoured to make them appear. We had taken a little dinner with us in a basket, and invited them to partake of it, which the mother refused to do, both for herself and her children, saying it was with them a fast day; adding, diffidently, that whether such observances were right or wrong, she felt it her duty to keep them strictly. The Jews, who are numerous in this part of the Rhine, greatly surpass the German peasantry in the beauty of their features, & in the intelligence of their countenance. But the lower classes of the German peasantry have, here at least, the air of people grievously opprest. Nursing mothers, at the age of seven or eight & twenty, often look haggard and far more decayed and withered than women of Cumberland & Westmoreland twice their age. This comes from being underfed, and overworked in their vineyards in a hot & glaring sun.

On the power of sound. Rydal Mount. 1828. I have often regretted that my tour in Ireland, chiefly performed in the short days of October in a carriage and four, (I was with M^r. Marshall) supplied my memory with so few images that were new, & with so little motive to write. The lines however in

༄

---

two days…spent *revised from* we spent two days rambling
or in *revised from* or at
at St. Goa *revised from* there

& in the *revised from* & the
underfed, and *inserted*
vineyards in *revised from* vineyards under
(I was with M^r. Marshall) *inserted*

[34]
this poem, "Thou too be heard, lone eagle!" &c. were suggested near the Giants' Causeway, or rather at the promontory of Fairhead where a pair of eagles wheeled above our heads and darted off as if to hide themselves in a blaze of sky made by the setting sun.

Peter Bell. Alfoxden, 1798. Founded upon an anecdote, which I read in a newspaper, of an ass being found hanging his head over a canal in a wretched posture. Upon examination a dead body was found in the water and proved to be the body of its master. The countenance, gait and figure of Peter were taken from a wild rover with whom I walked from Builth on the River Wye downwards nearly as far as the town of Hay. He told me strange stories. It has always been a pleasure to me through life to catch at every opportunity that has occured in my rambles, of becoming acquainted with this class of people. The number of Peter's Wives was taken from the trespasses in this way of a lawless creature who lived in the county of Durham, and used to be attended by many women, sometimes not less than half a dozen, as disorderly as himself—and a story went in the country that he had been heard to say while they were quarrelling, 'Why can't you be quiet? there's none so many of you.' —Benoni, or the child of sorrow, I knew when I was a school-boy. His

---

heard, *revised in pencil from* heard
1798 *DQ revised from* 1789
in this way *inserted*
and used *revised from* who used

went in *revised from* [?was told]
sorrow...when *entered over illegible erasure*
His *revised from* It

[35]
Mother had been deserted by a gentleman in the neighbourhood, she herself, being a gentlewoman by birth. The circumstances of her story were told me by my dear old Dame, Ann Tyson, who was her confidante. The Lady died broken-hearted.—In the woods of Alfoxden I used to take great delight in noticing the habits tricks and physiognomy of asses; and I have no doubt that I was thus put upon writing the poem out of liking for the creature that is so often dreadfully abused.—The crescent-moon which makes such a figure in the prologue assumed this character one evening while I was watching its beauty in front of Alfoxden House. I intended this poem for the volume before spoken of, but it was not published for more than 20 years afterwards.— The worship of the Methodists or Ranters is often heard during the stillness of the summer evening in the country with affecting accompaniments of rural beauty. In both the psalmody & the voice of the preacher there is, not unfrequently, much solemnity likely to impress the feelings of the rudest characters under favourable circumstances.

Naming of Places. It was an April Morn &c—Grasmere, 1800. This poem was suggested on the banks of the brook that runs through Easedale, which is in some parts of its course as wild &

Dame, Ann Tyson, *revised in pencil from* Dame Ann Tyson
makes *revised from* made

intended this *revised from* began to write the
wild MW *revised in pencil from* wide

[36] beautiful as brook can be. I have composed thousands of verses by the side of it

To Joanna Hutchinson.   Grasmere, 1800. The effect of her laugh is an extravagance; though the effect of the reverberation of voices in some parts of these mountains is very striking. There is in the Excursion an allusion to the bleat of a lamb thus reechoed, and described without any exaggeration, as I heard it on the side of Stickle Tarn from the precipice [   ] that stretches on to Langdale Pikes.

There is an Eminence &c.   1800. It is not accurate that the eminence here alluded to could be seen from our orchard-seat. It arises above the road by the side of Grasmere Lake, towards Keswick, and its name is Stone Arthur.

Point Rash Judgement.   1800. The character of the eastern shore of Grasmere Lake is quite changed since these verses were written, by the public road being carried along its side. The friends spoken of were Coleridge and my Sister, & the fact occurred strictly as recorded.

To Mary Hutchinson.   Two years before our marriage. The pool alluded to is in Rydal Upper Park.

When to the attractions of the busy world."   1805. The Grove still exists; but the plantation has been walled in, and is not so accessible as when my brother John wore the path in the manner

---

stretches *revised from* streches
Sister,...strictly *revised from* Sister. The facts spoken of occur strictly

to the *ed. emended from* to the'
the busy *revised from* this busy
The Grove *revised from* This Grove

[37] here described. The grove was a favorite haunt with us all while we lived at Town-End.—

Miscellaneous Sonnets. Part 1. In the cottage of Town-End, one afternoon, in 1801, my Sister read to me the Sonnets of Milton. I had long been well acquainted with them, but I was particularly struck on that occasion with the dignified simplicity and majestic harmony that runs through most of them—in character so totally different from the Italian, and still more so from Shakespeare's fine Sonnets. I took fire, if I may be allowed to say so, and produced three sonnets the same afternoon, the first I ever wrote, except an irregular one at School. Of these three the only one I distinctly remember is, "*I grieved for Bonaparte* &c." One was never written down; the third, which was I believe preserved, I cannot particularise.

Sonnet 6. There is a little unpretending Rill. This rill trickles down the hillside into Windermere near Low-wood. My Sister & I on our first visit together to this part of the country, walked from Kendal, & we rested to refresh ourselves by the side of the lake where the streamlet falls into it. This sonnet was written some years after in recollection of that happy ramble, that most happy day & hour.

Sonnet 8. The fairest brightest hues &c: Suggested at Hackett, which is on the craggy ridge that rises between the two Langdales & looks towards Windermere.

---

was a *revised from* was the
Part I. *inserted*
in 1801, *inserted*
the first *revised from* The first
One *revised from* One of the others

Low-wood *revised from* Lowwood
Suggested at Hackett…Windermere. *revised from* The cottage of Hackett was very often visited by us
Win-dermere *runs over to p. 38*

[38]
The cottage of Hackett was often visited by us, & at the time when this Sonnet was written, & long after, was occupied by the husband & wife described in the Excursion, where it is mentioned that she was in the habit of walking in the front of the dwelling with a light to guide her husband home at night. The same cottage is alluded to in the epistle to Sir G. Beaumont as that from which the female peasant hailed us on our morning journey. The Musician mentioned in the Sonnet was the Revd S. Tillbrook of Peterhouse, who remodelled the Ivy Cottage at Rydal after he had purchased it.

Sonnet 9. On a beautiful picture by G. Beaumont. This was written when we dwelt in the Parsonage at Grasmere, The principal features of the picture are Bredon Hill & Cloud Hill near Coleorton. I shall never forget the happy feeling with which my heart was filled when I was impelled to compose this Sonnet. We resided only two years in this house; and during the last half of the time, which was after this poem had been written, we lost our two children Thomas and Catherine. Our sorrow upon these events often brought it to my mind, & cast me upon the support to which the last line of it gives expression,

"The appropriate calm of blest eternity."

It is scarcely necessary to add that we still possess the picture.

Sonnet 11. Aerial Rock! &c A projecting point of

Revd *revised from* Rever
Ivy Cottage *revised from* ivy cottage
a beautiful picture *revised from* the sight
Bredon Hill & Cloud Hill near *revised from* Bredon & Cloud Hills by

which my *revised from* my
it to my mind *revised from* to my mind this sonnet

[39]

Loughrigg, nearly in front of Rydal Mount. Thence looking at it, you are struck with the boldness of its aspect; but walking under it, you admire the beauty of its details. It is vulgarly called Holme-scar, probably from the insulated pasture by the waterside below it

Sonnet 15. Wild Duck's Nest. I observed this beautiful nest in the largest island of Rydal Water.

Sonnet 19. Grief thou hast lost. I could write a treatise of lamentation upon the changes brought about among the cottages of Westmoreland by the silence of the Spinning Wheel. During long winter nights & wet days, the wheel upon which wool was spun gave employment to a great part of a family. The old man, however infirm, was able to card the wool, as he sate in the corner by the fire-side; and often, when a boy, have I admired the cylinders of carded wool which were softly laid upon each other by his side. Two wheels were often at work on the same floor, and others of the family, chiefly the little children, were occupied in teasing and cleaning the wool to fit it for the hand of the carder. So that all except the smallest infants were contributing to mutual support Such was the employment that prevailed in the pastoral vales. Where wool was not at hand, in the small rural towns, the wheel for spinning flax was almost in as constant use, if knitting was not preferred; which latter occupation had the advantage (in some cases disadvantage) that

---

looking *revised from* looked
largest *revised from* larger
Sonnet 19 *revised from* Sonnet 16
Wheel. *revised from* Wheel,
wheel...wool *revised from* wool...the wool

chiefly...children, *inserted*
occupied *revised from* employed
teasing *revised from* cl
smallest *revised from* meanest
had *revised from* that

[40]

not being of necessity stationary, it allowed of gossipping about from house to house, which good housewives reckoned an idle thing.

Sonnet 22. Decay of Piety. Attendance at church on prayer-days, Wednesdays and Fridays and holidays, received a shock at the revolution. It is now, however, happily reviving. The ancient people described in this Sonnet were among the last of that pious class, May we hope that the practise, now in some degree renewed, will continue to spread.

Sonnets 24, 25 & 26. Translations from Michael Angelo, done at the request of M^r. Duppa, whose acquaintance I made through M^r. Southey. M^r. Duppa was engaged in writing the life of Michael Angelo, and applied to M^r. Southey and myself to furnish some specimens of his poetic genius.

Sonnet 27. This was in fact suggested by my daughter Catherine long after her death.

Sonnets 28 & 29. The latter part of the first of these was a great favourite with my Sister Sara Hutchinson. When I saw her lying in death I could not resist the impulse to compose the Sonnet that follows.

Sonnet 30. This was composed on the beach near Calais in the autumn of 1802.

Sonnet 37. Personal Talk. Written at Town-End. The last line but two stood at first, better and more characteristically, thus:

Sonnet 22 *inserted*
Decay *revised from* The Decay

revolution *revised from* [?revalution]
Sara *EQ revised in pencil to* Sarah

[41]
   By my half-kitchen and half-parlour fire.

My Sister and I were in the habit of having the tea-kettle in our little sitting room; and we toasted the bread ourselves which reminds me of a little circumstance not unworthy of being set down among these minutiae. Happening both of us to be engaged a few minutes one morning when we had a young prig of a Scotch Lawyer to breakfast with us, my dear Sister, with her usual simplicity, put the toasting-fork with a slice of bread into the hands of this Edinburgh genius. Our little bookcase stood on one side of the fire. To prevent loss of time, he took down a book and fell to reading to the neglect of the toast, which was burnt to a cinder. Many a time have we laughed at this circumstance and other cottage-simplicities of that day. By the bye, I have a spite at one of this Series of Sonnets (I will leave the reader to discover which) as having been the means of nearly putting off for ever our acquaintance with dear Miss Fenwick, who has always stigmatised one line of it as vulgar and worthy only of having been composed by a country Squire.

   Sonnet 42.   Composed in Edinburgh, during my Scotch tour with Mary & Sara, in the year 1814. Poor Gillies never rose above that course of extravagance in which he was at that time living, & which

---

tea- *inserted*   when *revised from* while

[42]

soon reduced him to poverty and all its degrading shifts, mendicity being far from the worst. I grieve whenever I think of him; for he was far from being without genius; and had a generous heart—not always to be found in men given up to profusion. He was nephew of Lord Gillies the Scotch Judge and also of the historian of Greece. He was cousin of Miss Margaret Gillies, who painted so many portraits with success in our house.

Sonnet 43. Suggested by observation of the way in which a young friend, whom I do not choose to name, misspent his time and misapplied his talents. He took afterwards a better course, and became an useful member of society, respected, I believe, wherever he has been known.

Sonnet 44. Suggested in front of Rydal Mount, the rocky parapet being the summit of Loughrigg Fell opposite. Not once only, but a hundred times, have the feelings of this Sonnet been awakened by the same objects seen from the same place.

Sonnet 47, This young man, Raisley Calvert, to whom I was so much indebted, died at Penrith 179–

---

worst *revised from* world
heart—not *revised from* heart, which is not

also *inserted*
with *over illegible erasure*

[43]

Miscellaneous Sonnets. Part 2.

Sonnet 1.   Composed, almost ex tempore, in a short walk on the western side of Rydal Lake.

Sonnet 3.   Suggested in the wild hazel-wood at foot of Helm-Crag where the Stone still lies, with others of like form and character—though much of the wood that veiled it from the glare of day has been felled. This beautiful ground was lately purchased by our friend M^{rs}. Fletcher, the ancient owners, most respected persons, being obliged to part with it in consequence of the imprudence if not misconduct of a son. It is gratifying to mention that instead of murmuring and repining at this change of fortune they offered their services to M^{rs}. Fletcher, the husband as an out-door labourer & the wife as a domestic servant. I have witnessed the pride & pleasure with which the man worked at improvements of the ground round the house. Indeed he expressed them to me himself & the countenance & manner of his wife always denoted feelings of the same character, I believe a similar disposition to contentment under change of fortune is common among the class to which these good people belong. Yet, in proof that to part with their patrimony is most painful to them, I may refer to

---

character—though *revised from* character.   expressed them *revised from* spoke of it
Though   among *revised from* to

[44] those stanzas entitled "Repentance," no inconsiderable part of which was taken verbatim from the language of the speaker herself.

Sonnet 4. October 3ᵈ. or 4ᵗʰ 1802. Composed, after a journey over the Hambleton Hills, on a day memorable to me—the day of my marriage. The horizon commanded by those hills is most magnificent

The next day, while we were travelling, in a post-chaise up Wensley Dale, we were stopt by one of the horses proving restiff, and were obliged to wait two hours in a severe storm before the postboy could fetch from the Inn another to supply its place. The spot was in front of Bolton Hall, where Mary Queen of Scots was kept prisoner soon after her unfortunate landing at Workington. The place then belonged to the Scroopes and memorials of her are yet preserved there. To beguile the time I composed a sonnet. The subject was our own confinement contrasted with her's; but it was not thought worthy of being preserved.

Sonnet 6. September 1815. For me, who under kindlier laws &c This conclusion has more than once, to my great regret, excited painfully sad feelings in the hearts of young persons fond of poetry and poetic composition by contrast of their feeble and declining health with that state of robust constitution which

---

herself *MW revised in pencil from* himself   we *inserted*
3ᵈ· or 4ᵗʰ *inserted*

[45]

prompted me to rejoice in a season of frost and snow as more favorable to the Muses than summer itself.

Sonnet 7. Nov^br. 1. Suggested on the banks of the Brathay, by the sight of Langdale Pikes. It is delightful to remember these moments of far-distant days, which probably would have been forgotten if the impression had not been transferred to verse. The same observation applies to the next.

Sonnet. 8. Composed during a storm in Rydal Wood by the side of a torrent.

Sonnet 11. 1807. To Lady Beaumont. The winter garden of Coleorton, fashioned out of an old quarry under the superintendence and direction of M^rs. Wordsworth and my Sister Dorothy, during the winter & spring of the year we resided there.

Sonnet 21. Written on a journey from Brinsop Court Herefordshire.

Sonnet 22. 1807. Coleorton. This Old Man's name was Mitchell. He was, in all his ways and conversation, a great curiosity, both individually and as a representative of past times. His chief employment was keeping watch at night by pacing round the house, at that time building, to keep off depredators. He has often told me gravely of having seen the Seven Whistlers & the Hounds as here described. Among the groves of Coleorton, where I became familiar with the habits & notions

---

on…Brathay, *inserted*
next *revised from* next
Sonnet 8. Composed *revised from*
   8, composed

Sonnet. .. Beaumont *ed. added italics*
fashioned *revised from* which was fashioned
Sonnet 22. 1807 *ed. added italics*
no-tions *runs over to p. 46*

[46]
of Old Mitchell, there was also a labourer of whom I regret I had no personal knowledge; for, more than forty years after, when he was become an old man, I learnt that while I was composing verses, which I usually did aloud, he took much pleasure, unknown to me, in following my steps that he might catch the words I uttered, and, what is not a little remarkable, several lines caught in this way kept their place in his memory. My volumes have lately been given to him, by my informant, and surely he must have been gratified to meet in print his old acquaintance.

Sonnet 23. Suggested on the road between Preston & Lancaster where it first gives a view of the Lake Country, & composed on the same day, on the roof of the coach.

Sonnet 29. Also composed on the roof of a coach, on my way to France, Sep^br. 1802.

Sonnet 35. This parsonage was the residence of my friend Jones, and is particularly described in another note.

Sonnet 37. In this Vale of Meditation my friend Jones resided, having been allowed by his Diocesan to fix himself there without resigning his Living in Oxfordshire. He was with my wife & daughter and me when we visited these celebrated ladies who had retired, as one may say, into notice in

---

by my informant, *inserted*

[47]

this vale. Their cottage lay directly in the road between London & Dublin, and they were of course visited by their Irish Friends as well as innumerable strangers. They took much delight in passing jokes on our friend Jones's plumpness, ruddy cheeks & smiling countenance, as little suited to a hermit living in the Vale of Meditation, We all thought there was ample room for retort on his part, so curious was the appearance of these ladies, so elaborately sentimental about themselves and their *Caro Albergo,* as they named it in an inscription on a tree that stood opposite, the endearing epithet being preceded by the word, Ecco! calling upon the Saunterer to look about him. So oddly was one of these ladies attired that we took her, at a little distance, for a Roman Catholic Priest, with a crucifix and relics hung at his neck. They were without caps their hair bushy and white as snow which contributed to the mistake.

 Sonnet 39. See Note.

 Sonnet 41. This is taken from the account given by Miss Jewsbury of the pleasure she derived, when long confined to her bed by sickness, from the inanimate object on which this Sonnet turns.

 Sonnet 43. The fate of this poor dove, as described, was told to me at Brinsop Court, by the Young Lady

---

told to me *revised from* told me   by the *revised from* by a

[48]
to whom I have given the name of Lesbia.

Sonnet 44.   The infant was Mary Monkhouse, the only daughter of our friend and cousin Thomas Monkhouse.

Sonnet 45.   Lady [   ] Fitzgerald as described to me by Lady Beaumont

Sonnet 46.   Rotha, the daughter of my Son-in-law M^r. Quillinan.

Sonnet 47. Miserrimus.   Many conjectures have been formed as to the person who lies under this Stone. Nothing appears to be known for a certainty. ? —The Revd M^r. Morris, a Non-Conformist, a sufferer for conscience-sake; a worthy man, who having been deprived of his benefice after the accession of William 3^d. lived to an old age in extreme destitution, on the alms of charitable Jacobites.—

Sonnet 48.   My attention to these antiquities was directed by M^r. Walker, Son to the itinerant Eidouranian Philosopher. The beautiful pavement was discovered within a few yards of the front door of his parsonage, and appeared (from the site in full view of several hills upon which there had formerly been Roman encampments) as if it might have been the villa of the commander of the forces, at least such was M^r. W.'s conjecture.

Lady…Beaumont. *revised from* This Lady was described by Lady Beaumont Her name was

Sonnet 46 *ed. added italics*

The Revd *inserted*

a worthy *revised from* & worthy after *revised from* on

formerly *inserted*

[49]

Sonnet 49. Chatsworth. I have reason to remember the day that gave rise to this Sonnet, the 6th. of Novbr. 1830. Having undertaken, a great feat for me, to ride my daughter's pony from Westmoreland to Cambridge, that she might have the use of it—while on a visit to her Uncle at Trinity Lodge, on my way from Bakewell to Matlock I turned aside to Chatsworth, and had scarcely gratified my curiosity by the sight of that celebrated place before there came on a severe storm of wind & rain, which continued till I reached Derby, both man & pony in a pitiable plight. For myself I went to bed at noonday. In the course of that journey I had to encounter a storm worse if possible in which the pony could (or would) only make his way slant-wise. I mention this merely to add that, notwithstanding this battering, I composed, on pony-back, the lines to the memory of Sir George Beaumont, suggested during my recent visit to Coleorton.

Sonnet 50. This pleasing tradition was told me by the coachman at whose side I sate while he drove down the dale, he pointing to the trees on the hill as he related the story.

Sonnet 51. Filial Piety. This was also communicated to me by a coachman in the same way. In the course of my many coach rambles

---

that she…of it— *revised from* for her use
pony-back *revised from* horseback

at whose side *revised from* by whose side
course *revised in error to* courses

[50] and journeys which, during the daytime always, and often in the night, were taken on the outside of the coach, I had good & frequent opportunities of learning the character of this class of men. One remark I made that is worth recording, that whenever I had occasion especially to notice their well-ordered, respectful and kind behaviour to women, of whatever age, I found them, I may say almost always, to be married men.

Sonnet 52. To the Author's portrait. The six last lines of this sonnet are not written for poetical effect but as a matter of fact, which in more than one instance, could not escape my notice in the servants of the house.

Sonnet 53. In the month of January, [   ], when Dora and I were walking from Town End Grasmere across the vale, snow being on the ground, she espied in the thick though leafless hedge, a bird's nest half filled with snow. Out of this comfortless appearance arose this Sonnet, which was in fact written without the least reference to any individual object, but merely to prove to myself that I could, if I thought fit, write in a strain that poets have been fond of. On the 14th. of Feby. in the same year, my daughter, in a sportive mood, sent it as a Valentine under a fictitious name to her Cousin C.W.—

Sonnet 54. This Sonnet, though said to be written

---

sonnet *MW revised in pencil from* portrait reference to any *inserted*

could, if I thought fit, write in *revised from* could write to

[51]
on seeing the portrait of Napoleon was in fact composed some time after, extempore, in the wood at Rydal Mount—

Memorials of a Tour in Scotland, 1803.

Mʳ. Coleridge, my Sister & myself started together from Town End to make a tour in Scotland—August [   ].

Poor Coleridge was at that time in bad spirits, & somewhat too much in love with his own dejection, and he departed from us, as is recorded in my Sister's Journal, soon after we left Loch Lomond. The verses that stand foremost among these memorials were not actually written for the occasion, but transplanted from my epistle to Sir G. Beaumont

To the Sons of Burns. See, in connection with these verses, two other Poems upon Burns, one composed actually at the time, and the other though then felt not put into words till several years afterwards.

Ellen Irwin or the Braes of Kirtle. It may be worth while to observe that as there are Scotch Poems on this subject in the simple ballad strain, I thought it would be both presumptuous and superfluous to attempt treating it in the same way; and, accordingly, I chose a construction of stanza quite new in our language; in fact the same as that of Burgher's *Leonora,* except that the first & third line do not, in my stanzas, rhyme.

————

from Town End *inserted*   as that of *inserted, with* of *in MW's pencil*

[52]
At the outset I threw out a classical image to prepare the reader for the style in which I meant to treat the story, and so to preclude all comparison.

The Highland Girl.   This delightful creature & her demeanour are particularly described in my Sister's Journal. The sort of prophecy with which the verses conclude has through God's goodness been realized, and now, approaching the close of my 73rd year I have a most vivid remembrance of her and the beautiful objects with which she was surrounded. She is alluded to in the Poem of "The Three Cottage Girls" among my continental memorials. In illustration of this class of poems I have scarcely anything to say beyond what is anticipated in my Sister's faithful and admirable Journal.

Address to Kilchurn-Castle.   The first three lines were thrown off at the moment I first caught sight of the Ruin from a small eminence by the way side; the rest was added many years after.

Rob Roy's Grave.   I have since been told that I was misinformed as to the burial-place of Rob Roy. If so, I may plead in excuse that I wrote on apparently good authority, namely that of a well-educated Lady who lived at the head of the Lake within a mile or less of the point indicated as containing the remains of One so famous in that neighbourhood.

& her *revised from* is her
One *revised from* one

neighbourhood *revised from* neigbourhood in

[53]

Sonnet composed at ——— Castle. 1803. The castle here mentioned was Nidpath, near Peebles. The person alluded to was the then Duke of Queensbury. The fact was told me by Walter Scott

Sonnet. Fly some kind Harbinger. This was actually composed the last day of our tour between Dalston & Grasmere.

The Blind Highland Boy. The story was told me by George Mackreth for many years parish-clerk of Grasmere. He had been an eye-witness of the occurrence. The vessel in reality was a washing-tub, which the little fellow had met with on the shore of the loch.

Second Tour in Scotland. 1814.

In this Tour my wife and her Sister Sara were my companions.— The account of the *Brownie's Cell,* & the Brownies was given me by a man we met with on the banks of Loch Lomond, a little above Tarbet, and in front of a huge mass of rock by the side of which, we were told, preachings were often held in the open air. The place is quite a solitude, & the surrounding scenery very striking. How much is it to be regretted that, instead of writing such poems as the Holy fair & others, in which the religious observances of his country are treated with

---

1803. inserted
here mentioned *revised from* named in this
Nidpath *revised from* Nedpath
a man *revised from* the man

Tarbet *ed. emended from* Tarbert
preachings were *revised from* preachings are
observances *revised from* offices

[54]
so much levity and too often with indecency, Burns had not employed his genius in describing religion under the serious and affecting aspects it must so frequently take.

Cora Linn.   I had seen this celebrated Waterfall twice before. But the feelings to which it had given birth were not expressed till they recurred in presence of the object on this occasion.

Effusion, near Dunkeld.   I am not aware that this condemnatory effusion was ever seen by the owner of the place, He might be disposed to pay little attention to it; but were it to prove otherwise, I should be glad, for the whole exhibition is distressingly puerile.

Yarrow Visited.   As mentioned in my verses on the death of the Ettrick Shepherd, my first visit to Yarrow was in his company, We had lodged the night before at Traquhair where Hogg had joined us,—& also D^r. Anderson the Editor of the British Poets, who was on a visit at the Manse. D^r. A. walked with us till we came in view of the vale of Yarrow, & being advanced in life he then turned back. The Old Man was passionately fond of poetry though with not much of a discriminating judgment, as the volumes he edited sufficiently shew. But

---

genius *revised from* religion
before. *revised from* before this tour was made
place. *revised from* place,

Poets, who…walked *revised from* Poets. They walked *revised from* Poets. Dr. A. walked

[55]

I was much pleased to meet with him, and to acknowledge my obligation to his collection, which had been my brother John's companion in more than one voyage to India, & which he gave me before his departure from Grasmere never to return. Through these volumes I became first familiar with Chaucer, and so little money had I then to spare for books that, in all probability, but for this same work, I should have known little of Drayton, Daniel, and other distinguished poets of the Elizabethan age and their immediate successors till a much later period of my life, I am glad to record this, not for any importance of its own, but as a tribute of gratitude to this simple-hearted old man whom I never again had the pleasure of meeting. I seldom read or think of this poem without regretting that my dear Sister was not of the party, as she would have had so much delight in recalling the time when, travelling together in Scotland, we declined going in search of this celebrated stream, not altogether, I will frankly confess, for the reasons assigned in the poem on the occasion.——

[56]

Sonnets dedicated to Liberty.

Sonnet 12. Two Voices are there. This was composed while pacing to and fro between the Hall of Coleorton, then rebuilding, & the principal Farm-house of the Estate, in which we lived for 9 or 10 months. I will here mention that the Song on the Restoration of Lord Clifford, as well as that on the feast of Brougham Castle, as mentioned p. 29, were produced on the same ground.

Sonnet 13. London, Sep^{br}. 1802. This was written immediately after my return from France to London, when I could not but be struck, as here described, with the vanity and parade of our own country, especially in great towns and cities as contrasted with the quiet, and I may say the desolation, that the revolution had produced in France. This must be borne in mind, or else the reader may think that in this & the succeeding sonnets I have exaggerated the mischief engendered & fostered among us by undisturbed wealth.

Sonnet 12. *inserted*
then rebuilding, *inserted*

as mentioned p. 29, *inserted*
engendered & *inserted*

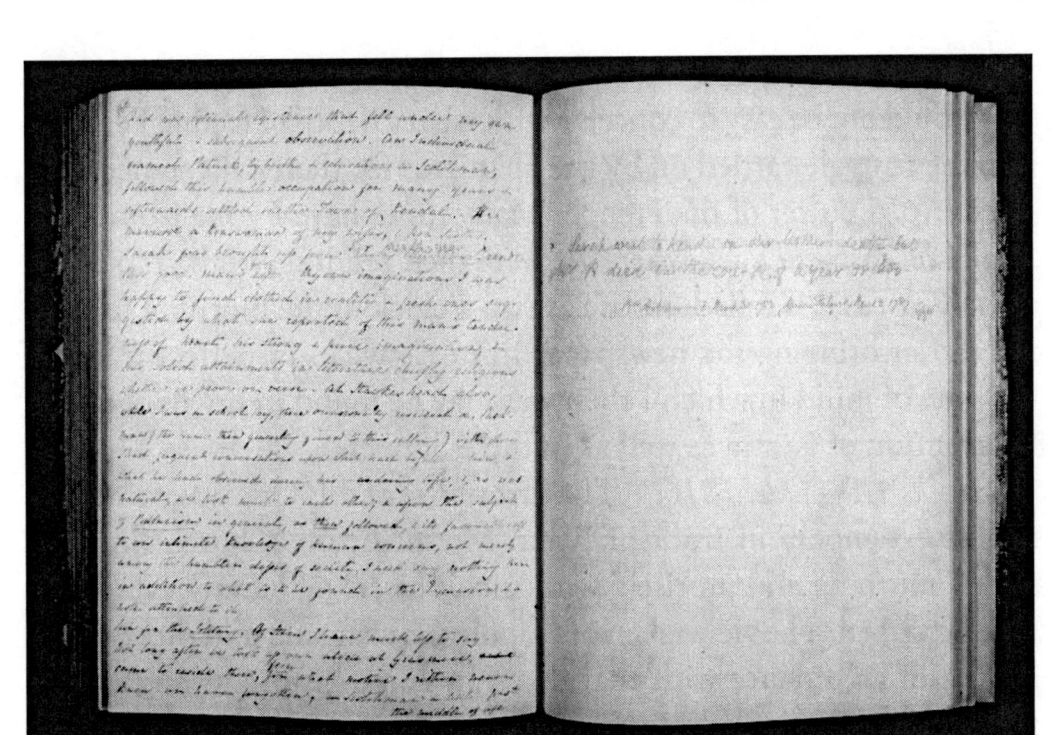

The opening between pp. 56 and 58 of the notebook is blank. EQ's pencil query at foot of p. 56 indicates he left space for the addition of notes to 'Sonnets relating to the expected Invasion' and to poems in the rest of parts I and II of the sonnets to *Liberty*, but no notes were supplied.

In the available space above is shown the notebook opening shown that is transcribed on p. 196 below. It shows DQ employing the left page for transcription and MW using the right for pencil commentary of her own. For a transcription of MW's pencil entry, see the editor's note to Notebook p. 160 on p. 374 below. This image is best viewed at a magnification of 200%. Image courtesy of Dove Cottage, The Wordsworth Trust.

[58]

It would not be easy to conceive with what a depth of feeling I entered into the struggle carried on by the Spaniards for their deliverance from the usurped power of the French. Many times have I gone from Allan Bank in Grasmere Vale, where we were then residing, to the top of the Raise-Gap, as it is called, so late as two o'clock in the morning to meet the carrier bringing the newspaper from Keswick. Imperfect traces of the state of mind in which I then was may be found in my tract on the Convention of Cintra as well as in these Sonnets.

Thanksgiving Ode. 1816. The first stanza of this Ode was composed almost extempore in front of Rydal Mount before Church-time, on such a morning and precisely with such objects before my eyes as are here described. The view taken of Napoleon's character and proceedings is little in accordance with that taken by some historians and critical philosophers. I am glad & proud of the difference, and trust that this series of poems, infinitely below the subject as they are, will survive to counteract in unsophisticated minds the pernicious and degrading tendency of those views

---

in Grasmere *revised from* and Grasmere
bringing *revised in pencil from* meeting

on such *revised from* & on such

[59]
and doctrines that lead to the idolatry of power as power, and in that false splendour to lose sight of its real nature and constitution as it often acts for the gratification of its possessor or without reference to a beneficial end—an infirmity that has characterised men of all ages, classes, & employments since Nimrod became a mighty hunter before the Lord.

Inscriptions. N°. 1. In the grounds of Coleorton these verses are engraved on a stone, placed near the Tree, which was thriving & spreading when I saw it in the Summer of 1841.

2. This Niche is in the sandstone rock in the winter-garden at Coleorton, which garden, as has been elsewhere said, was made under our direction out of an old unsightly quarry. While the labourers were at work M^rs. Wordsworth, my Sister & I used to amuse ourselves occasionally in scooping this seat out of the soft stone. It is of the size, with something of the appearance, of a stall in a Cathedral. This inscription is not engraven, as the former & the two following are, in the grounds.

6. The circumstance alluded to at the conclusion of these verses was told me by D^r. Satterthwaite, who was Incumbent of Bootle, a small town at the foot of Black Comb.

N°.1. *inserted*
Tree *revised from* tree
of the size *revised from* the size

This inscription *revised from* The inscription
Bootle *ed. emended from* Boodle

[60] He had the particulars from one of the engineers, who was employed in making trigonometrical surveys of that region.

8. Engraven, during my absence in Italy, upon a brass plate inserted in the stone.

9. The walk is what we call *the far-terrace,* beyond the Summer-house at Rydal Mount. The lines were written when we were afraid of being obliged to quit the place to which we were so much attached.

11. The monument of ice here spoken of I observed while ascending the middle road of the three ways that lead from Rydal to Grasmere. It was on my right hand, and my eyes were upon it when it fell as told in these lines.

12. Where the second quarry now is, as you pass from Rydal to Grasmere there was formerly a length of smooth rock that sloped towards the road on the right hand. I used to call it tadpole slope from having frequently observed there the water-bubbles gliding under the ice, exactly in the shape of that creature.

Written in the Album of a Child. This quatrain was extempore on observing this image, as I had often done, on the lawn of Rydal Mount. It was first written down in the Album of my God-daughter Rotha Quillinan.

☙

---

afraid of being *inserted*
from Rydal *revised from* from Gr
This quatrain was *revised from* These verses were

God-daughter Rotha Quillinan. *EQ entered first in pencil then in ink*

[61]

Lines in Lady Lonsdale's Album. This is a faithful picture of that amiable Lady as she then was. The youthfulness of figure & demeanour and habits, which she retained in almost unprecedented degree, departed a very few years after & she died without violent disease by gradual decay before she reached the period of old age.

The Egyptian Maid. In addition to the short notice prefixed to this poem it may be worth while here to say that it rose out of a few words casually used in conversation by my nephew Henry Hutchinson. He was describing with great spirit the appearance and movement of a vessel which he seemed to admire more than any other he had ever seen, & said her name was the Water-Lily. This plant has been my delight from my boyhood, as I have seen it floating on the Lake; & that conversation put me upon constructing & composing the poem. Had I not heard those words it would never have been written. The form of the stanza is new, & is nothing but a repetition of the first five lines as they were thrown off, & is perhaps not well suited to narrative, & certainly would not have been trusted to had I thought at the beginning that the poem would have gone to such a length.

---

was. The *revised from* was, the very few *revised from* fe

that conversation *revised from* the conversation

[62]

The River Duddon. It is with the little River Duddon as it is with most other rivers, Ganges & Nile not excepted,—many springs might claim the honor of being its head. In my own fancy I have fixed its rise near the noted Shire stones placed at the meeting point of the counties Westmoreland, Cumberland and Lancashire, They stand by the way-side on the top of the Wry-nose Pass, & it used to be reckoned a proud thing to say, that by touching them at the same time with feet and hands one had been in three counties at once. At what point of its course the stream takes the name of Duddon I do not know. I first became acquainted with the Duddon, as I have good reason to remember, in early boyhood. Upon the banks of the Derwent I had learnt to be very fond of angling. Fish abound in that large river, not so in the small streams in the neighbourhood of Hawkshead; and I fell into the common delusion that the further from home the better sport would be had. Accordingly one day I attached myself to a person living in the neighbourhood of Hawkshead who was going to try his fortune as an angler near the source of the Duddon. We fished a great part of the day with very sorry success; the rain pouring torrents and long before we got home I was worn out with fatigue; and if the good man had not carried me on his back, I must

[63]
have lain down under the best shelter I could find. Little did I think then it would have been my lot to celebrate, in a strain of love and admiration, the stream which for many years I never thought of without recollections of disappointment & distress.

During my college-vacation, and two or three years afterwards, before taking my Bachelor's Degree, I was several times resident in the house of a near relative who lived in the small town of Broughton. I past many delightful hours upon the banks of this river, which becomes an estuary about a mile from that place. The remembrances of that period are the subject of the 21st. Sonnet.— The subject of the 27th. is in fact taken from a tradition belonging to Rydal Hall, which once stood, as is believed, upon a rocky & woody hill on the right hand as you go from Rydal to Ambleside, & was deserted from the superstitious fear here described, & the present site fortunately chosen instead. The present Hall was erected by Sir Michael Le Fleming, and it may be hoped that at some future time there will be an edifice more worthy of so beautiful a position. With regard to the 30th. Sonnet it is odd enough that this imagination was realised in the year 1840 when I made a tour through this district with my wife & daughter, Miss Fenwick &

---

celebrate, in a strain of...admiration, the stream *revised from* celebrate the stream in a strain of...admiration
27th. *revised from* 27th. Sonnet
rocky & *inserted*
it may be hoped *revised from* we must hope this

imagination *revised from* the circumstance anticipated
1840 *revised from* 1740
when *revised from* when in company

[64]

her niece & M^r^. & Miss Quillinan. Before our return from Seathwaite Chapel, the party separated, M^rs^. Wordsworth, while most of us went further up the stream, chose an opposite direction, having told us that we should overtake her on our way to Ulpha. But she was tempted out of the main road to ascend a rocky eminence near it, thinking it impossible we should pass without seeing her. This however unfortunately happened, and then ensued vexation & distress, especially to me, which I should be ashamed to have recorded, for I lost my temper entirely. Neither I nor those who were with me saw her again till we reached the Inn at Broughton seven miles. This may perhaps in some degree excuse my irritability on the occasion, for I could not but think she had been much to blame. It appeared however, on explanation, that she had remained on the rock, calling out and waving her handkerchief as we were passing, in order that we also might ascend & enjoy a prospect which had much charmed her. "But on we went, her signals proving vain." How then could she reach Broughton before us? When we found she had not gone on to Ulpha Kirk, M^r^. Quillinan went back in one of the carriages in search of her. He met her on the road, took her up and by a shorter way conveyed her to Broughton, where we were all reunited ⁓

---

in some degree excuse *revised from* ex
rock, *revised from* rock an
us? When *revised from* us, when

on *revised from* on before
were all reunited *revised from* arrived an hour later

[65]
and spent a happy evening.

I have many affecting remembrances connected with this stream. These I forbear to mention, especially things that occurred on its banks during the later part of that visit to the seaside of which the former part is detailed in my epistle to Sir George Beaumont.

The White Doe of Rylstone.   The earlier half of this Poem was composed at Stockton upon Tees, when Mary & I were on a visit to her eldest brother M^r. Hutchinson at the close of the year 1807. The country is flat & the weather was rough. I was accustomed every day to walk to & fro under the shelter of a row of stacks in a field at a small distance from the town, & I there poured forth my verses aloud as freely as they would come. Mary reminds me that her brother stood upon the punctilio of not sitting down to dinner till I joined the party; and it frequently happened that I did not make my appearance till too late, so that she was made uncomfortable. I here beg her pardon for this & similar transgressions during the whole course of our wedded life. To my beloved sister the same apology is due.

When, from the visit just mentioned, we returned to Town-End, Grasmere, I proceeded with the poem, it may be worth while to note as a caution to others who may cast their eye on these memoranda,

---

I have many *revised to new paragraph*
that visit *revised from* the visit
& I there poured *revised from* & there poured it

frequently *revised from* as frequently
made *revised from* rendered
note *revised from* notice

[66]
that the skin having been rubbed off my heel by my wearing too tight a shoe, though I desisted from walking I found that the irritation of the wounded part was kept up by the act of composition, to a degree that made it necessary to give my constitution a holiday. A rapid cure was the consequence.

Poetic excitement when accompanied by protracted labour in composition has throughout my life brought on more or less bodily derangement. Nevertheless I am, at the close of my seventy third year in what may be called excellent health, so that intellectual labour is not necessarily unfavourable to longevity. But perhaps I ought here to add that mine has been generally carried on out of doors.

Let me here say a few words on this Poem in the way of criticism. The subject being taken from feudal times has led to its being compared to some of Walter Scott's poems that belong to the same age & state of society. The comparison is inconsiderate. Sir Walter pursued the customary & very natural course of conducting an action, presenting various turns of fortune, to some outstanding point on which the mind might rest as a termination or catastrophe. The course I attempted to pursue is entirely different. Everything that is attempted by the principal

---

wearing *revised from* having worn
necessarily unfavourable *revised from* generally preferred

being taken from *revised from* turning on
customary *revised from* common

[67]
personages in "the White Doe" fails, so far as its object is external and substantial. So far as it is moral & spiritual it succeeds. The heroine of the poem knows that her duty is not to interfere with the current of events either to forward or delay them, but

> To abide
> The shock, and finally secure
> O'er pain & grief a triumph pure.

This she does in obedience to her brother's injunction, as most suitable to a mind & character that, under previous trials, had been proved to accord with his. She achieves this not without aid from the communication with the inferior creature, which often leads her thoughts to revolve upon the past with a tender & humanizing influence that exalts rather than depresses her. The anticipated beatification, if I may so say, of her mind, and the apotheosis of the companion of her solitude are the points at which the poem aims, & constitute its legitimate catastrophe, far too spiritual a one for instant or widely-spread sympathy, but not therefore the less fitted to make a deep & permanent impression upon that class of minds who think & feel more independently than the many do of the surfaces of things, and interests transitory because belonging more to the outward & social forms of life than to its internal spirit. How insignificant a thing, for example, does personal

---

interfere *revised from* mix
had been proved *revised from* have been proved
creature, which *revised from* creature, who
influence that *revised from* influence whic

rather than *revised from* rather
& social forms of life *revised from* forms of life and society
than to its *rev from* than to the *rev from* than to its

[68]

prowess appear compared with the fortitude of patience & heroic martyrdom, in other words with struggles for the sake of principle, in preference to victory gloried in for its own sake.

Memorials of a Tour on the Continent in 1820.

I set out in company with my Wife & Sister and Mʳ. & Mʳˢ. Monkhouse then just married & Miss Horrocks. These two ladies, sisters, we left at Berne while Mʳ. Monkhouse took the opportunity of making an excursion with us among the Alps, as far as Milan. Mʳ. H. C. Robinson joined us at Lucerne, & when this ramble was completed we rejoined at Geneva the two ladies we had left at Berne, & proceeded to Paris, where Mʳ. Monkhouse & H.C.R. left us, & where we spent five weeks of which there is not a record in these poems.

Sonnet 5. Between Namur & Liege. The scenery on the Meuse pleases me more, upon the whole, than that of the Rhine, though the river itself is much inferior in grandeur. The rocks both in form & colour, especially between Namur & [Huy,] surpass any upon the Rhine, though they are in several places disfigured by quarries, whence stones were taken for the new fortifications. This is much to be regretted, for they are useless & the scars will remain perhaps for thousands of years. A like injury to a still greater degree has been inflicted, in my

---

then just married *inserted*
the opportunity *revised from* this opportunity
two *inserted*

[Huy] *see editor's note*
surpass *revised from* surpasses
were taken *EQ inserted in pencil*

[69] memory, upon the beautiful rocks of Clifton on the banks of the Avon. There is probably in existence a very long letter of mine to Sir Uvedale Price in which was given a description of the landscapes on the Meuse as compared with those on the Rhine.

Details in the spirit of these Sonnets are given both in Mary's Journals & my Sister's, & the reperusal of them has strengthened a wish long entertained that somebody would put together, as in one work, the notices contained in them, omitting particulars that were written down merely to aid our memory, & bringing the whole into as small a compass as is consistent with the general interests belonging to the scenes, circumstances & objects touched on by each writer.

Ecclesiastical Sonnets.

My purpose in writing this Series was, as much as possible to confine my view to the introduction progress and operation of the Church in England, both previous & subsequent to the Reformation: the Sonnets were written long before Ecclesiastical History & points of doctrine had excited the interest with which they have been recently enquired into & discussed. The former particular is mentioned as an excuse for my having fallen into error in respect to an incident which had been selected as setting forth the height to which the power of the Popedom over temporal sovereignty

---

the reperusal of them has *revised from* they
is consistent *revised from* was consistent

an incident *revised from* a fact

[70]
had attained, & the arrogance with which it was displayed. I allude to the last Sonnet but one in the first Series, where Pope Alexander the 3rd., at Venice, is described as setting his foot on the neck of the Emperor Barbarossa. Though this is related as a fact in history, I am told it is a mere legend of no authority. Substitute for it an undeniable truth, not less fitted for my purpose, namely the penance inflicted by Gregory the 7th. upon the emperor Henry the 4th. at [Canosa.]

Before I conclude my notice of these Sonnets, let me observe that the opinion I pronounced in favour of Laud (long before the Oxford Tract movement) and which had brought censure upon me from several quarters is not in the least changed. Omitting here to examine into his conduct in respect to the persecuting spirit with which he has been charged, I am persuaded that most of his aims to restore ritual practises which had been abandoned were good and wise, whatever errors he might commit in the manner he sometimes attempted to enforce them. I further believe that had not he, and others who shared his opinions and felt as he did, stood up in opposition to the reformers of that period, it is questionable whether the Church would ever have recovered its lost ground and become the blessing it now is, and

---

the 3rd., at Venice, *inserted in ink, perhaps in MW's hand*
[Canosa.] *see editor's note*
and which had *revised from* in fact had

ritual *revised from* spiritual
manner *revised from* way
it…whether *revised from* much that had been lost *inserted*

[71]
will, I trust, become in a still greater degree both to those of its communion & those who unfortunately are separated from it.—

I saw the figure of a lovely maid. Sonnet 1. Part 3. When I came to this part of the Series I had the dream described in this sonnet The figure was that of my daughter, and the whole past exactly as here represented. The sonnet was composed on the middle road leading from Grasmere to Ambleside; it was begun as I left the last house of the vale, and finished, word for word as it now stands, before I came in view of Rydal. I wish I could say the same of the 5 or 6 hundred I have written: most of them were frequently retouched in the course of composition, and not a few laboriously.

I have only further to observe that the intended Church which prompted these Sonnets was erected on Coleorton Moor towards the centre of a very populous parish, between three and four miles from Ashby-de-la-Zouche, on the road to Loughborough, & has proved, I believe, a great benefit to the neighbourhood.

I saw *revised from* [?He] saw   it was begun *revised from* & it was begun

[72]

Prefatory lines to Vol. 5.—If thou indeed &c— Like an untended watch-fire &c— These verses were written some time after we had become residents at Rydal Mount, and I will take occasion from them to observe upon the beauty of that situation, as being backed & flanked by lofty fells which bring the heavenly bodies to touch, as it were, the earth upon the mountain tops while the prospect in front lies open to a length of level valley, the extended lake, & a terminating ridge of low hills so that it gives an opportunity to the inhabitants of the place of noticing the stars in both the positions here alluded to, namely on the tops of the mountains, & as winter-lamps at a distance among the leafless trees.

Expostulation & Reply. This poem is a favourite among the Quakers, as I have learnt on many occasions. It was composed in front of the house of Alfoxden, in the Spring of 1798.

The Tables Turned. Composed at the same time.

Lines left upon a Yew-tree Seat. Composed in part at school at Hawkshead. The tree has disappeared, & the slip of common on which it stood, that ran parallel to the lake and lay open to it, has long been enclosed, so that the road has lost much of its attraction. This spot was my favourite walk in the evenings during the latter part of my School-time, The individual whose

[73] habits and character are here given was a gentleman of the neighbourhood, a man of talent and learning who had been educated at one of our Universities, & returned to pass his time in seclusion on his own estate. He died a bachelor in middle age. Induced by the beauty of the prospect, he built a small summerhouse on the rocks above the penninsula on which the ferry-house stands.

This property afterwards past into the hands of the late M[r]. Curwen. The site was long ago pointed out by M[r]. West in his Guide as the pride of the Lakes, and now goes by the name of "The Station". So much used I to be delighted with the view from it, while a little boy, that some years before the first pleasure-house was built I led thither from Hawkshead a youngster about my own age, an Irish Boy who was a servant to an Itinerant Conjuror. My motive was to witness the pleasure I expected the boy would receive from the prospect of the islands below & the intermingling water. I was not disappointed; and I hope the fact, insignificant as it may seem to some, may be thought worthy of note by others who may cast their eye over these notes.

Lines written while sailing in a boat at evening, 1789. This title is scarcely correct. It was during a solitary walk on the banks of the Cam that I was first struck with this appearance, & applied it to my own feelings in ☙

---

summerhouse on *revised from* summerhouse ab
ferry-house *revised from* ferry

"The Station" *revised from* the Station
delighted *revised from* disappointed
applied it to *revised from* applied to

[74]
the manner here expressed, changing the scene to the Thames, near Windsor. This, and the three stanzas of the following poem, "Remembrance of Collins" formed one piece; but, upon the recommendation of Coleridge, the three last stanzas were separated from the other.

Lines written in early Spring.   1798. Actually composed while I was sitting by the side of the brook that runs down from the *Comb,* in which stands the village of Alford, through the grounds of Alfoxden. It was a chosen resort of mine, The brook fell down a sloping rock so as to make a waterfall considerable for that country, and, across the pool below, had fallen a tree, an ash if I rightly remember, from which rose perpendicularly boughs in search of the light intercepted by the deep shade above. The boughs bore leaves of green that for want of sunshine had faded into almost lily-white: and, from the underside of this natural sylvan bridge depended long & beautiful tresses of ivy which waved gently in the breeze that might poetically speaking be called the breath of the water-fall. This motion varied of course in proportion to the power of water in the brook. When with dear friends I revisited this spot, after an interval of more than forty years, this interesting feature of the scene was gone. To the Owner of the place I could not but regret that the beauty of this retired part of the grounds had not tempted him to make it more accessible, by a path, not broad or

---

"Remembrance of Collins" *inserted* from *revised from* through Comb *revised from* comb

in...Alford, *entered, then deleted, after* brook breeze that *revised from* breeze m

[75] obtrusive; but sufficient for persons who love such scenes to creep along without difficulty.

A Character. The principal features are taken from that of my friend Robert Jones.

To my Sister. Composed in front of Alfoxden House. My little boy messenger on this occasion was the son of Basil Montagu, The larch mentioned in the first stanza was standing when I revisited the place in May 1841, more than 40 years after.— I was disappointed that it had not improved in appearance, as to size, nor had it acquired anything of the majesty of age, which, even though less perhaps than any other tree, the larch sometimes does.— A few score yards from this tree, grew, when we inhabited Alfoxden, one of the most remarkable beech-trees ever seen. The ground sloped both towards & from it. It was of immense size, and threw out arms that struck into the soil like those of the banyan tree, & rose again from it. Two of the branches thus inserted themselves twice, which gave to each the appearance of a serpent moving along by gathering itself up in folds. One of the large boughs of this tree had been torn off by the wind before we left Alfoxden, but five remained. In 1841, we could barely find the spot where the tree had stood. So remarkable a production of nature could not have been wilfully destroyed.

---

features *revised from* features in it
Alfoxden House *revised from* Alfoxden, House
My little boy…Montagu. *ed. transposed, in accord with ink markings, with* The larch…after.—

as to size *revised from* either to size
themselves *ed. emended from* themselves themselves
could not have been *revised from* could not be

[76]

Simon Lee. This old man had been huntsman to the Squires of Alfoxden, which, at the time we occupied it belonged to a minor. The old man's cottage stood upon the common a little way from the entrance to Alfoxden Park. But it had disappeared. Many other changes had taken place in the adjoining village, which I could not but notice with a regret more natural than well-considered. Improvements but rarely appear such to those who, after long intervals of time, revisit places they have had much pleasure in, It is unnecessary to add, the fact was as mentioned in the poem, and I have, after an interval of 45 years, the image of the old man as fresh before my eyes as if I had seen him yesterday. The expression when the hounds were out, "I dearly love their voice," was word for word from his own lips.

Lines written in Germany. 1798 & 9. A plague &c. A bitter winter it was when these verses were composed, by the side of my Sister in our lodgings at a draper's house in the romantic imperial town of Goslar on the edge of the Hartz Forest. In this town the German emperors of the Franconian line were accustomed to keep their court, & it retains vestiges of ancient splendour. So severe was the cold of this winter, that when we past out of the parlour warmed by the stove, our cheeks were struck by the air as by cold iron. I slept in a room over a passage that was not ceiled. The people

---

who, after…time, *revised from* who poem, and *revised from* poem.
When Goslar *MW revised in pencil from* Guslar
peo-ple *runs over to p.* 77

[77] of the house used to say, rather unfeelingly, that they expected I should be frozen to death some night. With the protection of a pelisse lined with fur, & a dog's-skin bonnet such as was worn by the peasants, I walked daily on the ramparts, or in a sort of public ground or garden in which was a pond. Here I had no companion but a Kings fisher, a beautiful creature that used to glance by me. I consequently became much attached to it. During these walks I composed the poem that follows, *The Poet's Epitaph*.—

To the Daisy. This and the other poems addressed to the same flower were composed at Town End, Grasmere, during the earlier part of our residence there. I have been censured for the last line but one, 'Thy function apostolical' as being little less than profane. How could it be thought so? The word is adopted with reference to its derivation implying something sent on a mission; &, assuredly, this little flower, especially when the subject of verse, may be regarded, in its humble degree, as administering both to moral & to spiritual purposes.

[78]

Matthew. Such a tablet as is here spoken of continued to be preserved in Hawkshead School, though the inscriptions were not brought down to our time. This and other poems connected with Matthew would not gain by a literal detail of facts. Like the Wanderer in the Excursion, this Schoolmaster was made up of several both of his class & men of other occupations. I do not ask pardon for what there is of untruth in such verses, considered strictly as matters of fact. It is enough, if, being true & consistent in spirit, they move & teach in a manner not unworthy of a poet's calling.

To the Spade of a Friend. This person was Thomas Wilkinson, a quaker by religious profession, by natural constitution of mind, or shall I venture to say by God's grace, he was something better. He had inherited a small estate & built a house upon it near Yanwath upon the banks of the Emont. I have heard him say that his heart used to beat, in his boyhood, when he heard the sound of a drum & fife. Nevertheless the spirit of enterprise in him confined itself in tilling his ground, & conquering such obstacles as stood in the way of its fertility. Persons of his religious persuasion do now, in a far greater degree than formerly, attach themselves to trade & commerce. He kept the old track. As represented in this poem, he employed his leisure hours in shaping pleasant

---

calling *revised from* career   Yanwath *revised from* Yanworth

[79] walks by the side of his beloved river, where he also built something between a hermitage & a summerhouse, attaching to it inscriptions after the manner of Shenstone at his Leasowes. He used to travel from time to time, partly from love of nature, & partly with religious friends in the service of humanity. His admiration of genius in every department did him much honor. Through his connexion with the family in which Edmund Burke was educated, he became acquainted with that great man, who used to· receive him with great kindness and condescension: and many times have I heard Wilkinson speak of those interesting interviews. He was honored also by the friendship of Elizabeth Smith, & of Thomas Clarkson & his excellent wife, & was much esteemed by Lord & Lady Lonsdale and every member of that family. Among his verses, (he wrote many) are some worthy of preservation—one little poem in particular upon disturbing by prying curiosity a bird while hatching her young in his garden. The latter part of this innocent and good man's life was melancholy. He became blind, & also poor by becoming surety for some of his relations. He was a bachelor. He bore, as I have often witnessed, his calamities with unfailing resignation. I will only add that while working in one of his fields, he unearthed a stone

༄

---

used *revised from* was wont   I will *revised from* I would

[80]

of considerable size, then another, then two more, & observing that they had been placed in order as if forming the segment of a circle, he proceeded carefully to uncover the soil and brought into view a beautiful Druid's temple of perfect though small dimensions. In order to make his farm more compact he exchanged this field for another, and, I am sorry to add, the new proprietor destroyed this interesting relic of remote ages for some vulgar purpose, The fact, so far as concerns Thomas Wilkinson, is mentioned in the note on a Sonnet on Long Meg & her Daughters.

Incident characteristic of a favourite Dog. This dog I knew well. It belonged to M^rs. Wordsworth's brother M^r. Thomas Hutchinson, who then lived at Sockburn on the Tees, a beautiful retired situation where I used to visit him & his sisters before my marriage. My Sister & I spent many months there after my return from Germany in 1799.

Fidelity. The young man whose death gave occasion to this poem was named Charles Gough, and had come early in the Spring to Patterdale for the sake of angling, While attempting to cross over Helvellyn to Grasmere he slipped from a steep part of the rock where the ice was not thawed, & perished. His body was discovered as is told in this poem. Walter Scott heard of the accident, and both he & I, without either of us knowing that the other had taken

---

Daughters *revised from* Daughter
Sockburn *revised from* Stock

Walter *revised from* Sir Walter
ta-ken *runs over to p. 81*

[81]

up the subject, each wrote a poem in admiration of the dog's fidelity. His contained a most beautiful stanza:

> How long didst thou think that his silence was slumber?
> When the wind waved his garment how oft didst thou start

I will add that the sentiment in the last four lines of the last stanza of my verses was uttered by a shepherd with such exactness that a traveller, who afterwards reported his account in print, was induced to question the man whether he had read them, which he had not.

Ode to Duty. This ode, written 1805, is on the model of Gray's *Ode to Adversity* which is copied from Horace's Ode to Fortune—

Many & many a time have I been twitted by my wife and sister for having forgotten this dedication of myself to the stern law-giver. Transgressor indeed I have been, from hour to hour, from day to day; I would fain hope however, not more flagrantly nor in a worse way than most of my tuneful brethren. But these last words are in a wrong strain. We should be rigourous to ourselves, & forbearing if not indulgent to others, & if we make comparisons at all it ought to be with those who have morally excelled us.

Who is the happy Warrior. The course of the great war with the French naturally fixed one's attention upon

---

add that *revised from* add that by a shepherd
by a shepherd *inserted*
a traveller *revised from* the traveller
afterwards *inserted*
his account *revised from* it
after in print, *the words* for his *inserted above then deleted*

Adversity *revised from* Duty
not [*with* not *revised from* nor]
more flagrantly *inserted*
nor *revised from* or
than most *revised from* from most
brethren *ed. emended from* brethen

[82]
the military character, and, to the honor of our country, there were many illustrious instances of the qualities that constitute its highest excellence. Lord Nelson carried most of the virtues that the trials he was exposed to in his department of the service necessarily call forth & sustain if they do not produce the contrary vices. But his public life was stained with one great crime, so that though many passages of these lines were suggested by what was generally known as excellent in his conduct, I have not been able to connect his name with the poem as I could wish, or even to think of him with satisfaction in reference to the idea of what a warrior ought to be. For the sake of such of my friends as may happen to read this note, I will add that many elements of the character here pourtrayed were found in my brother John who perished by shipwreck as mentioned elsewhere. His messmates used to call him the Philosopher, from which it must be inferred that the qualities & dispositions I allude to had not escaped their notice, He often expressed his regret, after the war had continued some time, that he had not chosen the Naval instead of the East-India Company's Service to which his family connexion had led him. He greatly valued moral & religious instruction for youth, as tending to make good sailors. The best, he used to say,

---

most of *inserted*
call *revised from* called

in reference *revised from* in reverence
such of my *revised from* such my

[83]

came from Scotland: the next to them from the north of England especially from Westmoreland & Cumberland, where, thanks to the piety & local attachments of our ancestors, endowed, or, as they are commonly called, free, Schools abound.

The Force of Prayer.   An appendage to the White Doe. My friend M`r`. Rogers has also written on the subject. The story is preserved in D`r`. Whitaker's History of Craven—a topographical writer of first-rate merit in all that concerns the past; but such was his aversion from the modern spirit as shewn in the spread of manufactories in those districts of which he treated, that his readers are left entirely ignorant both of the progress of these arts and their real bearing upon the comfort, virtues, & happiness of the inhabitants.

While wandering on foot through the fertile vallies & over the moorlands of the Apennine that divides Yorkshire from Lancashire, I used to be delighted with observing the number of substantial cottages that had sprung up on every side, each having its little plot of fertile ground won from the surrounding waste. A bright & warm fire if needed was always to be found in these dwellings. The father was at his loom; the children looked healthy & happy. Is it not to be feared that the increase of mechanic power has done away with many of these blessings, &

Westmoreland & *revised from* the hills of   blessings, *revised from* blessings?
virtues *revised from* conduct

[84] substituted many evils? Alas, if these evils grow, how are they to be checked, & where is the remedy to be found? Political economy will not supply it, that is certain: We must look to something deeper, purer & higher.

Dion. This poem was first introduced by a stanza that I have since transferred to the notes for reasons there given, & I cannot comply with the request expressed by some of my friends that the rejected stanza should be restored. I hope they will be content if it be hereafter immediately attached to the poem, instead of its being degraded to a place in the notes.

Canute. The first & last fourteen lines of this poem each make a sonnet, & were composed as such. But I thought that by intermediate lines they might be connected so as to make a whole. One or two expressions are taken from Milton's History of England.

Ode to Lycoris. The discerning reader who is aware that in the poem of Ellen Irwin, I was desirous of throwing the reader at once out of the old ballad, so as if possible to preclude a comparison between that mode of dealing with the subject & the mode I meant to adopt, may here perhaps perceive that this poem originated in the four last lines of the first stanza. These specks of snow reflected in the

---

hereafter *inserted*   I was *revised from* being

[85]

lake, & so transferred, as it were, to the subaqueous sky, reminded me of the Swans which the fancy of the ancient classic poets yoked to the car of Venus. Hence the tenor of the whole first stanza, & the name of Lycoris, which with some readers who think mythology & classical allusion too farfetched & therefore more or less unnatural or affected, will tend to unrealize the sentiment that pervades these verses. But surely one who has written so much in verse as I have done may be allowed to retrace his steps into the regions of fancy which delighted him in his boyhood, when he first became acquainted with the Greek & Roman Poets. Before I read Virgil I was so strongly attached to Ovid, whose Metamorphoses I read at School, that I was quite in a passion whenever I found him, in books of criticism, placed below Virgil. As to Homer, I was never weary of travelling over the scenes through which he led me. Classical literature affected me by its own beauty. But the truths of scripture having been entrusted to the dead languages, and these fountains having been recently laid open at the Reformation, an importance & a sanctity were at that period attached to

---

beauty. But...at that period [period *inserted*]...revived (*carrying over to p. 86*) *revised from*

beauty, but as [as *inserted*] it is obvious from the mould in which Milton's Lycidas is cast, that the dead languages being the

[86]
classical literature that extended, as is obvious in Milton's Lycidas for example, both to its spirit & form in a degree that can never be revived. No doubt the hackneyed & lifeless use into which mythology fell toward the close of the 17th. century, & which continued through the 18th., disgusted the general reader with all allusion to it in modern verse. And though, in deference to this disgust, & also in a measure participating in it, I abstained in my earlier writings from all introduction of pagan fable,—surely, even in its humble form, it may ally itself with real sentiment—as I can truly affirm it did in the present case.

A little onward. The complaint in my eyes which gave occasion to this address to my daughter first shewed itself as a consequence of inflammation caught at the top of Kirkstone when I was overheated by having carried up the ascent my eldest son a lusty infant. Frequently has the disease recurred since, leaving the eyes in a state which has often prevented my reading for months—& makes me at this day incapable of bearing without injury any strong light by day or night My acquaintance with books has therefore been far short of my wishes; and on this account to acknowledge the services daily and hourly done me by my family and friends this note is written.

---

to its *revised from* in
And though, *revised from* In deference
when I was *over illegible erasure*

having carried *revised from* carrying
light *revised from* candle light
night My *ed. emended from* night my

[87]

Ode to Lycoris.   This as well as the preceding & the two that follow were composed in front of Rydal Mount & during my walks in the neighbourhood. Nine tenths of my verses have been murmured out in the open air—& here let me repeat what I believe has already appeared in print. One day a Stranger having walked round the garden & grounds of Rydal Mount asked of one of the female servants who happened to be at the door permission to see her Master's Study. "This" said she leading him forward "is my Master's Library, where he keeps his books—but his study is out of doors." After a long absence from home it has more than once happened that some one of my cottage neighbours (not of the double coach-house cottages) has said "Well there he is, we are glad to hear him *booing* about again." Once more in excuse for so much Egotism, let me say these notes are written for my familiar friends & at their earnest request. Another time a gentleman whom James had conducted thro' the grounds asked him what kind of plants throve best there; after a little consideration, he answered "Laurels:" "That is" said the Stranger "as it should be; dont you know that the Laurel is the emblem of Poetry, & that Poets used on public occasions to be crowned with it." James stared when the question was first put, but was doubtless much pleased with the information.

---

neighbourhood. Nine *revised from* neighbourhood nine

Study. "This" *ed. emended from* Study "this"

of one *revised from* to be

again." Once *revised from* again" once

[88]

Pillar of Trajan   These verses had better perhaps be transferred to the class of "Italian Poems". I had observed in the Newspaper that the Pillar of Trajan was given as a subject for a Prize Poem in English Verse. I had a wish perhaps that my Son, who was then an undergraduate at Oxford, should try his fortune & I told him so: but he, not having been accustomed to write verse, wisely declined to enter on the task; whereupon I showed him these lines as a proof of what might without difficulty be done on such a subject.

Lines written in a blank Leaf of Macpherson's Ossian   This Poem should, for variety's sake, take its place among the itinerary Sonnets in one of the Scotch Tours. The verses— "or strayed from hope & promise, self betrayed" were, I am sorry to say, suggested from apprehensions of the fate of my Friend H.C. the subject of the verses addressed to *H.C. when 6 years old.* The piece w^h. follows, to *"Memory,"* arose out of similar feelings.

To The Lady le Fleming.   After thanking in prose Lady Fleming for the service she had done to her neighbourhood by erecting this Chapel I have nothing to say beyond the expression of regret that the Architect did not furnish an elevation better suited to the site in a narrow mountain pass & what is of more consequence better constructed in the interior for the purposes of worship—It has

---

should, *over illegible erasure*
follows, to "Memory," *commas added by ed.*

had done *revised from* has done

[89] no chancel—the Altar is unbecomingly confined, the Pews are so narrow as to preclude the possibility of kneeling—there is no vestry—& what ought to have been first mentioned, the font instead of standing at its proper place at the Entrance is thrust into the farther end of a little Pew—when these defects shall be pointed out to the Munificent Patroness they will it is hoped be corrected—

The Gleaner. This Poem was first printed in the Annual called the "Keepsake"—the Painter's name I am not sure of, but I think it was Holmes.

Gold & Silver Fishes. They were a present from Miss Jewsbury of whom mention is made in the note at the end of the next Poem. The fish were healthy to all appearance in their confinement for a long time but at last, for some cause we could not make out, they languished & one of them being all but dead they were taken to the pool under the old Pollard Oak—the apparently dying one lay on its side unable to move. I used to watch it and about the tenth day it began to right itself, & in a few days more was able to swim about with its companions—for many months they continued to prosper in their new place of abode—but one night by an unusually great flood they were swept out of the pool & perished to our great regret.

Liberty Sequel to the above The connection of this with the preceding Poem is sufficiently obvious.

Entrance *revised from* entrance

[90]

Incident at Bruges. This occur^d at Bruges in the year 1828. M^r. Coleridge my daughter and I made a Tour together in Flanders, upon the Rhine & returned by Holland. Dora & I while taking a walk along a retired part of the town heard the voice as here described & were afterwards informed that it was a Convent in which were many English—we were both much touched, I might say affected,—& Dora moved as appears in the Verses.

This Lawn. This lawn is the sloping one approaching the kitchen garden & was made out of it. Hundreds of times have I here watched the dancing of shadows amid a press of sunshine; & other beautiful appearances of light & shade, flowers & shrubs. What a contrast between this & the Cabbages & Onions & Carrots that used to grow there on a piece of ugly shaped unsightly ground! No reflexion however either upon Cabbages or Onions—the latter we know were worshipped by the Egyptians & he must have a poor eye for beauty who has not observed how much of it there is in the form & colour which cabbages & plants of that genus exhibit through the various stages of their growth & decay. A richer display of colour in vegetable nature can scarcely be conceived than Coleridge my Sister & I saw in a bed of Potatoe plants in blossom near a hut upon the moor between Inversneyd & Loch Katrine.

---

worshipped *ed. emended from* worshiped
Potatoe plants *revised from* Potatoes

Loch *revised from* loch

[91]
These blossoms were of such extraordinary beauty & richness that no one could have passed them without notice: but the sense must be cultivated through the mind before we can perceive these inexhaustible treasures of Nature for such they truly are without the least necessary reference to the utility of her productions, or even to the laws whereupon, as we learn by research, they are dependent. Some are of opinion that the habit of analysing decomposing, & anatomizing is inevitably unfavorable to the perception of beauty. People are led into this mistake by overlooking the fact that such processes being to a certain extent within the reach of a limited intellect we are apt to ascribe to them that insensibility of which they are in truth the effect & not the cause. Admiration & love, to which all knowledge truly vital must tend, are felt by men of real genius in proportion as their discoveries in Natural Philosophy are enlarged; and the beauty in form of a plant or an animal is not made less but more apparent as a whole by more accurate insight into its constituent properties & powers—A *Savant* who is not also a Poet in soul & a religionist in heart is a feeble & unhappy Creature.

Humanity These Verses & the preceding ones entitled "Liberty" were composed as one piece which Mʳˢ. W.—

---

as we learn *revised from* we learn   beauty in *revised from* beauty &

[92] complained of as unwieldly & ill proportioned; & accordingly it was divided into two on her judicious recommendation.

Thought on the Seasons   Written at Rydal Mount 1829.

To I—— W—— on the birth of her first Child   Written at Moresby near Whitehaven 1833, when I was on a visit to my Son then Incumbent of that small living. While I am dictating these notes to my Friend Miss Fenwick Jany. 24th. 1843. the Child upon whose birth these verses were written is under my roof & is of a disposition so promising that the wishes & prayers & prophecies, w^h. I then breathed forth in Verse are thro' God's mercy likely to be realized.

The Warning a Sequel to the foregoing.   These lines were composed during the fever spread thro' the Nation by the reform bill. As the motives which led to this measure & the good or evil which has attended or has risen from it, will be duly appreciated by future Historians, there is no call for dwelling on the subject in this place. I will content myself with saying that the then condition of the people's mind is not, in these verses, exaggerated.

The Labourers Noon-day Hymn   Bishop Ken's Morn^g & Ev^g. Hymns are as they deserve to be familiarly known. Many other hymns have also been written on the same subjects but not being aware of any being designed for Noon-day I was induced to compose these verses. Often one has occasion to observe Cottage children carrying in their baskets dinner to

---

these verses *revised from* they   As *ed. emended from* as

[93]
their Fathers engaged with their daily labours in the fields & woods. How gratifying would it be to me could I be assured that any portion of these Stanzas had been sung by such a domestic concert under such circumstances. A friend of mine has told me that she introduced this Hymn into a Village school which she superintended—& the Stanzas in succession furnished her with texts to comment upon in a way which without difficulty was made intelligible to the Children & in which they obviously took delight; & they were taught to sing it to the tune of the *old 100th* Psalm.

Ode composed on May Morning
To May These two Poems originated in these lines "How delicate &c—." My daughter & I left Rydal Mount upon a tour through our mountains with M^r. & M^{rs}. Carr in the month of May 1826. & as we were going up the Vale of Newlands I was struck with the appearance of the little Chapel gleaming thro' the veil of half opened leaves—& the feeling which was then conveyed to my mind was expressed in the Stanza that follows. As in the cases of "Liberty" and "Humanity" mentioned before, my first intention was to write only one Poem; but subsequently I broke it into two making additions to each part so as to produce a consistent & appropriate whole.

Lines suggested by a Portrait
Subject resumed This Portrait has hung for many years in our principal sitting room & represents J.Q. as she was when a girl. The picture, tho' it is somewhat

---

My *ed. emended from* my   principal *revised from* principle

[94]

thinly painted, has much merit in tone & general effect—it is chiefly valuable however from the sentiment that pervades it. The Anecdote of the saying of the Monk in sight of Titian's Picture was told in this house by M^r. Wilkie, & was, I believe, first communicated to the Public in this Poem the former portion of w^h. I was composing at the time. Southey heard the story from Miss Hutchinson & transferred it to the D^r.—but it is not easy to explain how my friend M^r. Rogers in a note subsequently added to his "Italy" was led to speak of the same remarkable words having many years before been spoken in his hearing by a monk or Priest in front of a picture of the Last Supper placed over a refectory-table in a Convent at Padua.

Bird of Paradise   I cannot forbear to record that the last seven lines of this Poem were composed in bed during the night on the day on w^h. my Sister S.H. died about 6.P.M and it was the thought of her innocent & beautiful life that, through faith, prompted the words "On wings that fear no glance of God's pure sight, no tempest from his breath." The reader will find two poems on pictures of this bird among my Poems. I will here observe that in a far greater number of instances than have been mentioned in these notes one Poem has as in this case grown out of another either because I felt the subject had been inadequately treated

---

Titian's *ed. emended from* Titians   time. *ed. emended from* time
the *revised from* at

[95]

or that the thoughts & images suggested in course of composition have been such as I found interfered with the unity indispensable to every work of Art however humble in character.

Yarrow Revisited   I first became acquainted with this great & amiable man in the year 1803. when my Sister & I, making a tour in Scotland, were hospitably received by him in Lasswade upon the banks of the Esk where he was then living, We saw a good deal of him in the course of the following week. The particulars are given in my Sister's journal of that Tour.

A Place of Burial   Similar places for burial are not infrequent in Scotland. The one that suggested this Sonnet lies on the banks of a small stream called the Wauchope that flows into the Esk near Langholme. Mickle who, as it appears from his Poem on Sir Martin, was not without genuine poetic feelings, was born & passed his boyhood in this neighbourhood, under his Father who was a Minister of the Scotch Kirk. The Esk, both above & below Langholme, flows through a beautiful country, and the two streams of the Wauchope & the Ewes w^h. join it near that place are such as a Pastoral Poet would delight in.

---

appears from *between these two words is an illegible deletion of several words*

[96]

On the sight of a Manse in the South of Scotland.   The Manses in Scotland and the gardens & grounds about them have seldom that attractive appearance which is common about our English Parsonages even when the Clergyman's income falls below the average of the Scotch Ministers. This is not merely owing to the one country being poor in comparison with the other but arises rather out of the equality of their Benefices so that no one has enough to spare for decorations that might serve as an example for others, whereas with us the taste of the richer Incumbent extends its influence more or less to the poorest. After all in these observations the surface only of the matter is touched. I once heard a conversation in which the Roman Catholic Religion was decried on account of its abuses, "You cannot deny however," said a Lady of the party repeating an expression used by Charles 2^d, "that it is the religion of a gentleman." It may be left to the Scotch themselves to determine how far this observation applies to the [   ] of their kirk, while it cannot be denied if it is wanting in that characteristic quality, the aspect of common life, so far as concerns its beauty, must suffer. Sincere Christian piety may be thought not to stand in need of refinement or studied ornament—but assuredly it is ever ready to adopt them, when they fall within its notice, as means allow: & this observation applies not only to manners, but to everything that a Christian, (truly so in spirit) cultivates & gathers round him however humble his social condition.

---

abuses. "You *ed. emended from* abuses "You

[97]

Roslin Chapel in a Storm   We were detained by incessant rain & storm at the small Inn near Roslin Chapel, & I passed a great part of the day pacing to & fro in this beautiful structure, which, though not used for public service, is not allowed to go to ruin. Here this Sonnet was composed—if it has at all done justice to the feeling which the place & the storm raging without inspired, I was as a prisoner— A Painter delineating the interior of the Chapel & its minute features under such circumstances would have, no doubt, found his time agreeably shortened. But the movements of the mind must be more free while dealing with words than with lines & colours—Such at least was then & has been on many other occasions my belief, & as it is allotted to few to follow both arts with success, I am grateful to my own calling for this & a thousand other recommendations which are denied to that of the Painter.

The Trosachs.   As recorded in my Sister's journal, I had first seen the Trosachs in her & Coleridge's company. The sentiment that runs thro' this Sonnet was natural to the season in which I again saw this beautiful spot, but this & some other Sonnets that follow were coloured by the remembrance of my recent visit to Sir Walter Scott & the melancholy errand on w^h. he was going

Loch Etive   "That make the Patriot Spirit"—It was mortifying to have frequent occasions to observe the bitter hatred of the lower orders of the Highlanders to their Superiors;

Chapel in a Storm *revised from* Castle in a Storm
inspired, *ed. emended from* inspired

many *revised from* every
Coleridge's *ed. emended from* Coleridges

[98]
love of country seemed to have passed into its opposite. Emigration was the only relief looked to with hope.

Sonnet composed on reading a Newspaper of the day   to be transferred to the Political Sonnets on order.

Eagles   "The last I saw was on the wing"   Off the Promontory of Fairhead, County of Antrim. I mention this because tho' my Tour in Ireland with M^r. Marshall & his Son was made many years ago, this allusion to the Eagle is the only image supplied by it to the Poetry I have since written. We travelled through that country in Oct^{br} & to the shortness of the days & the speed with w^h. we travelled (in a carriage & four) may be ascribed this want of notices, in my verse, of a country so interesting. The deficiency I am somewhat ashamed of, & it is the more remarkable as contrasted with my Scotch & Continental tours, of which are to be found in these Vols. so many Memorials.

Sound of Mull.   Touring late in the season in Scotland is an uncertain speculation, we were detained a week by rain at Bunaw on Loch Etive in a vain hope that the weather would clear up & allow me to shew my daughter the beauties of Glencoe: two days we were at the Isle of Mull on a visit to Major Campbell, but it rained incessantly & we were obliged to give up our intention of going to Staffa. The rain pursued us to *Tyndrum* where the 11th sonnet was composed in a storm.

Bothwell Castle.   In my Sister's journal is an account of Bothwell Castle as it appeared to us at that time.

Fairhead, County *ed. emended from* Fairhead County   11th *revised from* 12th

[99]

The Avon   "Yet is it one that other Rivulets bear"   There is the Shakespear Avon, the Bristol Avon, the one that flows by Salisbury & a small river in Wales, I believe, bear the name, Avon being in the ancient tongue the general name for river.

Inglewood Forest   The extensive forest of Inglewood has been enclosed within my memory. I was well acquainted with it in its ancient state. The Harts horn tree mentioned in the next Sonnet was one of its remarkable objects, as well as another tree that grew upon an eminence not far from Penrith; it was single & conspicuous & being of a round shape, tho' it was universally known to be a "Sycamore," it was always called the "Round Thorn" so difficult is it to chain fancy down to fact.

Countess' Pillar   Suggested by the recollection of Juliana's bower & other traditions connected with this ancient forest.

Highland Broach   (To be inserted among the Sonnets)   On ascending a hill that leads from Loch Awe towards Inverary, I fell into conversation with a woman of the humbler class who wore one of those Highland broaches. I talked with her about it, & upon parting with her, when I said with a kindness I truly felt "May that broach continue in your family thro' many generations to come, as you have already possessed it" she thanked me most becomingly & seemed not a little moved.

N.B.

The note that follows to stand first among those of *"Yarrow Revisited"*. It was overlooked in transcribing.

Salisbury *revised from* Salsbury   transcribing. *ed. emended from* transcribing
those Highland *revised from* these Highland

[100]

Yarrow Revisited. In the autumn of 1831 my daughter and I set off from Rydal to visit Sir Walter Scott before his departure for Italy. This journey had been delayed by an inflammation in my eyes till we found that the time appointed for his leaving home would be too near for him to receive us without considerable inconvenience. Nevertheless we proceeded & reached Abbotsford on Monday. I was then scarcely able to lift up my eyes to the light. How sadly changed did I find him from the man I had seen so healthy, gay, & hopeful a few years before when he said, at the Inn at Paterdale in my presence his daughter Anne also being there with M^r^. Lockhart my own Wife and daughter & M^r^. Quillinan, "I mean to live till I am *80.* & shall write as long as I live:' Though we had none of us the least thought of the cloud of misfortune which was then going to break upon his head I was startled and almost shocked at that bold saying w^h^. could scarcely be uttered by such a man sanguine as he was without a momentary forgetfulness of the instability of human life. But to return to Abbotsford, the Inmates & Guests we found there were Sir Walter—Major Scott, Anne Scott & M^r^. & M^rs^. Lockhart—M^r^. Liddell—his Lady and brother, & M^r^. Allan the Painter & M^r^. Laidlaw a very old friend of Sir W.'s. One of Burns' sons, an officer in the Indian Service, had left the house a day or two before and had kindly expressed his regret that he could not wait my arrival, a regret that I may truly say was mutual.   ☙

Wife and *inserted*

[101]

In the Evening Mr. & Mrs. Liddell sang, & Mrs. Lockhart chaunted old Ballads to her harp, & Mr. Allan, hanging over the back of a chair, told & acted odd stories in a humorous way. With this exhibition, & his daughter's singing, Sir Walter was much amused & indeed were we all as far as circumstances would allow. But what is most worthy of mention is the admirable demeanour of Major Scott during that E{vg}. He had much to suffer from the sight of his Father's infirmities & from the great change that was about to take place at the residence he had built & where he had long lived in so much prosperity & happiness, But what struck me most was the patient kindness with which he supported himself under the many fretful expressions that his Sister Anne addressed to him or uttered in his hearing, She, poor thing, as Mistress of that house, had been subject after her Mother's death, to a heavier load of care & responsibility, & greater sacrifices of time, than one of such a constitution of body & mind was able to bear. Of this Dora & I were made so sensible that as soon as we had crossed the Tweed on our departure we gave vent at the same moment to our apprehensions, that her brain would fail & she w{d}. go out of her mind, or that she would sink under the trials she had passed & those which awaited her. On Tuesday Morning Sir Walter Scott accompanied us & most of the party to Newark Castle on the Yarrow.

---

humorous *ed. emended from* humorous
With *ed. emended from* with

Yarrow. *ed. emended from* Yarrow

[102]

When we alighted from the carriages he walked pretty stoutly & had great pleasure in revisiting these his favorite haunts—of that Excursion the Verses "Yarrow revisited" are a memorial: notwithstanding the romance that pervades Sir W.'s works & attaches to many of his habits, there is too much pressure of fact for these verses to harmonize as much as I c^d. wish with the two preceding Poems. On our return in the afternoon we had to cross the Tweed directly opposite Abbotsford. The wheels of our carriage grated upon the pebbles in the bed of the stream that there flows somewhat rapidly—a rich but sad light of rather a purple than a golden hue was spread over the Eilden Hills at that moment & thinking it probable that it might be the last time Sir Walter would cross the stream I was not a little moved & expressed some of my feelings in the Sonnet beginning "A trouble" &c.— At noon on Thursday we left Abbotsford & in the morn^g. of that day Sir W. & I had a serious conversation tete-a-tete when he spoke with gratitude of the happy life which upon the whole he had led. He had written in my daughter's Album, before he came into the breakfast room that morning, a few Stanzas addressed to her & while putting the book into her hand, in his own Study standing by his desk, he said to her in my

---

Yarrow revisited *revised from* yarrow revisited
Sir W.'s *ed. emended from* Sir W.s
might *DQ added in pencil over illegible erasure*

tete-a-tete *ed. emended from* tete a tete
daughter's *ed. emended from* daughters

[103]

presence; "I should not have done any thing of this kind but for your Father's sake; they are probably the last verses I shall ever write." They shew how much his mind was impaired not by the strain of thought but by the execution, some of the lines being imperfect, & one Stanza wanting corresponding rhymes. One letter, the initial S, had been omitted in the spelling of his own name. In this interview also it was that upon my expressing a hope of his health being benefited by the climate of the country to which he was going— & by the interest he would take in the classic remembrances of Italy, he made use of the quotation from "Yarrow Unvisited" as recorded by me in the "Musings at Aquapendente" six years afterwards.

M^r. Lockhart has mentioned in his life of him what I heard from several quarters while abroad both at Rome & elsewhere, that little seemed to interest him but what he could collect or heard of the fugitive Stuarts & their adherents w^h. had followed them into Exile.

Both the "Yarrow Revisited" & the "Sonnet" were sent him before his departure from England. Some further particulars of the conversations who occurred during this visit I should have set down had they not been already accurately recorded by M^r. Lockhart.   ☙

---

sake; *ed. emended from* sake
execution, *ed. emended from* execution
letter,...S, *ed. supplied commas*
Italy, *ed. emended from* Italy

use of *revised from* [?allusion]
England. *ed. emended from* England
occurred *ed. emended from* occured
set down *revised from* recorded

[104]

The Russian Fugitive   Early in life this story had interested me & I often thought it would make a pleasing subject for an opera or Musical drama.

*   *   *

Memorials of a Tour in Scotland in 1833   My Companions were H.C. Robinson & my Son John.

Nun's Well, Brigham.   So named from the Religious House which stood close by. I have rather an odd anecdote to relate of the Nun's Well. One day the Landlady of a public house, a field's length from it, on the road side said to me "You have been to see the Nun's Well, Sir." "The Nun's Well! What is that?" said the Post man who in his royal livery stopt his Mail car at the door. The Landlady & I explained to him what the name meant & what sort of people the Nuns were. A country man who was standing by rather tipsy stammered out "Aye, those Nuns were good people, they are gone, but we shall soon have them back again." The Reform Mania was just then at its height.

To a Friend &— "*Pastor & Patriot*"   My Son John who was then building a Parsonage on his small living at Brigham.

Mary Queen of Scots   "Bright as a Star." I will mention for the sake of the Friend who is writing down these Notes that it was among the fine Scotch Firs near Ambleside

---

Memorials…1833 *ed. added italics*
My Companions *ed. emended from* my Companions

Queen of Scots *ed. emended from* Queen of Scotts

[105]

& particularly those near Green Bank that I have over & over again paused at the sight of this Image. Long may they stand to afford a like gratification to others! This wish is not uncalled for, several of their brethren having already disappeared.

N.B. The Poem of S*ᵗ. Bees* to follow at this place

Isle of Man.   My Son William is here the person alluded to as saving the life of the Youth, & the circumstances were as mentioned in the Sonnet.

Sonnet by a Retired Mariner   Mary's brother Henry

Bala Sala.   A thankful refugee, Supposed to be written by a friend (M*ʳ*. Cookson) who died there a few years after

Tynwald Hill   M*ʳ*. Robinson & I walked the greater part of the way from Castle-Town to Peel & stopped some time at Tynwald Hill. My Companions were an elderly man who in a muddy way (for he was tipsy) explained & answered as far as he could, my enquiries about this place & the ceremonies held here. I found more agreeable company in some little children, one of whom, upon my request, recited the Lord's prayer to me & I helped her to a clearer understanding of it as well as I could, but I was not at all satisfied with my own part—hers was much better done, & I am persuaded, that like other children, she knew more about it than she was able to express, especially to a Stranger.   ☙

Image. *ed. emended from* Image
uncalled for, *ed. emended from* uncalled for
refugee *ed .. emended from* refuge

My Companions *revised from* my Companions

[106]

Ailsa Cragg   The morning of the Eclipse was exquisitely beautiful while we passed the cragg as described in the Sonnet. On the deck of the Steam boat were several persons of the poor & labouring class, & I could not but be struck with their cheerful talk with each other, while not one of them seemed to notice the magnificent objects with w^h. we were surrounded; & even the phenomenon of the eclipse attracted but little of their attention. Was it right not to regret this? They appeared to me however so much alive in their own minds to their own concerns that I could not look upon it as a misfortune that they had little perception for such pleasures as cannot be cultivated without ease & leisure. Yet if one surveys life in all its duties & relations such ease & leisure will not be found so enviable a privilege as it may at first appear. Natural Philosophy, Painting & Poetry & refined taste are no doubt great acquisitions to society, but among those who dedicate themselves to such pursuits, it is to be feared that few are as happy & as consistent in the management of their lives as the Class of persons who at that time led me into this course of reflection. I do not mean by this to be understood to derogate from intellectual pursuits for that would be monstrous. I say it in deep gratitude for this compensation to those whose cares are limited to the necessities of daily life. Among them, self tormentors,

---

phenomenon *revised from* phominen

[107]

so numerous in the higher classes of society, are rare.

Arran   The mountain outline on the North of this Island as seen from the Firth of Clyde is much the finest I have ever noticed in Scotland or elsewhere.

Staffa   See note.

There said a Stripling   Mosgiel was thus pointed out to me by a young man on the top of the coach on my way from Glasgow to Kilmarnock. It is remarkable that tho' Burns lived some time here, & during much the most productive period of his poetical life, he nowhere adverts to the splendid prospects stretching towards the sea, & bounded by the Peaks of Arran, on one part, which in clear weather he must have had daily before his eyes. Yet this is easily explained, in one of his poetical effusions he speaks of describing "fair Nature's face" as a privilege on w^h. he sets a high value, nevertheless natural appearances rarely take a lead in his poetry. It is as a human being eminently sensitive & intelligent, & not as a Poet clad in his priestly robes & carrying the ensigns of sacerdotal office, that he interests & affects us. Whether he speaks of rivers, hills, & woods, it is not so much on account of the properties with which they are absolutely endowed, as relatively to local patriotic remembrances & associations, or as they ministered to personal feelings, especially those of Love, whether happy or otherwise; yet it is not *always* so. Soon after we had passed Mosgiel Farm we crossed

---

& bounded…Arran, *revised in ink and in pencil from* by the Peaks of Arran, & bounded

Yet. …explained, *revised in ink to* (Yet. …explained,)

effusions *EQ supplied in pencil*

especially *ed. emended from* especialy

[108]
the Ayr murmuring & winding thro' a narrow woody hollow. His line "Auld hermit Ayr staw thro' his woods" came at once to my mind with Irwin, Lugar, Ayr & Doon, Ayrshire streams over which he breathes a sigh as being unnamed in song, & surely his own attempts to make them known were as successful as his heart could desire.

The River Eden   "Nature gives thee flowers "that have no rival amidst British Bowers." This can scarcely be true to the letter but without stretching the point at all I can say that the soil & air appear more congenial with many upon the banks of this river, than I have observed in any other parts of Great Britain.

Monument of M^{rs}*. Howard*   Nollekins.   Before this monument was put up in the Chapel at Wetheral I saw it in the Sculptor's Studio. Nollekins, who by the bye was a strange & grotesque figure that interfered much with one's admiration of his works, shewed me at the same time the various models in clay which he had made one after another of the Mother and her Infant, the improvement on each was surprising & how so much grace beauty & tenderness had come out of such a head I was sadly puzzled to conceive. Upon a window seat in his parlour lay the casts of faces one of the Dutchess of Devonshire so noted in her day & the other of M^r. Pitt, taken after his death

---

staw *ed. emended from* sta[ ]
Irwin, Lugar, *ed. emended from* Irwin Lugar

Sculptor's *ed. emended from* Sculptors
one's *ed. emended from* ones

[109]

a ghastly resemblance, as these things always are, even when taken from the living subject & more ghastly in this instance from the peculiarity of the features. The heedless & apparently neglectful manner in which the faces of these two persons were left—the one so distinguished in London society & the other upon whose counsels & public conduct during a most momentous period depended the fate of this great Empire & perhaps of all Europe, afforded a lesson to which the dullest of casual visitors could scarcely be insensible. It touched me the more because I had so often seen M^r. Pitt upon his own ground at Cambridge & upon the floor of the House of Commons.

Nunnery.   I became acquainted with the walks of Nunnery when a boy—they are within easy reach of a day's pleasant excursion from the town of Penrith where I used to pass my summer holydays under the roof of my maternal grand Father. The place is well worth visiting tho' within these few years its privacy, & therefore the pleasure w^h. the scene is so well fitted to give, has been injuriously affected by walks cut in the rocks on that side the stream which had been left in its natural state.

Lowther   "Cathedral Pomp." It may be questioned whether this union was in the contemplation of the Artist

---

side *revised from* [?strea]

[110]
when he planned the Edifice. However this might be, a Poet may be excused for taking the view of the subject presented in this Sonnet

The Somnambulist.   This poem might be dedicated to my friends Sir G. Beaumont & Mr Rogers jointly. While we were making an Excursion together in this part of the Lake district we heard that Mr Glover the Artist, while lodging at Lyulph's Tower, had been disturbed by a loud shriek & upon rising he learnt that it had come from a young woman in the house who was in the habit of walking in her sleep: in that state she had gone down stairs & while attempting to open the outer door, either from some difficulty, or the effect of the cold stone upon her feet, had uttered the cry which alarmed him. It seemed to us all that this might serve as a hint for a poem, & the story here told was constructed & soon after put into verse by me as it now stands.

Evening Voluntaries

Lines composed on a high part of the coast of Cumberland.   The lines were composed on the road between Moresby & Whitehaven while I was on a visit to my Son then Rector of that place. This succession of Voluntaries, with the exception of the 8th. & 9th., originated in the concluding lines of the last paragraph of this Poem.

---

might be, *ed. emended from* might be
Lyulph's *ed. emended from* Lyulphs
Evening Voluntaries *ed. added italics*

Voluntaries,…originated, *revised from* Voluntaries, originated…9th,
8th *ed. emended from* 8th.

[111]
With this coast I have been familiar from my earliest childhood & remember being struck for the first time by the town & port of Whitehaven & the white waves breaking against its quays & piers as the whole came into view from the top of the high ground down which the road,—which has since been altered, then descended abruptly. My Sister when she first heard the voice of the sea from this point & beheld the scene spread before her burst into tears. Our family then lived at Cockermouth & this fact was often mentioned among us as indicating the sensibility for which she was so remarkable.

Not in the lucid intervals of life.   The lines following "Nor do words" were written with L. Byron's character as a Poet before me & that of others among his contemporaries who wrote under like influences.

The leaves that rustled.   Composed by the side of Grasmere Lake. The mountains that enclose the vale, especially towards Easedale, are most favorable to the reverberation of sound: there is a passage in the Excursion towards the close of the 4th. Book where the voice of the Raven in flight is traced thro' the modifications it undergoes as I have often heard it in that Vale & others of this district.

---

breaking *revised in pencil from* [?cras]hing
—which has *revised from* it has
contemporaries *ed. emended from*

cotemporaries *revised from* cotempories
Composed *revised from* composed

[112]

The sun has long been set.   Reprinted at the request of my Sister in whose presence the lines were thrown off

Had this effulgence.   Felt, & in a great measure composed, upon the little mount in front of our abode at Rydal. In concluding my notices of this class of Poems it may be as well to observe that among the Miscellaneous Sonnets are a few alluding to morning impressions which might be read with mutual benefit in connection with these Evening Voluntaries. See for example that one on Westminster Bridge—that 1st. on May, 2^{d}. on the song of the Thrush & the one beginning "While beams of orient light" &c.

The old Cumberland Beggar.   Observed & with great benefit to my own heart when I was a child—written at Race Down & Alfoxden in my 23^{d}. year. The political economists were about that time beginning their war upon mendicity in all its forms & by implication, if not directly, on Alms-giving also. This heartless process has been carried as far as it can go by the AMENDED poor-law bill, tho' the inhumanity that prevails in this measure is somewhat disguised by the profession that one of its objects is to throw the poor upon the voluntary donations of their neighbours, that is, if rightly interpreted, to force them into a condition

---

See *ed. emended from* see

May, *ed. emended from* May

year. The *ed. emended from* year The

neighbours, *ed. emended from* neighbours

[113]
between relief in the union poor House & Alms robbed of their Christian grace & spirit, as being *forced* rather from the benevolent than given by them, while the avaricious & selfish, & all in fact but the humane & charitable, are at liberty to keep all they possess from their distressed brethren.

The Farmer of Tilsbury Vale. The character of this man was described to me and the incident upon which the verses turn was told me by Mr. Poole of Nether Stowey with whom I became acquainted thro' our common friend S.T.C. During my residence at Alfoxden I used to see a great deal of him & had frequent occasions to admire the course of his daily life especially his conduct to his Labourers & poor neighbours—their virtues he carefully encouraged, & weighed their faults in the scales of Charity. If I seem in these verses to have treated the weaknesses of the farmer & his transgression too tenderly it may in part be ascribed to my having received the story from one so averse to all harsh judgement. After his death, was found in his escritoir a lock of grey hair carefully preserved with a notice that it had been cut from the head of his faithful Shepherd who had served him for a length of years. I need scarcely add that he felt for all men as his brothers. He was much beloved by distinguished

---

while *revised from* [?when]
brethren *ed. emended from* brethern
After brethren. *a sentence in ink was erased:* To throw the poor before the voluntary donations of their neighbours for the benefit of both parties by [?it.] Which is the best state of the case?
Poole *ed. emended from* Pool
a great deal *EQ revised in pencil to* much

[114]

persons— M^r. Coleridge, M^r. Southey, Sir H. Davy & many others, & in his own neighbourhood was highly valued as a Magistrate, a man of business & in every other social relation. The latter part of the Poem perhaps requires some apology as being too much of an echo to the "Reverie of Poor Susan."

The two Thieves.   This is described from the life as I was in the habit of observing when a boy at Hawkeshead school. Daniel was more than 80 years older than myself when he was daily, thus occupied, under my notice, no book could have so early taught me to think of the changes to which human life is subject, & while looking at him I could not but say to myself we may, any of us I, or the happiest of my play mates, live to become still more the object of pity than this old man, this half-doating pilferer.

Animal Tranquillity & decay   If I recollect right these verses were an overflowing from the old Cumberland Beggar.

---

any of us *revised from* one of us

[115]

Epitaphs.

Those from Chiabrera were chiefly translated when Mr. Coleridge was writing his Friend in wh. periodical my Essay on Epitaphs, written about that time, was first published—for further notice of Chiabrera in connection with his Epitaphs see "Musings at Aquapendente."

By a blessed husband This Lady was named Carleton, she, along with a sister, was brought up in the neighbourhood of Ambleside. The Epitaph, a part of it at least, is in the church at Bromsgrove where she resided after her marriage.

Elegiac Stanzas suggested by a picture of Peel Castle. Sir George Beaumont painted two pictures of this subject one of which he gave to Mrs. Wordsworth saying she ought to have it: but Lady B—— interfered & after Sir George's death she gave it to Sir Uvedale Price in whose house at Foxley I have seen it—rather grudgingly I own.

Invocation to the Earth. Composed immediately after the Thanksgiving Ode, to which it may be considered as a second Part.

Elegiac Stanzas On Mrs. Fermor. This lady had been a widow long before I knew her. Her husband was of the family of the Lady celebrated in the Rape of the Lock, & was, I believe, a Roman Catholic. The sorrow which

---

Friend *ed. emended from* friend
Epitaphs *ed. added italics*
Essay *revised from* Essy
along with *EQ revised in pencil to* &

Bromsgrove *revised from* Broomsgrove
of this subject *revised from* on this subject
ought *revised from* aught

[116]
his death caused her was fearful in its character as described in this poem, but was subdued in course of time by the strength of her religious faith. I have been for many weeks at a time an inmate with her at Coleorton Hall as were also Mary & my Sister. The truth in the sketch of her character here given was acknowledged with gratitude by her nearest relatives. She was eloquent in conversation, energetic upon public matters, open in respect to these but slow to communicate her personal feelings, upon these she never touched in her intercourse with me, so that I could not regard myself as her confidential friend & was accordingly surprised when I learnt she had left me a Legacy of £100 as a token of her esteem. See, in further illustration, the second stanzas inscribed upon her Cenotaph in Coleorton Church.

Elegaic Musings These verses were in fact composed on horseback during a storm whilst I was on my way from Coleorton to Cambridge—they were alluded to elsewhere—

Sister. The *ed. emended from* Sister. the   conversation, *ed. emended from* conversation

[117]

Once I could hail. "No faculty yet given me to espy the dusky shape". Afterwards, when I could not avoid seeing it, I wondered at this & the more so because like most children I had been in the habit of watching the Moon thro' all her changes & had often continued to gaze at it while at the full till half blinded.

To a good Man of most dear Memory. Light will be thrown upon the tragic circumstance alluded to in this Poem when after the death of Charles Lamb's Sister, his biographer Mʳ. Sergeant Talfourd shall be at Liberty to relate particulars which could not at the time when his memoir was written be given to the public. Mary Lamb was ten years older than her brother & has survived

---

Afterwards, when [when *inserted*]...blinded *revised from* It is not easy to account for this fact since I was in the habit as most boys are of gazing before the moon in all her changes, & often when she was at full I continued to do so till my eyes were almost blinded

alluded *revised from* here alluded

[118]
him as long a time. Were I to give way to my own feelings I should dwell not only on her genius & intellectual powers but upon the delicacy & refinement of manner which she maintained inviolable under most trying circumstances, She was loved & honored by all her brother's friends—& others—some of them strange characters, whom his philanthropic peculiarities induced him to countenance. The death of C. Lamb himself was doubtless hastened by his sorrow for that of Coleridge to whom he had been attached from the time of their being school-fellows at Christ's Hospital. Lamb was a good Latin scholar & probably would have gone to college upon one of the school foundations if it had not been for the impediment in his speech. Had such been his lot he would have probably been preserved from the indulgences of social humours & fancies which were often injurious to himself & causes of severe regret to his friends without really benefiting the object of his misapplied kindness.

When first descending. These verses were written extempore immediately after reading a notice of the Ettrick Shepherd's death, in the Newcastle Paper to the Editor of w^h. I sent a copy for publication. The persons lamented in these verses were all either of my friends or acquaintance. In Lockhart's life

---

his sorrow for *inserted*
if it had not been *EQ revised in pencil to* but

Lockhart's *ed. emended from* Lockharts

[119]
of Sir Walter Scott an account is given of my first meeting with him in 1803, How the Ettrick Shepherd & I became known to each other has already been mentioned in these notes. He was undoubtedly a man of original genius, but of coarse manners & low & offensive opinions. Of Coleridge & Lamb I need not speak here. Crabbe I have met in London at M^r. Rogers', but more frequently & favorably at M^r. Hoare's upon Hampstead Heath. Every spring he used to pay that family a visit of some length & was upon terms of intimate friendship with M^{rs}. Hoare & still more with her daughter in law who has a large collection of his letters addressed to herself. After the Poet's decease application was made to her to give up these letters to his biographer, that they, or at least part of them, might be given to the public. She hesitated to comply & asked my opinion on the subject "By no means" was my answer, grounded not upon any objection there might be to publishing a selection from these letters, but from an aversion I have always felt to meet idle curiosity by calling back the recently departed to become the object of trivial & familiar gossip. Crabbe obviously for the most part preferr'd the company of women to that of men, for this among other reasons that he did not like to be put upon the stretch in general conversation. Accordingly in miscellaneous society his talk was so

---

Scott *revised from* Scot
Poet's *ed. emended from* Poets
subject "By *ed. emended from* subject "By

conversation. Accordingly *ed. emended from* conversation accordingly

[120] much below what might have been expected from a man so deservedly celebrated that to me it seemed trifling. It must upon other occasions have been of a different character as I found in our rambles together on Hampstead Heath, & not so much so from a readiness to communicate his knowledge of life & manners as of Natural History in all its branches. His mind was inquisitive & he seems to have taken refuge from a remembrance of the distresses he had gone thro' in these studies & the employments to which they led. Moreover such contemplations might tend profitably to counterbalance the painful truths which he had collected from his intercourse with mankind. Had I been more intimate with him I should have ventured to have touched upon his office as a Minister of the Gospel, & how far his heart & soul were in it so as to make him a zealous & diligent labourer. In poetry, tho' he wrote much, as we all know, he assuredly was not so. I happened once to speak of pains as necessary to produce merit of a certain kind which I highly valued. His observation was "It is not worth while." You are right, thought I, if the labour encroaches upon the time due to teach truth as a steward of the mysteries of God—if there be cause to fear that, write less: but if poetry is to be produced at all, make what you do produce as good as you can. M^r. Rogers once told me that he expressed his regret to Crabbe

---

trifling *ed. emended from* trif'ing
have touched *revised in pencil to* touch
valued. His *ed. emended from* valued. his

You *ed. emended from* while."
you can. M^r. Rogers *ed. emended from* can M^r. Rogers

while."

[121] that he wrote in his later works so much less correctly than in his earlier. "Yes," replied he "but then I had a reputation to make; now I can afford to relax." Whether it was from a modest estimate of his own qualifications or from causes less creditable, his motives for writing verse & his hopes & aims were not so high as is to be desired. After being silent for more than twenty years he again applied himself to poetry upon the spur of applause he received from the periodical publications of the day, as he himself tells us in one of his prefaces. Is it not to be lamented that a man who was so conversant with permanent truth & whose writings are so valuable an acquisition to our country's literature should have *required* an impulse from such a quarter?

Mrs. Hemans was unfortunate as a Poetess in being obliged by circumstances to write for money, & that so frequently & so much that she was compelled to look out for subjects wherever she could find them & to write as expeditiously as possible. As a woman she was to a considerable degree a spoilt child of the world. She had been early in life distinguished for talent & poems of hers were published whilst she was a girl. She had also been handsome in her youth, but her education had been most unfortunate. She was totally ignorant of housewifery & could as easily have managed

[122] the spear of Minerva as her needle. It was from observing these deficiencies that one day, while she was under my roof, I *purposely* directed her attention to household economy & told her I had purchased Scales w^h. I intended to present to a young lady as a wedding present, pointed out their utility, (for her especial benefit) & said that no ménage ought to be without them. M^rs. Hemans, not in the least suspecting my drift, reported this saying in a letter to a friend at the time as a proof of my simplicity. Being disposed to make large allowances for the faults of her Education & the circumstances in w^h. she was placed I felt most kindly disposed towards her & took her part upon all occasions & I was not a little affected by learning that after she withdrew to Ireland a long & severe sickness, raised her spirit as it depressed her body. This I heard from her most intimate friends & there is striking evidence of it in a poem entitled [   ] written & published not long before her death. These notices of M^rs. Hemans would be very unsatisfactory to her intimate friends, as indeed they are to my self not so much for what is said but what for brevity's sake is left unsaid. Let it suffice to add there was much sympathy between us & if opportunity had been allowed me to see more of her I should have loved & valued her accordingly. ☙

---

ménage *ed. emended from* mênage
sickness *revised from* illness

her spirit *revised from* a spirit

[123]
As it is, I remember her with true affection for her amiable qualities & above all for her delicate & irreproachable conduct during her long separation from an unfeeling husband whom she had been led to marry from the romantic notions of inexperienced youth: upon this husband I never heard her cast the least reproach, nor even name him though she did not forbear wholly to touch upon her domestic position, but never so, as that any fault could be found with her manner of adverting to it.

The Ode. This was composed during my residence at Town-End, Grasmere, two years at least passed between the writing of the four first stanzas & the remaining part. To the attentive & competent reader the whole sufficiently explains itself, but there may be no harm in adverting here to particular feelings or *experiences* of my own mind on which the structure of the poem partly rests. Nothing was more difficult for me in childhood than to admit the notion of death as a state applicable to my own being. I have said elsewhere "a simple child that lightly draws its breath and feels its life in every limb, what should it know of death?" but it was not so much from [ ] of animal vivacity that *my* difficulty came

---

even *EQ revised in pencil to* did I ever hear her even
wholly *ed. emended from* wholy

rests. Nothing *ed. emended from* rests Nothing
the notion of *inserted*

[124]

as from a sense of the indomitableness of the spirit within me. I used to brood over the stories of Enoch & Elijah & almost to persuade myself that whatever might become of others I s^d be translated in something of the same way to heaven. With a feeling congenial to this I was often unable to think of external things as having external existence & I communed with all that I saw as something not apart from but inherent in my own immaterial nature. Many times while going to school have I grasped at a wall or tree to recall myself from this abyss of idealism to the reality. At that time I was afraid of such processes. In later periods of life I have deplored, as we have all reason to do, a subjugation of an opposite character & have rejoiced over the remembrances, as is expressed in the lines "obstinate questionings &c." To that dream-like vividness & splendour which invest objects of sight in childhood every one, I believe, if he would look back, could bear testimony, & I need not dwell upon it here—but having in the Poem regarded it as presumptive evidence of a prior state of existence, I think it right to protest against a conclusion which has given pain to some good & pious persons that I meant to inculcate such a belief.

[125]
It is far too shadowy a notion to be recommended to faith as more than an element in our instincts of immortality. But let us bear in mind that, tho' the idea is not advanced in revelation, there is nothing there to contradict it, & the fall of Man presents an analogy in its favor. Accordingly, a preexistent state has entered into the popular creeds of many nations, and among all persons acquainted with classic literature is known as an ingredient in Platonic philosophy. Archimedes said that he could move the world if he had a point whereon to rest his machine. Who has not felt the same aspirations as regards the world of his own mind? Having to wield some of its elements when I was impelled to write this Poem on the "Immortality of the soul" I took hold of the notion of preexistence as having sufficient foundation in humanity for authorizing me to make for my purpose the best use of it I could as a Poet.

---

recommended *revised from* recomended
in its favor *revised from* it is favor

wield *revised in pencil from* yield

[126]

Prelude to the Last Vol

These verses were begun while I was on a visit to my son John at Brigham & finished at Rydal. As the contents of this Vol to which they are now prefixed will be assigned to their respective Classes when my Poems shall be collected in one Vol: I should be at a loss where with propriety to place this Prelude being too restricted in its bearing to serve as a Preface for the Whole. The lines towards the conclusion allude to the discontents then fomented thro' the country by the Agitators of the Anti-Corn Law league: the particular causes of such troubles are transitory but disposition to excite & liability to be excited are nevertheless permanent & therefore proper objects for the Poet's regard.

Guilt & Sorrow.   Unwilling to be unnecessarily particular, I have assigned this Poem to the dates 93 & 94, but in fact much of the "Female Vagrant's" story was composed at least two years before, All that relates to her sufferings as a Soldier's wife in America & her condition of mind during her voyage home were faithfully taken from the report made to me of her own case by a friend who had been subjected to the same trials & affected in the same way. Mr. Coleridge, when I first became acquainted with him,

---

Anti-Corn Law league *revised from* Corn league
disposition *revised from* dispositions
Poet's *ed. emended from* Poets
unnecessarily *revised from* unnecessary
94, *ed. emended from* 94.
Vagrant's" *ed. emended from* Vagrant"s
made *over illegible erasure*

[127] was so much impressed with this Poem that it would have encouraged me to publish the whole as it then stood; but the Mariner's fate appeared to me so tragical as to require a treatment more subdued & yet more strictly applicable in expression than I had at first given to it This fault was corrected nearly 50 years afterwards when I determined to publish the whole, It may be worth while to remark that tho' the incidents of this attempt do only in a small degree produce each other & it deviates accordingly from the general rule by which narrative pieces ought to be governed, it is not therefore wanting in continuous hold upon the mind or in unity which is effected by the identity of moral interest that places the two personages upon the same footing in the reader's sympathies. My ramble over many parts of Salisbury plain put me, as mentioned in the preface, upon writing this Poem, & left upon my mind imaginative impressions the force of w^h. I have felt to this day. From that district I proceeded to Bath, Bristol, & so on to the banks of the Wye, where I took again to travelling on foot. In remembrance of that part of my journey which was in 93., I began the verses "Five years have passed &—"

---

sympathies *revised from* sympathy   93., *ed. emended from* 93.

[128]

The Forsaken.   This was an overflow from the affliction of Margaret, & excluded as superfluous there, but preserved in the faint hope that it may turn to account by restoring a shy Lover to some forsaken Damsel. My poetry having been complained of as deficient in interests of this sort, a charge w^h. the next piece beginning *"Lyre! tho' such power do in thy magic live"* will scarcely tend to obviate. The natural imagery of these verses was supplied by frequent, I might say intense, observation of the Rydal torrent. What an animating contrast is the ever changing aspect of that & indeed of every one of our mountain brooks to the monotonous tone & unmitigated fury of such streams among the Alps as are fed all the summer long by Glaciers & melting snows. A Traveller observing the exquisite purity of the great rivers such as the Rhone at Geneva & the Aare at Lucerne when they issue out of their respective Lakes might fancy for a moment that some power in nature produced this beautiful change with a view to make amends for those Alpine sullyings which the waters exhibit near their fountain heads: but alas! how soon does that purity depart before the influx of tributary waters that have flowed thro' cultivated Plains & the crowded abodes of Men.

---

account by *revised from* account in
torrent What *ed. emended from* torrent what
the ever *revised from* that

brooks *revised from* [?becks]
snows. A *ed. emended from* snows A
Rhone *revised in error* to Rhine

[129]

Address to the Scholars of the Village School— Were composed at Goslar in Germany. They will be placed among the Elegiac pieces.

Lines on the expected Invasion To take their place among the political pieces.

At the grave of Burns To be printed among the poems relating to my first tour in Scotland. For illustration see my Sister's journal. It may be proper to add that the second of these pieces tho' *felt* at the time was not composed till many years after.

Elegiac Verses. "There did we stop" &c The point is 2 or 3 yards below the outlet of Grisdale Tarn on a foot-road by which a horse may pass to Paterdale ridge of Helvellyn on the left, & the summit of Fairfield on the right.

At Applethwaite This was presented to me by Sir George Beaumont with a view to the erection of a house upon it, for the sake of being near to Coleridge then living, & likely to remain, at Greta Hall near Keswick. The *severe* necessities that prevented this arose from his domestic situation. This little property, with a considerable addition that still leaves it very small, lies beautifully upon the banks of a rill that gurgles down the side of Skiddaw & the orchard & other parts

---

Scotland. For *ed. emended from* Scotland. for   Helvellyn *ed. emended from* Helvelyn

[130]

of the grounds command a magnificent prospect of Derwent Water, the mountains of Borrowdale & Newlands. Not many years ago I gave the place to my daughter.

Epistle to Sir G. H. Beaumont Bart. This poem opened when first written with a paragraph that has been transferred as an introduction to the first series of my Scotch Memorials. The journey of which the first part is here described was from Grasmere to Bootle on the south west coast of Cumberland—the whole along mountain roads through a beautiful country & we had fine weather. The verses end with our breakfast at the head of Yewdale in a yeoman's house, which like all the other property in that sequestered vale has passed or is passing into the hands of M^r. James Marshall of Monk-Coniston, in M^r. Knotts the late owner's time called Waterhead. Our hostess married a M^r. Oldfield, a Lieut. in the Navy: they lived together for some time at Hackett, where she still resides as his widow. It was in front of that house, on the mountain side, near which stood the Peasant who while we were passing at a distance saluted us waving a kerchief in her hand as described in the Poem.

Water, *ed. emended from* Water
Not *DQ deleted (see editor's note)*
the head of *inserted*
in M^r. Knotts…called *revised from illegible*

erasure
widow. It *revised from* widow, & it
saluted *written over an illegible word*
Poem. *ed. emended from* Poem

[131]

The dog which we met soon after our starting had belonged to Mr. Rowlandson who for 40 years was curate at Grasmere in place of the Rector who lived to extreme old age in a state of insanity. Of this Mr. R. much might be said both with reference to his character & the way in which he was regarded by his parishioners. He was a man of a robust frame, had a firm voice & authoritative manner, of strong natural talents of which he was himself conscious for he has been heard to say (it grieves me to add with an oath) "if I had been brought up at college by — I would have been a Bishop." Two vices used to struggle in him for mastery, avarice & the love of strong drink: but avarice as is common in like cases always got the better of its opponent, for though he was often intoxicated it was never I believe at his own expence. As has been said of one in a more exalted station he could take any *given* quantity. I have heard a story of him w{h}. is worth the telling. One summer's morning our Grasmere curate, after a night's carouse in the vale of Langdale, on his return home having reached a point near which the whole Vale of Grasmere might be seen with the Lake immediately below him,

---

parishioners. He *revised from* parishioners. he
frame, *ed. emended from* frame
authoritative *ed. emended from* authoratitive *revised from* authorititive
I would have *revised from* I should have

mastery, *ed. emended from* mastery
avarice *revised from* averice
is common *revised from* is mostly common
one in *inserted*
night's *ed. emended from* nights

[132] stept aside & sat down upon the turf; after looking for some time at the landscape, then in the perfection of its morning beauty, he exclaimed "Good God that I should have led so long such a life in such a place!" This no doubt was deeply felt by him at the time but I am not authorized to say that any noticeable amendment followed: penuriousness strengthened upon him as his body grew feebler with age, He had purchased property & kept some land in his own hands but he could not find in his heart to layout the necessary hire for labourers at the proper season & consequently he has often been seen in half dotage working his hay in the month of November by moon light, a melancholy sight which I myself have witnessed. Notwithstanding all that has been said, this man on account of his talents and superior Education, was looked up to by his parishioners who without a single exception lived at that time (& most of them upon their own small inheritances) in a state of Republican Equality, a condition favorable to the growth of kindly feelings among them & in a striking degree exclusive to temptations to gross vice & scandalous behavior. As a Pastor their curate did little or nothing for them, but what could more strikingly set forth

---

stept *revised from* he stept

[133]

the efficacy of the Church of England thro' its Ordinances & Liturgy than that in spite of the unworthiness of the Minister his Church was regularly attended, &, tho' there was not much appearance in his flock of what might be called animated piety, intoxication was rare & dissolute morals unknown. With the bible they were for the most part well acquainted & as was strikingly shewn when they were under affliction must have been supported & comforted by habitual belief in those truths which it is the aim of the Church to inculcate. *Loughrigg Tarn* this beautiful pool & the surrounding scene are minutely described in my little book upon the Lakes. Sir G.H.B. in the earlier part of his life was induced by his love of nature & the art of painting to take up his abode at Old Brathay about three miles from this spot, so that he must have seen it under many aspects & he was so much pleased with it that he purchased the Tarn with a view to build such a residence as is alluded to in this Epistle. Baronets & Knights were not so common in that day as now & Sir M¹. Le Fleming not liking to have a rival in this kind of distinction so near him, claimed a sort of Lordship over the Territory & shewed dispositions little in unison with those of Sir G Beaumont who was eminently a lover of peace. The project of building

---

efficacy *ed. emended from* effacacy
the Minister *revised from* its Minister

there was not *ed. emended from* their was not
might be *revised from* ought to be

[134]

was in consequence given up, Sir G.B. retaining possession of the Tarn. Many years afterwards a Kendal tradesman born upon its banks applied to me for the purchase of it & accordingly it was sold for the sum that had been given for it & the money was laid out under my direction upon a substantial oak fence for a certain number of Yew trees to be planted in Grasmere Church Yard; two were planted in each enclosure with a view to remove after a certain time the one which throve the least. After several years the stouter plant being left the others were taken up & placed in other parts of the same church yard & were adequately fenced at the expence & under the care of the late M^r. Barber, M^r. Greenwood & myself: the whole eight are now thriving & are already an ornament to a place w^h. during late years has lost much of its rustic simplicity by the introduction of iron palisades to fence off family burying grounds, & by numerous monuments some of them in very bad taste, from which this place of burial was in my memory quite free. See the lines in the vith book of the Excursion beginning "Green is the Church yard"—The Epistle to which these notes refer tho' written so far back as 1804 was carefully revised so late as 1842, previous to its publication.

---

up, *ed. emended from* up
free. See *ed. emended from* free see
vith book *revised in pencil from* th book

so *over illegible erasure*
publication. *ed. emended from* publication

[135]

I am loth to add that it was never seen by the person to whom it is addressed. So sensible am I of the deficiencies in all that I write, & so far does every thing that I attempt fall short of what I wish it to be, that even private publication, if such a term may be allowed, requires more resolution than I can command. I have written to give vent to my own mind & not without hope that sometime or other kindred minds might benefit by my labours: but I am inclined to believe I should never have ventured to send forth any verses of mine to the world if it had not been done on the pressure of personal occasions, Had I been a rich man my productions like this Epistle, the Trajedy of the Borderers, &cet, would most likely have been confined to M.S.

A Night Thought. These verses were thrown off extempore upon leaving M^{rs}. Luff's house at Fox Ghyll one evening. The good woman is not disposed to look at the bright side of things, & there happened to be present certain ladies who had reached the point of life where *youth* is ended & who seemed to contend with each other in expressing their dislike of the country & the climate. One of them had been heard to say she could not endure a country where there was "neither sunshine nor Cavaliers."

---

loth *revised from* loath
any verses *revised from* my verses

evening. The *revised from* evening. the

[136]

Farewell lines.   These lines were designed as a farewell to Charles Lamb & his Sister who had retired from the throngs of London to comparative solitude in the village of Enfield Hert[ds].

Love lies bleeding   It has been said that the English, though their Country has produced so many great Poets, is now the most unpoetical nation in Europe. It is probably true; for they have more temptation to become so than any other European people. Trade, commerce, & manufactures, physical science & mechanic arts, out of which so much wealth has arisen, have made our country men infinitely less sensible to movements of imagination & fancy than were our Forefathers in their simple state of society. How touching & beautiful were in most instances the names they gave to our indigenous flowers or any other they were familiarly acquainted with! Every month for many years have we been importing plants & flowers from all quarters of the globe many of which are spread thro' our gardens & some perhaps likely to be met with on the few commons which we have left. Will their botanical names ever be displaced by plain English appellations which will bring them home to our hearts by connection with our joys & sorrows? It can never be, unless society treads back her steps towards those simplicities which have been banished by the undue influence of Towns spreading & spreading in every direction so that city life with every generation takes more & more the lead of rural. Among the Ancients, Villages were reckoned the seats of barbarism.

Country *revised from* nation
have made *revised from* & made

appellations *revised from* appelations

[137]

Refinement, for the most part false, increases the desire to accumulate wealth; & while theories of political economy are boastfully pleading for the practise, inhumanity pervades all our dealings in buying & selling. This selfishness wars against disinterested imagination in all directions, &, evils coming round in a circle, barbarism spreads in every quarter of our Island. Oh for the reign of justice, & then the humblest man among us would have more power & dignity in & about him than the highest have now!

Address to the Clouds. These verses were suggested while I was walking on the foot road between Rydal Mount & Grasmere; the clouds were driving over the top of Nabb scar across the Vale—they set my thoughts agoing & the rest followed almost immediately.

The Bird of Paradise This subject has been treated of before (see a former note). I will here only by way of comment direct attention to the fact that pictures of animals & other productions of nature as seen in conservatories, menageries & museums &c—would do little for the national mind, nay they would be rather injurious to it, if the imagination were excluded by the presence of the object, more or less out of a state of nature: If it were not that we learn to *talk* & think of the Lion & the Eagle, the Palm tree & even the Cedar from the impassioned introduction of them so frequently into Holy Scripture & by Great Poets, & Divines who write as Poets, the spiritual part of our nature & therefore the higher part of it

---

barbarism *revised from* barbarism, note). *ed. emended from* note)

nature *revised from* nature, Eagle, *ed. emended from* Eagle

[138]
would derive no benefit from such intercourse with such objects.

Maternal Grief   This was in part an overflow from the Solitary's description of his own & his wife's feelings upon the decease of their children, &, I will venture to add *for private notice solely,* is faithfully set forth from my Wife's feelings & habits after the loss of our two children within half a year of each other.

*Memorials of a tour
In Italy*

During my whole life I had felt a strong desire to visit Rome & the other celebrated cities & regions of Italy but did not think myself justified in incurring the necessary expence till I received from M^r. Moxon the publisher of a large edition of my Poems a sum sufficient to enable me to gratify my wish without encroaching upon what I considered due to my family. My excellent friend H. C. Robinson readily consented to accompany me & in March 1837 we set off from London to which we returned in Augst., earlier than my companion wished or I should myself have desired had I been like him, a batchelor. These Memorials of that Tour touch upon but a very few of the places & objects that interested me, & in what they do advert to are for the most part much slighter than I could wish. More particularly do I regret that there ↄ

---

objects *revised from* subjects *(but initial* s *of* subjects *not deleted)*   &, I will *revised from* —I will   Memorials…Italy *ed. added italics*

[139]
is no notice in them of the south of France nor of the Roman antiquities abounding in that district especially of the Pont de Degard which together with its situation impressed me full as much as any remains of Roman Architecture to be found in Italy. Then there was Vaucluse, with its fountain, its Petrarch, its rocks of all seasons, its small plots of lawn in their first vernal freshness & the blossoms of the peach & other trees embellishing the scene on every side. The beauty of the stream also called forcibly for the expression of sympathy from one who from his childhood had studied the brooks & torrents of his native mountains. Between two & three hours did I run about climbing the steep & rugged craggs from whose base the water of Vaucluse breaks forth, "Has Laura's Lover;' often said I to myself, "ever sat down upon this Stone? Or has his foot ever pressed that turf?" Some, especially of the female sex, would have felt sure of it, my answer was (impute it to my years) "I fear not." Is it not in fact obvious that many of his love verses must have flowed, I do not say from a wish to display his own talent, but, from a habit of exercising his intellect in that way rather than from an impulse of his heart? It is otherwise with his Lyrical Poems & particularly with the one upon the degradation of his country: there he pours out his reproaches, lamentations

---

Italy. Then *ed. emended from* Italy Then
stream *revised from* river

especially *ed. emended from* especialy
particularly with *revised from* particularly at

[140] and aspirations like an ardent & sincere Patriot. But enough; it is time to turn to my own effusions such as they are.

Aquapendente. "Had his sunk eye kindled at those dear words that spake of Bards & Minstrels." His, Sir W. Scott's, eye did in fact kindle at them for the lines "Places forsaken now" & the two that follow were adopted from a Poem of mine which nearly 40 years ago was in part read to him & he never forgot them. "Old Helvellyn's brow where once together in his day of strength we stood rejoicing." Sir H^y. Davy was with us at the time. We had ascended from Paterdale & I could not but admire the vigor with which Scott scrambled along that horn of the mountain called "Striding Edge". Our progress was necessarily slow & beguiled by Scott's telling many stories & amusing anecdotes as was his custom. Sir H. Davy would have probably been better pleased if other topics had occasionally been interspersed & some discussion entered upon; at all events he did not remain with us long at the top of the mountain but left us to find our way down its steep side together into the Vale of Grasmere where at my cottage M^{rs}. Scott was to meet us at dinner. He said, "When I am there although 'tis fair 'twill be another Yarrow." See among these

---

scrambled…called *written over pencil which was entered over an illegible erasure*
Striding *revised from* striding

Our *ed. emended from* our
Scott's *ed. emended from* Scotts

[141]

the one upon Yarrow Revisited.

"A few short steps painful they were" This, tho' introduced here, I did not know till it was told me at Rome by Miss Mackensie of Seaforth, a lady whose friendly attentions during my residence at Rome I have gratefully acknowledged with expressions of sincere regret that she is no more. Miss M. told me that she accompanied Sir Walter to the Junicular Mount & after showing him the grave of Tasso in the church upon the top, & a mural monument there erected to his memory, they left the church & stood together on the brow of the hill overlooking the city of Rome; his daughter Anne was with them & she, naturally desirous, for the sake of Miss Mackensie especially, to have some expression of pleasure from her Father, half reproached him for showing nothing of that kind either by his looks or voice. "How can I;' replied he, "having only one 'eg to stand upon & that in extreme pain." So that the prophecy was more than fulfilled.

"*Over waves rough & deep*".   We took boat near the light-house at the point of the right horn of the bay, which makes a sort of natural port for Genoa, but the wind was high & the waves long & rough, so that I did not feel quite recompensed by the view of the city, splendid as it was,

---

notes *EQ inserted*
This *ed. emended from* this
DQ added Junicular *to the gap in pencil*

the top, & *revised from* the top of which
can *ed. emended from* can"

[142]

for the danger apparently incurred. The boatman (I had only one) encouraged me, saying we were quite safe, but I was not a little glad when we gained the shore, tho' Shelley & Byron—one of them at least who seemed to have courted agitation from every quarter—would have probably rejoiced in such a situation, more than once I believe were they both in extreme danger even on the Lake of Geneva. Every man however has his fears of some kind or other; &, no doubt, they had theirs—of all men whom I have ever known Coleridge had the most of passive courage in bodily peril, but no one was so easily cowed when moral firmness was required in miscellaneous conversation or in the daily intercourse of social life.

"How lovely didst thou appear, Savona." There is not a single bay along this beautiful coast that might not raise in a traveller a wish to take up his abode there each as it succeeds seems more inviting than the other, but the desolated convent on the cliff in the bay of Savona struck my fancy most, & had I, for the sake of my own health or of that of a dear friend, or any other cause, been desirous of a residence abroad, I should have let my thoughts loose

---

incurred. The *revised from* incured, the Shelley *ed. emended from* Shelly

ever *inserted*

[143]

upon a scheme of turning some part of this building into a habitation provided as far as might be with English comforts. There is close by it a row or Avenue I forget which of tall Cypresses, I could not forbear saying to myself—"What a sweet family walk or one for lonely musings would be found under the shade"! but there probably the trees remain little noticed & seldom enjoyed. "This flowering broom's dear neighbourhood" The Broom is a great ornament thro' the months of March & April to the vales & hills of the Appenines in the wild parts of which it blows in the utmost profusion & of course successively at different elevations as the season advances, it surpasses ours in beauty & fragrance but speaking from my own limited observation only I cannot affirm the same of several of their wild spring flowers, the primroses in particular which I saw not unfrequently but thinly scattered & languishing compared with ours.

The note at the close of the Poem upon the Oxford movement was intrusted to my friend M^r. Frederick Faber. I told him what I wished to be said & begged that as he was intimately acquainted with several of the Leaders of it he would express my thought in the way least likely to be taken amiss by them. Much of the work they are undertaking was grievously wanted & God grant their endeavours may continue to prosper as they have done.

---

comforts. There *ed. emended from* comforts. there
Cypresses. I *ed. emended from* Cypresses I
enjoyed. "This *ed. emended from* enjoyed "This

affirm *revised from* afirm
Faber. I *ed. emended from* Faber I
wanted & *revised from* wanted—

[144]

Sonnets.

The Pine Tree of Monte Mario. Sir G. Beaumont told me that when he first visited Italy Pine trees of this species abounded, but that on his return thither which was more than 30. years after, they had disappeared from many places where he had been accustomed to admire them & had become rare all over the Country especially in & about Rome. Several Roman Villas have within these few years passed into hands of foreigners who, I observed with pleasure, have taken care to plant this tree which in course of years will become a great ornament to the city & to the general landscape. May I venture to add here that having ascended the Monte Mario I could not resist embracing the trunk of this interesting monument of my departed friend's feelings for the beauties of nature, & the power of that Art which he loved so much & in the practice of which he was so distinguished.

Is this ye Gods. Sight is at first a sad enemy to imagination & to those pleasures belonging to old times with which some exertions of that power will always mingle: nothing perhaps brings this truth home to the feelings more than the city of Rome; not so much in respect to the impression made at the moment when it is first seen & looked at as a whole; for then the imagination may be invigorated & the mind's eye quickened

---

Sonnets. *ed. added italics*
landscape. May *ed. emended from* landscape May

whole; *revised from* whole,
mind's *ed. emended from* minds

[145]
to perceive as much as that of the [.] But when particular spots or objects are sought out disappointment is I believe invariably felt. Ability to recover from this disappointment will exist in proportion to knowledge & the power of the mind to reconstruct out of fragments & parts & to make details in the present subservient to more adequate comprehension of the past.

At Rome.b.   I have a private interest in this Sonnet for I doubt whether it would ever have been written but for the lively picture given me by Anna Ricketts of what they had witnessed of the indignation & sorrow expressed by some Italian noblemen of their acquaintance upon the surrender which circumstances had obliged them to make of the best portion of their family mansions to Strangers.

Albano "*Days passed*"   This sonnet is founded on simple fact & was written to enlarge, if possible, the views of those who can see nothing but evil in the intercessions countenanced by the Church of Rome: that they are in many respects lamentably pernicious must be acknowledged; but on the other hand they who reflect while they see & observe cannot but be struck with instances which will prove that it is a great error to condemn in all cases such mediation as purely idolatrous. This remark bears with especial force upon addresses to the Virgin.

Cuckoo at Laverna.   Among a thousand delightful feelings connected in my mind with the voice of the Cuckoo,

---

passed *revised from* pass

[146]
there is a personal one which is rather melancholy, I was first convinced that age had rather dulled my hearing by not being able to catch the sound at the same distance as the younger companions of my walks & of this failure I had a proof upon the occasion that suggested these verses. I did not hear the sound till M^r. Robinson had twice or thrice directed my attention to it.

Vallombrosa I must confess, though of course I did not acknowledge it in the few lines I wrote in the Stranger's book kept at the Convent, that I was somewhat disappointed at Vallombrosa. I had expected as the name implies a deep & narrow valley overshadowed by enclosing hills, but the spot where the convent stands is in fact not in a valley at all but a cove or crescent open to an extensive prospect. In the book before mentioned I read the notice in the English language that if anyone would ascend the steep ground above the convent & wander over it he would be abundantly rewarded by magnificent views, I had not time to act upon this recommendation & only went with my young guide to a point, nearly on a level with the site of the Convent, that overlooks the Vale of Arno for some leagues.

To praise great & good men has ever been deemed one of the worthiest employments of poetry, but the objects of admiration vary so much with time & circumstances, & the noblest of mankind have been found when intimately known to be of characters so imperfect, that no eulogist can

---

melancholy. I *ed. emended from* melancholy I   on a level *over illegible erasure*

[147]
find a subject which he will venture upon with the animation necessary to create sympathy unless he confines himself to a particular act or he takes something of a one-sided view of the person he is disposed to celebrate. This is a melancholy truth, & affords a strong reason for the poetic mind being chiefly exercised in works of fiction; the Poet can then follow wherever the spirit of admiration leads him unchecked by such suggestions as will be too apt to cross his way if all that he is prompted to utter is to be tested by fact. Something in this spirit I have written in the note attached to the Sonnet on the King of Sweden & many will think that in this poem & elsewhere I have spoken of the Author of Paradise Lost in a strain of panegyrick scarcely justifiable by the tenour of some of his opinions whether theological or political & by the temper he carried into public affairs in which unfortunately for his genius he was so much concerned.

Sonnet at Florence. Upon what evidence the belief rests that this stone was a favorite seat of Dante I do not know, but a Man would little consult his own interest as a Traveller if he should busy himself with doubts as to the fact. The readiness with which traditions of this character are received & the fidelity with which they are preserved from generation to generation are an evidence of feelings honorable to our nature. I remember how, during one of my rambles in the course of a college vacation, I was pleased on being shown at [Ilam] a seat

---

Man *revised from* man [Ilam] *see editor's note*
I was pleased *revised from* how I was pleased

[148]

near a kind of rocky cell at the source of the river [Manifold] on which it was said that Congreve wrote his "old Bachelor"—one can scarcely hit on any performance less in harmony with the scene—but it was a local tribute paid to intellect by those who had not troubled themselves to estimate the moral worth of that Author's comedies, & why should they? He was a man distinguished in his day—& the sequestered neighbourhood in which he often resided was perhaps as proud of him as Florence of her Dante. It is the same feeling, tho' proceeding from persons one cannot bring together in this way without offering some apology to the Shade of the great Visionary.

The Baptist.   It was very hot weather during the week we stayed at Florence, & having never been there before I went thro' much hard service & am not therefore ashamed to confess I fell asleep before this picture & sitting with my back towards the Venus de Medicis. Buonaparte in answer to one who had spoken of his being in a sound sleep up to the moment when one of his great battles was to be fought, as a proof of the calmness of his mind and command over anxious thoughts said frankly that he slept because from bodily exhaustion he could not help it. In like manner it is noticed that Criminals on the night previous to their execution seldom awake before they are called—a proof that the body is the master of us for more than we need be willing to allow. Should this note by any possible chance be seen

---

at the source *revised from* [?near] the source
[Manifold] *see editor's note*
Congreve *revised from* Congrave
intellect *revised from* in[?]

He *ed. emended from* he
being in a sound *revised from* being sound
allow. *ed. emended from* allow

[149]
by any of my country men who might have been in the Gallery at the time (& several persons were there) & witnessed such an indecorum, I hope he will give up the opinion which he might naturally have formed to my prejudice.

Florence. Rapt above earth & *the following one.* However at first these two Sonnets from M. Angelo may seem in their spirit somewhat inconsistent with each other I have not scrupled to place them side by side as characteristic of their great Author & others with whom he lived. I feel nevertheless a wish to know at w^t. periods of his life they were respectively composed. The latter, as it expresses, was written in his advanced years when it was natural that the Platonism that pervades the one should give way to the Christian feeling that inspired the other— between both, there is more than poetic affinity.

Among the Ruins of a Convent. The Political Revolutions of our time have multiplied on the Continent objects that unavoidably call forth reflections such as are expressed in these verses, but the ruins in those countries are too recent to exhibit in any thing like an equal degree the beauty with which time & nature have invested the remains of our Convents & Abbeys. These verses it will be observed take up the beauty long before it is matured as one cannot but wish it may be among some of the desolations of Italy, France, & Germany.

Sonnet 20 & 21st. I had proof in several instances that

[150]
the Carbonari, if I may still call them so, & their favourers are opening their eyes to the necessity of patience & are intent upon spreading knowledge actively but quietly as they can. May they have resolution to continue in this course! for it is the only one by which they can truly benefit their country.

"Fair Land" & the concluding Sonnet. We left Italy by the way which is called the "Nuova Strada de Allmagna" to the east of the high passes of the Alps which take you at once from Italy into Switzerland. This road leads across several smaller heights & winds down different Vales in succession so that it was only by the accidental sound of a few German words I was aware we had quitted Italy, & hence the unwelcome shock alluded to in the two or three last lines of the Sonnet with which this imperfect series concludes.

Composed by the Sea-shore. These lines were suggested during my residence under my Son's roof at Moresby on the coast near Whitehaven, at the time when I was composing those verses among the Evening Voluntaries that have reference to the Sea. In some future edition I purpose to place it among that Class of Poems. It was in that neighbourhood I first became acquainted with the ocean & its appearances & movements. My Infancy & early childhood

---

truly…country *revised from* benefit their country truly
Switzerland. This *ed. emended from* Switzerland. this
sound *revised from* hearing

[151]

were passed at Cockermouth about eight miles from the coast, & I well remember that mysterious awe with which I used to listen to anything said about storms & shipwrecks. Sea-shells of many descriptions were common in the town, & I was not a little surprised when I heard M[r]. Landor had denounced me as a Plagiarist from himself for having described a boy applying a sea shell to his ear & listening to it for intimations of what was going on in its native element: This I had done myself scores of times & it was a belief among us that we could know from the sound whether the tide was ebbing or flowing.

The Norman Boy. The subject of this Poem was sent me by M[rs]. Ogle, to whom I was personally unknown, with a hope on her part that I might be induced to relate the incident in Verse, & I do not regret that I took the trouble, for not improbably the fact is illustrative of the boy's early piety & may concur with my other little pieces on Children to produce profitable reflection among my youthful readers. This is said however with an absolute conviction that Children will derive most benefit from books which are not unworthy the perusal of persons of any age. I protest with my whole heart against those productions so abundant in the present day, in which the doings of children are dwelt upon as if they were incapable of being interested in anything else. On this subject

---

Sea-shells *revised from* sea-shells
Plagiarist *revised from* Plagairism

ebbing or *revised from* ebbing &
present day *revised from* current day

[152]
I have dwelt at length in the poem on the growth of my own Mind.

Poor Robin

I often ask myself what will become of Rydal Mount after our day—will the old walls & steps remain in front of the house & about the grounds, or will they be swept away with all the beautiful mosses & Ferns & Wild Geraniums & other flowers which their rude construction suffered & encouraged to grow among them? This little wild flower "Poor Robin" is here constantly courting my attention & exciting what may be called a domestic interest with the varying aspects of its stalks & leaves & flowers. Strangely do the tastes of men differ according to their employment & habits of life. "What a nice well would that be" said a labouring man to me one day, "if all that rubbish was cleared off." The *"rubbish"* was some of the most beautiful mosses & lichens & ferns, & other wild growths, as could possibly be seen. Defend us from the tyranny of trimness & neatness showing itself in this way! Chatterton says of freedom "Upon her head wild weeds were spread," & depend upon it if "the marvellous boy" had undertaken to give Flora a garland, he would have preferred what we are apt to call weeds to garden-flowers. True taste has an eye for both. Weeds have been called flowers out of place. I fear the place most people would assign to them is too limited, Let them come near to our abodes, as surely they may without impropriety or disorder.

---

the varying aspects *revised from* a Strangely *revised from* strangely
off." The *ed. emended from* off." the

seen. Defend *ed. emended from* seen Defend
True *revised from* true

[153]

The Cuckoo Clock   Of this clock I have nothing further to say than what the Poem expresses except that it must be here recorded that it was a present from the dear friend for whose sake these notes were chiefly undertaken & who has written them from my dictation.

The wishing-gate destroyed   See printed note upon this.

The Widow on Winandermere side.   The facts recorded in this Poem were given me and the Character of the person described by my highly esteemed friend the Revd R.P. Graves who has long officiated as Curate at Bowness to the great benefit of the parish & neighbourhood. The individual was well known to him. She died before these verses were composed. It is scarcely worth while to notice that the Stanzas are written in the Sonnet-form which was adopted when I thought the matter might be included in 28 lines.

Cenotaph on M^rs. Fermor   See the Verses on M^rs. F.

Epitaph in Langdale Church yard.   Owen Lloyd, the subject of this Epitaph, was born at Old Brathay n^r. Ambleside & was the son of Charles Lloyd & his wife Sophia (nee Pemberton) both of Birmingham who came to reside in this country soon after their marriage. They had many children, both sons & daughters, of whom the most remarkable was the subject of this Epitaph. He was educated under M^r. Dawes of Ambleside, D^r. Butler of Shrewsbury, & lastly at Trin: Col. Cambridge where he would have been greatly distinguished as a Scholar, but for inherited infirmities of bodily constitution which from early childhood affected his mind. His love for the neighbourhood in which he was born

---

notes were *revised from* notes
are Church *revised from* church
Brathay *revised from* Brathey

n^r. *EQ revised in pencil to* near
née *ed. emended from* nèe
Epitaph. He *ed. emended from* Epitaph. he

[154]
& his sympathy with the habits & characters of the mountain yeomanry, in conjunction with irregular spirits that unfitted him for facing duties in situations to which he was unaccustomed, induced him to accept the retired Curacy of Langdale. How much he was beloved & honoured there, & with what feelings he discharged his duty under the oppression of severe malady is set forth tho' imperfectly in this Epitaph.

Sonnet A Poet &—.   I was impelled to write this Sonnet by the disgusting frequency with which the word *artistical,* imported with other impertinencies from the Germans, is employed by writers of the present day, for artistical let them substitute artificial & the Poetry written on this system both at home & abroad will be for the most part much better characterised.

Sonnet   *"The most alluring clouds"* &c.   Hundreds of times have I seen hanging about and above the Vale of Rydal clouds that might have given birth to this Sonnet which was thrown off on the impulse of the moment one evening when I was returning home from the favorite walk of ours along the Rotha under Loughrigg.

"Feel for the wrongs"   This Sonnet is recommended to the perusal of the Anti Corn Law Leaguers, the Political Economists, & of all those who consider that the Evils under which we groan are to be removed or palliated by measures ungoverned by moral & religious principles.

Aspects of Xtianity in America   See Notes.

Duke of Wellington   This was composed while I was ascending Helvellyn in company with my daughter & her husband.

---

yeomanry *ed. emended from* yomanry
Langdale. How *revised from* Langdale how

Anti *inserted*
Helvellyn *revised from* Helvelyn

[155]
She was on horseback & rode to the very top of the hill without once dismounting—a feat which it was scarcely possible to perform except during a season of dry weather & a guide with whom we fell in on the mountain told us he believed it had *never* been accomplished before by anyone.

Portentous Change

To a Painter   The picture which gave occasion to this & the following Sonnet was from the pencil of Miss M. Gillies, who resided for several weeks under our roof at Rydal Mount.

To a Red breast   Almost the only verses composed by our lamented Sister S.H.

Floating Island.   My poor Sister takes a pleasure in repeating these verses which she composed not long before the beginning of her sad illness.

If with old love of you dear hills.   This and the following Sonnet were composed on what we call the "far Terrace" at Rydal Mount where I have murmured out many thousands of my Verses.

At Dover from the Pier's Head.   For the impressions on w^h. this Sonnet turns I am indebted to the experience of my daughter during her residence at Dover with our dear friend Miss Fenwick.

"Oh what a Wreck."   The sad condition of poor M^{rs}. Southey put me upon writing this. It has afforded comfort to many persons whose friends have been similarly affected.

---

husband. She *ed. emended from* husband she   fell in on *revised from* fell in at
very top *revised from* top

[156]

Intent on gathering Wool. Suggested by a conversation with Miss F⎯⎯ who along with her Sister had during their childhood found much delight in such gatherings for the purpose here alluded to.

The Borderers a Tragedy. Of this dramatic work I have little to say in addition to the short printed note which will be found attached to it. It was composed at Race Down in Dorset:ʳᵉ during the latter part of the year 95 & in the course of the following year. Had it been the work of a later period of life it would have been different in some respects from what it is now. The plot would have been something more complex & a greater variety of characters introduced to relieve the mind from the pressure of incidents so mournful. The manners also wᵈ. have been more attended to—my care was almost exclusively given to the passions & the characters, & the position in which the persons in the Drama stood relatively to each other that the reader (for I had then no thought of the Stage) might be moved & to a degree instructed by lights penetrating somewhat into the depths of our nature. In this endeavour I cannot think upon a very late review that I have failed. As to the scene & period of action little more was required for my purpose than the absence of established Law & Government, so that the Agents might be at liberty to act on their own impulses. Nevertheless I do remember that having a wish to colour the manners in some degree

---

had then no *revised from* never impulses. nevertheless
impulses. Nevertheless *ed. emended from*

[157] from local history more than my knowledge enabled me to do I read Ridpath's history of the Borders but found there nothing to my purpose. I once made an observation to Sir Walter Scott in which he concurred that it was difficult to conceive how so dull a book could be written on such a subject. Much about the same time, but a little after, Coleridge was employed in writing his Tragedy of Remorse, & it happened that soon after thro' one of the Mr. Pooles Mr. Knight the actor heard that we had been engaged in writing Plays & upon his suggestion mine was curtailed, & I believe Coleridge's also was offered to Mr. Harris Manager of Covent Garden. For myself I had no hope nor even a wish (tho' a successful Play would in the then state of my finances have been a most welcome piece of good fortune) that he should accept my performance so that I incurred no disappointment when the piece was *judiciously* returned as not calculated for the stage. In this judgement I entirely concurred, & had it been otherwise it was so natural for me to shrink from public notice that any hope I might have had of success would not have reconciled me altogether to such an exhibition. Mr. C—'s play was as is well known brought forward several years after thro' the kindness of Mr. Sheridan. In conclusion I may observe that while I was composing this play I wrote a short essay illustrative of that constitution & those tendencies of human nature which make the apparently *motiveless* actions of bad men intelligible to careful observers. This was partly done with reference to the character of Oswald, & his persevering endeavour to lead the man he   ↝

Ridpath's *ed. emended from* Ridpaths

[158]
disliked into so heinous a crime, but still more to preserve in my distinct remembrance what I had observed of transition in character & the reflections I had been led to make during the time I was a witness of the changes through which the French Revolution passed.

The Excursion.

Something must now be said of this Poem but chiefly, as has been done through the whole of these notes, with reference to my personal friends, & especially to Her who has perseveringly taken them down from my dictation. Towards the close of the first book, stand the lines that were first written beginning "Nine Tedious years" & ending "last human tenant of these ruined walls." These were composed in /95. at Race Down & for several passages describing the employment & demeanour of Margaret during her affliction I was indebted to observations made in Dorsetshire & afterwards at Alfoxden in Somersetshire where I resided in 97. & 98. The lines towards the conclusion of the 4th. book, "Despondency corrected," beginning, "For the Man who in this Spirit" to the words "intellectual soul" were in order of time composed the next either at Race Down or Alfoxden, I do not remember which. The rest of the Poem was written in the Vale of Grasmere chiefly during our residence at Allan Bank. The long Poem on my own education was, together with many minor Poems, composed while we lived at the Cottage at Town End. Perhaps my purpose of giving an

---

"last *ed. emended from* last   or Alfoxden *ed. emended from* or Allfoxden

[159]

additional interest to these my Poems in the eyes of my nearest & dearest Friends may be promoted by saying a few words upon the character of the Wanderer, the Solitary, & the Pastor, & some other of the persons introduced—and first of the principal one the Wanderer.—My lamented friend Southey (for this is written a month after his decease) used to say that had he been born a Papist, the course of life which would in all probability have been his, was the one for which he was most fitted & most to his mind, that of a Benedictine Monk in a Convent furnished, as many once were & some still are, with an inexhaustible Library. *Books,*—as appears from many passages in his writings & was evident to those who had opportunities of observing his daily life—were in fact *his passion*; & *wandering,* I can with truth affirm, was mine, but this propensity in me was happily counteracted by inability from want of fortune to fulfil my wishes. But had I been born in a class which would have deprived me of what is called a liberal education, it is not unlikely that being strong in body, I should have taken to a way of life such as that in which my Pedlar passed the greater part of his days. At all events I am here called upon freely to acknowledge that the character I have represented in his person is chiefly an idea of what I fancied my own character might have become in his circumstances. Nevertheless much of what he says & does

---

upon *revised from an illegible word*
the course *revised from* that the course
Books,—as *revised from* Books, were in fact, as
life—were in fact *revised from* life, were way of *revised from* way in
become in *revised from* become.

[160] had an external existence that fell under my own youthful & subsequent observation, An Individual named Patrick, by birth & education a Scotchman, followed this humble occupation for many years & afterwards settled in the Town of Kendal. He married a kinswoman of my wife's, & her Sister Sarah was brought up from early Childhood under this good man's eye. My own imaginations I was happy to find clothed in reality & fresh ones suggested by what she reported of this man's tenderness of heart, his strong & pure imagination, & his solid attainments in literature chiefly religious whether in prose or verse. At Hawkeshead also, while I was a school boy, there occasionally resided a Packman (the name then generally given to this calling) with whom I had frequent conversations upon what had befallen him & what he had observed during his wandering life, &, as was natural, we took much to each other, & upon the subject of *Pedlarism* in general, as *then* followed, & its favourableness to an intimate knowledge of human concerns, not merely among the humbler classes of society. I need say nothing here in addition to what is to be found in the Excursion & a note attached to it.

Now for the *Solitary.* Of Him I have much less to say. Not long after we took up our abode at Grasmere, came to reside there, from what motive I either never knew or have forgotten, a Scotchman a little past the middle of life

---

Kendal. He *revised from* Kendal—be came *written twice, the first deleted* from *DQ entered for* first *and from* above,

underscoring the latter to show replacement forgotten, *revised from* forgotten—

[161]

who had for many years been Chaplain to a Highland Regim^r. He was in no respect, as far as I know, an interesting character, tho' in his appearance there was a good deal that attracted attention as if he had been shattered in fortune & not happy in mind. Of his quondam position I availed myself to connect with the Wanderer, also a Scotchman, a character suitable to my purpose the elements of which I drew from several persons with whom I had been connected & who fell under my observation during frequent residences in London at the beginning of the French Revolution. The chief of these was, one may *now* say, *a* M^r. Fawcett, a preacher at a dissenting meeting-House at the Old Jewry. It happened to me several times to be one of his congregation thro' my connection with M^r. Nicholson of Cateaton S^t., Strand, who, at a time when I had not many acquaintances in London, used often to invite me to dine with him on Sundays, & I took that opportunity (M^r. N. being a Dissenter) of going to hear Fawcett who was an able & eloquent man. He published a Poem on War, w^h. had a good deal of merit & made me think more about him than I should otherwise have done. But his Xtianity was probably never very deeply rooted, &, like many others in those times of like shewy talents, he had not strength of character to withstand the effects of the French revolution & of the wild & lax opinions which had done so much towards producing it & far more in carrying it forward in its extremes. Poor Fawcett, I have been told, became pretty much such a person as I have described;

Regim^r. He *ed. emended from* Regimt. he
no *MW's pencil over erased* this *probably in response to EQ's query opposite*
Cateaton St., Strand *EQ revised in pencil from* Catherine St. *revised in pencil from* Cat[ ] St

more *revised from* a[?bout]
But *revised from* but
have been *revised from* was

[162]
& early disappeared from the Stage, having fallen into habits of intemperance, which I have heard (tho' I will not answer for the fact) hastened his death. Of him I need say no more: there were many like him at that time which the world will never be without but w[h]. were more numerous then for reasons too obvious to be dwelt upon.

The Pastor   To what is said of the Pastor in the Poem I have little to add but what may be deemed superfluous. It has ever appeared to me highly favorable to the beneficial influence of the Church of England upon all gradations & Classes of Society that the patronage of its benefices is in numerous instances attached to the estates of noble families of ancient Gentry, & accordingly I am gratified by the opportunity afforded me in the Excursion to pourtray the character of a country clergyman of more than ordinary talents, born & bred in the upper ranks of society so as to partake of their refinements, & at the same time brought by his pastoral office & his love of rural life into intimate connection with the peasantry of his native district. To illustrate the relation which in my mind this Pastor bore to the Wanderer & the resemblances between them, or rather the points of community in their nature, I likened one to an Oak & the other to a Sycamore, &, having here referr'd to this comparison, I need only add I had no one individual in my mind, wishing rather to embody this idea than to break in upon the simplicity of it by traits of individual character or any peculiarity of opinion.

& early *revised in pencil from* early
the words 'many', 'time', 'which' *and* 'w[h].' *EQ double-underscored in pencil*

superfluous. *ed. emended from* superfluous
any peculiarity *EQ revised in pencil to* of any peculiarity

[163]

And now for a few words upon the scene where these interviews & conversations are supposed to occur. The scene of the first book of the Poem is, I must own, laid in a tract of country not sufficiently near to that which soon comes into view in the second book to agree with the fact. All that relates to Margaret & the ruined cottage &c was taken from observations made in the South West of England & certainly it would require more than seven leagued boots to stretch in one morning from a common in Somersetshire or Dorsetshire, to the heights of Furness Fells & the deep vallies they embosom. For thus dealing with space I need make, I trust, no apology; but my friends may be amused by the truth.

In the Poem I suppose that the Pedlar & I ascended from a plain country up the vale of Langdale & struck off a good way above the Chapel to the Western side of the Vale. We ascended the hill & thence looked down upon the circular recess in which lies Blea Tarn chosen by the Solitary for his retreat. After we quit his cottage, passing over a low ridge, we descend into another Vale that of Little Langdale towards the head of which stands embowered or partly shaded by Yews & other Trees something between a Cottage & a Mansion or Gentleman's house such as they once were in this country. This I convert into the Parsonage, & at the same time & as by the waving of a magic wand, I turn the comparatively confined Vale of Langdale, its Tarn, & the rude Chapel

---

boots *emended from* books
Vale. We *ed. emended from* Vale

we retreat. After *ed. emended from* retreat. after

[164]
which once adorned the Valley, into the stately & comparatively spacious Vale of Grasmere & its ancient Parish Church, & upon the side of Loughrigg-fell at the foot of the Lake & looking down upon it & the whole Vale & its encompassing mountains, the Pastor is supposed by me to stand, when at Sunset he addresses his companions in words which I hope my readers will remember or I should not have taken the trouble of giving so much in detail the materials on which my mind actually worked.

Now for a few particulars of *fact* respecting the persons whose stories are told or characters described by the different speakers. To Margaret I have already alluded. I will add here that the lines beginning "She was a woman of a steady mind" "—live on earth a life of happiness" faithfully delineate as far as they go, the character possessed in common by many women whom it has been my happiness to know in humble life, & that several of the most touching things which she is represented as saying & doing are taken from actual observation of the distresses & trials under which different persons were suffering, some of them Strangers to me, & others daily under my notice.

I was born too late to have a distinct remembrance of the origin of the American war, but the state in w^h. I represent Robert's mind to be I had frequent opportunities of observing at the commencement of our rupture with France in 93, opportunities of which I availed myself in the Story of the Female Vagrant as told in the Poem on Guilt & Sorrow. The account given by the Solitary towards the close of

---

words *ed. emended from* wwords
particulars of *ed. emended from* particulars of,

mind to be *revised from* mind to be in 93, *ed. emended from* 93.

[165]
the 2ᵈ. Book in all that belongs to the character of the Old Man was taken from a Grasmere Pauper who was boarded in the last house quitting the Vale on the road to Ambleside; the character of his hostess, & all that befell the poor man upon the mountain, belongs to Paterdale. The woman I knew well; her name was Ruth Jackson, & she was exactly such a person as I describe. The Ruins of the old Chapel, among which the old man was found lying, may yet be traced, & stood upon the ridge that divides Paterdale from Boardale & Martindale, having been placed there for the convenience of both districts. The glorious appearance disclosed above & among the mountains was described partly from what my friend Mʳ. Luff who then lived in Paterdale witnessed upon this melancholy occasion & partly from what Mary & I had seen in company with Sir G. & Lady Beaumont above Hartshope Hall in our way from Paterdale to Ambleside.

And now for a few words upon the Church, its Monuments, & of the Deceased who are spoken of as lying in the surrounding Churchyard. But first for the one picture given by the Wanderer of the Living. In this nothing is introduced but what was taken from Nature & real life. The Cottage was called Hackett & stands as described on the Southern extremity of the ridge which separates the two Langdales: the Pair who inhabited it were called Jonathan & Betty Yewdale. Once when our

---

lying *revised from* laying   described on *revised from* described at

[166]
children were ill, of whooping cough I think, we took them for change of air to this cottage & were in the habit of going there to drink tea upon fine summer afternoons so that we became intimately acquainted with the characters, habits & lives of these good, & let me say, in the main, wise, people. The Matron had in her early youth been a servant in a house at Hawkeshead where several boys boarded while I was a school boy there. I did not remember her as having served in that capacity; but we had many little anecdotes to tell to each other of remarkable boys, incidents, & adventures which had made a noise in their day in that small town. These two persons were induced afterwards to settle at Rydal where they both died.

Church & Churchyard. The Church, as already noticed, is that of Grasmere. The interior of it has been improved lately & made warmer by underdrawing the roof & raising the floor, but the rude & antique majesty of its former appearance has been impaired by painting the rafters. And the oak benches with a simple rail at the back dividing them from each other have given way to seats that have more the appearance of Pews. It is remarkable that excepting only the Pew belonging to Rydal Hall, that to Rydal Mount, the one to the Parsonage & I believe another, the Men & Women still continue, as used to be the Custom in Wales, to sit separate from each other. Is this practice as old as the Reformation? and when & how did it originate? In the Jewish synagogues & in Lady Huntingdon's Chapels the sexes are divided in the same way. In the adjoining church yard greater changes have taken place. It is now not a little crowded with Tomb stones

---

say, in the main, *revised from* say [?wise]

persons were induced afterwards to settle *EQ queried and revised in pencil to* persons afterwards settled

other. Is *ed. emended from* other Is

originate? In *ed. emended from* originate? in

place. It *ed. emended from* place. it

[167]

and near the school house which stands in the Church yard is an ugly structure built to receive the Hearse which is recently come into use. It would not be worth while to allude to this building or the Hearse Vehicle it contains, but that the latter has been the means of introducing a change much to be lamented in the mode of conducting funerals among the Mountains. Now the Coffin is lodged in the Hearse at the door of the house of the Deceased & the Corpse is so convey'd to the Church yard gate; all the solemnity which formerly attended its progress, as described in this Poem is put an end to, so much do I regret this, that I beg to be excused for giving utterance here to a wish that should it befall me to die at Rydal Mount, my own body may be carried to Grasmere Church after the manner in which, till lately, that of every one was borne to that place of Sepulture, namely on the shoulders of neighbours no house being passed without some words of a funeral Psalm being sung at the time by the attendants bearing it. When I put into the mouth of the Wanderer, "Many precious rites & customs of our rural ancestry are gone or stealing from us," "this I hope will last for ever," & what follows, little did I foresee that the observance & mode of proceeding w^h. had often affected me so much would so soon be superceded. Having said much of the injury done in this Church-yard let me add that one is at liberty to look forward to a time when by the growth of the Yew Trees, thriving there, a solemnity will be spread over the place that will in some degree make amends for the old simple character which has already been so much encroached upon & will be still more every year. I will here set down by way of memorial

---

to *over illegible erasure*
my own *revised from* that my own
Sepultore *revised from* Sepulchre

rites & customs *revised from* rights & manners

[168]
that my Friend Sir G. Beaumont having long ago purchased the beautiful piece of Water called Loughrigg Tarn on the banks of which he intended to build, I told him that a person in Kendal who was attached to the place wished to purchase it. Sir George finding the possession of no use to him consented to part with it & placed the purchase money £20. at my disposal for any local use which I thought proper. Accordingly I resolved to plant Yew Trees in the Church Yard & had four pretty strong large oak enclosures made, in each of w^h. was planted, under my own eye & principally if not entirely by my own hand, two young trees, with the intention of leaving the one that throve best to stand. Many years after M^r. Barber, who will long be remembered in Grasmere, M^r. Greenwood, the chief landed proprietor, & myself had four other enclosures made in the church-yard at our own expence in each of w^h. was planted a tree taken from its neighbour & they all stand thriving admirably, the fences having been removed as no longer necessary. May the trees be taken care of hereafter when we are all gone & some of them will perhaps at some far distant time rival in majesty the Yew of Lorton & those which I have described as growing in Borrowdale where they are still to be seen in grand assemblage.

And now for the persons that are selected as lying in the Church yard. But first for the Individual whose grave is prepared to receive him.

༄

---

principally *ed. emended from* prinipaly   *to* Greenwood (…proprietor)
Greenwood,…proprietor, *EQ revised in pencil*

[169]

His story is here truly related; he was a school-fellow of mine for some years. He came to us when he was at least 17. years of age very tall, robust & full grown. This prevented him from falling into the amusements & games of the school; consequently he gave more time to books. He was not remarkably bright or quick but by industry he made a progress more than respectable. His parents not being wealthy enough to send him to college when he left Hawkeshead he became a schoolmaster with a view to preparing himself for holy orders. About this time he fell in love as related in the Poem & every thing followed as there described except that I do not know exactly when & where he died. The number of youths that came to Hawkeshead School from the families of the humble yeomanry to be educated to a certain degree of Scholarship as a preparation for the Church was considerable, & the fortunes of these persons in after life various of course, & of some not a little remarkable, I have now one of this class in my eye who became an Usher in a preparatory school & ended in making a large fortune. His manners when he came to Hawkeshead were as uncouth as well could be; but he had good abilities with skill to turn them to account & when the Master of the School to w^h. he was Usher died he stept into his place & became Proprietor of the Establishment—he contrived to manage it with such address & so much to the taste of what is called High Society & the fashionable

---

related;…He…school; *ed. emended from*
  related…he…school

[170]
world that no school of the kind, even till he retired, was in such high request—Ministers of State, the wealthiest gentry, & nobility of the first rank vied with each other in bespeaking a place for their sons in the Seminary of this fortunate Teacher. In the solitude of Grasmere while living as a married man, in a Cottage of £8 p^r. annum rent I often used to smile at the tales which reached me of the brilliant career of this quondam clown, for such in reality he was in manners & appearance before he was polished a little by attrition with *gentlemen's* sons trained at Hawkeshead, rough & rude as many of our juveniles were. Not 200. yards from the Cottage in Grasmere just mentioned to which I retired, this gentleman, who many years afterwards purchased a small estate in the neighbourhood, is now erecting a boat-house with an upper story to be resorted to as an entertaining-room when he & his associates may feel inclined to take their pastime on the Lake. Every Passenger will be disgusted with the sight of this Edifice not merely as a tasteless thing in itself, but as utterly out of place & peculiarly fitted as far as it is observed (& it obtrudes itself on notice at every point of view) to mar the beauty & destroy the pastoral simplicity of the Vale. For my own part & that of my household it is our utter detestation standing by a shore to which, before the high road was made to pass that way, we used daily & hourly to repair for seclusion & for the shelter of a grove under which I composed many of my Poems,

[171]

The Brothers especially, & for this reason we gave the grove that name, "That which each man loved & prized in his peculiar Nook of Earth dies with him or is changed." So much for my old School fellow & his exploits. I will only add that as the foundation has twice failed from the Lake no doubt being intolerant of the intrusion there is some ground for hoping that the impertinent structure will not stand.

The Miner next described as having found his treasure after twice ten years of labour, lived in Paterdale & the story is true to the letter. It seems to me however rather remarkable that the strength of mind which had supported him through this long unrewarded labour did not enable him to bear its successful issue. Several times in the course of my life I have heard of sudden influxes of great wealth being followed by derangement, & in one instance the shock of good fortune was so great as to produce absolute Idiotcy. But these all happened where there had been little or no previous effort to acquire the riches & therefore such a consequence might the more naturally be expected than in the case of the Solitary Miner. In reviewing his story one cannot but regret that such perseverance was not sustained by a worthier object. Archimedes leapt out of his bath & ran about the streets proclaiming his discovery in a transport of joy, but we are not told that he lost either his life or his senses in consequence.

The next character to whom the Priest is led by contrast with the resoluteness displayed ☙

The Brothers *underscored in pencil*
changed." So *ed. emended from* changed" So
intolerant *revised from* intol[?]

derangement, *comma added in pencil*
naturally *ed. emended from* naturaly

[172] by the foregoing is taken from a person born & bred in Grasmere by name Dawson, & whose talents, dispositions & way of life were such as are here delineated. I did not know him, but all was fresh in memory when we settled at Grasmere in the beginning of the Century. From this point the conversation leads to the mention of two Individuals who by their several fortunes were at different times driven to take refuge at the small and obscure town of Hawkeshead on the skirt of these Mountains. Their stories I had from the dear old Dame with whom, as a school-boy, & afterwards, I lodged for nearly the space of ten years. The elder, the Jacobite, was named Drummond & was of a high family in Scotland; the Hanoverian Whig bore the name of Vandepat, & might perhaps be a descendant of some Dutchman who had come over in the train of King William. At all events his zeal was such that he ruined himself by a contest for the representation of London or Westminster undertaken to support his party & retired to this corner of the world, selected as it had been by Drummond, for that obscurity which since visiting the Lakes became fashionable it has no longer retained. So much was this region considered out of the way till a late period, that persons who had fled from justice used often to resort hither for concealment & some were so bold as to not unfrequently make excursions from the place of their retreat for the purpose of committing fresh offences. Such was particularly the case with two brothers of the name of Weston who took up their abode at Old Brathay, I think about 70 years ago. They were High-way-Men & lived there some time without being discovered

---

delineated *revised from* deleniated
Mountains. Their *ed. emended from* Mountains Their

Brathay *revised from* Brathey

[173]

tho' it was known that they often disappeared in a way and upon errands which could not be accounted for. Their horses were noticed as being of a choice breed & I have heard from the Relf family, one of whom was a Saddler in the town of Kendal, that they were curious in their Saddles & housings & accoutrements of their horses. They as I have heard, & as was universally believed, were in the end both taken & hanged.

"Tall was her stature, her complexion dark and saturnine. This person lived at Town End & was almost our next neighbour. I have little to notice concerning her beyond what is said in the Poem. She was a most striking instance how far a woman may surpass in talent, in knowledge & culture of mind those with & among whom she lives & yet fall below them in Xtian virtues of the heart & spirit. It seemed almost, & I say it with grief, that in proportion as she excelled in the one she failed in the other. How frequently has one to observe in both sexes the same thing. & how mortifying is the reflection!

As on a sunny bank the tender Lamb. The story that follows was told to M^{rs}. Wordsworth & my Sister by the Sister of this unhappy young woman, every particular was exactly as I have related. The party was not known to me tho' she lived at Hawkeshead, but it was after I left school. The Clergyman who administered comfort to her in her distress I knew well. Her Sister who told the story was the wife of a leading Yeoman in the Vale of Grasmere & they were an affectionate Pair & greatly respected by everyone who knew them. Neither lived to be old, & their Estate which was perhaps the most considerable then in the Vale & was endeared to them

---

a way *revised from* [?hours]
Relf *EQ revised in pencil to* Relph
horses. They *ed. emended from* horses They

& among *inserted*
told to *revised from* told

[174]
by many remembrances of a salutary character not easily understood or sympathised with by those who are born to great affluence, past to their eldest Son according to the practice of these Vales, who died soon after he came into possession; he was an amiable & promising youth, but was succeeded by an only brother a good natured man, who fell into habits of drinking by which he gradually reduced his property & the other day the last acre of it was sold, & his wife & children, & he himself still surviving, have very little left to live upon, which it would not perhaps have been worth while to record here but that through all trials this woman has proved a model of patience, meekness, affect^te forebearance, & forgiveness. Their eldest Son, who thro' the vices of his Father has thus been robbed of an ancient family inheritance, was never heard to murmur or complain against the cause of their distress & is now deservedly the chief prop of his Mother's hopes.

Book VII. The Clergyman & his family described at the beginning of this book were during many years our principal associates in the Vale of Grasmere unless I was to except our very nearest neighbours. I have entered so particularly into the main points of their history that I will barely testify in prose that with the single exception of the particulars of their journey to Grasmere, which however was exactly copied from, in another instance, the whole that I have said of them is as faithful to the truth as words can make it. There was much talent in the family & the eldest son was distinguished for poetical talent of which a specimen is given in my Notes to the Sonnets on the Duddon. Once when in our Cottage at Town-End

---

with the single…another instance, *EQ revised in pencil to* (with the single…another instance)

copied from, *comma added in pencil*

[175]

I was talking with him about Poetry, in the course of conversation I presumed to find fault with the versification of Pope of whom he was an enthusiastic Admirer; he defended him with a warmth that indicated much irritation, nevertheless I would not abandon my point & said, "in compass & variety of sound your own versification surpasses his." Never shall I forget the change in his countenance & tone of voice; the storm was laid in a moment, he no longer disputed my judgment & I passed immediately in his mind, no doubt, for as great a critic as ever lived. I ought to add he was a Clergyman & a well educated man, & his verbal memory was the most remarkable of any Individual I have known except a M^r. Archer, an Irishman who lived several years in this neighbourhood, & who in this faculty was a prodigy: he afterwards became deranged & I believe continues so if alive.

Then follows the character of Robert Walker for which see notes to the Duddon—

—That of the *Deaf Man* whose Epitaph may be seen in the Church yard at the Head of Hawes water, & whose qualities of mind & heart & their benign influence in conjunction with his privation I had from his relatives on the spot.

The *blind Man* next commemorated was John Gough of Kendal a man known far beyond his neighbourhood for his talents & attainments in Natural History and Science.

Of the *Infants Grave* next noticed I will only say it is an exact picture of what fell under my own observation; & all persons who are intimately acquainted with Cottage Life

---

Poetry, in *revised from* Poetry, &
Archer,…neighbourhood, *commas added in pencil*
believe *EQ revised in pencil to* fear

Then *revised from* The
privation *revised from illegible erasure*
Science. Of *ed. emended from* Science Of

[176] must often have observed like instances of the working of the domestic affections.

"*A volley thrice repeated.*" This young Volunteer bore the name of Dawson & was younger brother if I am not mistaken to the Prodigal of whose character & fortunes an account is given towards the beginning of the preceding book. The Father of the family I knew well: he was a man of literary education, & [   ] experience in society much beyond what was common among the inhabitants of the Vale. He had lived a good while in the Highlands of Scotland as a Manager of Iron Works at Bunaw & had acted as clerk to one of my predecessors in the office of Distributor of Stamps, when he used to travel round the country collecting & bringing home the money due to Government in gold, which, it may be worth while to mention for the sake of my Friends, was deposited in the cell or Iron-closet under the west window which still exists with the Iron doors that guarded the property. This of course was before the time of bills & notes. The two sons of this person had no doubt been led by the knowledge of their Father to take more delight in Scholar ship & had been accustomed in their own minds to take a wider view of social interests than was usual among their associates, The premature death of this gallant young man was much lamented & as an attendant upon the funeral I myself witnessed the ceremony & the effect of it as described in the Poem.

"Tradition tells that in Eliza's golden days", "A knight came on a Warhorse", "The House is gone." The pillars of the Gate way in front of the Mansion remained when we first took up our abode at Grasmere. Two or three cottages still remain

---

thrice *so PW (1841); written in ink as alternate above* twice
sake *EQ underscored in pencil*
associates. The *ed. emended from*

associates The Poem. "Tradition *ed. emended from* Poem "Tradition

[177]
which are called Nott Houses from the name of the Gentleman (I have called him a knight) concerning whom these Traditions survive. He was the Ancestor of the Knott family formerly considerable proprietors in the district. What follows in the discourse of the Wanderer upon the changes he had witnessed in Rural Life by the introduction of Machinery, is truly described from what I myself saw during my boy-hood & early youth & from what was often told me by persons of this humble calling. Happily, most happily for these Mountains, the mischief was diverted from the banks of their beautiful streams & transferred to open & flat Countries abounding in coal where the agency of Steam was found much more effectual for carrying on those demoralizing works. Had it not been for this invention, long before the present time, every torrent & river in this district would have had its factory large & populous in proportion to the power of the water that could there be commanded. Parliament has interfered to prevent the night work which was once carried on in these Mills as actively as during the day time, & by necessity still more perniciously—a sad disgrace to the proprietors & to the nation which could so long tolerate such unnatural proceedings. Reviewing at this late period, *1843*, what I put into the mouths of my Interlocutors a few years after the commencement of the Century, I grieve that so little progress has been made in diminishing the evils deplored, or promoting the benefits of education which the Wanderer anticipates. The results of Lord Ashley's labours to defer the time when Children might legally be allowed to work in factories

---

Happily, *comma added in pencil*

[178]

& his endeavours to still further limit the hours of permitted labour have fallen far short of his own humane wishes & those of every benevolent & right-minded man who has carefully attended to this subject & in the present Session of Parliament (1843) Sir James Graham's attempt to establish a course of religious education among the children employed in factories has been abandoned in consequence of what might easily be foreseen, the vehement & turbulent opposition of the Dissenters; so that for many years to come it may be thought expedient to leave the religious instruction of Children entirely in the hands of the several denominations of Christians in the Island, each body to work according to its own means & in its own way. Such is my own confidence, a confidence I share with many others of my most valued friends, in the superior advantages both religious & social who attend a course of instruction presided over, & guided by, the Clergy of the Church of England, that I have no doubt that if but once its Members, Lay & clerical, were duly sensible of those benefits, their Church would daily gain ground, & rapidly, upon every shape & fashion of Dissent: & in that case a great majority in Parliament being sensible of these benefits, the Ministers of the Country might be emboldened, were it necessary, to apply funds of the State to the support of Education on Church Principles, Before I conclude I cannot forbear noticing the strenuous efforts made at this time in Parliament by so many persons to extend manufactoring & commercial industry at the expence of agricultural, tho' we have recently had abundant proofs that the apprehensions expressed by the Wanderer were not groundless

"I spake of mischief by the Wise diffused

---

still further limit *reordered in pencil to* limit still further

[179]
>   With gladness, thinking that the more it spreads
>   The healthier, the securer we become;
>   Delusion which a moment may destroy!

The Chartists are well aware of this possibility & cling to it with an ardor & perseverance which nothing but wiser and more brotherly dealing towards the many on the part of the wealthy few can moderate or remove.

Book IX. towards conclusion.

>   "While from the grassy mountain's open side
>   "We gazed—"

The point here fixed upon in my imagination is half way up the northern side of Loughrigg fell from which the Pastor & his companions are supposed to look upwards to the sky & mountain tops, & round the Vale with the Lake lying immediately beneath them.

>   "But turned not without welcome promise given
>   "That he would share the pleasures & pursuits
>   "Of yet another summer's day, consumed
>   "In wandering with us."

When I reported this promise of the Solitary, & long after, it was my wish, & I might say intention, that we should resume our wanderings & pass the borders into his native country where as I hoped he might witness in the Society of the Wanderer some religious ceremony—a sacrament say, in the open fields, or a preaching among the Mountains, which by recalling to his mind the days of his early Childhood, when he had been present on such occasions in company with his Parents & nearest Kindred, might have dissolv'd his heart into tenderness & so done more towards restoring the Christian Faith in which he had been educated, & with that, contentedness & even cheerfulness of mind, than all that the Wanderer & Pastor by their several effusions & addresses had been unable to effect—an issue

---

perseverance which *revised from* perseverance [?when/where]   (*notes continue on p. 180*)

[180]

like this was in my intentions—But alas!

> —Mid the Wreck of is & was
> Things incomplete & purposes betrayed
> Make sadder transits o'er thought's optic glass
> Than noblest objects utterly decayed.

Rydal Mount June 24th.
    1843.
S^t. John Baptist day

To dearest Miss Fenwick are we obliged for these notes every word of which was taken down by her kind pen from my Father's dictation. The former portion was transcribed at Rydal by M^r. Quillinan, the latter by me & finished at the Vicarage Brigham this *Twenty fifth day of Augst. 1843. D.Q.*

---

179 mountain's *ed. emended from* mountains us." *EQ appended a long pencil dash* mind, than *revised from* mind, & unable *DQ queried* able

180 thought's *ed. emended from* thoughts was *revised from* were

Editor's Notes

1   *My heart leaps up when I behold*   Probably composed 26 March 1802.
    Town-End   See Glossary.
    To a Butterfly   ('Stay near me—do not take thy flight!'). Composed 14 March 1802.
    Foresight   Composed 28 April 1802.
    my Daughter Catherine   Catherine Wordsworth. The Wordsworths moved to Allan Bank in June 1808. Catherine was born in September of that year and the family moved to the Rectory in June 1811; Catherine died at the Rectory 5 June 1812. However, as Reed points out, the manuscript drafts from which WW drew for this poem must date after December 1812 (*Chronology: MY*, p. 677). WW may have conflated the time of composition with the time of the incident.
    Address to a Child, During a Boisterous Winter Evening. By a Female Friend of the Author   DW composed the poem between 28 November and around 5 December 1805, and showed it to WW when he returned home about 6 December. WW inserted lines 34–6 in late 1814 before publishing it with his own poems in 1815.
    The Mother's Return; By the Same   Perhaps composed 5 May 1807. 'D°.' is 'Ditto'.
    Alice Fell; Or, Poverty   Robert Grahame was a solicitor in Glasgow. James Grahame (1765–1811), his brother, was a poet and dramatist whose *The Sabbath, A Poem*, was published in 1804, and whose *Poems* appeared in 1807.
    Clarkson   See Glossary.

2   *till it was restored*   EQ's pencil note reads, 'see Coleridge's Biog. Lit'—that is, STC's expressed view that this and several other poems in the same 'homely mode' would have been 'more delightful in prose' (*Biographia Literaria*, Chapter 4).
Lucy Gray; Or, Solitude   Probably composed between 6 October 1798 and 23 February 1799.
Edward Quillinan   See the Introduction and Glossary.
Goslar   See Glossary.
Crabbe   See Glossary.

3   *Alfoxden*   See Glossary.
We are Seven. Goodrich Castle   The ruins of Goodrich Castle are at Ross, Herefordshire, on the east bank of the Wye, a few miles north of Tintern Abbey. See WW's note to *Ode: Intimations of Immortality* on p. 123 for his discussion of the differences between adult and childhood conceptions of death.
Salisbury Plain   A large tract of chalk upland north of Salisbury in Wiltshire, on the road from London to Bristol.
Vale of Clwydd   See WW's reference to this walking tour in his note to *Peter Bell*, p. 34. See also the Glossary entries for Calvert, with whom he began the tour, and for Jones.
Coleridge   See Glossary.
In the Spring of the year 1798   The walking tour with STC and DW, during which *The Rime of the Ancient Mariner* was planned, actually took place in mid-November 1797 (see Chronology: *EY*, p. 210 and n. 37; Moorman, I, 346–9; *LB* [Owen], pp. vii–viii).
Linton   Usually spelled Lynton. West of Alfoxden along the Bristol Channel, a few miles east of Porlock. The Valley of Stones, or Valley of Rocks as it is now called, is twelve miles west of Lynton on the coast of Bristol Channel. In a surviving fragment of a letter DW described the place as 'A valley at the top of one of those immense hills which open at each end to the sea, and is from its rocky appearance called the Valley of Stones' (DW to Mary Hutchinson?, November 1797; *EY*, p. 194).

4   *Phillips the Bookseller...D^r. Aikin*   Richard Phillips (1767–1840), was a bookseller and publisher in Leicester and London. In 1793 he was found guilty of selling Thomas Paine's *Rights of Man* and was sentenced to eighteen months imprisonment. On his release he set up business in St Paul's Churchyard, London, and began the *Monthly Magazine* in 1796 with Dr John Aikin (1747–1822) as editor (the *New Monthly Magazine* was founded in 1814; see Nathaniel Teich, 'Correcting the Reference to the *Monthly Magazine* in the Fenwick Note to WW's "We are Seven",' *WC* 1 [1970] pp. 55–6). Aikin, physician and author, was the brother of Mrs Barbauld (see note to *The Idle Shepherd Boys*, p. 11) and a contributor to the magazine along with Southey, John Wolcot ('Peter Pindar'), and others. Phillips was a friend of Joseph Priestley and a patron of many radical contemporaries. Under Phillips' and Aikin's influence the *Monthly Magazine* was strongly anti-government.

Quantock Hills   See Glossary.

towards Watchet   On the coast of Bristol Channel, near Alfoxden.

his friend M^r. Cruikshank   John Cruikshank (bapt. 25 January 1773) was the land agent to Lord Egmont at Nether Stowey and a neighbour of STC. He helped to raise funds to assist STC when his journal *The Watchman* failed in 1796.

Shelvocke's Voyages   George Shelvocke (fl. 1690–1728), privateer and author of *Voyage round the World, by the Way of the Great South Sea, performed in the years 1719, 20, 21, 22...*(London, 1726; 2nd edn, 1757).

Editor's Notes 220

5   *by Dulverton*   A market town in southwestern Somersetshire.
we began to talk of a volume   See Gill, *A Life* (pp. 148–50), for a discussion of the personal and financial pressures on WW and STC and the complex negotiations among WW, STC and Cottle, their publisher, under which the scheme for publishing the *Lyrical Ballads* was formed. WW inscribed a copy of *Lyrical Ballads* (1798) to his nephew John Wordsworth on 6 March 1844, 'This Volume was published in conjunction with Mr Coleridge, at Bristol, by our common Friend Mr Cottle, and immediately before its publication Mr Coleridge my Sister and I went into Germany' (Wordsworth Library copy, The Wordsworth Trust). For Cottle see the note to *Tintern Abbey*, p. 30.

6   *supernatural subjects*   EQ inserted '? natural' above in pencil. W. J. B. Owen has suggested that the copyist made an elision from 'supernatural subjects and subjects taken from common life' (*Wordsworth and Coleridge, Lyrical Ballads, 1798* [2nd edn, Oxford, 1969, corr. 1971] p. 136).
our friend James Tobin's name   James Webbe Tobin (1767–1814) was a contemporary and acquaintance of WW, friend of the Pinneys, STC, Lamb and Godwin, and a member of the Bristol firm of Pinney and Tobin. John Tobin (1770–1804), James' brother, was a dramatist whose plays achieved wide success only after his death from tuberculosis in 1804. 'Jim', two sentences on, is the copyist's mistake for 'Jem'.

8   *Sir —— Meyrick's impertinent structure* Sir Samuel Rush Meyrick (1783–1848) was a lawyer and antiquarian who tried unsuccessfully to buy the ruins of Goodrich Castle at Ross on the Wye. In 1827 he built a mansion, the 'new castle' of WW's note, on the hill opposite the ruins, which he called Goodrich Court and where he housed his collection of ancient arms and armour.

Anecdote for Fathers, Showing How the Practice of Lying May be Taught Probably written shortly after the incident took place, between early March or early April and around 16 May 1798. When Basil was living with WW and DW at Racedown (see Glossary), WW said the boy, named Basil after his father, 'lies like a little devil' (in a letter of 7 March 1796; *EY*, p. 168). For Montagu see Glossary.

Liswyn Farm John Thelwall's farm in Wales (see *LY*, IV, 249, and Geoffrey Little, 'Tintern Abbey and Llyswen Farm', *WC*, 8 [1977] 80–2). Kilve, too, is a real place, though they have been taken to represent Alfoxden and Racedown respectively, the two places where young Basil had lived with the Wordsworths. 'Citizen John' Thelwall (1764–1834) gave up the law to become a Jacobin reformer, writer and lecturer on politics and (later) on elocution. As a young man he had been apprenticed to a tailor in London. He was an impressive orator; in 1794 he was sent to prison in the Tower of London with Thomas Hardy (founder in 1792 of the London Corresponding Society), John Horne Tooke and others on a charge of high treason, but they were all acquitted. In 1797 he left London for the farm in Wales. He was a friend of Godwin (briefly), and of STC and WW.

9   *Nether Stowey*   See Glossary.

a spy being sent by government—   As comical as it seemed in retrospect, the episode of 'Spy-nosy', when Sir Robert Peel's Tory government sent a spy to Somersetshire to observe the suspicious movements of STC and WW, was symptomatic of a dangerous time (see Gill, *A Life*, pp. 127–9). STC told the same story WW tells but with more point, as recorded in *Specimens of the Table Talk of Samuel Taylor Coleridge* (R.N. Coleridge [ed.] 2 vols [London, 1835] I, 190–1); in this account STC remarked that it was a place to forget 'treason' and Thelwall replied that it was 'a place to make a man forget there is any necessity for treason'.

Rural Architecture   Probably composed between 13 September and 10 October 1800.

10   *The Pet Lamb. A Pastoral*   Composed by 15 September 1800. Barbara and her younger sister, Hannah, lived with their father, George Lewthwaite, at Grove Cottage, on the road between Town End and the Swan. Their mother, Anne, died in childbirth in May 1797. Hannah was employed by DW to help with MW's and WW's first two children, John (b. 1803) and Dorothy (Dora) (b. 1805).

Ambleside   See Glossary.

with her babe in her arm   That is, 'her dead babe', as *Memoirs* reads; the child was stillborn.

I chose the name   In March 1801. WW's brother John (see Glossary) told Mary Hutchinson that WW had her sister Joanna in mind when he drew the portrait of the 'Maiden' in *The Pet Lamb* (see *John Wordsworth's Letters*, ed. Carl H. Ketcham [Cornell University Press, Ithaca, NY, 1969] pp. 94, 201).

Lindley Murray (1745–1826)   An educator who included WW's poem in *Introduction to the English Reader,* published in 1809.

11 *The Idle Shepherd Boys; Or, Dungeon-Ghyll Force A Pastoral*   Composed by 9 July 1800.
Southey   See Glossary.
Helvellyn   See Glossary.
There, sometimes...lonely cheer   From the poem *Fidelity,* ll. 25–6.
a review ascribed to Mrs. Barbauld   Anna Letitia Barbauld (1743–1825), poet and writer, whose collected *Works* did not appear until 1825 (2 vols, with a *Memoir by Lucy Aikin,* her niece), but whose poems were published in various magazines during her lifetime, including the *Monthly Magazine,* edited by her brother, Dr John Aikin (see WW's note to *We Are Seven,* notebook p. 3). Besides her poetry and journalism, she wrote several books for children and edited a fifty-volume collection of the British novelists. She addressed one of her poems to STC (*To Mr. C—ge*), praising him as a 'Youth beloved / Of Science-of the Muse beloved'. He had visited her in Bristol in 1797.

12 *Influence of Natural Objects in Calling Forth and Strengthening the Imagination in Boyhood and Early Youth. From an Unpublished Poem* ('Wisdom and Spirit of the universe')   Composed in Goslar in the winter of 1798–9 and first published in STC's *The Friend* 28 December 1809 (see *Prelude,* I, 428–89).
The Longest Day. Addressed To —— (*Addressed To My Daughter, Dora* [*PW* 1850]). The occasion was 21 June 1817; the earliest manuscript of the poem is dated 5 September 1817. For Dora Wordsworth see Glossary.
Rydal Mount See   Glossary.
Dear Native Regions   The title is *Extract from the Conclusion of a Poem, Composed in Anticipation of Leaving School.*
Hawkshead   See Glossary.
Hall of Coniston   The 'old hall' with its 'neglected mansion-house' of the 1799 *Prelude* (II, 140–8) was the seat of the Flemings from 1226 (in the reign of Richard III), when the manor of Coniston passed

to Richard Le Fleming, until the death of William Fleming in 1653. Thereafter the manor of Rydal, which passed to Thomas Le Fleming in 1409 (in the reign of Henry IV), became the family seat. Coniston Hall, mentioned by West (*Guide to the Lakes in Cumberland, Westmorland and Lancashire,* London, 1777), 'appears upon the bank of the lake…and though now abandoned and in ruins, it has the air of grandeur and magnificence'. See also WW's appreciative description in *An Unpublished Tour* (*Prose,* II, 307–9). Parts of the building may date from the thirteenth century, but much of what remains was rebuilt in the fifteenth ('Coniston Hall', by H. Swainson Cowper, in *Transactions of the Cumberland and Westmoreland Archaeological Society,* 9 [1888] art. 32, pp. 438–47). Sir Michael Le Fleming, the first of the line, is said to have obtained lands in Furness (Lancaster County) and in Cumberland at the time of the Conquest. WW was correct to use the 'Le' before 'Fleming' since the ancient form of the name was restored by Sir William Fleming, an Antiquarian, in 1757 and used by his heirs thereafter. See also the Glossary, under 'Le Fleming'.

The Poem of which it was the conclusion *The Vale of Esthwaite.* Probably composed in spring or early summer of 1787 and never published by WW. See *Poems, 1807–1820,* pp. 141–2, for WW's further use of this image and an account of his 'recomposing' this poem for the first collective edition, *Poems* (1815). He dated the poem '1786' in 1815 and in 1820. For *The Vale of Esthwaite,* see *Poems, 1785–1795,* p. 407ff.

13 *An Evening Walk, Addressed to a Young Lady* EQ's revision somewhat obscures the timing of composition, so the original reading has been restored. 'At School' refers to WW's final year at Hawkshead School, probably in the spring of 1787. 'After [he] left' school and went to Cambridge, his first and second college vacations were in 1788 and 1789. These are the dates WW assigned to the poem in editions from 1836. The poem was much revised before it was published in 1793.
Waving his hat ... the intercepted flocks The words as they appeared in *PW* (1841) ll. 181–4, except 'loud' for 'bounds' in l. 183 of 1841.
Dunmail Raise See Glossary.
And fronting ... in stronger lines *PW* (1841) ll. 213–14. Cf. 'a Tree, of many, one', *Ode: Intimations of Immortality,* l. 51.

14 *14 years of age* WW emerged a 'dedicated spirit' after such an experience, as told in *The Prelude* (1805) IV, 330–45, but there he assigns the occasion to his first 'summer vacation', July 1788.
Esthwaite See Glossary.
discarded from the poem of Dion For this passage in an early version of *Dion*, see *Poems, 1807–1820*, pp. 213–14.
the late Mr. Curwen John Christian (1756–1828) took the name Curwen in 1790 after his wife Isabella inherited the Curwen estates from her father, Henry Curwen of Workington Hall. Isabella Curwen bought Belle Isle in Lake Windermere (see Glossary entry for 'Windermere') in 1781 and after her marriage to John Christian they acquired other islands and properties on the lake, including 'The Station' above the ferry landing. WW gave the same account of the introduction of swans to the islands in his *Unpublished Tour* (*Prose*, II, 335). On Belle Isle John (Christian) Curwen built a circular mansion and extended the gardens in the early 1780s, much to the Wordsworths' later disgust (cf. *Journals*, I, 155 [8 June 1802], and the several versions of *Guide Through the District of the Lakes* in *Prose*, II, 209, 267, 411n.).

15   *Descriptive Sketches Taken During a Pedestrian Tour Among the Alps*   Probably composed between late November 1791 and December 1792.

Lungarne & *Sarnen*   See *Descriptive Sketches,* ll. 222 ff. (*PW* [1841]).

The Female Vagrant   WW dated the poem '1792' in editions from 1840 through 1843 (though he had given the date as '1793' in editions of 1815 and 1820). In the Advertisement to *Guilt and Sorrow* he dated the composition of the poem 1793–4. *The Female Vagrant* may have been composed as early as 1791, though no manuscript version survives to confirm an early date; but work on *Salisbury Plain,* of which it was a part, is correctly dated in this note as 1793–4 (EQ entered this date in pencil in a gap in the only full manuscript of the notes, this portion of which he also transcribed). *Salisbury Plain* was revised in 1795–9 as *Adventures on Salisbury Plain* when WW thought of publishing it with Joseph Cottle in Bristol, and it was largely rewritten in 1841 and published as *Guilt and Sorrow; or, Incidents upon Salisbury Plain* in 1842 among *Poems, Chiefly of Early and Late Years.* In his note published with *Guilt and Sorrow* WW confirmed the 1793–4 dating but added the information that the story that formed the basis for *The Female Vagrant* was composed 'at least two years before'. (See WW's note to *The Excursion* below, p. 164; *SPP,* p. 7; and the note to *The Female Vagrant* in *LB, 1797–1800,* pp. 343–4.) After the 1843 edition *The Female Vagrant* was not published separately. This note and all the notes on notebook pp. 16–17 were copied on separate sheets by IF, probably using DC MS. 153 rather than her own notes as guide (see the note About the Text, p. xxxvii).

16 *The Brothers*   WW probably completed about half of the poem before the end of December 1799 and finished it before 5 April 1800. The 'fact' was related to WW while on a tour of the Lake District with STC and, during the earlier part of the tour, WW's sailor brother John, in the autumn of 1799. At Ennerdale Water WW and STC heard the story of Jerome Bowman, who had died after breaking his leg near Scalehow Force, and another story of a man who 'broke his neck before this by falling off a Crag…—supposed to have layed down & slept—but walked in his sleep, & so came to this crag, & fell off—This was at Proud Knot on the mountain called Pillar up Ennerdale—his Pike staff stuck midway & stayed there till it rotted away' (*STCN*, I, entry 540). Ennerdale begins at 'The Pillar', the mountain above Ennerdale Water; the river of the same name flows through the lake to the Irish Sea. WW gave a similar account of the poem's source to Sir John Taylor Coleridge (*Memoirs,* II, 305). See also his note to *Hart-Leap Well* on p. 29 of the notebook. Besides the stories heard at Ennerdale Water, the character and experiences of WW's brother John provided important elements for the portrait of Leonard. See also WW's letter to Charles James Fox of 14 January 1801 in which he emphasised the qualities he admired in Lake District 'statesmen', the very qualities on which he founded the characters of the figures in *The Brothers* and in *Michael* (*EY,* pp. 314–15; see also his note to *Michael* on p. 20 of the notebook).

Artegal and Elidure   Composed mainly in late 1814 to early 1815. John Milton's *The History of Britain* (1670) is the work quoted; another source, mentioned in the epigraph to the poem, and also heavily drawn upon by Milton, is Geoffrey of Monmouth's *History of the Kings of Britain* (see *Poems, 1807–1820,* pp. 531–3, for the relevant passages).

The Sparrow's Nest   Probably composed around March-April, certainly by 7 May 1802.

Cockermouth...Derwent   See Glossary entries.

To a Butterfly ('I've watched you now a short half-hour'). Composed 20 April 1802.

A Farewell   Composed in late May to 14 June 1802. Gallow Hill (or Gallowhill), near the coast in North Yorkshire, was where MW's brothers, George and Thomas Hutchinson, began farming together in 1800. WW and DW did not set off for Gallow Hill until 9 July 1802. After a short stay they went on to Calais to see Annette Vallon and Annette's and WW's daughter Caroline at the end of August, returning to Gallow Hill at the end of September. WW and Mary Hutchinson were married from Gallow Hill Farm, in Brompton Church, on 4 October 1802.

Stanzas Written In My Pocket-copy of Thomson's Castle of Indolence   Probably composed 9–11 May 1802. In 1796 STC described himself to John Thelwall thus: 'I cannot breathe thro' my nose—so my mouth, with sensual thick lips, is almost always open. In conversation I am impassioned, and oppose what I deem [error] with an eagerness, which is often mistaken for personal asperity—but I am ever so swallowed up in the *thing*, that I perfectly forget my *opponent*' (*STCL*, I, p. 260). Hartley Coleridge (1796–1849), eldest son of STC. See WW's poem *To H.C.* and his note to *Written in a Blank Leaf of Macpherson's Ossian* on notebook p. 88.

17 *I met Louisa in the Shade* Louisa. After Accompanying Her On a Mountain Excursion. The first line in 1841 was 'Though, by a sickly taste betrayed'; by the time WW dictated this note he had restored the original first line and did so in print in 1845. The poem was composed in early 1802, certainly by 9 February of that year; however, it was not published until 1807 in *Poems, in Two Volumes,* the preparations for which were made closer to WW's remembered date in late 1806.

Strange fits of passion have I known and *She dwelt among the untrodden ways* were composed between 6 October and 28 December 1798. *I travelled among unknown men* was probably composed in 1801. The correct wording of the second two poems was supplied above and below the line, though the original wording was not struck out in the notebook. I have nevertheless adopted the correct wording. 'She dwelt beside the Springs [banks] of Dove', is the poet's or the copyist's elision of ll. 1–2 and was never a version of l. 1 of WW's text.

Ere with cold beads of midnight dew De Selincourt has suggested the 'friend' was one of several suitors for Dora W's hand at this time (see *LY,* I, 423–4 and note) .

Look at the fate of summer flowers Its title is *To* ——. After the words 'some dear friends of mine' the note continued, 'I've heard', but this start of a sentence was deleted. Dora has been suggested as one of the subjects; in April and May 1824 Dora and her father were in London seeing the 'sights' and enjoying the society of London friends (*LY,* I, 260). EQ's pencil note identifies 'S.C.'—that is, STC's daughter, Sara—as one of the 'friends.' Mrs Coleridge and her daughter spent periods of a fortnight or more at Rydal Mount, as they did for example in April–May 1825; the Coleridge, Southey and Wordsworth families visited back and forth often during these years when their children were growing up and after STC moved permanently to the South. It is certainly possible that EQ, whether or not in consultation with Dora, censored material recorded by IF: alongside similar commentary based on hearsay EQ wrote 'gossip' on notebook p. 135.

'Tis said, that some have died for love (so *PW* [1841]). Despite WW's date of '1800', manuscript evidence suggests an early version of the poem may have been written in Germany in 1799.

There is a change, and I am poor A Complaint. Probably composed between 30 October 1806 and early April 1807. The 'Friend' is STC, as EQ's penciled note confirms. EQ revised 'Town-End' in pencil to 'Coleorton'. During this period the Wordsworth family was living in the Farm House at Coleorton as guests of Sir George and Lady Beaumont (see Glossary).

Let other bards of angels sing The title is *To* ——.

How rich that forehead's calm expanse. JC added to *PW* (1857P) that 'Mrs. Wordsworth's impression is that the Poem was written at Coleorton: it was certainly suggested by a Print at Coleorton Hall' (printed in *PW* [1857]). WW and DW spent a month at Coleorton in February–March 1824 while Mary remained at Rydal Mount to care for young Willy.

Oh dearer far than light and life are dear The title is *To* —— (and the first line begins "O dearer far"). Perhaps written during or shortly after WW's and MW's visit, in mid-September 1824, to the Thomas Hutchinson's farm at Hindwell where they found Thomas Monkhouse 'in a very alarming state of health'; WW considered Monkhouse, as he told Sir George Beaumont, one of his 'best friends' (*LY*, I, 279). Monkhouse died the following spring.

Lament of Mary Queen of Scots. On the Eve of a New Year WW dated this poem 1817 in editions from 1836; it was first published in the *River Duddon* volume (1820).

18 *But now he upraises…why I am here* From *The Convict*, ll. 41–2; the poem was composed in 1796 and published in *Lyrical Ballads* in 1798. WW did not reprint it.

I read Hearne's Journey For the head note to *The Complaint of a Forsaken Indian Woman* WW drew on the work of Samuel Hearne (*1745–92*): *A Journey from Prince of Wale's Fort in Hudson's Bay to the Northern Ocean, undertaken…for the discovery of copper mines, a North West passage, etc. in the years 1769–1772* (London, 1795). WW's poem was probably composed between early March and around 16 May 1798.

The Last of the Flock The poem was probably composed between early March and around 16 May 1798. In a letter to John Kenyon, c. 24 September 1836, WW said of the poem's origin, 'notwithstanding what has here been said in verse, I never in my whole life saw a man weep *alone* in the roads; but a friend of mine *did* see this poor man weeping *alone,* with the Lamb, the last of his flock, in his arms' (*LY,* III, 292). The friend was very likely Thomas Poole.

Repentance. A Pastoral Ballad With her husband, Thomas, and his five daughters by a previous marriage, Peggy Ashburner lived in one of the cottages, just north of the Wordsworths' cottage in Town End, Grasmere. DW recorded her conversation with Peggy Ashburner on 24 November 1801, in her journal (I, 83; for Gordon Graham Wordsworth's brief account of the Ashburners see *Journals,* Appendix I, vol. II, 433). The poem was probably composed 24 November 1801 to mid-1802 and much revised before publication in 1820.

The Affliction of Margaret The poem may have been composed in 1800, in the spring of 1802 or between late March 1804 and early January 1807. The only manuscript of the poem is among the printer's copy for *Poems, in Two Volumes (1807)*.

The Cottager to her Infant. By a Female Friend DW probably composed

< Return to Fenwick Notes | Continue through Editor's Notes>>

the poem by between 28 November and 6 December 1805. WW added two stanzas between the second and third stanzas of DW's poem, which were then deleted in the two manuscripts where they appear. It seems likely the adding and deleting took place before copy was sent to the printer for *Poems,* 1815, where DW's three-stanza version first appeared.

The Sailor's Mother   Composed 11 and 12 March 1802. For the 'Wishing-Gate' see WW's notes to *The Wishing-Gate* and *The Wishing-Gate Destroyed* (notebook pp. 32 and 153).

Penrith   See Glossary.

19 *The Childless Father* A version was composed in Germany in 1799. WW may recall revising the poem at Town End before sending it to be printed in *Lyrical Ballads,* 1800. EQ has inadvertently underscored the place and date as well as the title.

The Emigrant Mother Composed 16 and 17 March 1802. WW's visit to Mary and her brother George Hutchinson (not at Sockburn, but at Middleham, beyond Bishop Auckland) took place in early April 1802.

Vaudracour and Julia Probably composed between early October and late autumn 1804. See de Selincourt's note on the sources of the story in his edition of *The Prelude, or Growth of a Poet's Mind* (2nd edn, Oxford: Clarendon Press, 1959) pp. 591–2.

The Idiot Boy Composed between early March and around 16 May 1798.

Thomas Poole See Glossary.

20   *Michael. A Pastoral Poem.*   *The Brothers* was completed nine months before *Michael* was begun (see note to *The Brothers* above); *Michael* was composed between 11 October and 9 December 1800 and published (with *The Brothers*) in *Lyrical Ballads* at the end of January 1801. In his letter to Charles James Fox on 14 January 1801, written to help promote the sales of *Lyrical Ballads,* 1800, WW stressed the special qualities of the Lake District 'statesmen', qualities on which Michael's character and story are modeled (*EY,* pp. 314–15). He also emphasised to Thomas Poole the importance in *Michael* of the 'manners of the "Statesmen" ': 'I have attempted to give a picture of a man, of strong mind and lively sensibility, agitated by two of the most powerful affections of the human heart: the parental affection, and the love of property, *landed* property, including the feelings of inheritance, home, and personal and family independence'; in writing *Michael,* he said, he had Poole's 'character often before my eyes' (9 April *1801; EY,* p. 322). For a summary of other sources for the poem see *LB, 1797–1800,* pp. 400–3.

The Sheepfold   EQ's note identifies the site as Greenhead Ghyll (see Glossary entry for Greenhead Ghyll).

Luke   The 'family' mentioned as providing WW with the model for Luke was that of John Benson (d. 1808) of Grasmere, who owned the house at Town End where WW lived (now Dove Cottage).

The Armenian Lady's Love   In his head note to the poem WW acknowledged his debt to *Orlandus,* by his 'friend, Kenelm Henry Digby' (1800–80). *Orlandus* is the fourth book of Digby's study of medieval chivalry, *The Broad Stone of Honour: The True Sense and Practice of Chivalry* (4 vols, 1826 and 1828–9, an enlarged edition, done after his conversion to Catholicism, of his earlier book *The Broad Stone of Honour: Or, Rules for the Gentlemen of England,* which was published anonymously in 1822). In March 1829 WW received a gift of *Orlandus* through a mutual friend, the Revd William Whewell. In his letter to Whewell, WW praised Digby's writing and found in it 'as much truth as there can be in Pictures where only one side is looked at' (*LY,* II, 47). It seems likely the poem was composed shortly after 13 March 1829, but perhaps as late as 1830, the date WW assigned to it. WW and Digby met at Cambridge in November 1830, evidently at Digby's request (*LY,* II, 354; *Letters of Dora Wordsworth,* p. 78). The poem was first published in 1835. The story of the Armenian lady, as told by Digby, appears on pp. 385–6 of *Orlandus* (in the four-volume edition cited above).

Loving and Liking: Irregular Verses, Addressed to a Child   To EQ's query of the date written in ink, '1802', MW added, 'This date is a mistake'. It was then corrected in pencil to 1832, probably by MW. A fragment of the poem appears in DW's journal for 12 February 1831 to 7 September 1833 (Levin, p. 215). A note in 1836 identifies the author as the one who composed *Addressed to a Child, During a Boisterous Winter Evening. By a Female Friend of the Author.* In 1845 the subtitle 'By my Sister' was added to *Loving and Liking.*

The Redbreast. (Suggested in a Westmoreland Cottage.)   MW, in a letter to Jane Marshall on 27 December 1834, gave a similar account of DW and her companionable robin (*MWL*, pp. 135–6). See also the note to *In the Woods of Rydal,* notebook p. 47.

21 *Her Eyes are Wild* Titled *The Mad Mother* in *Lyrical Ballads* (1798–1805), it was probably composed between early March and around 16 May 1798. The 'Lady of Bristol' may have been Mrs John Estlin of Bristol, whose story 'of the Maniac who walked round & round' was noted by STC in his journal (*STCN*, I, entry 230).

The Waggoner 1805 is also the date WW placed below the poem in 1836, but it was composed in January 1806 and read to Charles Lamb, as WW noted in the dedication of the poem to Lamb, in 1806 (in April–May). The 'fact' referred to is explained by a note WW published with the poem in the edition of 1836–7:

> Several years after the event that forms the subject of the foregoing poem, in company with my friend, the late Mr. Coleridge, I happened to fall in with the person to whom the name of Benjamin is given. Upon our expressing regret that we had not, for a long time, seen upon the road either him or his waggon, he said:—"They could not do without me: and as to the man who was put in my place, no good could come out of him; he was a man of no *ideas*."
>
> The fact of my discarded hero's getting the horses out of great difficulty with a word, as related in the poem, was told me by an eye-witness.

John Watson, the original of Benjamin, was employed by William Jackson (1748–1809), Southey's landlord at Greta Hall, and brother-in-law to WW's landlord, John Benson, at Dove Cottage. The conversation reported in this note probably occurred during WW's residence at Allan Bank, where STC was house-guest from June 1808 to September 1810.

A Morning Exercise The close association with *To a Sky-Lark* ('Ethereal Minstrel'), also dated 1825, tends to confirm WW's correction of the date of *A Morning Exercise* from 1828 (below the printed text). In 1845 what had been the second stanza of *Sky-Lark* was inserted after l. 42 in this poem. The poem was not published until 1832.

A Flower-Garden, At Coleorton Hall, Leicestershire is the full title. WW and DW spent a month at Coleorton, the Beaumont estate, from mid-February to mid-March 1824. For Beaumont and Coleorton see Glossary entries.

A whirl-blast from behind the hill   Composed 18 or 19 March 1798.

with dear friends   EQ identified them, in pencil opposite, as 'Mrs. Wordsworth, Miss Fenwick and M^r. & M^{rs}. Quillinan, May, 1841' and added 'two days after our marriage'. He then queried whether 'W.Wth. J^r.' (Willy) was of the party (see Introduction).

The Oak and the Broom. A Pastoral   Composed certainly by 4 August 1800. DW described a walk along this 'track' with WW and STC in her journal for 23 April 1802 (*Journals*, I, 136–7). For further topographical details and information on sources for this and *The Waterfall and the Eglantine* see *LB, 1797–1802*, pp. 384–5.

Nab-Scar   See Glossary.

The Waterfall and the Eglantine   Composed certainly by 4 August 1800. EQ wrote in pencil that 'W. W shewed me the place', dating his own note '1848'.

To a Sexton   Probably composed between 6 October 1798 and 23 February 1799 while WW was living in Goslar.

To the Daisy ('In youth from rock to rock I went'), *To the same flower* ('With little here to do or see'), and *The Green Linnet.*   To the first two poems, and a third 'Daisy' poem, 'Sweet Flower! belike one day to have', WW assigned the date 1802 in the edition of 1807; in editions from 1836 the second and third were assigned to 1805 and 1803 respectively. *The Green Linnet* was assigned the date 1803 in editions from 1836. However, 'In youth', 'With little here' and *The Green Linnet* were probably composed between 16 April and 8 July 1802, though the two 'Daisy' poems may not have been completed until March 1804–March 1805.

22 *To the Small Celandine* ('Pansies, lilies, kingcups, daisies'). Below the text in editions from 1836 WW assigned the date 1803 and added two years when he composed this note. But this poem and its companion, 'Pleasures newly found are sweet', were both composed between 30 April and 1 May 1802. EQ added a pencil note: '?has not Chaucer noticed it?'

The Redbreast chasing the Butterfly WW adopted this title in 1845. *The Redbreast and Butterfly* was the title in editions from 1827 through 1843; prior to that it was *The Redbreast and the Butterfly.* Though WW assigned the poem to 1806 in editions from 1836, he actually composed it on 18 April 1802, as recorded in his sister's Grasmere journal.

Song for the Spinning Wheel. Founded Upon a Belief Prevalent Among the Pastoral Vales of Westmoreland In editions from 1836 WW dated the poem 1812; in naming the source of the 'belief' in 1843 he may have associated the poem's composition with the final year of his residence at Town End, where the 'old neighbour' very probably lived, perhaps Peggy Ashburner, his 'next door' neighbour. The text of the poem is closely associated with two sonnets, the earliest manuscripts for which do not predate 1814, 'Grief, thou hast lost an ever ready friend' and one he never published, 'Through Cumbrian Wilds, in many a mountain cove'. (For the connections among the poems see *Poems, 1807–1820,* pp. 520–1 and 530–1.)

Hint from the Mountains For Certain Political Pretenders When WW learned, on 10 December 1817, that his cousin William Crackanthorpe of Newbiggin Hall was planning to stand in opposition to the Lowther interest in the 1818 election, he became an active worker for the Lowther cause (see *Poems, 1807–1820,* p. 547).

On Seeing a Needlecase in the Form of a Harp, The Work of E.M.S. Edith May Southey (1804–71), daughter of Robert Southey (the 'Laureate's Child'), spent two months at Rydal Mount, helping to nurse her friend Dora W, from mid-January to early March 1827. Dora sent a copy of the poem to Mrs Eliot on 6 April 1827 (Cornell University Library).

The Contrast, The Parrot and the Wren   EQ has noted in pencil 'addressed to Dora'. The poem was probably composed in August–September 1824; WW seems to have completed it when MW wrote to EQ in 27 September 1824, that 'Wm. has been writing verses on Mrs. Luff's Birds which I dare say Doro will send you should she fall in with Franks' (that is, the opportunity for a free post; *MWL*, p. 117). Mrs Letitia Luff (see Glossary), after her husband died abroad, returned to Rydal in May 1824, complete with her 'living Stock, three singing Birds of gay plumage' which she brought with her from Mauritius (DW to HCR, 23 May 1824, *LY,* I, 270). She stayed first at Rydal Mount, and then in Spring Cottage at Rydal until she took possession of Fox-Ghyll in 1825. She seems not to have moved into the house until late spring because of the many renovations she undertook. WW may be amalgamating her later residence at Fox-Ghyll with her long preliminary stay at Spring Cottage in 1824. Fox-Ghyll, or Fox Ghyll, successively the home of several of Wordsworth's friends, was situated under Loughrigg, across the vale from Rydal Mount.

The Danish Boy. A Fragment   Probably composed between 6 October 1798 and 23 February 1799, and almost certainly before late April 1799. In the editions of 1827 and 1832, WW included this end-of-volume note to l. 11 ('The shadow of a Danish Boy'): 'THESE Stanzas were designed to introduce a Ballad upon the story of a Danish Prince who had fled from Battle, and, for the sake of the valuables about him, was murdered by the Inhabitant of a Cottage in which he had taken refuge. The House fell under a curse, and the Spirit of the Youth, it was believed, haunted the Valley where the crime had been committed.' For a full discussion of additional fragments of the 'ballad' and possible sources see *LB, 1797–1800,* p. 397.

Song for the Wandering Jew (the published title). Possibly composed in Germany in 1799, but certainly by mid-August 1800. For a summary of the legend and WW's use of it see *LB, 1797–1800,* p. 388–9.

<To return to the Fenwick Notes use the Previous View Button twice

23 *Stray Pleasures*   WW met Lamb often during the eight weeks he spent in London in April–May 1806; the poem was probably composed before mid-November when it was settled that a volume of poems WW was preparing for the press would in fact make up two volumes (*Poems, in Two Volumes*, 1807).

Charles Lamb   See Glossary.

the river Saone   WW and Robert Jones reached Chalon-sur-Saône on 27 July 1790.

The Pilgrim's Dream; Or, The Star and the Glow-worm   Probably composed in the summer of 1818; before June 1919. See WW's note to *Inscribed Upon a Rock* on notebook p. 60.

Loughrigg Fell   See Glossary.

What so monstrous…a glow-worm   An elision of two lines from *Peter Bell;* the full stanza reads:

> In vain, through every changeful year,
> Did Nature lead him as before;
> A primrose by a river's brim
> A yellow primrose was to him,
> And it was nothing more.
>   (ll. 246–50)

The Poet and the Caged Turtledove   Probably composed in early December 1828. In the earliest manuscript of the poem DW has headed it, '"Twenty minutes exercise upon the Terrace last night (at the beginning of December)" but the scene within doors'; and Dora W mentioned the poem in a letter to Maria Jewsbury of 11 September 1829 (*LY*, II, 127). In a pencil note EQ associated the poem with Dora W. For Maria Jewsbury see WW's notes to *Sonnet 41* ('While Anna's') on notebook p. 47 and *Liberty* on notebook p. 89; also see Glossary.

24 *A Wren's Nest*   Probably composed in the spring of 1833. Dora's field was originally purchased by WW as a building site for a house when he thought Lady Anne Le Fleming would not permit him and his family to remain at Rydal Mount (see Glossary). When the lease on Rydal Mount was renewed, he subsequently gave the field to Dora and laboriously planted it with daffodils.

Rural Illusions   Perhaps composed around April 1829, but certainly by 5 August when WW sent a copy of the poem in his letter to DW, who was away from Rydal Mount, and very ill, at Whitwick (near Coleorton), John Wordsworth's first curacy (*LY*, II, 105–6).

The Kitten and Falling Leaves   Composed possibly between early October 1804 and early 1805; perhaps late 1805 or early 1806.

There was a Boy   First appearing as a first-person narrative in an early manuscript of *The Prelude,* the lines were sent as a free-standing poem to STC in late November or very early December 1798. Not part of the 1799 *Two-Part Prelude,* the account does appear in the longer versions (*Prelude* V, 389–422). WW discussed the poem in his *Preface* to *Poems,* 1815 (*Prose*, III, 35n.).

William Raincock   EQ inserted 'NB' in pencil by this passage. Thompson supplies information about the identity of the boy who died and reports some of the exploits of William Raincock and other Hawkshead boys (including 'Bill Wordsworth') as recorded in reminiscences by his brother Fletcher Raincock (see *Wordsworth's Hawkshead,* pp. 55-6, 211-13).

25 *To the Cuckoo* ('O blithe New-comer! I have heard'). Perhaps composed largely 23 to 26 March 1802, and possibly added to around and on 14 May and 3 June 1802.

A Night-piece DW recorded the incident described in the poem in her journal entry for 25 January 1798, although which account preceded the other is uncertain; the poem must have been composed on 25 January or shortly afterward (see *LB, 1797–1800,* p. 453). The 'road' mentioned is that between Holford and the Castle of Comfort inn in Somerset (Lawrence, *Coleridge and Wordsworth in Somerset,* p. 164). Titled *A Fragment* in its early manuscript version, the poem was first published in 1815. The correct phrasing of the quoted passage in the note is 'he looks up—the clouds are split Asunder' (ll. 11-12).

The Yew-trees Titled simply *Yew-trees.* Probably composed in its earliest form between 23 September and 5 October 1804, or shortly after, when WW visited Lorton Vale (see *Poems, 1800–1807,* pp. 605–6). The earliest extant manuscript dates from June 1811. WW told HCR on 9 May 1815, that *A Night-Piece* and *Yew-trees* were 'among the best [of his Poems of Imagination] for the imaginative power displayed in them' (*HCR Books,* I, 166). He included an account of the Borrowdale Yews in *Select Views* (*Prose,* II, 275).

at Lorton That is, at High Lorton, north of Crummock Water.

the road…to Stonethwaite South of Derwentwater, in Borrowdale.

26 *Nutting*   DW copied a version of the poem in a letter to STC, written from Goslar, Germany, on 21 or 28 December 1798 (see *Chronology: EY,* p. 259, n. 61, for the date of the letter), but WW continued to revise *Nutting* until he sent it to the printer for inclusion in the second volume of *Lyrical Ballads* (1800) in August 1800.

the ancient family of Sandys   Edwin Sandys (1516?–1588), archbishop of York, was probably born at Hawkshead, where, in 1585 he founded and endowed a grammar school. He was a graduate of St Johns College, Cambridge, and the link between St Johns and Hawkshead School lasted at least until the end of the eighteenth century, both in bringing masters to Hawkshead and in sending students on to Cambridge. Of Archbishop Sandys' seven sons, George (1578–1644) was a recognised poet and translator, and local descendants of the Sandys family remained active supporters of the school into WW's time. The woods lie south of Esthwaite Water and Graythwaite Hall itself is two and a half miles south of the lake.

She was a Phantom of delight (so *PW* [1841]). Composed probably between 14 October 1803, and 6 March 1804; perhaps early in 1804. WW told Justice Coleridge that the poem was written 'on my dear wife' (*Memoirs,* II, 306).

The Nightingale   That is, 'O Nightingale! thou surely art'. WW never titled the poem in print. In the notebook EQ queried the presence of nightingales at Town End and MW wrote a reply, 'at Coleorton', signing it, 'MW'; the poem was composed between early February and early April 1807, during or shortly after the Wordsworths' stay at Hall Farm on the Beaumont estate at Coleorton.

Three years she grew in sun and shower   Beside the line is EQ's unanswered pencil query: '—?who?—'. See WW's note to *Written in Germany, On One of the Coldest Days of the Century,* notebook p. 76. WW perhaps composed the poem in late February 1799 when he and DW left Goslar by walking through the Hartz forest; but more likely it was composed earlier, in December 1798, during a walk in the forest from

Goslar, which was situated, as WW described it, 'on the edge' of the forest (*EY*, p. 249; see the note to this poem in *LB, 1797–1800*, p. 392).

A slumber did my spirit seal   Composed in December 1798. For the composition of the other three 'Lucy' poems see WW's and the editor's notes to 'Strange fits of passion I have known' (notebook p. 17; editor's notes p. 203).

The Daffodils   This title is bracketed with the first line above to form one entry. WW never used *The Daffodils* as a title in print though the poem is often referred to thus in early manuscripts, family letters and journals. WW published the following note to the poem in 1815: 'The subject of these Stanzas is rather an elementary feeling and simple impression (approaching to the nature of an ocular spectrum) upon the imaginative faculty, than an *exertion* of it. The one which follows [that is, *The Reverie of Poor Susan*] is strictly a Reverie; and neither that, nor the next after it in succession, 'The Power of Music', would have been placed here [that is, among Poems of the Imagination] except for the reason given in the foregoing note'. WW composed the poem probably between late March 1804 and early April 1807, possibly by the end of 1804. The incident took place two years earlier, as described by DW in her journal entry for 15 April 1802 (*Journals*, 1,131).

the two best lines   EQ—in reply to his own pencil query 'Mrs Wordsworth—but which?'—added in pencil, 'And flash upon that inward eye Which is the bliss of solitude'. In *PW* (1857P) the ascription of 'the two best lines' to Mary is deleted and it was omitted from *PW* (1857).

<To return to the Fenwick Notes use the Previous View Button twice

27   *Ulswater*   See Glossary.

The Reverie of Poor Susan   Published in *Lyrical Ballads,* 1800, and probably composed at Goslar before 28 December 1798. For the dating and for possible sources of the poem see *LB, 1797–1800,* p. 386; for WW's comment on 'reverie' see his note to 'I wandered lonely as a cloud' (notebook p. 26).

Power of Music (so *PW* [1841]). Composed probably between 4 April and 10 November 1806. For WW's comment on this poem as 'reverie' see his note to 'I wandered lonely as a cloud' (notebook p. 26).

Star-gazers   Observed, probably in the company of Charles Lamb, when WW was in London in April and May 1806; the poem was composed between 4 April and 14 November 1806.

The cock is crowing   *Written in March, While Resting on the Bridge at the Foot of Brother's Water.* DW noted the composition of this poem on 16 April 1802, in her journal. Joanna Baillie (1762–1851) was a Scottish dramatist and poet whose work was much admired by Sir Walter Scott. WW met her in 1812 after she had moved to Hampstead (*MY,* II, 22). He contributed two sonnets, 'A volant Tribe of Bards on earth are found' and 'Not Love, not War, nor the tumultuous swell', to her *Poetic Miscellanies,* published in 1823.

The Beggars   The printed title lacks the article. The incident took place on 27 May 1800, as DW noted in her journal two weeks later; WW composed the poem 13 and 14 March 1802, as noted again by DW in her journal entries for those days: 'After tea I read to William that account of the little Boys belonging to the tall woman and an unlucky thing it was for he could not escape from those very words, and so he could not write the poem'; but 'before he rose' the next morning he had finished the poem. In 1808 WW told HCR that the poem was written to 'exhibit the power of physical beauty and health and vigor in childhood even in a state of moral depravity' (*HCR,* I, 53).

Gipsies   Composed probably around but not before 26 February 1807. Castle Donington is seven miles northeast of Coleorton, about half-way between Coleorton and Derby.

Ruth   Unlike most poems composed at Goslar *Ruth* does not appear in any manuscripts of that period; the first mention of the poem is in DW's journal, the entries for 27 July and 22 August 1800. In his note to l. 58 of the poem WW referred to William Bartram's *Travels through North and South Georgia…*(Philadelphia, 1791; London, 1792 and 1794); much of the poem is indebted to this work. For a summary account of this and other possible sources see *LB, 1797–1800*, pp. 389–90.

Resolution and Independence   The meeting with the old man took place on 3 October 1800, the date DW entered her account of him in her journal. WW began composing the poem, first called 'The Leech Gatherer', 3 May 1802, and completed it by 12 July when DW copied it out 'for Coleridge and for us'. In WW's and DW's letter to Sara and Mary Hutchinson of 14 June 1802, they defended the matter-of-fact style of the early version of the poem (*EY,* pp. 364–7; for a transcription see *Poems, 1800–1807,* pp. 316–23). WW commented at length on the final version in the *Preface* to *Poems,* 1815 (*Prose,* III, 32–3).

28 *over Barton Fell…towards Askam* Barton Fell lies along the eastern shore of Ullswater, south of Pooley Bridge and Eusemere (the home of the Thomas Clarksons) and west of Askham Fell, which lies east of the village of Askham.

The Thorn Begun probably on 19 March and completed probably by 20 April 1798. For a summary account of the locale and the probable sources see the editors' note to the poem in *LB, 1797–1800*, pp. 350–2. WW's own discussion of the poem's dramatic structure appears in the Advertisement to *Lyrical Ballads,* 1798, and in an end-of-volume note in the subsequent editions of *Lyrical Ballads* (reprinted in *LB, 1797–1800*).

which Wilkie thought his best David Wilkie (1785–1841), painter; friend of B. R. Haydon and Sir George Beaumont, and a frequent visitor of galleries abroad. See WW's note to *Lines Suggested by a Portrait From the Pencil of F. Stone* and *The Foregoing Subject Resumed*, notebook pp. 93–4.

it reminds one too much of Wilson Probably John Wilson (1774–1855), whose many sea-scapes and coastal scenes were shown at three London exhibitions between 1807 and 1856. Wilson's son, also John (d. 1875), painted landscapes. Neither painter should be confused with John Wilson (Christopher North), friend of WW and contributor to *Blackwood's Magazine*.

29 *Goody Blake and Harry Gill. A True Story*   On 6 March 1798 WW asked Cottle for a copy of Darwin's *Zoonomia*. He composed the poem probably between that date and around 16 May 1798. Erasmus Darwin (1731–1802), physician, botanist and poet, published his *Zoonomia, or the Laws of Organic Life,* in two volumes in 1794–6. The 'incident' WW referred to is an example of what Darwin called 'Mutable Madness', a condition in which 'patients are liable to mistake ideas of sensation for those from irritation, that is, imaginations for realities' (II, 356). The passage is printed in *LB, 1797–1800* (pp. 344–5), along with discussion of other possible sources.

Hart-Leap Well   Probably composed by 4 August 1800. The head note printed with the poem identifies the well as 'a small spring of water, about five miles from Richmond in Yorkshire, and near the side of the road that leads from Richmond to Askrigg. Its name is derived from a remarkable Chase, the memory of which is preserved by the monuments spoken of in the second Part of the following Poem, which monuments do now exist as I have there described them'. WW and DW made their 'wild winter journey' from Sockburn (see Glossary) between 17 and 20 December 1799 and heard the story the first day out. WW treated the journey and the place again in *Home at Grasmere* (see *H at G*, MS. B, ll. 218–56). See *LB, 1797–1800,* p. 378, for information on sources and topographical details.

The Horn of Egremont Castle   WW's note printed with the poem adds that 'this Story is a Cumberland Tradition'. Egremont Castle is a twelfth- to thirteenth-century ruin on the River Eden, which flows from Ennerdale Water to the Irish Sea. Hutton John, home of the Hudlestons, 'pleasantly situated, though of a character somewhat gloomy and monastic' (*Guide, Prose,* II, 166), is six miles west of Penrith on the road to Keswick 'in a sequestered Valley upon the River Dacor' (now spelled Dacre; WW's note printed with the poem).

Song at the Feast of Brougham Castle, Upon the Restoration of Lord Clifford, the Shepherd, to the Estates and Honours of His Ancestors (in its full printed title). The poem was composed probably between 30 October and early December 1806. Brougham Castle is a twelfth-century ruin two miles west of Penrith on the road to Appleby. WW's note, first published with the poem in 1807, details the history of Henry Lord Clifford (1455?–1523), 'the subject of this Poem', and praises Lady Anne Clifford, Countess of Pembroke (1590–1676), for restoring this and other castles in the vicinity. After her death the castles were demolished or left to decay.

30 *Tintern Abbey*   The full printed title is *Lines, Composed a Few Miles Above Tintern Abbey, on Revisiting the Banks of the Wye During a Tour. July 13, 1798*. WW and DW began their four-day ramble through the Wye valley from Bristol, probably on 10 July, spending the first night at Tintern. WW probably started composition of the poem that evening and completed it as they walked down the hill from Clifton to Bristol four days later (so he told the Duke of Argyle many years after, *PW*, II, 517). WW printed an end-of-volume note to the poem in *Lyrical Ballads* (1798): 'I have not ventured to call this Poem an Ode; but it was written with a hope that in the transitions, and the impassioned music of the versification would be found the principal requisites of that species of composition.' See *LB, 1797–1800* (pp. 357–9), for an account of possible sources and influences, including WW's several tours of Wales. See also Hayden, *Wales and Ireland*, pp. 27–37.

The Lyrical Ballads…Cottle   Joseph Cottle (1770–1853), was a Bristol bookseller and poet; he published *Lyrical Ballads* as well as the early work of STC, Southey and Charles Lloyd.

It is no Spirit who from heaven hath flown   Composed probably between 21 May 1802, and 6 March 1804. Sara Hutchinson (see Glossary) was visiting the Wordsworths from 8 November 1802 to 7 January 1803, and from 1 to 28 April 1803.

French Revolution, As It Appeared to Enthusiasts at its Commencement. Reprinted from 'The Friend'   Probably composed around late November or December 1804; published 26 October 1809 in *The Friend*. In the note printed with the poem WW identified this and two other poems, *There was a Boy* and *Influence of Natural Objects*, as coming from 'the unpublished Poem of which some account is given in the Preface to the EXCURSION'. In the Preface, published with *The Excursion* in 1814, he refers to the unfinished *Recluse*, to which *The Prelude* was to have been the introductory piece, and includes the blank verse *Prospectus*, 'On Man, on Nature, and on Human Life'.

Yes, it was the mountain Echo (thus its printed form). Composed 15 June 1806, or shortly thereafter. Thomas Wordsworth, their third child, was born in 1806 and died in 1812.

31 *To a Sky-Lark* (in its printed form). WW told Barron Field in 1828 that he felt he 'succeeded in the second "Skylark", and in the conclusion of the poem titled *A Morning Exercise,* in my notice of this bird' (*LY,* I, 644); the poem was probably composed in the spring of 1825. EQ added a pencil note to 'Rydal Mount': 'where there are no skylarks—but the poet is everywhere—'.

Laodamia   Composed between about mid-October and about 27 to 29 October 1814 and revised extensively before publication in February 1815. The note WW published with the poem refers the reader to three of the 'Ancients': 'For the account of these long-lived trees [ll. 167–74], see Pliny's "Natural History", ib. xvi. cap. 44; and for the features in the character of Protesilaus, see the "Iphigenia in Aulis" in Euripides. Virgil places the Shade of Laodamia in a mournful region, among unhappy Lovers,

⸺⸺His Laodamia
  It Comes.⸺⸺'

For an account of WW's many revisions and of his probable sources see *Poems, 1807–1820,* pp. 143–52, 529–30.

Dear Child of Nature   Titled *To a Young Lady, Who had been Reproached for Taking Long Walks in the Country.* Composed probably between 23 and 27 January, certainly by 9 February 1802.

The Pass of Kirkstone   Until 1836 titled *Ode. The Pass at Kirkstone.* Composed beginning perhaps about 3 June 1817, before 9 June; completed at least through l. 60 by 27 June. For the dating see *Poems, 1807–1820,* p. 545. For Kirkstone Pass see Glossary.

To ⸺, On Her First Ascent to the Summit of Helvellyn (its full printed title). For Helvellyn see Glossary. Composed probably 1816, not before May and perhaps after 2 August; possibly as late as 1819 (for the dating see *Poems, 1807–1820,* p. 542).

Mr. Montagu Burgoyne (1750–1836) was a politician who wrote on parliamentary reform and allotments of land for the labouring poor. Miss Blackett was probably either Elizabeth, Burgoyne's daughter and wife of Christopher Blackett, or the latter's sister Dorothy (see Eric C. Walker, 'Wordsworth, "Miss Blackett", and Montagu Burgoyne' *N&Q* n.s. 34 [March 1987] pp. 26–7).

<To return to the text use the Previous View Button

32 *Water-Fowl* In earliest form composed probably in March or April 1800 as part of *Home at Grasmere,* the lines WW wrote to celebrate his return to the Lakes after many years' absence. He included a version of these lines in his *A Description of the Scenery of the Lakes in the North of England* (1823) and in the *Poetical Works* of 1827 he published them as a separate poem, *Water-Fowl,* based on revisions of *Home at Grasmere* done in 1812–14 (see *H at G*, pp. 8, 54–7, especially ll. 292–314 and note).

View from the Top of Black Comb (in its printed form). The ascent of Black Comb took place in August 1811; the poem was composed beginning perhaps in late August to early September 1811, but perhaps not completed until 1813. For the several versions of the poem and its dating see *Poems, 1807–1820*, pp. 98–101. The fell 'stands at the southern extremity of Cumberland: its base covers a much greater extent of ground than any other mountain in these parts; and from its situation, the summit commands a more extensive view than any other point in Britain' (WW's published note to *View from the Top of Black Comb*).

See also WW's note to *Epistle to Sir George Howland Beaumont, Bart.*, notebook p. 130, and his description of the view in *Guide* (*Prose*, II, 166), where he quotes a passage from *The Minstrels of Winandermere*, a poem by his Hawkshead classmate and friend, Charles Farish.

The Haunted Tree. To ——— (in its printed form). Composed in the late spring or early summer of 1819, the poem was titled simply *To ———* when it was first published in *River Duddon* (1819). The addressee ('O Lady! fairer in thy Poet's sight/Than fairest spiritual Creature of the groves') has not been identified (but see *Poems, 1807–1820*, p. 550, for the suggestion that it is DW).

The Triad Probably composed early in 1828, certainly by early March (*LY*, I, 590–1). The three 'sisters' are presented in the poem in the same order as they are named in the note. Edith May Southey (1804–71) married Revd J. W. Warter in 1834 and Sara Coleridge (1802–52) married her cousin Henry Nelson Coleridge in 1829.

The Wishing-Gate (in its printed form). Probably composed early in 1828, certainly by early March (*LY*, I, 590). The note to *The Wishing-Gate Destroyed* is on notebook p. 153. The gate was on the south side of the middle road between Rydal and Grasmere.

The Primrose of the Rock   EQ wrote '1821' in the notebook, but WW gave the date as 1831 in editions from 1836. The rock was long a favoured spot: in 1802 DW first called it 'Glow-worm Rock' and noted its tuft of primroses in her journal (24 April 1802), and in 1808 WW composed a long blank verse poem, never completed, called *The Tuft of Primroses* (see *'The Tuft of Primroses' with Other Late Poems for 'The Recluse'*, ed. Joseph F. Kishel, Ithaca and London, 1986). For topographical details see McCracken, p. 23.

from Grasmere to Rydal   JC added 'along the middle road' (*PW* [1857]). Though long a resident of Rydal Mount, WW thought of the familiar walk as commencing at Dove Cottage.

Presentiments   WW dated the poem '1830' in editions from 1836 on.

Vernal Ode   The 'Ditto' refers to 'Rydal Mount' above. Composed in April 1817 and published in *River Duddon* (1820) where it was titled *Ode.—1817*; it took its present title in 1827. For the earliest version see *Poems, 1807–1820*, pp. 233–6.

Devotional Incitements   Probably composed around May-June 1832 (*LY*, II, 673–4).

A Jewish Family (in its printed form). The tour took place between 22 July and 6 August. The only other poem produced by this tour is *Incident at Bruges* (see notebook p. 90). EQ added a pencil note: 'the three went from my house in Bryanstone Street London'; the trip was suddenly agreed upon in London between STC and WW in June 1828, the first lengthy reunion between them since the rupture of their friendship in 1810 (*LY*, I, 614–15); the trip lasted from 22 June to 6 August.

33 *Mr. Aders at Gotesburg* Charles Aders, a London merchant, and his wife were art connoisseurs and collectors living in London and Godesberg, Germany, and were well known for their musical and cultural gatherings. The trip was planned at a breakfast meeting at the Aders' in Euston Square. Their circle of friends included Charles Lamb, HCR, the Wordsworths, STC and William Blake. Dora's journal of this tour gives a detailed account (Wordsworth Library, DC MS. 110) and is generously quoted in Hayden, *Europe II* (pp. 22–48). Of the encounter with the Jews she wrote, 'When Mr. Coleridge told this Rachel how much he admired her Child—"Yes, said she, she is beautiful," (adding with a sigh) "but see these rags and misery"—pointing to its frock which was made up of a thousand patches' (*Europe II,* p. 37). St Goar is between 17 and 18 miles downstream from Bingen, the southernmost point of their tour (roughly 60 miles upstream from Godesberg).

On the Power of Sound (in its printed form). In a letter to George Huntley Gordon, 15 December 1828, WW said that 'during the last week' he had written 'some stanzas on the Power of Sound' (*LY,* I, 689). The trip to Ireland mentioned took place in September and early October 1829; the poem was first published in 1835.

Mr. Marshall John Marshall (1765–1845), a Leeds linen manufacturer and, from 1810, resident of Halsteads at Watermillock, Ullswater; he purchased the Patterdale Hall Estate in 1824 and employed some of his extensive lands for plantations of native trees and plants (*Grasmere Journals,* p. 167). He married Jane Pollard, DW's friend from her Halifax days. See WW's note to *Eagles. Composed at Dunollie Castle in the Bay of Oban,* notebook p. 98.

34 *Giants' Causeway...Fairhead*   In County Antrim, Northern Ireland. See WW's note to *Eagles. Composed at Dunollie Castle in the Bay of Oban*, notebook p. 98.

Peter Bell. A Tale   Composed beginning 20 April 1798 and complete enough for WW to have read it to Hazlitt a month or so later, between 23 May and 12 June ('My First Acquaintance with Poets' in *The Complete Works of William Hazlitt* [ed. P. P. Howe, in 21 vols; London, 1930] XVII, 118). The poem was extensively revised during the two decades before it was published, in April 1819 (see *Peter Bell*, ed. John E. Jordan, Cornell University Press, Ithaca, NY, 1985, pp. 1–9).

walked...as far as the town of Hay   In the summer of 1793 WW traveled, mostly on foot, from Salisbury Plain in Wiltshire, where he parted from Raisley Calvert, to Bristol and up the Wye Valley to visit his friend Robert Jones in Plas-yn-Llan, Llangynhafal. He seems to have reached Builth and then walked back nearly to Hay with the tinker.

35 *Ann Tyson*   See Glossary.

Poems on the Naming of Places   This grouping first appeared in *Lyrical Ballads* of 1800 and was retained through all of the lifetime editions.

It was an April Morn ('It was an April morning: fresh and clear'). Composed probably between April and 13 October 1800; certainly by 15 October 1800. Easedale Beck is the name of the 'brook'; Emma's Dale or Dell is in Easedale (see Glossary and McCracken, pp. 107–10, 239–40). To the name given the place in the last line of the poem, 'Emma's dell', EQ added a pencil note, 'who was Emma'. After they settled in Grasmere in late 1799 WW adopted 'Emma', and its variant, 'Emmeline', as a poetic name for DW.

36 *To Joanna* (its title in print). Composed probably around but by 23 August 1800. For WW's manuscript note to the poem see *LB, 1797.*
1800, pp. 398–9. See the entry for Joanna Hutchinson in Glossary. The 'precipice' is Harrison Stickle, the 'huge breast of rock' described in *Excursion* IV, 402–12.

Langdale Pikes   See Glossary entry for 'Langdale'.

There is an Eminence &c.   "There is an Eminence,—of these our hills' is found in the same manuscript with *The Brothers*. Sharing some lines with the longer poem, "There is an Eminence" was composed by 18 December 1800, perhaps earlier in the same year, around January. For dating see *Chronology: MY*, p. 55 and note, and the notes to this poem and *The Brothers* in *LB, 1797–1800* (pp. 379–82).

Stone Arthur rises beside Greenhead Ghyll to the east of the village of Grasmere (see McCracken, pp. 35, 234, 236).

Point Rash Judgement   'A narrow girdle of rough stones and crags' was never titled in print, though DW called it 'Point Rash Judgment' in her journal entry for 10 October 1800. The 'two beloved Friends' are mentioned in l. 6. The walk probably took place, despite WW's setting the scene on a 'calm September morning' (l. 7), on 23 July 1800, the day STC noted in his journal an encounter with the ailing fisherman described in the poem; the next day STC and his wife Sara ended their three and a half week stay in Grasmere (*STCN*, I, entry 761; see also *Grasmere Journals*, p. 159). WW probably composed a version of the poem between this date and 18 December, very likely completing it by 6 November when he 'said' the poem to DW and Charles and Priscilla Lloyd, as noted by DW in her journal entry of that date. See McCracken, pp. 101–2, 234–5, for more on the changes to the 'eastern shore of Grasmere Lake'. For the connection between WW's encounter with the fisherman and his portrait of the 'old man' of *Resolution and Independence*, see *Chronology: EY*, p. 74, and the note to 'A narrow girdle of rough stones and crags' in *LB, 1797–1800*, p. 399.

To Mary Hutchinson   *To M.H.* (its title in print). WW and Mary Hutchinson (see Glossary) were married 4 October 1802, from her brothers' farm at Gallow Hill. DW entered the date 'Sat Dec^b. 28 99' below her copy of the poem in DC MS. 25; their walk took place within a few days of DW's and WW's arrival in Grasmere on 20 December 1799. For dating see *Chronology: EY,* pp. 284–5, and the note to this poem in *LB, 1797–1800,* pp. 399–400.

Rydal Upper Park   The ground above Rydal Hall and part of the estate. See the Glossary and McCracken, pp. 194n., 243–4.

When, to the attractions of the busy world (in its printed form). John Wordsworth (see Glossary) visited Dove Cottage from the end of January to the end of September 1800. 'The Firgrove', as DW called it, lay on the middle road between Grasmere and Rydal; she later transferred the name of the wood to the poem (*Journal* I, 57–8), but WW never adopted the title in print. The poem was composed 29–30 August 1800, much revised before 6 March 1804 when a copy was prepared for STC, and revised again before publication, possibly between 9 September and late October 1814. When it was first published in 1815—where the poem was dated '1802'—WW appended this note to ll. 109–11: 'This wish was not granted; the lamented Person, not long after, perished by shipwreck, in discharge of his duty as Commander of the Honourable East India Company's Vessel, the Earl of Abergavenny'. See also WW's notes to *Elegiac Verses,* notebook p. 129, and *Character of the Happy Warrior,* notebook pp. 81–2.

37 *Miscellaneous Sonnets. Part 1*   DW noted in her journal, 21 May 1802, that 'Wm wrote two sonnets on Buonaparte after I had read Milton's sonnets to him'. Only 'I grieved' has been identified.

an irregular one at School   The poem referred to is *Sonnet, on seeing Miss HELEN MARIA WILLIAMS weep at a Tale of Distress,* published in the *European Magazine* of March 1787 (vol. 11, p. 202). WW composed at least five sonnets before April 1802. See *Poems, 1800–1807,* p. 409.

Sonnet 6   The 'happy ramble' occurred in early April 1794; they traveled by coach from Halifax to Kendal; from Kendal they walked to Grasmere, where they spent the night, and walked on to Windy Brow in Keswick the next day. Low Wood lies between the town of Windermere and Ambleside on the Keswick road. For Kendal and Keswick see Glossary entries.

Sonnet 8 ('The fairest, brightest hues of ether fade'). Probably based on several visits to Hackett; composed probably 1–8 September 1812.

the two Langdales   See Glossary entry for 'Langdale'.

38   *The same cottage is alluded to*   See *Excursion*, V, 750–66, and *Epistle to Sir George Howland Beaumont, Bart.*, ll. 203–8. See also the notes to these poems below.

Revd S. Tillbrook   Samuel Tilbrooke, of Peterhouse, Cambridge. This remodeling of Ivy Cottage should not be confused with later work done by William Ball in 1835, when it was renamed Glen Rothay.

Sonnet 9 Upon the Sight of a Beautiful Picture, Painted by Sir G. H. Beaumont, Bart.   Composed after 11 June 1811, probably within a few days (see *Poems, 1807–1820*, p. 514). In a letter to Haydon, 13 January 1816, WW described the sonnet as 'a favorite of mine, and I think not unworthy of the subject'; he proposed that it be paired with the sonnet addressed to Haydon ('High is our calling, Friend') and published in the *Champion*, but this plan was never carried out (*MY*, II, 274 and note). For Haydon see Glossary.

in this house   That is, the Parsonage, across the road from the church in Grasmere.

we lost our two children   Thomas Wordsworth (1806–12) and Catherine Wordsworth (1808–12), both buried in Grasmere churchyard. Composed probably in the first two or three weeks in June 1811. For dating see *Poems, 1807–1820*, p. 514.

Sonnet 11. Aerial Rock!   ('Aerial Rock—whose solitary brow'). Composed perhaps about 1 December 1815; by late May to early June 1819. See also WW's note for 'I watch, and long have watched, with calm regret' on notebook p. 42. For dating see *Poems. 1807–1820*, pp. 534–5.

39 *Sonnet 15 The Wild Duck's Nest* (in its printed form). The poem was composed probably between 1815 and March 1819. Originally part of *The River Duddon* series of sonnets, it was published instead in *The Waggoner, A Poem. To which are added, Sonnets* (1819). For information on dating see *Sonn*, pp. 50–1.

Sonnet 19 ('Grief, thou hast lost an ever ready friend'). One of the several manuscripts of this sonnet dates from 1814. Perhaps composed in 1812, possibly as early as 1806; but by 9 September–late October 1814 (for dating and the sonnet's connections with the unpublished sonnet, 'Through Cumbrian Wilds', and with *Song for the Spinning Wheel*, see *Poems, 1807–1820*, pp. 520–1). See also WW's *Michael*, ll. 84–7, 108–9; his *Brothers*, ll. 20–5, 30–3; his letter to Charles James Fox, 14 January 1801 (*EY*, pp. 312–15); his note to *Song for the Spinning Wheel, Founded upon a Belief Prevalent Among the Pastoral Vales of Westmoreland*, notebook p. 22; and his account of the production of wool for market by 'estatesmen' in *Guide* (*Prose*, II, 224).

40   *Sonnet 22*   *Decay of Piety* appears in a notebook used chiefly for sonnets intended for *Ecclesiastical Sonnets,* written largely in 1821–2, and was probably written at the same time.

Sonnets 24, 25 & 26   These sonnets are *From the Italian of Michael Angelo* ('Yes! hope may with my strong desire keep pace'), probably composed in 1805, certainly by 24 August when Southey sent a copy to Duppa; *From the Same* ('No mortal object did these eyes behold'), probably begun in 1805 and completed between 7 November 1805 and 8 September 1806 when WW sent a copy to Sir George Beaumont; and *To the Supreme Being* ('The prayers I make will then be sweet indeed'), also probably begun in 1805 and completed perhaps by 1 August 1806 when WW sent a copy of one of these sonnets to Beaumont, perhaps this one (see *MY,* I, 65, 79).

Mr. Duppa   Richard Duppa (1770–1831) published his *The Life and Literary Works of Michel Angelo Buonarotti with his Poetry and Letters* in 1806; it included translations by WW and Southey.

Sonnet 27 ('Surprised by joy-impatient as the Wind'). Catherine Wordsworth (b. 1808) died on 4 June 1812; WW probably composed the sonnet near the time of preparing his poems for the edition of 1815, certainly by late October 1814.

Sonnets 28 & 29   These sonnets are 'Methought I saw the footsteps of a throne', composed probably around early February 1807, and *November, 1836* ('Even so for me a Vision sanctified'), referred to as 'the Sonnet that follows'. Sara Hutchinson was seriously ill in May 1835 and died 23 June 1835. See *LY,* III, 65–76, for WW's letters to family and friends concerning Sara's death. The sonnet was at least conceived and probably composed in part at the time and completed in November 1836.

Sonnet 30   This sonnet began 'A fairer face of evening cannot be' in *PW* (1841); WW altered it in 1845 to its original form, 'It is a beauteous Evening, calm and free'. Composed probably between 1 and 29 August 1802.

Sonnet 37. Personal Talk   WW placed this sequence in 'Poems of Sentiment and Reflection' in editions of 1845 and 1849–50. He composed the four sonnets probably between 21 May 1802 and 6 March 1804.

41   *By the bye, I have a spite* The line 'stigmatized' by IF is l. 6 of the first sonnet, 'Sons, mothers, maidens withering on the stalk'. For information about IF see the Introduction.

Sonnet 42 ('From the dark chambers of dejection freed'). Possibly composed 25–30 August 1814 (the dates of the tour with MW and Sara Hutchinson), but probably in the following October. For dating see *Poems, 1807–1820,* p. 528.

Poor Gillies Robert Pearce Gillies (1788–1858), poet and journalist. Despite his efforts to sustain a literary career he ran constantly into debt. He published *Memoirs of a Literary Veteran* in 1851 in which he described his encounters with WW, Hogg, and other literary figures he knew.

42 *Lord Gillies*   Adam Gillies (1760–1842), during his career, was ordinary judge of the Royal College of Justice, lord commissioner of the jury court and judge of the court of the exchequer in Scotland. An older brother, the historian and classical scholar John Gillies (1747–1836), wrote a once popular 'History of Greece' (1786) that WW may have known as a schoolboy or undergraduate. For Robert Gillies' cousin, Margaret Gillies, see the note to *To a Painter* on notebook p. 155.

Sonnet 43 ('Fair Prime of life! were it enough to gild'). EQ's pencil note, 'take first the beam', chides WW by alluding to Luke 6,41: 'cast out first the beam out of thine own eye'. De Selincourt noted that the poem was probably composed at the same time as *Retirement* ('If the whole weight of what we think and feel'), which he tentatively dated 1826 (*PW*, III, 326).

Sonnet 44 ('I watch, and long have watched, with calm regret'). Composed after May 1813, probably after October 1814, by May–June 1819; perhaps about December 1, 1815. See also WW's notes to 'Aerial Rock' and *November 1* (notebook pp. 38, 45). For dating see *Poems, 1807–1820*, pp. 534–5.

Sonnet 47   *To the Memory of Raisley Calvert* was composed probably between 21 May 1802 and 6 March 1804. Calvert died around 9 January and was buried on 12 January 1795; in the notebook the final digit of the date was not supplied. For more information about Calvert see Glossary.

43   *Sonnet 1* ('Scorn not the Sonnet; Critic, you have frowned'). Probably composed between 1820 and 1827, certainly by early April 1827; published in 1827.

Sonnet 3 ('Mark the concentred hazels that enclose'). Composed probably between late March–April 1807 (when *Poems, in Two Volumes* had gone to press) and late October 1814 (when copy for *Poems,* 1815, had been sent off). Helm Crag stands at the northern head of Grasmere Vale, with Easedale to the west.

our friend M^{rs}. Fletcher   Mrs Elizabeth Fletcher (1770–1858) built a new house at Lancrigg Farm in Easedale in 1840; she was a long-time visitor to the Lakes and a friend of the Wordsworths and the Thomas Arnolds of Fox How. In her *Autobiography of Mrs. Fletcher, of Edinburgh*, published in Carlisle in 1871, she gives an account of her acquaintance with WW.

Indeed he expressed them   JC emended 'them' to 'those feelings' in 1857.

44 *Repentance*   The full title is *Repentance. A Pastoral Ballad.* See notebook p. 18 above.

Sonnet 4 Composed after a Journey Across the Hambleton Hills, Yorkshire (the spelling 'Hambleton' was changed from 'Hamilton' in the edition of 1832). Composed on the return journey from Gallow Hill, in Yorkshire, on the afternoon of WW's marriage to Mary Hutchinson, 4 October 1802. The hills above Wensleydale and, beyond them, The Pennines form the western 'horizon' commanded from the Hambleton Hills, which lie between Helmsley, Northallerton and Stokesley in the North Riding of Yorkshire. To the east lay the North York Moors and the North Sea. The stop at Bolton Hall in Wensleydale occurred the next day and the sonnet mentioned is 'Hard was thy Durance, Queen, compared with ours', only the first line of which is known to survive (preserved in DW's retrospective account of their trip to Calais, the marriage of William and Mary, and the return to Grasmere in her journal entry for 9 July to 8 October 1802).

then belonged to the Scroopes   The last male representative of the Scrope family of Bolton was William Scrope (1772–1852), an artist and classical scholar.

Sonnet 6 September, 1815 (While not a leaf seems faded; while the fields'). The title dates the incident itself while the poem was composed about 2 December 1815 and sent in WW's letter to B. R. Haydon on 21 December (*MY*, II, 258; *PW*, III, 425); it was published first in the *Examiner* for 11 February 1816.

For me, who under kindlier laws &c   That is, the final sestet of the sonnet, which praises winter as a season 'potent to renew, / 'Mid frost and snow, the instinctive joys of song / And nobler cares than listless summer knew'. Perhaps WW has Dora in mind; the lake district winter was especially hard on her fragile state of health.

45   *Sonnet 7 November 1* ('How clear, how keen, how marvellously bright'). Composed about 1 December 1815 and included in the same letter to Haydon (see the preceding sonnet and note). The River Brathay flows from Elterwater in Langdale (see Glossary), through Clappersgate, into Lake Windermere.

Sonnet 8   The title from 1827 on was *Composed During a Storm;* its title when it appeared in the *Westmoreland Gazette* for 6 February 1819 was *Composed during One of the Most Awful of the Late Storms, Feb.* 1819. It was probably composed in January 1819, certainly by 3 February 1819. Rydal Wood is in Upper Rydal Park, above Rydal Hall (see Glossary).

Sonnet 11 To the Lady Beaumont ('Lady! the songs of Spring were in the grove'). Composed probably around early February 1807. DW, WW, MW and the children were staying at the Beaumonts' Hall Farm at Coleorton. Detailed correspondence regarding the garden between DW and WW and Sir George and Lady Beaumont, who were spending the winter in London, began in November 1806 and carried through January 1807 (*MY,* I, 92–131).

Sonnet 21 St. Catherine of Ledbury.   Brinsop Court, about five miles northwest of Hereford, was the home of Thomas Hutchinson, MW's brother, and his family, from February 1825. WW's visit to Brinsop Court in December 1827 and his return journey at the end of January 1828 are thought to be associated with this sonnet and two others, 'Four fiery steeds' and 'Wait, prithee, wait' (*LY,* II, 14n.; see WW's notes to these poems on notebook pp. 46–7).

Sonnet 22 ('Though narrow be that old Man's cares, and near'). Probably composed between 30 October 1806 and early April 1807.

< Return to Fenwick Notes | Continue through Editor's Notes>>

46 *Sonnet 23* ('Four fiery steeds impatient of the rein'). Probably composed between 11 December 1827 and 24 January 1828.

Sonnet 29 Composed upon Westminster Bridge, Sept. 3, 1802. Perhaps begun 31 July 1802 (the morning of his and DW's journey by coach from London to Dover), and probably completed 3 September, four days after their return to London. Despite its title, WW dated the poem '1803' in the edition of 1820.

Sonnet 35 A Parsonage in Oxfordshire. Composed 14 July 1820 while on his continental tour with MW. At first part of the planned sequence of *Ecclesiastical Sonnets* (1820), it was relegated instead to a note to that series (see the following note) and then given a place in 'Miscellaneous Sonnets' in *PW* (1827). In editions after 1843 WW continued to add to and rearrange the Miscellaneous Sonnets. This sonnet and several of those following were installed in a new 'Part III' in 1845.

described in another note WW published a note with sonnet xiv, part III, *Ecclesiastical Sonnets* (1822), and in editions from 1827, which read in part: 'A parsonage-house generally stands not far from the church; this proximity imposes favourable restraints, and sometimes suggests an affecting union of the accommodations and elegancies of life with the outward signs of piety and mortality. With pleasure I recal to mind a happy instance of this in the residence of an old and much-valued Friend in Oxfordshire. The house and church stand parallel to each other, at a small distance; a circular lawn or rather grass-plot, spreads between them; shrubs and trees curve from each side of the dwelling, veiling, but not hiding, the church. From the front of this dwelling, no part of the burial-ground is seen; but, as you wind by the side of the shrubs towards the steeple-end of the church, the eye catches a single, small, low, monumental headstone, moss-grown, sinking into, and gently inclining towards, the earth. Advance, and the church-yard, populous and gay with glittering tombstones, opens upon the view. This humble, and beautiful parsonage called forth a tribute, for which see' this sonnet.

< Return to Fenwick Notes | Continue through Editor's Notes>>

Sonnet 37 To the Lady E. B. and the Hon. Miss P. Composed in the Grounds of Plass Newidd, near Llangolen, 1824. Composed in September 1824. On September 2, during a tour of Wales with MW and Dora W and his friend Robert Jones, WW and his party called on these two celebrated recluses of Llangolen, Lady Eleanor Butler, sister of the Duke of Ormonde, and the Hon. Miss Ponsonby, cousin of the Earl of Bessborough (see DW's and WW's accounts of this visit in their separate letters to the Beaumonts, 18 and 20 September 1824; *LY,* I, 274, 276–7). Jones (see Glossary) held the curacy at Glyn Mavyn as well as the living in Oxfordshire.

daughter EQ's vigilant pencil noted 'Dora'.

47 *Caro Albergo* Italian for 'dear house'.

Sonnet 39 In the Woods of Rydal ('Wild Redbreast! hadst thou at Jemima's lip'). In the note printed with the poem WW cites other examples of the redbreast's behavior. Probably composed between early May 1820 and early January 1827, certainly by April 1827. See also WW's note to *The Redbreast,* notebook p. 20.

Sonnet 41 ('While Anna's peers and early playmates tread'). Maria Jane Jewsbury (1800–33) first visited WW at Rydal Mount on 23 May 1825, and joined the Wordsworth family during their month's holiday at Kent's Bank on Morecombe Bay in July and August The Wordsworths then visited her in Manchester in mid-November. The sonnet was composed between mid-July 1825 and early January 1827, but probably around the time of these first encounters.

Sonnet 43 To ———. ('"Wait, prithee, wait!" this answer Lesbia threw'). For the probable date of composition see the note above to *St. Catherine of Ledbury.* The 'Young Lady' is identified in a manuscript of the poem as Ellen Loveday Walker, the Daughter of the Rector of Brinsop. WW had composed an imitation of Catullus' *Carmina* V, *To Lesbia,* probably in 1787, perhaps during his first months at Cambridge, and later turned it over to STC, who published it in the *Morning Post* for 11 April 1798. For Brinsop Court see the editor's note to 'Sonnet 21', *St. Catherine of Ledbury* (notebook p. 45).

48 *Sonnet 44 The Infant M—— M——.* The child, Mary Monkhouse, was born 21 December 1821; the manuscript is dated 12 November 1824. Thomas Monkhouse, Mary (Hutchinson) Wordsworth's cousin, married Jane Horrocks of Preston in 1820.

Sonnet 45 To ——, In Her Seventieth Year. MW enclosed a copy of the poem in her letter to Lady Beaumont, on 9 December 1825, describing it as 'a corrected copy of the sonnet suggested by you' (*LY*, I, 413–14). The Lady is perhaps Lady Maria Fitzgerald, first wife of Sir Maurice Fitzgerald who represented Kerry in the Irish and imperial parliaments from 1794 to 1831. She died in 1827.

Sonnet 46 To Rotha Q——. Rotha, second daughter of Jemima and Edward Quillinan, was born in Rydal, in a house beside the river Rotha, in September 1821; her mother, Edward's first wife, died 25 May 1822. WW stood as Rotha's godfather at her christening; the poem was probably composed around and certainly by 19 November 1824 (*LY*, I, 286).

Sonnet 47. Miserrimus 'Miserrimus' is the first word of the sonnet (*A Grave-Stone Upon the Floor in the Cloisters of Worcester Cathedral*). EQ's pencil parentheses surround '?—The Revd…Jacobites—'. His pencil note follows: 'See Hist of Monuments from which M^r. Q. has an extract—' (the book has not been identified).

Revd M^r. Morris Thomas Morris (1660–1748); WW's sonnet was probably composed around but by 23 January 1828 (*SHL*, pp. 358–9), and was first published with four other poems in *The Keepsake* in December 1828.

Sonnet 48 Roman Antiquities Discovered at Bishopstone, Herefordshire. Associated with WW's visit to Brinsop Court in December 1828, the sonnet was probably composed around but by early March 1828; it was among five sonnets submitted with three longer poems for publication in *The Keepsake* but did not appear there (*LY*, II, 14 and n., 74).

Eidouranian Philosopher Adam Walker (1731?–1821), author and inventor, was born in Patterdale and, mainly through self-education, rose to become a lecturer in astronomy at Manchester and, later, in London and at various public schools. He invented an 'eidouranion,' a type of transparent orrery, which he used to illustrate his astronomy lectures. The son WW spoke to was probably Adam John Walker, who was Vicar and Rector of Bishopstone, Herefordshire, from 1809–39.

49   *Sonnet 49*   Titled *1830* ('Chatsworth! thy stately mansion, and the pride'). WW sent a copy of the sonnet to Dorothy on 8 November 1830, from Coleorton; he had visited Chatsworth the day before (*LY,* II, 340).

a visit to her Uncle   Revd Christopher Wordsworth (1774–1846), WW's younger brother, was Master of Trinity College, Cambridge.

lines to the memory of Sir George Beaumont   That is, *Elegiac Musings in the Grounds of Coleorton Hall, the Seat of the Late Sir G. H. Beaumont, Bart.,* composed 17 November 1830. See WW's and DQ's notes to this poem on notebook p. 116.

Sonnet 50   *A Tradition of Oken Hill in Darley Dale, Derbyshire.* 'Oken' was changed to 'Oker' in the edition of 1849–50. WW's sonnet was probably composed around but by early March 1828 and was first published with four other poems in *The Keepsake* in December 1828. In November 1830 when WW revisited the dale he wrote to DW that, though he 'recognized the two Trees that gave occasion to my Sonnet on the parting of the two Brothers', he could discover no 'such tradition from the people whom I questioned, but a little Boy told me that two very large Willows had stood close by where we were, called Scotch Trees; and that the spot which he pointed to was called Scotchman's Turn, from a Scotchman who had been murthered there' (*LY,* II, 340).

Sonnet 51   Titled *Filial Piety. (On the Way-side between Preston and Liverpool.)* Composed certainly by 4 February 1828, according to a dated copy in Edith May Southey's album, but probably nearer the time of WW's hearing the anecdote in late January 1828. The sonnet was first published with four other poems in *The Keepsake* in December 1828. 'Thomas Scarisbrick was killed by a flash of lightning whilst building a turf-stack in 1779. His son James Scarisbrick, who was then thirty years old, completed the stack, and ever after during his life reverently kept it in repair as a memorial to his father. James died in 1824, consequently for forty-five years he had tended this rude monument, and to further perpetuate the remembrance of it he left to his grandchildren sets of goblets and decanters, on each of which are incised his own and his wife's monogram and a representation of the turf-stack between two trees.... [The farm was located] about a mile north of Ormskirk, and abutted to the Preston highway.... The turf-stack stood between two large sycamore trees.... [It] was pulled down and its turf used for field drainage on the farm within six years after the death of James Scarisbrick in 1824' (James Bromley, 'The Story of a Sonnet,' *The Atheneum,* 17 May 1890, p. 641). The anecdote echoes curiously against the story of WW's *Michael,* written nearly three decades earlier.

50   *Sonnet 52 To the Author's Portrait.* Henry William Pickersgill, R.A. (1782–1875), on commission from St John's College, did a preliminary chalk portrait at Rydal Mount in the first week of September 1832 and completed the half–length portrait in oils at his studio in London by the following May. In a letter to Maria Kinnaird on 15 October 1832, Dora W reported every one pleased with the picture and added, 'All I need say is none of the females of this house could gaze upon it for 6 minutes with eyes undimmed by tears' (*LY,* II, 554 and n.). Dora sent a copy of the sonnet to EQ on 3 October 1832, adding the comment, 'We do feel grateful to M^r. P. for giving us such a portrait of such a father!' It seems clear from this that WW based his sonnet on the chalk drawing; he and his family, when they finally saw the finished oil painting in the following spring, were less than satisfied (*LY,* II, 589n.).

Sonnet 53 ('Why art thou silent! Is thy love a plant'). Composed 18 January 1830, according to Dora's note with the copy of the poem sent as a valentine, signed 'Kate Barker', to her cousin, CWjr. The blank space was left for the date but was not filled in. The 'valentine' survives among manuscripts in the Cornell University Library.

Sonnet 54 To B. R. Haydon, on Seeing his Picture of Napoleon Buonaparte on the Island of St. Helena. Composed around 11 June 1831 (*LY,* II, 396). WW saw the painting two months earlier while visiting the painter's studio in London (12 April 1831). WW's note is followed by a heavily deleted and only partially legible paragraph in ink: '(I omit [mention of another] recollection that I have of the [*8 to 10 illegible words.*] M^r. Haydon's [execution in] the picture'. EQ then inserted his own pencil note referring to the thought expressed in the sonnet: 'but it was said in prose in Haydon's studio for I was present–relate the facts and why it was versified—'. For Haydon see Glossary.

51 *Memorials of a Tour in Scotland, 1803* For topographical details see Hayden, *Scotland*, pp. 10–30, and throughout. The date, left blank by EQ, was 14 August 1803.

Sisters Journal DW's *Recollections*.

The verses that stand foremost Departure from the Vale of Grasmere. August, 1803. This portion of *Epistle to Sir George Howland Beaumont, Bart.* was composed perhaps about 30 August 1811 when WW was vacationing with his family at the seaside town of Bootle; but the poem (minus these lines) was not published until 1842 (see notebook p. 130). Around January 1827 the 32 lines of *Departure* were 'transplanted' from this longer poem, which had nothing to do with the 1803 tour in Scotland, and published with the *Memorials of a Tour in Scotland, 1803* (renamed from its more explicit title *Poems Written During a Tour in Scotland*), in editions from 1827. For dating see *Poems, 1807–1820*, p. 514.

To the Sons of Burns, After Visiting the Grave of Their Father (the full printed title). When the poem was first published in 1807, its title was *Address to the Sons of Burns after visiting their Father's Grave. (August 14th, 1803)*. Chiefly composed probably between early September 1805 and 21 February 1806; completed between April 1820 and early January 1827. The other two poems are *Ejaculation at the Grave of Burns* ('composed...at the time'—18 August 1803; completed in its early form between late March 1806 and early 1807, revised and first published in 1842) and *Thoughts suggested the Day Following, on the Banks of the Nith, near the Poet's Residence* (written 'several years afterwards'; perhaps conceived at the time and composed in part between late March 1806 and early 1807 but probably completed after preparations began in March 1841 for *Poems, Chiefly of Early and Late Years*).

Burns See Glossary.

Ellen Irwin: Or, The Braes of Kirtle (in its printed form). Probably written in Germany between 6 October 1798 and 23 February 1799, but by the preparation of printer's copy for *Lyrical Ballads* (1800) in July

1800. For sources and dating see *LB, 1797–1800,* pp. 382–3. Gottfried August Bürger (1747–94) was an important figure in the revival of interest in folk song and the language of the people in Germany and elsewhere in Europe in the late eighteenth century. His *Leonora* (1773), a spectral romance in ballad form, was well known to STC and WW in William Taylor's translation when they began composing poems for *Lyrical Ballads* (1798); WW and DW bought a copy of Bürger's poems, in the original German, in Hamburg on their way to Goslar in September 1798.

52 *The Highland Girl* *To a Highland Girl. (At Inversneyde, Upon Loch Lomond.)* Composed probably between 14 October 1803 and 6 March 1804, possibly around 21 November 1803. DW's 'Journal' mentioned here is her *Recollections*. *To a Highland Girl,* and the incident which occasioned it, is recalled in ll. 53–65 of *The Three Cottage Girls,* which appeared in *Memorials of a Tour on the Continent, 1820,* in 1822.

Address to Kilchurn-Castle, Upon Loch Awe (in its printed form). Begun 31 August 1803 and probably completed between April 1820 and January 1827.

Rob Roy's Grave Composed probably between early September 1805 and 21 February 1806. The burial ground WW saw was in Glen Gyle. Rob Roy's actual burial site is on the shore of Loch Voil. See Hayden, *Scotland,* pp. 25–6.

53 *Sonnet. Composed at —— Castle* (in its printed form). Composed 18 September 1803. Sir William Douglas, fourth Duke of Queensbury (1724–1810). Around 1798 he stripped the grounds at Drumlanrig and around Neidpath Castle of the larger part of their trees to provide a dowry for Maria Fagniani, whom he supposed to be his daughter. Peebles lies a few miles south of Edinburgh.

Walter Scott   See Glossary.

Sonnet ('Fly, some kind Harbinger, to Grasmere-dale'). The poem's title in manuscript is 'Sonnet September 25th, 1803'; it was completed by 21 November 1803. Dalston is thirty miles north of Grasmere, on the road from Carlisle.

The Blind Highland Boy   Probably composed between late March 1804 and around March 1806. When he revised the poem for publication in 1815, WW expanded an earlier note thus: 'It is recorded in Dampier's Voyages that a Boy, the Son of a Captain of a Man of War, seated himself in a Turtle-shell and floated in it from the shore to his Father's Ship, which lay at anchor at the distance of half a mile. Upon the suggestion of a Friend, I have substituted such a Shell for that less elegant vessel in which my blind voyager did actually intrust himself to the dangerous current of Loch Levin, as was related to me by an Eyewitness.' George M. Mackereth (or Mackareth; 1751–1832), the 'eye-witness', was parish clerk in Grasmere from 1785 until shortly before his death; he lived with his large family at Knott Houses, a farm-house near the Swan, and owned a horse frequently borrowed by the Wordsworth's while they lived at Town End.

Second Tour in Scotland. 1814   That is, *Memorials of a Tour in Scotland. 1814*. The touring party, comprised of WW, MW and Sara Hutchinson, left Grasmere 18 July and returned 9 July 1814. See Hayden, *Scotland*, pp. 31–48.

Brownie's Cell   That is, *Suggested by a Beautiful Ruin upon one of the Islands of Loch Lomond, a Place Chosen for the Retreat of a Solitary Individual, from whom this Habitation Acquired the name of The Brownie's Cell*. For the locale of *Brownie's Cell* see Hayden, *Scotland,* pp. 25, 63. The poem was composed possibly in part 5 August 1814 or shortly after; probably not completed until around but by January 1820. WW reached Pulpit Rock on Loch Lomond on the 1814 tour on 5 August where he was told the legend of Brownie's cell by the last remaining member of the MacFarlane family; he had first visited Pulpit Rock in September 1803 during his tour with DW. See *Chronology: MY,* pp. 562–3, and *Poems, 1807–1820,* pp. 525–6.

54 *Cora Linn Composed at Cora Linn, In Sight of Wallace's Tower.* The falls of Cora Linn and Wallace's Tower are a mile south of Lanark on the Clyde. WW reached this point on 25 July 1814; the poem was probably begun at this time, though it was not published until 1820 (see *Poems, 1807–1820*, pp. 524–5). His two previous visits were in 1801 and 1803. See Hayden, *Scotland,* pp. 3–4.

Effusion, near Dunkeld That is, *Effusion, In the Pleasure-Ground on the Banks of the Bran, near Dunkeld.* WW perhaps revisited the Duke of Atholl's pleasure-ground 19 August 1814. The incident is recollected from WW and DW's earlier visit to the pleasure-ground 9 September 1803. The quotation from the journal of his 'Fellow-Traveller' at the head of the poem comes from Dorothy's *Recollections.* The poem was not included in the first publication of the 1814 *Tour* in 1820. It was probably completed between April 1820 and January 1827 (see *Poems, 1807–1820,* pp. 526–7).

Yarrow Visited, September, 1814 Composed chiefly between 1 and 16 September 1814 (*SHL*, p. 79); a revised version of this poem appears in letters of 11 and 12 November 1814 (DW to Catherine Clarkson and WW to Robert Pearce Gillies, respectively). For another reference to this poem see the note to *Extempore Effusion Upon the Death of James Hogg* on notebook p. 118. See also *Poems, 1807–1820,* pp. 527–8.

Hogg See Glossary.

D^r. Anderson Dr Robert Anderson (1750–1830), of Edinburgh, was an editor and biographer of British poets. His chief work, *A Complete Edition of the Poets of Great Britain,* appeared in thirteen volumes in 1792–5, and a fourteenth volume was added in 1807. WW's inscribed and annotated copy of this edition, annotated even more extensively by STC, is in the Folger Library, Washington, D.C.

Editor's Notes

55 *known little of Drayton, Daniel* Michael Drayton (1563–1631) and Samuel Daniel (1562–1619). Both produced sonnet sequences and Daniel wrote the *Defence of Rhyme* in which he argued for the fitness of the English language for rhymed verse.

travelling together in Scotland In *Yarrow Unvisited,* composed during the 1803 tour of Scotland, the speaker declines his companion's invitation to visit Yarrow because, of

> Yarrow Stream unseen, unknown,...
> We have a vision of our own;
> Ah! why should we undo it?'

See WW's notes to the third Yarrow poem, *Yarrow Revisited,* on notebook pp. 95 and 99 below.

56 *Sonnets dedicated to Liberty* In 1845 WW changed the heading to *Poems Dedicated to National Independence and Liberty.*

Sonnet 12 Thought of a Briton on the Subjugation of Switzerland. Probably composed between 30 October 1806 and January 1807.

as mentioned on p. 29 That is, notebook p. 29, where WW's notes to both *The Horn of Egremont Castle* and *Song at the Feast of Brougham Castle, upon the Restoration of Lord Clifford, the Shepherd, to the Estates and Honours of His Ancestors* are found. See also his published note to the latter poem for his history of the Cliffords.

Sonnet 13 Written in London, September, 1802 ('O Friend! I know not which way I must look'). Composed probably by 22 September 1802.

58 *the top of Raise-Gap* That is, the highest point of Dunmail Raise, the pass between Grasmere and Wythburn, on the road to Keswick. For Keswick see Glossary.

my tract on the Convention of Cintra That is, *Concerning the Relations of Great Britain, Spain, and Portugal…as Affected by the Convention of Cintra* (1809). The tract was written in the winter of 1808–9 and published in installments in the *Courier* in December 1808 and January 1809 and as a pamphlet in May 1809. A general revolt in Spain against the invading French army and the impending imposition of Joseph Bonaparte as King of Spain led to the defeat of the French at Lisbon, with the help of the British under Wellesley. But the agreement signed permitted the French to withdraw with its army, arms, and honour, intact. WW, Southey and others were incensed and tried to rouse public opinion against the 'Convention'. See Gill, *A Life*, p. 274.

Thanksgiving Ode *Ode. The Morning of the Day Appointed for a General Thanksgiving. January 18, 1816*. This is the version of 1815–43, before WW split one poem into two in 1845. The poem was composed around, and by, 18 March 1816. For discussion of the poem before and after division and the texts of all versions see *Poems, 1807–1820*, pp. 177–200, 536, and 426–35. EQ's pencil note:

> In a letter to Southey about the rhythm of this Ode, WW, in comparing the first paragraph of the Aeneid with that of the Jerusalem Liberated, says that the measure of the latter has "the pace of a set of recruits shuffling to *vulgar* music upon a parade & receiving from the adjutant or drill sergeant the command to halt at every 20 steps."
>
> Mr. W. had no ear for instrumental music; or he w^d. not have applied this vulgar sarcasm to military-march music. Besides, awkward recruits are never drilled to music at all. The Band on parade plays to perfectly drilled troops. Ne sutor ultra crepidam ['*Let the cobbler stick to his last,*' from Pliny].
>
> In the letter to Southey which EQ mentions, WW made no mention

< Return to Fenwick Notes | Continue through Editor's Notes>>

of the *Thanksgiving Ode* or of music, vulgar or otherwise; he actually compared the measure of *Jerusalem Delivered* with 'the pace of a set of recruits shuffling on the drill ground, and receiving from the adjutant or drill-serjeant the command to halt at every ten or twenty steps' ([1815], *MY*, II, 268). In a later letter to Southey, probably around June 1816, WW did discuss the 'irregular frame of the metre' of the *Thanksgiving Ode,* but without reference to Virgil or Tasso (*MY*, II, 324–5). The text of both letters derives from Knight's edition of the *Letters of the Wordsworth Family* (3 vols, 1907).

historians and critical philosophers   WW may be thinking of Carlyle's 1840 lecture on 'The Hero as King', the sixth and final lecture in his series *On Heroes, Hero-Worship and The Heroic in History* (later published in London, 1841). For Carlyle, Napoleon—like Oliver Cromwell in England—was for a time one of 'the most important of Great Men', a 'true Democrat' who had a 'heart-hatred for anarchy' and saw the necessity to 'bridle in that great devouring, self-devouring French Revolution' (pp. 316, 386–7). Sir Walter Scott published a *Life of Napoleon Buonaparte, Emperor of the French* in 1827 (Edinburgh and London). Planned first as 'a brief and popular abstract of the life of the most wonderful man, and the most extraordinary events, of the last thirty years' Scott's nine-volume *Life* praised Napoleon's 'splendid personal qualities—his great military actions and political services to France'. See also the editor's note to *In Allusion to Various Recent Histories and Notices of the French Revolution* ('Portentous change'), the heading for which appears—without any accompanying note by WW—on notebook p. 155.

59 *Inscriptions. Nº. 1*   That is, *In the Grounds of Coleorton, the Seat of Sir George Beaumont, Bart., Leicestershire. 1808* ('The embowering rose, the acacia, and the pine'). Composed not later than about mid-October 1811; possibly in 1808. For the complex history of the composition and revision of these four inscriptions associated with Coleorton (*In the Grounds of Coleorton; In a Garden of the Same; Written at the Request of Sir George Beaumont, Bart., and in his Name, for an Urn, Placed by Him at the Termination of a Newly-Planted Avenue, in the Same Grounds;* and *For a Seat in the Groves of Coleorton*) see *Poems, 1807–1820*, pp. 100–8, 519–20.

2. *This Niche*   *In a Garden of the Same* ("This Niche," l. 8 of 'Oft is the medal faithful to its trust'). Composed 29 October 1811 (*MY,* I, 513–14; see also *Poems, 1807–1820,* pp. 518–19). WW's note to *To the Lady Beaumont* on notebook p. 45 refers to the making of this quarry garden which WW, DW and MW helped to plan in 1806–7.

the former & *the two following*   See the editor's note to *In the Grounds of Coleorton* where the four inscriptions are listed.

6. *The circumstance alluded to*   *Written with a Slate Pencil on a Stone, on the Side of the Mountain of Black Comb* ('Stay, bold Adventurer; rest awhile thy limbs'). The poem was begun perhaps in late August or early September 1811, but perhaps not completed until 1813. For the dating see *Poems, 1807–1820,* p. 518. WW's source was the Revd James Satterthwaite (1773–1827). See WW's published note to *View from the Top of Black Comb* cited above (notebook p. 32).

60   *making trigonometrical surveys*   That is, preparing Ordnance Survey maps. The surveyors (or 'engineers'), using triangulation to measure distance and height, began their work in 1791 and had completed the job by 1840.

8. *Engraven* ('In these fair vales hath many a Tree')   The poem's title in 1835 was *Inscription Intended for a Stone in the Grounds of Rydal Mount*, but the title was dropped in the one-volume editions from 1845 and in 1849–50. The poem was dated in the earliest manuscript 26 June 1830. The engraving was done after WW left for Italy in March and before he returned to Rydal Mount in September 1837.

9. *The walk*   The quoted words refer to l. 5 of 'The massy Ways, carried across these heights'. For the threatened removal from Rydal Mount see the entry for 'Le Fleming' in the Glossary. WW's lease for Rydal Mount expired at the end of 1825 and in December Lady Le Fleming told him she would not renew it. But the threat of removal subsided by the end of October 1826. Probably composed between January and early October 1826. See Kishel, *Tuft of Primroses,* pp. 8–13, for discussion of another poem arising from the same circumstances, *Composed when a probability existed of our being obliged to quit Rydal Mount as a Residence.*

11. *The monument of ice*   *Inscribed Upon a Rock* ('Pause, Traveller! whosoe'er thou be'). Part of a sequence called *Inscriptions Supposed to be Found in and Near a Hermit's Cell,* and composed in 1818, perhaps at the beginning of the year (see *Poems, 1807–1820,* pp. 263–4, 547). WW's description indicates the overhanging rock beside the road leading from the main road, just beyond the White Moss slate quarry, over the Common to How Top Farm. The Wordsworths called it 'Glow-worm Rock', as WW explains in his note to *The Pilgrim's Dream, or the Star and the Glow-worm,* notebook p. 23. *The Primrose and the Rock* concerns the same feature of the landscape. (See McCracken, pp. 20–4.)

12. Where the second quarry ('Hast thou seen, with flash incessant'.)   Like the previous poem, part of a sequence called *Inscriptions Supposed to be Found in and Near a Hermit's Cell,* and composed in 1818, perhaps at the beginning of the year. The location seems to have been close to that described in *Inscribed Upon a Rock,* but a few yards before the road rises to the Common.

Written in the Album of a Child   First called *Written in an Album* (1835), the poem was titled *Written in the Album of a Child* in 1837 and it became *To a Child, Written in Her Album* in 1845 when it was moved to 'Miscellaneous Poems'. In the album, now in the Wordsworth Library, Grasmere, the poem is dated Rydal Mount, 3^d July 1834.

my God-daughter Rotha   EQ's daughter by his first wife, Jemima. See WW's note to *To Rotha Q*—— on notebook p. 48 and the editor's note.

61 *Lines in Lady Lonsdale's Album* The published title is *Lines Written in the Album of the Countess of Lonsdale. Nov. 5, 1834*. The poem was probably composed at the time or shortly before. It was moved to 'Miscellaneous Poems' in editions of 1845 and 1849–50. Lady Augusta Lonsdale died 6 March 1838. Her husband, Sir William Lowther, Lord Lonsdale (1757–1844), on succeeding his cousin, James Lowther, in 1802, offered to settle the debt for wages and expenses, around £4,500, owed to John Wordsworth, WW's father, when he died in 1783, and made good the offer a short time later to the sum of £8,500, including interest. WW dedicated *The Excursion* (1814) to the second earl and through the earl's offices WW was appointed to the Distributorship of Stamps. Lord Lonsdale had been WW's friend and patron since 1806 when he purchased a small estate in Patterdale and presented it to the poet.

before she reached the period of old age EQ's pencil note: 'query was she not 70? [?W^m.] J.' Perhaps his intention was to ask William Wordsworth Jr, who, with Lord Lonsdale's help, had finally taken over his father's duties as Stamp Distributor for Cumberland and Westmoreland in 1842 (Moorman, II, 510–11, 556–7).

The Egyptian Maid; Or, The Romance of the Water Lily (in its printed form). Probably composed between 18–25 November 1828; WW told George Huntley Gordon on 25 November 1828, that he had 'just concluded a kind of romance'; in a letter written the same day MW told EQ that it was written 'within the last 8 days' and WW added that 'it rose out of my mind like an exhalation' (*LY*, I, 663, 666–7). In the 'short notice prefixed to this poem' WW cited the 'History of the renowned Prince Arthur and his Knights of the Round Table' as the source for 'names and persons' and 'the beautiful work of ancient art, once included among the Townley Marbles, and now in the British Museum' as the inspiration for the 'carved Lotus cast upon the beach/By the fierce waves, a flower in marble graven' (ll. 125–6).

Henry Hutchinson The son of John Hutchinson (1768–1831) of Stockton-on-Tees, Mary's elder brother. For other Hutchinson siblings see Glossary.

<To return to the text use the Previous View Button

62 *The River Duddon. A Series of Sonnets.*   Composed, variously, between May 1802 and April 1820, but chiefly between late November 1818 and the April 1820 (See *Sonn*, pp. 49–55). For Duddon see Glossary.
Wry-nose Pass   Between the Langdales and the Duddon Valley.
I first became acquainted   This first visit probably occurred in 1782; WW is known to have returned to the Duddon Valley in 1788–9, 1794, 1804, 1808 and twice in 1811.

63 *During my college-vacation*   WW stayed at Broughton with his cousin Mary Wordsworth Smith and her husband John, about a mile from Duddon Bridge, in Furness in August and in September 1789 and again, with Dorothy, in August of 1794; he may have visited the Smiths during his first summer vacation in 1788 as well. His visits and his cousin's early death are referred to in Sonnet XXI ('Whence that low voice?—A whisper from the heart' in *PW [1841]*).
the 21st. sonnet   Composed in November 1818.
The subject of the 27th.   The 27th sonnet is 'Fallen, and diffused into a shapeless heap', composed between 1815 and March 1819.
Rydal Hall   See Glossary.
the 30th. Sonnet ('Who swerves from innocence, who makes divorce'). Probably composed between December 1820 and April 1820. Besides the Wordsworths and Dora the party included IF, EQ and his daughter Rotha. They made the tour in July 1840.

64 *Seathwaite Chapel*   In Seathwaite, on the Duddon.
on our way to Ulpha   Ulpha lies two miles south of Seathwaite, along the river.
Ulpha Kirk   The church at Ulpha.

65   *in my epistle*   *Epistle to Sir George Howland Beaumont, Bart.* Composed in 1811. See WW's note to this poem on notebook p. 130.

The White Doe of Rylstone; Or, The Fate of the Nortons   The first canto was written by early November 1807 when 'Part I' was read to De Quincey; WW left Grasmere to join Mary at Stockton-on-Tees on 1 December and by the 24th, when they left for home, 1,200 lines had been completed, the 'earlier half' of the poem. Composed chiefly between 16 October 1807 and 16 January 1808, and revised the following April, the poem was given its final form around November 1814 to late January 1815. For dating see *Chronology: MY*, pp. 45, 700–2, and *The White Doe of Rylstone; or The Fate of the Nortons, by William Wordsworth*, ed. Kristine Dugas (Cornell University Press: Ithaca, 1988), pp. 29–31; and for discussion of circumstances surrounding composition of this poem see Dugas' introduction to her edition.

Mr. Hutchinson   MW's brother John Hutchinson (1768–1833), who lived at Stockton-on-Tees.

67   *To abide…a triumph pure*   Quoted from ll. 1070–2 of *The White Doe*.

68   *Memorials of a Tour on the Continent, 1820* (in its printed form). See also WW's notes published with the poems. Many of the poems among these 'Memorials' were written a year after he returned to England, between early October 1821 and the end of January 1822, for at the later date DW reported to HCR, who was of the party and who had visited Rydal Mount in early October 1821, that 'My Brother…has written some beautiful poems since you left us' (*LY,* I, 92). On 28 December 1821 MW told John Kenyon that 'The *Poet* has been busily engaged upon subjects connected with our Continental journey' and that 'Miss W. is going on with her journal, which will be ready to *go to press* interspersed with her brother's poems' (*LY,* I, 100); and less than a month later DW wrote to Catherine Clarkson on 16 January 1822 that WW 'began (as in connection with my *Recollections of a Tour in Scotland*) with saying "I will write some Poems for your journal," and I thankfully received two or three of them as a tribute to the journal, which I was making from notes, memoranda taken in our last summer's journey on the Continent; but his work has grown to such importance (and has continued growing) that I have long ceased to consider it in connection with my own narrative of events …' (*LY,* I, 104; for DW's *Journal of a Tour on the Continent, 1820,* see *Journals,* II). As WW mentions at the end of the notes to this section, a similar journal was kept by MW (Wordsworth Library manuscript), and WW drew upon both accounts while composing the poems. See also Hayden, *Europe I,* pp. 41–109. The *Memorials of a Tour on the Continent, 1820,* were sent to the press at the end of January and appeared in March 1822. WW made later additions to the series in 1827 and 1838. See *Sonn,* 351–356.

M^r. & M^{rs}. *Monkhouse…& Miss Horrocks*   Jane Horrocks, of Preston, married Thomas Monkhouse, MW's cousin, in 1820; her sister, 'Miss Horrocks', accompanied them on the tour.

H.C. Robinson See Glossary.

Sonnet 5 ('What lovelier home could gentle Fancy choose'). Composed between 29 November 1821 and 31 January 1822.

[*Huy*] EQ left a blank space and then supplied 'Huyes' in pencil. *Memoirs* has 'Huy' while *PW* (1857) has 'Liege'. It seems likely that WW said Huy, which lies between Namur and Liège (the comma is editorial).

69   *the banks of Avon*   The river located south of Glasgow and Bothwell Castle, in Scotland. See WW's remark in the note to *The Avon. (A Feeder of the Annan.)* notebook p. 99.

Sir Uvedale Price   See WW's and the editor's notes to *Elegiac Stanzas Suggested by a picture of Peele Castle, in a Storm, Painted by Sir George Beaumont,* notebook p. 115. WW's letter to Price has not been located.

Mary's Journals & *my Sister's*   In the winter of 1821, urged on by her brother, DW prepared her journal of the continental tour for publication, and later was pressed by HCR to revise it, but she decided not to publish it (see her letter to HCR, 23 May 1824; *LY,* I, 271).

Ecclesiastical Sonnets. In Series   WW explained the personal origin in the 'Advertisement' of the *Ecclesiastical Sketches,* as the volume was called when first published in March 1822:

> During the month of December, 1820, I accompanied a much beloved and honoured Friend [Sir George Beaumont] in a walk through different parts of his estate [Coleorton], with a view to fix upon the site of a new Church which he intended to erect It was one of the most beautiful mornings of a mild season, our feelings were in harmony with the cherishing influences of the scene; and, such being our purpose, we were naturally led to look back upon past events with wonder and gratitude, and on the future with hope. Not long afterwards, some of the Sonnets which will be found towards the close of this series were produced as a private memorial of that morning's occupation.
>
> The Catholic Question, which was agitated in Parliament about that time, kept my thoughts in the same course; and it struck me that certain points in the Ecclesiastical History of our Country might advantageously be presented to view in verse. Accordingly, I took up the subject, and what I now offer to the Reader was the result.
>
> When this work was far advanced, I was agreeably surprised to find that my friend, Mr. Southey, was engaged with similar views, in writing a concise History of the Church *in* England. If our

< Return to Fenwick Notes | Continue through Editor's Notes >>

Productions, thus unintentionally coinciding, shall be found to illustrate each other, it will prove a high gratification to me, which I am sure my Friend will participate [*dated 24 January 1822*].

The sonnets mentioned in the *Advertisement* as arising from his visit to Coleorton in 1820 are the three titled *Church to be Erected, Continued,* and *New Church-Yard* (section III, sonnets xxix–xxxi, in 1841), all probably composed in December 1820. Three others, given the collective title *Inside of King's College Chapel, Cambridge* (III, xxxiii–xxxv, in 1841), were written a few days before this while WW was visiting his brother Christopher at Trinity Lodge, Cambridge. The series was extensively added to in subsequent years. For a detailed history of the composition of the series, see *Sonn*, pp. 127–136.

70   *Gregory the 7th...at [Canosa]*   In Italy. EQ left the space blank. The sonnet referred to is *Scene in Venice* ('Black Demons hovering o'er his mitred head'). Pope Gregory VII (Hildebrand, c. 1025–85), in his struggle with Henry IV (1050–1106), Emperor of Germany, over the centralization of the powers and wealth of the Church, excommunicated the Emperor. Henry pleaded for absolution at Canosa, where he intercepted Gregory as he returned to Rome, and Gregory pardoned him (presumably with 'penance'). However, Henry continued to defy the Pope and was excommunicated a second time and 'deposed': he in turn deposed Gregory, electing Clement III as Pope, and besieged Rome in 1084, driving Gregory into exile. Pope Alexander III (Bandinelli; d. 1181) excommunicated Frederick I (Barbarossa; 1123–50) in 1160 and accepted his homage in 1177.

      the Oxford Tract movement   William Laud (1573–1645) became Archbishop of Canterbury under Charles I in 1633 and supported the king in his struggle against Parliament. For his pains he was tried for treason in 1640 and executed in 1645. While in power he defended the Anglican Church as a national institution against the claims of both Rome and the Puritans. He is treated in the sonnet *Laud* ('Prejudged by foes determined not to spare'). The 'Oxford Movement' or 'Tractarian Movement', as it is usually called, began at Oxford in 1833 with a sermon by John Keble on national apostasy, an attack upon those who regarded the Anglican Church as no more than a 'merely human institution'. John Henry Newman and Edward Pusey joined Keble in producing several 'Tracts for the Times' in which they defended their higher conception of the Church. See WW's remarks on Frederick Faber and the Oxford movement in his note to *Musings Near Aquapendente*, notebook p. 143.

71   *I saw the figure of a lovely maid*   The first sonnet in Part III, *From the Restoration to the Present Times*.

      my daughter   EQ's note, 'Dora?' and what is possibly MW's reply, 'Dora', are both entered in pencil.

      I have only further to observe...a great benefit to the neighbourhood   See the introductory note to *Ecclesiastical Sonnets* above.

72 *Prefatory lines to Vol. 5* ('If thou indeed derive thy light from Heaven'). Probably composed between May 1813 and January 1827 and published for the first time among 'Poems of Sentiment and Reflection' in 1827, this poem was placed first in volume five in 1837 as a 'prefatory' poem to this class. When the one-volume edition was being prepared in 1845, WW instructed the printer to place it at the beginning of the single volume 'as a sort of Preface' (WW to Edward Moxon, 5 November 1845, *LY*, IV, 717). It remained as 'prefatory lines' to all his poems through the edition of 1849–50. For dating see *Poems, 1807–1820*, p. 525

Like an untended watch-fire &c   WW's new residence in 1813, Rydal Mount is situated east of Nab Scar with a prospect across the valley to Loughrigg Fell opposite and the sky above it:

Expostulation and Reply   The first poem in 'Poems of Sentiment and Reflection'; it was composed, along with *The Tables Turned*, on or shortly after 23 May 1798. In the Advertisement to *Lyrical Ballads, 1798*, WW said the two poems 'arose out of conversation with a friend who was somewhat unreasonably attached to modern books of moral philosophy'; the friend was probably William Hazlitt who discussed philosophy with WW on 23 May 1798 or shortly after. For dating and the identity of the friend, see *LB, 1797–1800*, pp. 355–6.

The Tables Turned; An Evening Scene on the Same Subject   See the note to *Expostulation and Reply* above.

Lines Left upon a Seat in a Yew-tree, which stands near the lake of Esthwaite, on a desolate part of the shore, commanding a beautiful prospect (in its printed form). See Glossary entry for Esthwaite. Composed perhaps in part in 1786 or 1787 but probably reached something like its present form in early 1797, between 8 February and July, at Racedown. In 1815 and 1820 WW dated it 1795 and in 1836–7 he assigned it to 1796, the year he and DW began residence at Racedown. For dating and sources see *LB, 1797–1800*, pp. 341–3.

73 *a gentleman of the neighbourhood*   EQ's pencil note, 'Query—Mr. Nott', is incorrect. The man whose story WW adapted to his poetic purposes was the Revd William Braithwaite of Satterhow (*Wordsworth's Hawkshead*, pp. 256–64, 376).

The Station   Thomas West referred to Braithwaite's ownership and improvement of this 'station' in a note added to his *Guide to the Lakes in Cumberland, Westmorland and Lancashire* (London, 1799). WW described the Station and the Pleasure House in his *Select Views* (in *Prose*, II, 263). For John Curwen see WW's note to *An Evening Walk*, notebook p. 14.

Lines Written While Sailing in a Boat at Evening   The date is underscored in the notebook but is not part of the published title. A sonnet version left in manuscript may have been composed while WW was at Cambridge, probably in 1789, the date he assigned to *Lines* in the edition of 1836; in its long form the poem was probably composed in early 1797, certainly by 29 March, and was revised as two poems between 29 March 1797 and 30 May 1798. For dating see *Chronology: EY*, pp. 305–6, and *LB, 1797–1800*, pp. 354–5. In a note printed with the second poem, titled *Remembrance of Collins, Composed on the Thames Near Richmond*, WW mentioned William Collins' *Ode on the Death of Mr. Thomson* (1749), which memorialises the author of *The Seasons*, James Thomson (1700–48), whose grave is at Richmond. WW in his turn pays tribute to Collins (1721–59). 'Windsor' in the Fenwick note may be an error for 'Richmond', thirteen miles further east along the Thames.

74   *Lines Written in Early Spring*   EQ's pencil note: 'See Dr. C^r. W's Mem p. 114 vol. 1—' (where WW's note is printed). EQ's pencil note, and perhaps many others of his, were entered after WW's death in 1850, when CWjr, WW's nephew, began preparing the *Memoirs,* which appeared the next year. The poem was probably composed in April 1798, perhaps around 12 and 13 April (see DW's journal entries for these dates).

     the Comb   The hill behind Alfoxden to the south (see Glossary for Alfoxden). The dell with the brook running through it is near Holford (not 'Alford') and was a retreat favoured by DW, WW and STC. For other accounts of the place, contemporary and modern, see WW's note to *Anecdote for Fathers* on notebook p. 9 and *LB, 1797–1800,* pp. 349–50.

75   *A Character*   Probably composed between 30 March 1797 and 12 October 1800. Jones spent a week at Dove Cottage in September 1800; the manuscript of the poem can be dated around 12 October 1800. For dating and for STC as a possible inspiration for the poem, see *Chronology: EY,* pp. 323–4, and *LB, 1797–1800,* pp. 396–7. For other references to Jones in the Fenwick notes see the index.

     To My Sister. Written at a Small Distance From My House, and Sent By My Little Boy   Probably composed between 1 and 9 March 1798, a period when DW reported sunny, pleasant days (see *LB, 1797–1800,* p. 345).

     In 1841, we could barely find the spot   That is, when WW, MW, the newly married Dora and Edward Quillinan, and IF visited Alfoxden and its surroundings after Dora's marriage. See Glossary entries for Dora W and EQ.

76 *Simon Lee, The Old Huntsman With an Incident in Which He Was Concerned*   Probably composed between early March and around 16 May 1798. For the literal basis of the poem see *LB, 1797–1800*, pp. 345–6.
But it had disappeared   That is, in 1841, when WW revisited the place.
image of the old man   EQ, who was an avid hunter, added this pencil note: 'but the *running* huntsman w^d. not so well apply to Somersetshire as to Darbyshire though people run out after hounds on foot everywhere—'.
Lines written in Germany   That is, *Written in Germany, On One of the Coldest Days of the Century*. This poem was probably composed between 6 October 1798 and 23 February 1799. DW reported Christmas day, 1798, as the coldest day of the century (*EY*, p. 243); WW dated the poem both 1798 (editions before 1836) and 1799 (editions after 1836).
ceiled   Lined with wood strips, plaster, etc. (OED).

77 *The Poet's Epitaph*   *A Poet's Epitaph* (in its printed form) was composed between 6 October 1798 and 23 February 1799. Though falling on its own line in the notebook, it was clearly the end of the note to *Written in Germany* as WW dictated it and no separate note was added. For sources see *LB, 1797–1800*, p. 396.
To the Daisy ('Bright Flower! whose home is everywhere'). Probably composed in part between 16 April and 8 July 1802; possibly not fully developed or written out until between 6 March 1804 and around March 1805. The date assigned in 1836 was 1803. The 'other poems' to the daisy composed about the same time are 'In youth from rock to rock I went', and 'With little here to do or see'; a fourth, 'Sweet Flower! belike one day to have', an elegy for WW's brother John, was composed in 1805. EQ added a pencil note in a six-line blank space at the foot of the page: 'some thing omitted here—see Miss F's notes—', but nothing was added. The next poem in *PW* (1841) is *Matthew*, the subject of the next note.

78 *Matthew* ('If Nature, for a favourite child'). Probably composed, with other 'Matthew' poems (*The Two April Mornings; The Fountain. A Conversation; Address to the Scholars of the Village School;* and the 'Mathew' elegies, 'Could I the priest's consent have gained' and 'Remembering how thou didst beguile') between 6 October 1798 and 23 February 1799 (for the latter see *LB, 1797–1800,* pp. 297–302, 458).

Schoolmaster was made up of several T. W. Thompson suggests three Hawkshead men: John Harrison, schoolmaster, Thomas Cowperthwaite, iron monger, and John Gibson, attorney (*Wordsworth's Hawkshead,* pp. 151–90). William Taylor, a headmaster at Hawkshead School, has also been suggested by Moorman and others (see *LB, 17971800,* pp. 390–1).

To the Spade of a Friend. (An Agriculturist.) Composed While We Were Labouring Together in his Pleasure-Ground (in its printed form). Probably composed between 18 August and 26 October 1806. Thomas Wilkinson (1751–1836), whose farm, the Grotto at Yanwath near Penrith, WW first visited in 1801, was a friend of STC and, as WW mentions, Thomas Clarkson; like Clarkson he was active in opposing the slave trade. WW read Wilkinson's *Tour in Scotland* in manuscript, borrowing from it when he composed his poem, *The Solitary Reaper.* Wilkinson himself described the incident treated in *To the Spade of a Friend:* 'I had promised Lord Lonsdale to take William Wordsworth to Lowther when he came to see me, but when we arrived at the Castle he was gone to shoot moor-game with Judge Sutton. William and I then returned, and wrought together at a walk I was then forming; this gave birth to his verses' (reported in Mary Carr, *Thomas Wilkinson: A Friend of Wordsworth* [London, 1905] p. 69). WW described Wilkinson in 1805 as 'an amiable inoffensive man; and a little of a Poet too' (*EY,* p. 626). See also *MY,* I, 105, for WW's letter to Wilkinson (30 November 1806) in which he mentioned and enclosed his verse tribute.

79   *Shenstone at his Leasowes*   William Shenstone (1714–63) landscaped his estate at the Leaseowes, near Halesowen, which was famous for its picturesque beauty.

Edmund Burke (1729–97). Burke's attack on the ideology and consequences of the French Revolution, *Reflections on the Revolution in France* (1790), made him WW's worthy opponent in the poet's radical years. Like Burke, however, WW came later to fear the threat of revolutionary chaos in Britain.

Elizabeth Smith (1776–1806), a self-taught linguist and translator, died at age 30 at Coniston and was buried at Hawkshead, where there is a tablet to her memory in the parish church. She and her father, Colonel George Smith, lived for a time at Patterdale before moving to Coniston in 1801. DW gives a brief account of her in a letter to Mary Laing in 1828 (*LY*, I, 571).

Lord & Lady Lonsdale   William Lowther, 2nd Earl of Lonsdale (1787–1872), and Lady Augusta Lonsdale (d. 1834). See WW's and the editor's notes to *Lines Written in the Album of the Countess of Lonsdale. Nov. 5, 1834*, notebook p. 61.

80 *note on a Sonnet on Long Meg & her Daughters*   In WW's published note to this sonnet, *The Monument Commonly Called Long Meg and Her Daughters, Near the River Eden* (in 'Itinerary Sonnets. Composed or Suggested During a Tour, in the Summer of 1833'), he describes this stone circle, which survives in the present day, and praises its 'singularity and dignity of appearance'; in this note, however, he does not mention Wilkinson or the destruction of the circle he uncovered. This sonnet on Long Meg and Her Daughters was composed between 6 January and July 1821, not long after WW's surprised discovery of the 'monument' just before Christmas, 1820 (*LY,* I, 4–5). Published first in his *Description of the Scenery of the Lakes in the North of England,* third edition, 1822, then among the 'Miscellaneous Sonnets' until 1836–7, when he included it in the Tour. The stone circle is six miles north-east of Penrith.

Incident Characteristic of a Favourite Dog   Probably composed between 14 August and 23 December 1806, along with its companion poem, *Tribute to the Memory of the Same Dog.*

Thomas Hutchinson   See Glossary.

Fidelity   Probably composed between 14 August and 10 November 1805, but by 2 March 1806. Gough fell to his death in the early spring of 1805 and the incident was widely discussed in the neighbourhood and in published accounts. WW also gave a brief account in his *Guide* (*Prose,* II, 167). Scott treated the same incident in his *Helvellyn.*

Patterdale   See Glossary.

<To return to the text use the Previous View Button

81 *Ode to Duty* Composed probably early in 1804, certainly by 6 March, with additions between late March 1804 and early December 1806.

Gray's Ode to Adversity EQ's pencil note: 'but is not the first stanza of Gray's from a chorus of Aeschylus?—And is not Horace's ode also modelled on the Greek?' WW's familiarity with the poetry of Thomas Gray (1716–71) and with the odes of Quintus Horatius Flaccus (65–8 BC) very probably dates from his school days at Hawkshead.

Who is the happy Warrior The first words of *Character of the Happy Warrior*. Probably composed between around December 1805 and early January 1806.

82 *Lord Nelson* Viscount Horatio Nelson (1758–1805), admiral in the Napoleonic War. His 'great crime' was his treachery to the patriots of Naples in 1799 when he hanged Francesco Caracciolo 'from the yard-arm of the *Minerva*' (Moorman, II, 63).

my brother John Captain John Wordsworth went down with his ship, the *Earl of Abergavenny*, off the Isle of Portland near Weymouth, 5 February 1805. Sara Hutchinson brought news of his death to the Wordsworths in Grasmere on 11 February 1805.

83 *The Force of Prayer; Or, The Founding of Bolton Priory. A Tradition* (in its printed form). In the 1815 and 1820 collected editions WW dated the poem '1808', the date of the completion of *The White Doe*, but *The Force of Prayer* was composed first. DW transcribed it on 18 October 1807 in her letter to Jane Marshall, adding that WW wrote it 'about a month ago' (*MY*, I, 168). See also WW's note to *The White Doe of Rylstone* on notebook p. 65.

M'. *Rogers* Samuel Rogers' *The Boy of Egremond* treats the same subject (for Samuel Rogers see Glossary).

D'. *Whitaker's History of Craven* Dr Thomas Dunham Whitaker (1759–1821), antiquarian and topographer, author of *The History and Antiquities of the Deanery of Craven, in the County of York* (see 2nd edn, London, 1812, p. 368). For a summary of discussion of the source of WW's poem see *Poems, 1807–1820*, p. 496.

<To return to the text use the Previous View Button

84 *Dion. (See Plutarch)*   Probably composed in 1816, perhaps after about 18 March. The initial stanza of 19 lines, beginning 'Fair is the Swan, whose majesty, prevailing', was first removed to the end-of-volume notes in 1836 and remained there despite WW's intention to place it directly below the poem. As he explained the 1836 note, the stanza was 'displaced on account of its detaining the reader too long from the subject, and as rather precluding, than preparing for, the due effect of the allusion to the genius of Plato'. For a discussion and presentation of sources see *Poems, 1807–1820* pp. 539–41. See also WW's note to *Evening Walk* on notebook p. 14, where he describes the swans on Windermere and their connection to the discarded stanza.

Canute   That is, *A Fact, and an Imagination; Or, Canute and Alfred, on the Sea-Shore.* Probably composed in 1816, perhaps in its original form as two sonnets, by about March 11. For dating and sources, including the appropriate passages in John Milton's *The History of Britain* (1670), see *Poems, 1807–1820,* pp. 538–9.

Ode to Lycoris. May, 1817   See the note to the second poem to Lycoris on notebook p. 87 (the note to *A little onward*, which precedes *Ode to Lycoris* in *PW* [1841], was apparently dictated out of sequence). Composed, as the full title indicates, in May 1817. Alan G. Hill, in 'Wordsworth, Boccaccio, and the Pagan Gods of Antiquity' (*Review of English Studies*, ns 45, no. 57 [1994], pp. 26–41), has suggested that the Fenwick note to *Ode to Lycoris* is linked to the passage on pagan myth in *The Excursion* (IV, I. 624ff.), and to Boccaccio's *Genealogia Deorum Gentilium* (ed. Vincenzo Romano; Bari, 1951; pp. 341–4). See Charles G. Osgood, *Boccaccio on Poetry, Being the Preface and the Fourteenth and Fifteenth Books of Boccaccio's Genealogia Deorum Gentilium in an English Version with Introductory Essay and Commentary* (Princeton, 1930), pp. 39, 44. WW seems to have known Boccaccio's work. In his article Hill argues that WW was paying tribute to the poetry of Keats and Shelley (without naming them) in the Fenwick note and points out that in his supporting letter regarding the copyright reform bill in 1842 WW had listed Shelley among writers of 'eminence' who had 'died early' (citing *LY,* IV, 293).

Ellen Irwin: Or, The Braes of Kirtle   See WW's note to this poem, notebook p. 51.

86 *A little onward* ('"A little onward lend thy guiding hand'). Composed in 1816, probably in the spring or summer, perhaps 2 May or after 2 August 1816. For dating see Ketcham's *Poems, 1807–1820*, p. 542. On WW's 'complaint' Ketcham remarks: 'The eye disease to which WW refers was probably trachoma. It affected chiefly his eyelids, but is capable of attacking the cornea and damaging vision.' Dora W began her transcription of the notes with this poem, though the title was entered by EQ. The poem actually precedes *Ode to Lycoris* in *PW* (1841). Dora then continued with the note to the second poem to Lycoris. WW may have omitted the note to 'A little onward' when the notes were first recorded and supplied one on Dora's request as she began her turn at transcription. EQ has written 'Dora' in pencil beside the title, perhaps to indicate her handwriting but more likely, as Ketcham suggests, to identify WW's 'Antigone' (in l. 11 of 'A little onward') as Dora (see *Poems, 1807–1820*, p. 542).

my eldest son   John Wordsworth (see Glossary).

87 *Ode to Lycoris*   That is, *To the Same* ('Enough of climbing toil!—Ambition treads'). Composed mainly in June 1817 and 1818, but portions of it date back to 1799–1800 (see *Poems, 1807–1820*, pp. 251–5, 546). See also the note to the first poem to Lycoris above. The three poems referred to as having been composed 'in front of Rydal Mount' are *Ode to Lycoris; September, 1819;* and *Upon the Same Occasion.*

booing about again   Canon Rawnsley recorded an account of WW's 'booing' given by a gardener's boy who had worked at Rydal Mount (*Wordsworthiana: A Selection of Papers Read to the Wordsworth Society*, ed. William Knight [London: Macmillan & Co., 1889], pp. 90–1).

James   WW's gardener.

88   *The Pillar of Trajan* (in its printed form). Although WW dated the poem '1823' in editions from 1836, it was composed in 1825–6, the year in which 'The Pillar of Trajan' was set as the subject for the Newdigate prize at Oxford (*PW*, III, 502). The poem was first published in 1827 among 'Poems of Sentiment and Reflection' and was moved to 'Memorials of a Tour in Italy, 1837', in 1845 and 1849–50.

Lines written…Ossian   Composed in 1824 and published in 1827 as *Written in a Blank Leaf of Macpherson's Ossian* among 'Poems of Sentiment and Reflection'. The poem was printed with 'Poems Composed or Suggested During a Tour, in the Summer of 1833', in 1845. In 1760, James Macpherson (1736–96) published *Fragments of Ancient Poetry* which he claimed to have translated from the Gaelic poems of Ossian. *Fingal* (1762) and *Temora* (1763) quickly followed and all were much admired. Their authenticity was challenged by Samuel Johnson and others, though their influence on WW's early verse was considerable. See the various discussions and annotations in *Poems, 1785–1797*, pp. 401–706.

"or strayed .. betrayed"   WW quotes from ll. 47–8 of *Stanzas Written in a Blank Leaf of Macpherson's Ossian*.

my Friend H.C.   David Hartley Coleridge (1796–1849), poet and periodical writer, eldest son of STC (see WW's poem *To H.C.*, and his note to *Stanzas Written In My Pocket-copy of Thomson's Castle of Indolence* on notebook p. 16). Raised at Greta Hall by Southey (see Glossary entry for Southey) after his parents separated, Hartley was disappointed in his career at Oxford, where he was unable to retain his fellowship at Oriel College through his indifference to authority and fondness for wine. Though unsuccessful in keeping discipline in his first teaching job, at Ambleside, he held temporary posts at Sedbergh with success. His poetry and prose were collected after his death by his brother Derwent and published in 1851.

The piece w^h. follows   That is, *Memory* ('A pen—to register; a key—'). WW assigned the poem to 1823 in editions from 1836.

To the Lady Fleming, On Seeing the Foundation Preparing for the Erection of Rydal Chapel, Westmoreland (in its printed form). See the Glossary for Le Fleming. A version of '80 lines' had been composed by 21 December 1822 when DW mentioned it to HCR as recent work (*LY*, I, 180); WW added to it in the new year and published it in 1827.

After thanking in prose   Having been sent a copy of the poem soon after it was written, Lady Fleming asked WW not to 'place her name' with his 'Verses upon Rydall Chapel'. The 'prose' WW may thus refer to his initial letter, which has not come to light, and his reply to her demurrer in late January 1823 in which he urged her to allow him to publish the poem as addressed to her (*LY*, I, 185–6 and note). Presumably she was won over, for the poem so appeared in print.

89   *the possibility of kneeling*   JC added 'with comfort' *PW* (1857P).

they will…be corrected   EQ's pencil note: '? have they not been corrected, in part at least—1843'.

The Gleaner. (Suggested by a Picture.)   Composed in March 1828 expressly for publication in *The Keepsake* (1829), an annual edited by Frederick Mansel Reynolds. For its *Keepsake* appearance WW left the title to Reynolds, who called it 'The Country Girl'. In editions from 1832 WW included it in his *Poetical Works* as *The Gleaner.* James Holmes (1777–1860) was a painter and water colourist of genre, portraits and miniatures. Some of his genre pictures were engraved for publications, such as *The Amulet, The Literary Souvenir* and *The Keepsake.* His untitled painting of a country girl holding a sheaf of corn was engraved by Charles Heath (1785–1848) for *The Keepsake* as an illustration for WW's poem. WW wrote to M and Dora W in early March 1828, 'I have written one little piece, 34 lines, on the Picture of a beautiful Peasant Girl bearing a Sheaf of Corn. The Person I had in my mind lives near the Blue Bell, Tillington—a sweet Creature, we saw her when going to Hereford' (*LY,* I, 590).

Gold and Silver Fishes in a Vase   This poem and its sequel, *Liberty,* were composed in November 1829.

note at the end of the next Poem   WW's published note to *Liberty* is given below.

Liberty. (Sequel to the Above.) [Addressed to a Friend: The Gold and Silver Fishes having been Removed to a Pool in the Pleasure-Ground of Rydal Mount.] (in its printed form). Maria Jane Jewsbury (see Glossary), the friend of the sub-title and the donor of the fish, is memorialised in WW's published note to this poem:

> There is now, alas! no possibility of the anticipation [that 'Life's book' for her 'may lie unclosed, till age/Shall with a thankful tear bedrop its latest page'], with which the above Epistle concludes, being realised: nor were the verses ever seen by the Individual for whom they were intended She accompanied her husband, the Revd Wm. Fletcher, to India, and

died of cholera, at the age of thirty-two or thirty-three years, on her way from Shalapore to Bombay, deeply lamented by all who knew her.

Her enthusiasm was ardent, her piety steadfast; and her great talents would have enabled her to be eminently useful in the difficult path of life to which she had been called. The opinion she entertained of her own performances, given to the world under her maiden name, Jewsbury, was modest and humble, and, indeed, far below their merits: as is often the case with those who are making trial of their powers, with a hope to discover what they are best fitted for. In one quality, viz., quickness in the motions of her mind, she had, within the range of the Author's acquaintance, no equal.

90 *Incident at Bruges*   The tour took place in July 1828; the poem was composed between 29 November and 19 December 1828. See Hayden, *Europe II*, pp. 22–3. First published in 1835, the poem was included in 'Poems of Sentiment and Reflection' in collected editions from 1836 to 1843; in 1845 it was moved to 'Memorials of a Tour of the Continent, 1820'. See *Sonn*, p. 355.

This Lawn ('This Lawn, a carpet all alive'). Composed in 1829 and published in 1835. The 'kitchen garden' is the one at Rydal Mount (*Memoirs*).

A richer display of colour   This sight impressed DW as well; she recalled two years after the tour: 'We passed by one patch of potatoes that a florist might have been proud of; no carnation-bed ever looked more gay than this square plot of ground on the waste common. The flowers were in very large bunches, and of an extra-ordinary size, and of every conceivable shade of colouring from snow-white to deep purple. It was pleasing in that place, where perhaps was never yet a flower cultivated by man for his own pleasure, to see these blossoms grow more gladly than elsewhere, making a summer garden near the mountain dwellings' (*Recollections*).

91 *Savant*   A learned person, especially one professionally engaged in scientific research.

Humanity   The original, single poem was composed as a sequel to *Gold and Silver Fishes* in December 1829 and divided, on MW's advice, shortly afterwards; all three poems were published in 1835.

92 *Thought on the Seasons* From 1845, *Thoughts on the Seasons*. WW enclosed the poem in a letter to his nephew, John Wordsworth at Cambridge, 7 December 1832, as having been composed 'in the Summer house [at Rydal Mount] at the end of the Terrace, whe[n the] wind was blowing high the other Evening' (*LY,* II, 573; the MS. is torn).

To I—— W—— The full title is *To ——. Upon the Birth of Her First-born Child, March, 1833*, and it is addressed to Isabella (Curwen) Wordsworth, wife of WW's son, John. Her parents were Isabella and John Curwen of Workington Hall and Belle Isle on Windermere (see WW's note to *An Evening Walk* above.) The daughter whose birth is celebrated was WW's grandchild, Jane Stanley (1833–1912). At the end of the note, in pencil, EQ asked 'Jane?'

Moresby See Glossary.

The Warning, A Sequel to the Foregoing The poem is a sequel to *To ——. Upon the Birth of Her First-born Child, March,* 1833 and was composed in March 1833 or shortly after, when the 'fever' over the Reform Bill was high, though the Bill itself was passed in June 1832.

The Labourer's Noon-day Hymn Thomas Ken (1637–1711) was Bishop of Bath and Wells; his 'Hymns for Morning, Evening, and Midnight' appeared in his *Manual for Winchester Scholars,* the edition of 1695. WW's poem was probably composed in 1834, before mid-July, and was published in January 1835.

93   *old 100th Psalm*   The popular psalm melody, so named from its use for the familiar 100th psalm in Day's psalter (1563): 'All people that on earth do dwell, Sing to the Lord with cheerful voice.'

    Ode composed on May Morning…To May   The two titles are joined with a bracket *Ode, Composed on May Morning* and *To May* were probably begun as one poem around May 1826, added to as either one or two poems around 15 November 1830, and completed as two poems before mid-July 1834. In editions from 1836 WW said that the *Ode* was composed in 1826 and *To May* between 1826 and 1834; both were published in 1835. He wrote to William Rowan Hamilton on 26 November 1830, speaking of one or both of these poems, that 'as I passed through the tame and manufacture-disfigured country of Lancashire I was reminded by the faded leaves of Spring, and threw off a few stanzas of an ode to May' (*LY*, II, 353). Exactly when WW toured the 'mountains' with Dora is not easily established. In May 1826 he was preoccupied with the Westmorland election and with planning the new house he proposed to build if forced to leave Rydal Mount, though it is possible he and Dora took her pony-chaise to the Newlands valley west of Derwentwater at that time. A later May excursion seems less feasible: late in May of 1827 he took Dora to Harrogate for her health, traveling by 'pony-chaise' (DW to John Wordsworth, 6 June 1827 [*LY*, I, 530]), but they would not have passed through the 'vale of Newlands' on their way to Yorkshire. The earliest manuscript of *To May* is dated 1829 but WW was in Cambridge and Whitlock in May of that year and in Cambridge and London in May of 1828. A mountain tour was proposed in May of 1830 but Dora became ill and it was cancelled.

    How delicate &c   From *To May*, ll. 81–8.

    M^r. & M^{rs}. Carr   Perhaps Dr and Mrs. Thomas Carr of Grasmere.

    the Stanza that follows   'Keep, lovely May,/…This modest charm of not too much' (ll. 93–5).

    Lines Suggested by a Portrait from the Pencil of F. Stone (in its printed form).

Composed in September 1834 and first published in 1835. Frank Stone, R.A. (1800–59), originally from Manchester, went to London in 1831 where his water colours and oil portraits gained a wide popularity in the forties and fifties.

Subject resumed   That is, *The Foregoing Subject Resumed.* Bracketed with the previous title and composed at the same time; also first published in 1835.

J.Q.   Jemima Quillinan, elder daughter of Edward Quillinan and his first wife, also called Jemima.

94 *Anecdote…told…by Mr. Wilkie*   David Wilkie, painter (see the note to *The Thorn*, notebook p. 28, above); the anecdote of the Monk (ll. 95–117) turns on the Monk's belief, when conscious of his own and his fellows' mutability, that the 'solemn Company' of Titian's painting of the Last Supper, which hangs on the refectory wall, 'are in truth the Substance, we the Shadows'. On 23 February 1837, two years after the publication of WW's poem, HCR noted in his diary having breakfasted with Samuel Rogers, who on that occasion read him a note to his *Italy* (a collection of verse and prose tales) that contained the same anecdote as WW's poem but with himself as auditor. HCR recorded that WW 'amplified' Roger's note in his poem, assenting to Roger's view that his own 'prose is better than the poem' (*HCR Books*, II, 512). However, WW's poem was composed and published before Rogers' version of the anecdote was written. According to the Rydal Mount Visitor's Book, Wilkie visited WW in September 1834. DC MS. 130, the earliest manuscript of WW's poem that contains the anecdote, bears MW's notation of Wilkie's having related the story at Rydal Mount a few days before WW introduced it into his poem and Sara Hutchinson's note of the date and place '1834, Rydal'. Rogers' note to a passage in *A Funeral* in which he describes Raphael's 'Transfiguration' was first published in an edition of *Italy* four years later, and a year after his conversation with HCR (Moxon: London, 1838; p. 263). WW's claim to priority seems just, though Rogers and Wilkie, who had certainly met by the early 1840s and probably earlier, may have shared the story or had a common source.

Miss Hutchinson   Sara Hutchinson (see Glossary).

Bird of Paradise   That is, *Upon Seeing a Coloured Drawing of the Bird of Paradise in an Album*; composed in part on 23 June 1835 at Rydal Mount, the day Sara Hutchinson died.

On wings that fear…no tempest from his breath   Ll. 37–8 of the poem.

The reader will find two poems   The second poem is *Suggested by a Picture of the Bird of Paradise* ('The gentlest Poet, with free thoughts endowed'), published in 1842. See the note below on notebook p. 137.

95   *Yarrow Revisited*   The full title of the sequence is *Yarrow Revisited, and Other Poems, Composed* (*Two Excepted*) *During a Tour in Scotland, and on the English Border, in the Autumn of* 1831. Notes in several hands draw attention to the fact that a second note to this sequence of poems is inserted out of order below and should precede this one in sequence. For a history of its composition see *Sonn*, pp. 481–8.

  great & amiable man   Someone, perhaps CWjr, has inserted 'Sir Walter Scott' in brackets above 'man' in the first sentence (*Memoirs* reads thus). In the second note WW gives the details of the tour, which took place from 13 September to 17 October 1831 (see notebook pp. 100–3). Most of the poems published in this series in 1835 were composed during the tour as the half-title claims, but several (more than the 'two excepted' of the 1836 half-title), were composed two years later, in the period September 1833 to December 1834. See also Hayden, *Scotland*, pp. 49–65.

A Place of Burial in the South of Scotland (in its printed form) ('Part fenced by man, part by a rugged steep'). Composed between 22 and 28 September 1831.

Mickle   William Julius Mickle (1755–88), poet and translator. His *Sir Martyn, a Poem in the Manner of Spenser* (London, 1777) was first published under the title of *The Concubine*. The following stanza from *Sir Martyn* is reminiscent of WW's early sonnet, 'With Ships the sea was sprinkled far and nigh':

> Bright through the fleeting clouds the sunny ray
>   Shifts o'er the fields, now gilds the woody dale,
> The flockes now whiten, now the ocean bay
>   Beneath the Radiance glistens clear and pale;
> And white from farre appeares the frequent sail,
>   By Traffick spread. Moord where the land divides,
> The British red-cross waving in the gale,
>   Hulky and black, a gallant warre ship rides,
> And over the greene wave with lordly port presides.
>
>   (canto II, stanza xviii)

96 *On the Sight of a Manse in the South of Scotland* ('Say, ye far-travelled clouds, far-seeing hills'). Composed between 23 September and 4 December 1833.

observation applies to the [   ] of their kirk   A pencil note was added to the gap: 'p. 101—M.S. Miss F.—' Dora evidently could not read IF's handwriting here and left an appropriate space for the word, but it was never filled. A word like 'conduct' seems probable. *Memoirs* repeats 'religion' from the first part of the sentence, though it seems unlikely that DQ would fail to recognize 'religion' a second time in the same passage.

97 *Roslin Chapel Composed in Roslin Chapel, During a Storm* ('The wind is now thy organist;—a clank'). Composed between 29 September and 7 October 1831. The chapel is in Scotland, between Peebles and Edinburgh.

if it has…as a prisoner   *Memoirs* emends to 'and I shall be satisfied if it has at all done justice…', but the elliptical expression makes sense in context: 'If it [the poem] has…done justice to the feeling…[it should be clear that] I was as a prisoner'.

The Trosachs ('There's not a nook within this solemn Pass'). Composed between 22 and 28 September 1831. In his note WW refers to the tour of 1803; see DW's *Recollections*.

melancholy errand   For additional comment on Scott's trip to Italy to improve his failing health see the second note to *Yarrow Revisited* on notebook pp. 100–3, especially p. 103.

Loch Etive   That is, *Composed in the Glen of Loch Etive* ('"This Land of Rainbows (spanning glens whose walls'). Composed between 29 September and 7 October 1831. WW quotes 1. 13.

98 *Sonnet…day* *Composed After Reading a Newspaper of the Day* ('"People! your chains are severing link by link'). Composed between 3 July and 31 December 1834 and published in 1835, with a note explaining its accidental omission from the sequence 'Yarrow Revisited'; it was transferred to 'Sonnets Dedicated to Liberty and Order' in 1845.

Eagles. Composed at Dunollie Castle in the Bay of Oban (in its printed form) ('Dishonoured Rock and Ruin! that, by law'). Composed between 4 and 7 October 1831. WW quotes ll. 4–5. WW sent a copy of the poem to W. R. Hamilton in a letter of 27 October 1831, providing this commentary: 'At Dunally Castle, a ruin seated at the tip of one of the horns of the bay of Oban, I saw the other day one of these noble creatures cooped up among the ruins, and was incited to give vent to my feelings as you shall now see—' (*LY,* II, 441). See also WW's note to *On the Power of Sound,* notebook p. 33.

Mr. Marshall…son John Marshall, of Halsteads on Ullswater and his son James. For Marshall see WW's and the editor's notes to *On the Power of Sound,* notebook p. 33.

Octo^br EQ's pencil note beside Dora's abbreviation: '?October?'; September is the correct month.

travelled through that country See Hayden, *Wales and Ireland,* pp. 53–75.

Sound of Mull In the Sound of Mull ('Tradition, be thou mute! Oblivion, throw') was composed between 29 September and 7 October 1831.

Bonaw Now spelled Bonawe, situated between Loch Awe and Loch Etive in northwestern Scotland.

Glencoe Also spelled Glen Coe; located in Appin, south of Fort William, Scotland.

Major Campbell Colonel and Mrs Campbell, former tenants of Allan Bank, moved to the Isle of Mull in 1823. They had visited the Wordsworths earlier in the summer of 1831 (*LY,* I, 168 and n.; *LY,* II, 428 and n.).

the 11th sonnet   That is, *In the Sound of Mull.*

Bothwell Castle. (Passed Unseen, on Account of Stormy Weather.) (in its printed form) ('Immured in Bothwell's towers, at times the Brave'). Composed between 23 September 1833 and 12 August 1834. WW first visited the Castle in 1803, as recorded by DW in her *Recollections* for 22 August 1803. The Castle lies eight-and-a-half miles southeast of Glasgow.

99 *The Avon. (A Feeder of the Annan.)* (in its printed form) ('Avon—a precious, an immortal name!'). Composed between 15 and 27 October 1831. See WW's remark in his note to *Between Namur & Liege* (notebook p. 68). WW quotes the second line.

Inglewood Forest   Suggested by a View from an Eminence in Inglewood Forest ('The forest huge of ancient Caledon') was composed between 23 October 1833 and 4 December 1834. The forest now lies north of Penrith on the River Eden but used to surround the town as well.

in the next Sonnet   Hart's-horn Tree, Near Penrith ('Here stood an Oak, that long had borne affixed'). In his printed note WW identified and quoted his source in the account by J. Nicolson and R. Burn, *History and Antiquities of the Counties of Westmorland and Cumberland* (2 vols; London, 1777). Composed between 3 July and 12 August 1834.

Countess' Pillar ('While the poor gather round till the end of time').   Composed between 3 July and 12 August 1834. The pillar is on the road from Penrith to Appleby, about two miles from Appleby. A few miles further, in Brougham near Whinfell Forest, is where Julian Bower (or Julian's Bower) is found. The latter is associated in folklore with Roger de Clifford, the eighth Lord Clifford (1299–?1327), who, though unmarried, 'had some illegitimate children by one Julian of the Bower; for whom he built a little house hard by Whinfell, which still bears her name' (Nicolson and Burn, *The History…of Westmorland and Cumberland*, I, 278), but the site is probably more ancient, perhaps of Roman origin (A. H. Smith, *The Place-Names of Westmorland* [Cambridge, 1977] II, 130). In his printed note to *The Hart's-horn Tree* in the same series WW listed Julian's Bower, Brougham and Penrith Castles, Penrith Beacon, Arthur's Round Table, Maybrough, the Giant's Cave, and Long Meg and her daughters among the many other traditions of the forest, all associated with sites in or within a few miles of Penrith. DQ's 'Juliana' in the text may reflect a local form of the legend in which 'Julian' was transformed into 'Juliana'.

The Highland Broach ('If to Tradition faith be due'). Composed between 10 and 17 October. In 1845 WW inserted the poem between the two sonnets *Highland Hut* and *The Brownie*.

100 *Yarrow Revisited* Two interpolated notes, one by each copyist, point to the earlier note on this sequence.

Abbotsford On the Tweed, southeast of Edinburgh. WW and Dora W left Rydal Mount for Abbotsford on 13 September, reaching their destination on 19 September, and returning home on 17 October 1831.

M^r. *Lockhart* John Gibson Lockhart (1794–1854), biographer of Sir Walter Scott (*Memoirs of the Life of Sir Walter Scott, Bart.,* 10 vols., Boston and New York, 1901) and of Robert Burns, and contributor to *Blackwood's Magazine.* He married Scott's eldest daughter, Sophia, in 1820 and settled on Scott's estate for five years. He accepted the editorship of the *Quarterly Review* and moved to London in 1825. See his account of Scott's 1825 visit to WW and WW's 1831 visit to Scott in *Life of Scott,* VIII, 38–9, and X, 77–80.

M^r. *Liddell* Henry Liddell (later Earl of Ravensworth) and his brother Tom first visited Scott at Abbotsford on 2 April 1831 (Lockhart's *Life of Scott* [see previous note] X, 42).

M^r. *Allan* Sir William Allan (1782–1850) painted pictures of historical subjects and scenes of Russian life. Sir Walter Scott helped him find a British audience for his paintings, and Allan in turn painted scenes from the history of Scotland, some suggested by Scott, and several portraits of Scott and his family. He was a renowned and lively raconteur and mimic.

M^r. *Laidlaw* William Laidlaw (1780–1845) was a friend of James Hogg, to whom he was distantly related. Both Laidlaw and Hogg assisted Scott with materials for his *Minstrelsy of the Scottish Border* in 1801, and Laidlaw became Scott's steward at Abbotsford in 1817, where he continued to serve as a valuable servant, counselor and friend. When Scott faced financial ruin and could no longer employ him, Laidlaw stayed on as his amanuensis.

<To return to the text use the Previous View Button

101 *during that ev^g* (evening). DQ added in pencil: 'This is a mistake dear Father it was the following Ev^g when the Liddells were gone and only ourselves and M^r. Allan present—'.

102 *the two preceding Poems* That is, *Yarrow Unvisited* and *Yarrow Visited*.
Eildon Hills These hills stretch south and east from Abbotsford.
A trouble &c 'A trouble, not of clouds, or weeping rain', l. 1 of *On the Departure of Sir Walter Scott from Abbotsford, for Naples*.

103 *"Musings at Aquapendente"* See the note to *Musings Near Aquapendente*, notebook p. 141. DQ has begun the next sentence on a new line, after a gap, indicating a new paragraph.
"Yarrow Revisited" & the "Sonnet" That is, the poem *Yarrow Revisited*, composed between 7 and 21 October 1831 and *On the Departure of Sir Walter Scott for Naples*, composed between 22 and 28 September 1831.

104 *The Russian Fugitive* WW told George Huntley Gordon on 29 January 1829 that he 'lately wrote a Tale (350) verses the Scene of which is laid in Russia, though it is not even tinged with Russian imagery' (*LY*, II, 26). His head note to the poem identifies the source: 'Peter Henry Bruce, having given in his entertaining Memoirs the substance of the following Tale, affirms, that, besides the concurring reports of others, he had the story from the Lady's own mouth.' See *Memoirs of Peter Henry Bruce, Esq., a Military Officer, in the Services of Prussia, Russia and Great Britain. Containing An Account of his Travels in Germany, Russia, Tartary, Turkey, and the West Indies, &c., And Also Several very interesting private Anecdotes of the Czar, Peter I. of Russia* (London, 1782) pp. 91–4.

Memorials of a Tour in Scotland in 1833 In 1835 titled *Sonnets. Composed or Suggested During a Tour in Scotland, in the Summer of 1833*. In 1841 the word *Sonnets* was altered to *Itinerary Sonnets* and in 1845 became more broadly *Poems*. WW, his son John, and HCR left Rydal Mount for John Wordsworth's home at Brigham on 12 July and, shortly after, for the Isle of Man, exploring Robert Burns country on their return; WW and his son returned on the 25th, leaving HCR at Inverary to continue his tour of Scotland. In an account of their travels to his family at Rydal from Greenock on 17 July 1833 (*LY*, II, 629–32), WW mentions several of the sights featured in the poems inspired by this tour. But the ten final sonnets included in this 'Tour' were written in response to a second journey in early August, with MW, to Carlisle and back along the River Eden, 'by Corby and Nunnery, both charming places', with visits of several days at Lowther Castle and Halsteads on Ullswater (WW to John Kenyon, 23 September 1833; *LY*, II, 641). By the date of his letter to John Kenyon, WW had composed twenty-two sonnets based on the 'two Excursions'. On December 4, 1833, he wrote to Alexander Dyce that his 'fortnight's tour in the Isle of Man, Staffa, Iona, etc.', had 'produced between 30 and 40 sonnets' (*LY*, II, 665). See also *Sonn*, pp. 561–72.

< Return to Fenwick Notes | Continue through Editor's Notes>>

Nun's Well, Brigham ('The cattle crowding round this beverage clear'). Composed between 23 September and 5 October 1833. For Brigham see WW's note to *To a Friend* on notebook p. 104.

The Reform Mania The demand for religious toleration brought the repeal of the Test Act in 1828 and the passing of the Catholic Emancipation Act in April 1829. But there was much political and social turmoil attendant upon the introduction, debate, final passing and implementation of the Reform Bill from 1831 through 1833. As the Bill was passed in June of 1832, WW refers here to enthusiastic efforts to extend the reforms the bill brought in, efforts which, WW feared, would trample upon ancient customs and values.

To a Friend. (On the Banks of the Derwent.) (in its printed form) ('Pastor and Patriot!—at whose bidding rise'). Composed between 23 September and 4 December 1833. On 12 July WW stayed with his son John at Brigham, a village two miles west of Cockermouth near the river Derwent (see the Glossary). WW quotes the first three words of the sonnet. In mid-January 1834 WW sent the poem to Lady Beaumont, explaining, 'Were you ever told that my Son is building a parsonage house on a small Living, to which he was lately presented by the Earl of Lonsdale? The situation is beautiful, commanding the windings of the Derwent both above and below the site of the House; the mountain Skiddaw terminating the view one way, at a distance of 6 miles-and the ruins of Cockermouth Castle appearing nearly in the centre of the same view. In consequence of some discouraging thoughts—expressed by my Son when he had entered upon this undertaking, I addressed to him the following Sonnet, which you may perhaps read with some interest at the present crisis' (*LY,* II, 689). On 20 February 1834 Dora W sent the sonnet to EQ, adding that it was 'addressed to John whose spirit failed him somewhat on finding he should be obliged to lay out so much money on his parsonage which might be taken from him any day by the reformed parliament—but it will do for any poor parson who is building for his parish' (WL MS.).

< Return to Fenwick Notes | Continue through Editor's Notes>>

Mary Queen of Scots. (*Landing at the Mouth of the Derwent, Workington.*) (in its printed form) ('Dear to the Loves, and to the Graces vowed'). WW quotes the 1835 text of the sonnet in his note, rather than the revised 1841 text:

> Bright as a Star (that, from a sombre cloud
> Of pine-tree foliage poised in air, forth darts,
> When a soft summer gale at evening parts
> The gloom that did its loveliness enshroud).
> (ll.5–8)

The poem was composed between 23 September and October 29 1833. In his note published with the poem WW cites the historian Robertson, who described her landing and her respectful reception at Workington.

105 *Green Bank*   A hamlet three miles west of Kendal.

The Poem of S^t. Bees   That is, *Stanzas suggested in a Steam-Boat off St. Bees' Heads, on the Coast of Cumberland.* WW adopted this arrangement in editions of 1845 and 1849–50. The poem was composed between March 1833 and August 1834, probably nearer the later date. See *Sonn,* pp. 566–8, for dating.

Isle of Man ('A Youth too certain of his power to wade'). Probably composed between 12 August and 23 September 1833. John, not William Jr (Willy; 1810–83), accompanied his father on the tour. The incident could have occurred when Willy and DW visited his aunt, Joanna Hutchinson, on the Isle of Man in June or July 1828 (MW to EQ, 26 July 1828; *MWL,* p. 126).

Sonnet by a Retired Mariner   That is, *By a Retired Mariner. (A Friend of the Author.)* ('From early youth I ploughed the restless sea'). Composed between 26 August and 25 September 1833. Henry Hutchinson (1769–1839) lived in retirement with his sister Joanna on the Isle of Man from 1830 until his death. Henry told the story of his 'retirement' from his life at sea in a lively poem, *The Retrospect of a Retired Mariner in Nine Cantos, written by Himself* (Stockton, 1836). In 1800 he quit his ship without collecting his pay in protest against a captain who controlled his crew by flogging them. He is the subject of the immediately preceding sonnet, *Isle of Man* ('Did pangs of grief for lenient time too keen').

Bala Sala   At *Bala-Sala, Isle of Man. (Supposed to be Written by a Friend of the Author.)* ('Broken in fortune, but in mind entire'). Composed between 23 and 29 September 1833.

A thankful refugee   The notebook reads 'refuge' but WW quotes 1. 7 of the sonnet, 'A grey-haired, pensive, thankful Refugee'. Thomas Cookson of Kendal, after some financial losses, retired with his wife to the Isle of Man. He died a few months after WW's visit; in a letter to Robert Jones on 29 October 1833 WW enclosed the sonnet written earlier as a 'memorial' of the 'situation and character' of his now 'lamented friend Mr Cookson' (*LY*, II, 651). In his long letter to his family, 17 July 1833, WW described the place thus: 'Bala Sala is a little wood-embosomed Village by the side of a stream upon which stands the ruined walls of an old Abbey, a pretty sequestered place—thronged with Blackbirds and thrushes of extraordinary size and power of song the upper part of the old Tower is overgrown with a yellow Lychen which has the appearance of a gleam of perpetual evening sunshine' (*LY*, II, 630).

Tynwald Hill ('Once on the top of Tynwald's formal mound'). Composed between 12 August and 23 September 1833. The hill is on the Isle of Man.

My Companions were Both *Memoirs* and *PW* (1857) emend to 'One of my companions was' but WW includes the children mentioned in the next sentence. WW wrote to his family at Rydal, 17 July 1833: 'Halted again at the Tynewald, St John's, and here eleven cottage children gathered about us, and nearly on the top of Tynewald (dearest D. knows what it is) sate an old Gullion with a telescope in his hand through which he peeped occasionally having the advantage of seeing things double, for as he frankly owned he had got a drop too much' (*LY*, II, 631).

106 *Ailsa Cragg*   That is, *In the Frith of Clyde, Ailsa Crag. (July 17.)* ('Since risen from ocean, ocean to defy'). Composed between 12 August and 23 September 1833. The title was altered in 1845 to *In the Frith of Clyde, Ailsa Crag. (During an Eclipse of the Sun, July 17)*. 'Ailsa Craig the peaks of Arran and the whole land and sea views most beautiful in sunshine with curling vapours, and an eclipse of the sun between 5 and 6 this morning into the bargain' (WW to his family at Rydal, 17 July 1833; *LY*, II, 630).

struck with   Beside 'with' EQ entered 'by? , in pencil.

Natural Philosophy   That is, the natural sciences.

107 *Arran*   The first word in *On the Frith of Clyde. (In a Steam-Boat.)* ('Arran! a single-crested Teneriffe'). Composed between 12 August and 23 September 1833.

Firth   A northern spelling of 'Frith' (OED).

Staffa   That is, the second *Cave of Staffa* ('Thanks for the lessons of this Spot-fit school'); composed between 12 August and 23 September 1833. WW refers to the published note in which he explains how he returned to the Cave after the disappointing visit described in the first sonnet in the sequence of three ('We saw, but surely, in the motley crowd').

There said a Stripling ('"There!" said a Stripling, pointing with meet pride'). Composed between 12 August and 23 September 1833. The young man points to Mosgiel Farm in Ayreshire where Robert Burns 'ploughed up the Daisy' (1. 4). In a letter to Allan Cunningham on 14 June 1834 WW described this tour and added that he passed 'for the first time...through Burns's Country, both in Renfrewshire and Ayrshire.... It gave me much pleasure to see Kilmarnock, Mauchlin, Mossgeil farm, the Air [that is, the river Ayr], which we crossed where he winds his way most romantickly thro' rocks and woods—and to have a sight of Irwin and Lugar, which naebody sung till he named them in immortal verse' (*LY*, II, 722).

one of his poetical effusions   EQ queried a blank after 'poetical' left by DQ, then filled it with the word 'effusions'.

108 *"Auld hermit Ayr staw thro' his woods"* From Burns' poem, *The Vision*. stanza xiv; 'staw' means 'strays'. See Glossary entry for Burns.

The River Eden, Cumberland (in its printed form) ('Eden! till now thy beauty had I viewed'). In transcribing ll. 6–7 after the title of the poem DQ showed the line-break with a quotation mark. In all published versions l. 7 reads 'no rivals among'. The sonnet was composed between 12 August and 23 September 1833. WW made the excursion with MW along the River Eden in August 1833. In his note printed with the poem WW admitted to the fanciful derivation of the river's name in the poem and offered another based on the Cumberland word 'dean', for valley. The likeliest etymology, however, traces the word to an Indo-European base with the general sense of 'water'.

Monument of Mrs. Howard, (by Nollekens,) In Wetheral Church, Near Corby, on the Banks of the Eden. (in its printed form) ('Stretched on the dying Mother's lap, lies dead'). Observed during the same excursion, August 1833; composed between 23 September 1833 and 12 August 1834. Joseph Nollekens, R.A. (1737–1823) was a sculptor whose carved portraits were in popular demand in England from 1770 when he first came to notice until 1819 when he suffered a stroke. His studio, which WW visited, was in London. Besides the monument and busts mentioned here, his sitters included George III, many members of the royal court, Charles James Fox, Oliver Goldsmith, Dr Johnson, and the Duke of Wellington. He was of grotesque appearance, with a short stature and large head, and of mercurial temperament. In June 1834, summarising his previous summer's excursion to the Isle of Man and through 'Burns's Country' (in a letter to Allan Cunningham who published a book on Robert Burns and later one on British painters, sculptors and architects), WW complained about the 'sorry piece of sculpture' which commemorates Burns in the Dumfries churchyard and contrasts it with the bust of Mrs Howard of Corby which he saw on the August excursion of 1833 in the church at Wetheral, five miles east of Carlisle. He then added, 'I first saw it many years ago in the

< Return to Fenwick Notes | Continue through Editor's Notes>>

Studio of Nollekens, in London. How a man of such a physiognomy and figure could execute a work with so much feeling and grace, I am at a loss to conceive!' (*LY,* II, 722–3). This earlier sighting may have occurred during a visit to London in April-May 1806 (*Chronology: MY,* p. 316).

Dutchess of Devonshire   'Dutchess' is a variant spelling of 'Duchess' in the early nineteenth century. Georgiana Spenser (1757–1806), married the fifth duke of Devonshire, William Cavendish, in 1774, and quickly became an undisputed leader of English society in fashion and style as well as in her generosity to persons of talent. She was also a notorious gambler and ran heavily into debt. She was a friend of Fox, campaigning for him in the Westminster election of 1784, and she entertained Samuel Johnson, both of whom were subjects of Nollekens' craft (her poetic tribute to Fox's 'Virtue', 'Zeal' and 'Wisdom' as a political leader and visionary, was prompted by the bust of Fox: *Lines by Georgiana, Duchess of Devonshire on the Bust of Charles Fox, at Wooburn*). Her poem, *Passage of the Mountain of St. Gothard* (1799), occasioned Coleridge's *Ode to Georgiana, Duchess of Devonshire*, 'O lady, nursed in pomp and pleasure/Whence learned you that heroic measure?' (ll. 5–6). She was among those eminent persons Coleridge singled out to receive a copy of the 1800 *Lyrical Ballads* accompanied by a complimentary letter dictated by Coleridge and probably signed by WW. Though hers is not among those busts listed as Nollekens' 'principal performances' by his biographer, those of her husband and two of his brothers are listed (John Thomas Smith, *Nollekens and his Times* [2 vols., London, 1828] vol. II, p. 72). The casting of masks, sometimes 'death–masks', as in Pitt's case, was much in fashion.

Mr. Pitt   William Pitt (1759–1806) was member of parliament for Cambridge University from 1784. He became prime minister at 25, and led the government until his death at 47.

109 *in this instance*   EQ added in pencil, '(of Mr. Pitt?)'

Nunnery ('The floods are roused, and will not soon be weary'). Observed during the excursion in August 1833; composed between 12 August and 23 September 1833. 'Nunnery Dell' (l. 13), is on the stream called Croglin Water as it meets the River Eden, nine miles north of Penrith.

my maternal grand Father   Christopher Crackanthorpe (Cookson), 1745–99.

Lowther ('Lowther! in thy majestic Pile are seen'). Composed between 12 August and 18 September 1833. WW quotes l. 2. Lowther Castle, the seat of Lord Lonsdale, is about five miles south of Penrith. On their return from Carlisle in August 1833 WW and MW spent several days there as guests of the Lonsdales. 'Reform Mania' was much on his mind.

110 *The Somnambulist.*   Though he dated the poem 1833 in editions from 1836, he wrote to Rogers in July 1830 that the poem 'is one of several Pieces, written at a heat, which I should have much pleasure in submitting to your judgement', but in the same paragraph claimed he had 'not written a verse these twelve months past' (*LY,* II, 309). The excursion to Ullswater with Beaumont and Rogers took place in the summer of 1826, when some of the poem may have been composed. Manuscripts of the poem and other evidence suggest a version was completed between 28 November and 18 December 1828.

M^r. Glover   John Glover (1767–1849), landscape-painter, much admired for his technique with water-colours. In 1824 he had helped to found the Society of British Artists. He owned a house and land at Ullswater where he intended to retire, but in 1831 he immigrated to Australia

Lyulph's Tower   Near Aira Force, above the western shore of Ullswater.

Lines composed…Cumberland   That is, *On a High Part of the Coast of Cumberland. Easter Sunday, April 7. The Author's Sixty-third Birthday.* The poem was placed second among the *Evening Voluntaries* in 1841. Composed on 7 April 1833.

my Son then Rector of that place   EQ deleted 'that place' in pencil and queried 'which' (Whitehaven or Moresby). John was Rector of Moresby, where WW stayed at the end of March through 7 April 1833. The '8th & 9th' poems in the sequence as it stood in 1841 were composed much earlier: 'The sun has long been set' in 1802 and *Composed Upon an Evening of Extraordinary Splendour and Beauty* in 1817 (see below). Manuscript evidence confirms WW's statement about the origin of the 1833 'voluntaries', though he worked on them during the next year before publishing them in *Yarrow Revisited* in 1835. However, poems XII and XIII (*PW* [1841]), both called *To the Moon,* were composed after the publication of *Yarrow Revisited* and were added to the set in the *Poetical Works* of 1836–7.

111 *Not in the lucid intervals of life* The poem was probably composed between April 1833 and January 1835. The lines on Byron (ll. 7–15) are lacking in the earliest manuscript version. Byron died in 1824; his letters were published in 1830 and 1832.
The leaves that rustled 'The leaves that rustled on this oak-crowned hill'; probably composed between April 1833 and January 1835.
the voice of the Raven in flight EQ added in pencil (from *Excursion,* IV, 1175–6, 1178):

                Often, at the hour
When issue forth the first pale stars, is heard,—
One voice, the solitary raven etc etc

112 *The sun has long been set* Though dated 1804 in editions from 1836, the poem was composed on 8 June 1802 and published in 1807, but dropped until reinstated in 1835.
Had this effulgence That is, *Composed Upon an Evening of Extraordinary Splendour and Beauty.* Though dated 1818 in editions from 1836, the poem was composed in the summer of 1817 and published in 1820. The sonnet was moved from 'Poems of Imagination' to this series in 1836–7.
Westminster Bridge... "While beams of orient light" &c The four sonnets referred to are *Composed upon Westminster Bridge, Sept. 3, 1803* ('Earth has not anything to show more fair', 1802), *Composed on May-Morning, 1838* ('If with old love of you, dear Hills! I share'), ''Tis He whose yester evening's high disdain' (1838), and 'While beams of orient light shoot wide and high' (1843).
The Old Cumberland Beggar (in its printed form). Begun as *Description of a Beggar* between mid-1796 and mid-1797 at Racedown, the poem was expanded in early 1798, between 25 January and 5 March, at Alfoxden, further revised before 10 October 1800 and published in the second volume of *Lyrical Ballads* later that year. For dating and discussion of the poem's growth see *Chronology: EY,* pp. 342–3; for sources see *LB, 1797–1800,* pp. 393–5. The phrase 'in my 23^d year' is probably the copyist's mistake for 'in my 25th year'; WW and DW went to live at Racedown in September 1795.

113 *The Farmer of Tilsbury Vale* Probably composed between 30 March 1797 and 18 July 1800, but perhaps chiefly in Goslar between 6 October 1799 and early 1800. The poem was first published in the *Morning Post* for 21 July 1800, though WW misdated it as '1803' in editions from 1836. The presence of this poem along with the closely linked poems, *The Reverie of Poor Susan* and *A Character*, in an early state of what appear to be the Goslar sections of two manuscripts (DC MSS. 15 and 16), and WW's dating of *Poor Susan* as '1799' (the date he assigned to most Goslar poems), together suggest that these poems were probably first written in Germany. For dating and sources see *LB, 1797–1800,* pp. 456–7, and *Chronology: EY,* pp. 324–6. WW's source was Thomas Poole.

114 *Southey...Davy* See Glossary entries.
 The Two Thieves; Or, The Last Stage of Avarice (in its printed form). Probably composed in 1800, by 29 July. Daniel Mackreth and his grandson, also Daniel, were residents of Hawkshead; the 'daughter at home' (l. 42) was based on Elizabeth Mackreth (see *Wordsworth's Hawkshead,* pp. 191–3). WW revisited Hawkshead in November 1799.
 Animal Tranquillity and Decay. A Sketch (in its 1841 printed form). When first published in *Lyrical Ballads* in 1798 the poem was called *Old Man Travelling*. For its origin in composition for *Old Cumberland Beggar* see *LB, 1797–1800,* pp. 356, 453, and associated transcriptions. Both poems were composed between the latter half of 1796 and early June 1797. For dating see *Chronology: EY,* pp. 342–3.

115 *Chiabrera* Gabriello Chiabrera (1552–1638); WW calls him 'gentle Chiabrera' in *Musings Near Aquapendente* (1. 236).

his Friend in w^h. periodical That is, *The Friend* (1808–9).

By a blessed husband ('By a blest Husband guided, Mary came'). First published in 1835. The churchyard where Mary Carleton is buried is in Bromsgrove, Worcestershire.

Elegiac Stanzas, Suggested by a Picture of Peele Castle, in a Storm, Painted by Sir George Beaumont (in its printed form). Composed probably between around 20 May and 27 June 1806. An engraving based on the painting of Piel Castle appeared as frontispiece to the second volume of WW's *Poems,* 1815. The 'two pictures' referred to are both oil paintings. The larger is now in the Leicester Museum and Art Gallery (*Sir George Beaumont of Coleorton, Leicestershire, a catalogue of works by Sir George Beaumont at Leicester Museum and Art Gallery* [Nottingham, ?1973], frontispiece, and p. 56); the smaller, the one WW preferred and probably the one given to Price, is illustrated in Felicity Owen and David Blayney Brown, *Collector of Genius, A Life of Sir George Beaumont* [New Haven, 1988] p. 64, and is now in private hands. It has not been possible to determine which painting inspired the poem. The ruins of Piel Castle lie on Piel Island off the southern tip of Furness. WW was its 'neighbour once' (1. 1) for a month in August 1794 when he and DW stayed with their cousin Mrs. Barker in Rampside.

Sir George's death…Sir Uvedale Price Beaumont died in 1827. Sir Uvedale (1747–1829) and Lady Price, both avid landscape gardeners, were friends of the Beaumonts. Through Beaumont WW first met the Prices at their Foxley estate in Herefordshire in 1810 and often stayed there with his family, especially after MW's brother Thomas Hutchinson took Brinsop Court Farm, near Hereford, in 1825.

Invocation to the Earth. February, 1816 (in its printed form). The date in the title is probably the date of composition. The poem was called simply *Elegiac Verses* when WW published it in *Thanksgiving Ode, January 18, 1816. With Other Short Pieces, Chiefly Referring to Recent Public*

Events (1816).

Elegiac Stanzas. (Addressed to Sir G.H.B. Upon the Death of His Sister-in-Law.) 1824 (in its printed form). Lady Beaumont's sister, Frances Fermor, died in December 1824. The poem was probably composed in January 1825 and a copy sent to the Beaumonts by early February (*LY,* I, 323). Pope's poem celebrates Arabella Fermor.

Editor's Notes 335

116 *these…these*   EQ queried the two occurrences of 'these' in this sentence.

second stanzas inscribed upon her Cenotaph   That is, *Cenotaph* ('By vain affections unenthralled'; see WW's note on *Cenotaph,* notebook p. 153). Composed, and engraved, in January or February 1825 but not published until 1842. MW sent a copy of the poem to Lady Beaumont 25 February 1825 (*LY,* I, 324). The word 'second' probably means they were composed 'second', after *Elegiac Stanzas;* the manuscript of the two-stanza poem is annotated below the last line, 'Words inscribed upon her Tomb at her own request', but this surely refers to Christ's words from the New Testament, 'I am the way, the truth, and the life', which close the epitaph and to which it refers.

Elegiac Musings in the Grounds of Coleorton Hall, the Seat of the Late Sir G. H. Beaumont, Bart. (in its printed form). The poem was composed on 17 November 1830.

alluded to elsewhere   See WW's note to *1830* ('Chatsworth! thy stately mansion, and the pride'), notebook p. 49 above. DQ added to the entry for *Elegiac Musings,* in ink in the main text and running over from page 116 to 117: '(My Father was on my poney who he rode all the way from Rydal to Cambridge that I might have the comfort & pleasure of a horse at Cambridge—the storm of wind & rain on this day was so violent that the coach in which my Mother & I travelled the same road was all but blown over & had the coachman drawn up as he attempted to do at one of his halting places we must have been upset. My Father & his poney were several times entirely blown out of the road. D.Q.)'

117 *Once I could hail* 'Once I could hail (howe'er serene the sky)' was preceded by an epigraph from the *Ballad of Sir Patrick Spence,* in Percy's *Reliques,* 'Late, late yestreen I saw the new moone/Wi' the auld moone in hir arme'. WW quotes the third and and part of the fourth lines of his poem. It was composed around but by 25 July 1826 when he sent a 'Copy of [these] Verses, part of which were written this very morning in the delightful wood that borders our garden on the side towards Rydal Water', to John Kenyon, and was published in 1827 among 'Epitaphs and Elegaic Pieces'; it was placed among 'Miscellaneous Poems' in the editions of 1845 and 1849–50. In the same letter to Kenyon WW added, 'You may be inclined to think from these verses that my tone of mind at present is somewhat melancholy—it is not by any means particularly so except from the shade that has been cast over it recently by poor Southey's afflictions.—I laugh full as much as ever, and of course talk more nonsense; for, be assured that after a certain Period of life old sense slips faster away from one than new can be collected to supply the loss. This is true with all men, and especially true when the eyes fail for the purposes of reading and writing as mine have done' (*LY,* I, 474–5).

To a good Man of most dear Memory Given the title *Written after the Death of Charles Lamb* in the 1845 edition. Lamb died December 27, 1834. WW composed the first version as an epitaph in November 1835 and expanded it to its present length in December; it was privately printed in January 1836 and included in WW's *Poetical Works* in 1836–7; it also appeared in Talfourd's edition of *Letters of Charles Lamb* in 1837.

tragic circumstances That is, the circumstances surrounding Mary Lamb's recurrent bouts of madness until her own death in 1847 (born 1764); during one of these, in 1796, she attacked her mother with a knife, fatally wounding her. Mary recovered, and, except for a short period in an asylum at Islington in 1796–7, she was cared for by her brother Charles until his death.

M[r]. Sergeant Talfourd Sir Thomas Noon Talfourd (1795–1854) was a jurist, author, dramatist, Member of Parliament and ardent advocate of international copyright. As executor of the estate of his friend, Charles Lamb, he published several volumes of 'memoirs' of Lamb, including the edition of letters to which WW was a reluctant contributor of his Lamb's letters to him.

118 *Christ's Hospital* The Blue Coat School, founded by Edward VI in 1552 as a home for orphans and other poor children, had developed by the end of the eighteenth-century into one of the most famous schools in England. Its Grammar school, in London, where Coleridge and Lamb were both students and boarders, trained boys in Greek and Latin in preparation for the Universities.

impediment in his speech A severe stutter.

When first descending 'When first, descending from the moorlands' (in its printed form), the first line of *Extempore Effusion Upon the Death of James Hogg*. Hogg died 21 November 1835. WW composed the first version of the poem soon after and on November 30th sent a copy to John Hernaman, editor of the *Newcastle Journal*, where it appeared 5 December 1835 (*LY*, III, 127 and note). In the note published with the poem WW listed the five writers whom he memorialised in the poem to Hogg: Walter Scott, STC, Charles Lamb, George Crabbe, and Felicia Hemans (see Glossary entries for all six).

119 *my first meeting with him* That is, with Scott; see Lockhart's *Life of Scott*, II, 109–14.

already mentioned in these notes See the note to *Yarrow Visited* on notebook p. 54, above. However, this note chiefly concerns 'Dr. Anderson', their companion for part of the journey.

M^r. Hoare's Mr and Mrs Samuel Hoare of Hampstead, he a banker and a Quaker and she an active churchwoman, often entertained and housed the Wordsworths during their visits to London.

121 *Is it not...from such a quarter* DQ added in pencil, with reference to Crabbe: 'Daddy dear I don't like this—think how many reasons there were to *depress* his Muse—to say nothing of his duties as a Priest & probably he found poetry interfered with them—he did not *require* such praise to make him write, but it just put it into his head to try again & gave him the courage to do so—'.

Hemans See Glossary.

122 *a poem entitled* The blank left by DQ was never filled in. EQ's pencil note: 'Do you mean "A Sonnet["] entitled "Sabbath Sonnet" composed by Mrs Hemans April 26th 1835, a few days before her death? "How many blessed groups this hour are wending".' This poem was published, with head note as quoted by EQ ('composed...death' followed by 'And Dedicated to her Brother'), in *The Works of Mrs Hemans; with a Memoir of Her Life, by Her Sister* (7 vols., Edinburgh and London, 1839) VII, 288. The sonnet EQ names (he misquotes 'wending' for 'bending') follows a sequence of seven sonnets titled 'Thoughts During Sickness', also composed shortly before she died on 16 May 1835. It is unlikely that any of these poems were published before her death, though the *Sabbath Sonnet* appeared in *Memorials of Mrs. Hemans*, by Henry F. Chorley (2 vols; London, 1836) II, 341. De Selincourt has suggested that the sonnet WW means is *Flowers and Music in a Room of Sickness;* in a letter to Mrs Hemans in September 1834 he praised the poem among those in her *Scenes and Hymns of Life* which she had recently sent him: 'The feelings are sweetly touched throughout this poem, and the imagery very beautiful' (*PW,* IV, 461; *LY,* II, 736).

123 *The Ode* This simple form of the title was used on its first publication in 1807; in *Poems,* 1815, WW changed it to *Ode. Intimations of Immortality from Recollections of Early Childhood.* Probably some or all of stanzas 1–4 composed 27 March 1802. Further composition, possibly including some or, less probably, all of stanzas 5–8, on 17 June 1802. Most of the last seven stanzas probably composed, and the poem completed, early 1804, by 6 March.

as I have said elsewhere EQ's pencil note: 'but this first st. of We are Seven is Coleridges Jem & all.—' WW quotes the first four lines of *We Are Seven* (see WW's note to this poem, notebook p. 6).

from [ ] of animal vivacity DQ left a blank; EQ penciled in 'the source'. *Memoirs* and *PW* (1857) supply 'feelings' but a word like 'excess' or 'surplus' or 'abundance' seems required.

124 *s^d*   DQ's highly compact rendition of 'should'.

126 *Prelude to the Last Vol.*   Before turning to *The Excursion* in volume six of *PW* (1841), WW here picked up *Poems, Chiefly of Early and Late Years,* the volume 'last' published. By this time WW and his publisher were treating the 1842 volume as a seventh volume in the 1841 set.

These verses   'In desultory walk through orchard grounds.' WW spent 'only one day' at Brigham at the end of November 1841, before going on to Lowther Castle for a week (*LY,* IV, 269; for Brigham see WW's and editor's notes to *To a Friend, On the Banks of the Derwent,* notebook p. 105). In the edition of 1842 WW dated the poem 26 March 1842. In editions of 1845, and its stereotypes, and 1849–50 he placed it among the 'Miscellaneous Poems' and titled it *Prelude Prefixed to the Volume entitled 'Poems Chiefly of Early and Late Years'.*

The Anti-Corn Law league   This League, formed in 1839 of local associations opposed to legislation that kept the price of grain artificially high and supported by wealthy manufacturers who wanted free trade in general, launched a propaganda campaign to discredit rich landlords and greedy farmers. Pressure was intense and sustained, linking up with more revolutionary movements at times (like Chartism in 1842), eventually resulting in the repeal of the protectionist Corn Laws in 1846.

Guilt and Sorrow; Or, Incidents upon Salisbury Plain (in its printed form). Composed summer 1793 to May 1794 as 'Salisbury Plain'; revised and enlarged in 1795 as 'Adventures on Salisbury Plain'; greatly altered again in 1841–2 and published in 1842 as *Guilt and Sorrow.* For dating, sources and the texts of all three versions see Stephen Gill's *The Salisbury Plain Poems of William Wordsworth* (Ithaca: Cornell University Press, 1975). *The Female Vagrant* (see WW's note to this poem on notebook p. 15) was excerpted from the second version and published in *Lyrical Ballads* in 1798. In the note published with *Guilt and Sorrow* in 1842 WW added these comments:

< Return to Fenwick Notes | Continue through Editor's Notes>>

During the latter part of the summer of 1793, having passed a month in the Isle of Wight, in view of the fleet which was then preparing for sea off Portsmouth at the commencement of the war, I left the place with melancholy forebodings. The American war was still fresh in memory. The struggle which was beginning, and which many thought would be brought to a speedy close by the irresistible arms of Great Britain being added to those of the allies, I was assured in my own mind would be of long continuance, and productive of distress and misery beyond all possible calculation. This conviction was pressed upon me by having been a witness, during a long residence in revolutionary France, of the spirit which prevailed in that country. After leaving the Isle of Wight, I spent two days in wandering on foot over Salisbury Plain, which, though cultivation was then widely spread through parts of it, had upon the whole a still more impressive appearance than it now retains.

The monuments and traces of antiquity, scattered in abundance over that region, led me unavoidably to compare what we know or guess of those remote times with certain aspects of modern society, and with calamities, principally those consequent upon war, to which, more than other classes of men, the poor are subject. In those reflections, joined with some particular facts that had come to my knowledge, the following stanzas originated.

In conclusion, to obviate some distraction in the minds of those who are well acquainted with Salisbury Plain, it may be proper to say, that of the features described as belonging to it, one or two are taken from other desolate parts of England.

127 *my ramble over many parts of Salisbury Plain* The projected tour to the West Country in the summer of 1793 was abandoned when WW and Calvert parted company after the latter's spirited horse destroyed their conveyance, a 'whiskey,' as they crossed Salisbury Plain. Calvert departed on horseback while Wordsworth set out on foot to visit Robert Jones in North Wales. After reaching Bristol, he crossed the Severn estuary to Chepstow and traveled along the Wye valley, through Tintern and Goodrich and on to Hay and Builth before proceeding north to reach the Vale of Clwyd, where Jones lived. For WW's other references to this journey see notebook pp. 3 and 34.

the verses "Five years have passed &c—" The *Tintern Abbey* poem. See notebook p. 30.

128 *The Forsaken* ('The peace which others seek they find'). Probably composed between around 1800 and around early January 1807, perhaps especially around 1800, spring 1802, or between late March 1804 and around early January 1807, but probably revised extensively around June 1842 when copy for *Poems, Chiefly of Early and Late Years* was in preparation. *The Affliction of Margaret* first appeared in *Poems, in Two Volumes* (1807).

"*Lyre! tho' such power do in thy magic live*" In this ode-like poem, moved to 'Poems of the Imagination' in the editions of 1845 and 1849–50, the poet asks the source of inspiration, the lyre, to 'recall' the 'not unwilling Maid,…The lovely Fugitive', whose presence gives rise to deep contemplation and gentle pleasure in the natural scene—the 'Rydal torrent' of the note. For the location see the Glossary entry for Rydal Hall. 'Lyre' was first published in 1842 and was probably composed around that time. But the image of eddying foam balls in a turbulent current of water appeared first in the sonnet, *Composed on the Banks of a Rocky Stream* ('Dogmatic Teachers, of the snow-white fur'), composed possibly in 1820 (before May, when WW left Rydal Mount for his tour of the continent) and published in the four-volume *Miscellaneous Poems* in July of the same year (*MWL*, p. 65 and note). WW used the image again in *On the Banks of a Rocky Stream* ('Behold an emblem of our human mind'), an inscription published for the first time in the edition of 1849–50.

the Rhone at Geneva & the Aare DQ or EQ miscorrected 'Rhone' to 'Rhine' and EQ, misreading 'Aare' as 'Ruce', entered 'Reuss?' on the facing page. Their confusion over the names of these rivers was compounded in *Memoirs* and *PW* (1857) which read 'Rhine' for 'Rhone' and 'Rheuss' (or 'Reuss') for 'Aare'. DQ has written 'Aare' not 'Reuss', though at Lucerne the river is called the Reuss, an affluent of the Aare; Geneva is situated on the Rhone at its western outlet from Lake Leman.

129 *Address to the Scholars of the Village School of* —— (in its printed form). The three elegies which make up the *Address* are 'I come, ye little noisy Crew', *Dirge* ('Mourn, Shepherd, near thy old grey stone'), and *By the Side of the Grave Some Years After* ('Long time his pulse hath ceased to beat'). When preparing poems for publication in *Poems, Chiefly of Early and Late Years* in 1841 and 1842 WW selected and arranged passages from the so-called 'Mathew elegies' which he had composed in Goslar in the winter of 1798–9. *Address* was moved to 'Epitaphs and Elegiac Pieces' in 1845. For a discussion of the development of these early materials into what became *Address to the Scholars* see Appendix VI of *LB, 1797–1800*.

Lines on the Expected Invasion. 1803 (in its printed form). Probably composed between 14 October 1803 and early January 1804, possibly by 31 October 1803; probably revised extensively around June 1842 when copy for *Poems, Chiefly of Early and Late Years* was in preparation. The poem was transferred to 'Poems Dedicated to National Independence and Liberty' in 1845.

At the Grave of Burns. 1803 (in its printed form) ('I shiver, Spirit fierce and bold'). The poem was probably composed 18 August 1803 or shortly after; completed in its early form between late March 1804 and early 1807. WW added to it when he was working on *Epitaph* for Charles Lamb and *Extempore Effusion on the Death of James Hogg* in December 1835, and revised it again for publication in *Poems, Chiefly of Early and Late Years,* around June 1842. The 'second piece' is *Thoughts Suggested the Day Following on the Banks of Nith, Near the Poet's Residence* ('Too frail to keep the lofty vow'). Part of *Thoughts,* including what is now the penultimate stanza, was composed at the time he revised *At the Grave of Burns,* in December 1835, when he said he had written it as 'a record of what passed in my mind when I was in sight of his residence on the banks of the Nith, at the same period'. He then added, 'So that I have to the best of my power done my duty to that great, but like many of his Brother Bards, unhappy man' (*LY,* III, 135). But as he explained to Henry Reed, he added a new conclusion in mid-December 1839 (*LY,* III, 750–1). In 1842 WW appended a note to *Thoughts* in which he quotes excerpts from the section for 'August 18th, 1803' in DW's journal of their 1803 tour (see *Journals,* I, 198–202). And to a manuscript of the poem prepared for publication in 1842 (DC MS. 151/4) he added this note which, in the end, he did not publish:

> With the Poems of Burns I became acquainted almost immediately upon their first appearance in the volume printed at Kilmarnock in 1796 [*a mistake for* 1786]. Their effect upon my mind has been sufficiently expressed above. Familiarity with the dialect of the border Counties of Cumb^d and West^d made it easy for me not only to understand but to feel them. It was not so with his Contemporary or rather his Predecessor Cowper,—as appears from one of his letters. This is to be regretted; for the simplicity the truth and the vigour of Burns would have strongly recommended him, notwithstanding occasional coarseness, to the sympathies of Cowper, and ensured the approval of his judgement. It gives me pleasure, venial I trust, to acknowledge at this late day, my obligations to these two great authors, both then and at a later period, when my taste and natural tendencies were under an injurious influence from the dazzling manner of Darwin, and the extravagance of the earlier Dramas of Schiller. May these few words serve as a warning to youthful Poets who are in danger of being carried away by the inundation of foreign Literature, from which our own is at present suffering so much, both in style and points of far greater moment. True it is that in the poems of Burns, as now collected, are too many reprehensible passages; but their immorality is rather the ebulition of natural temperament and a humour of levity, than a studied thing: whereas in these foreign Writers, and in some of our own Country not long deceased, the evil, whether of voluptuousness, impiety, or licentiousness, is courted upon system, and therefore is greater, and less pardonable .

WW probably contrasts Burns with Byron (described as 'an eminent deceased Poet of our own age' in an earlier version of this note), among others. Before revision he acknowledged Percy's *Reliques,* with Burns' poems, as having 'powerfully counteracted the mischievous influence' of Erasmus Darwin and Johann Christoph Friedrich von Schiller.

Elegiac Verses in Memory of My Brother. John Wordsworth, Commander of the E. I. Company's Ship The Earl of Abergavenny, in which He Perished by Calamitous Shipwreck. Feb. 6th, 1805. Composed near the Mountain track that leads from Grasmere through Grisdale Hawes, where it descends towards Patterdale. 1805 (its full title in print). The earliest version of this elegy was probably composed 8 June 1805. WW revised it in late 1841 but certainly by 26 March 1842 before publishing it in *Poems, Chiefly of Early and Late Years.* WW misquotes the opening line of the third stanza, 'Here did we stop; and here looked round'. John Wordsworth's last sojourn with DW and WW at Town End was from the end of January to the end of September 1800, when he left to prepare for his captaincy of the East Indiaman, *The Earl of Abergavenny.* See also WW's notes to 'When; to the attractions of the busy world', notebook p. 36, and *Character of the Happy Warrior,* notebook pp. 81–2.

Grisedale Tarn WW wrote of this spot, 'A sublime combination of mountain forms appears in front while ascending the bed of this valley [from Patterdale], and the impression increases till the path leads almost immediately under the projecting masses of Helvellyn' where the Tarn lies (*Guide, Prose,* II, 167). DW was present at the parting, too (*EY,* p. 598).

At Applethwaite, Near Keswick. 1804 (in its printed form) ('Beaumont! it was thy wish that I should rear'). Probably composed between 14 October 1803 and 6 March 1804; revised around but before June 1842. Beaumont's gift, made before he had met WW, was one of several unsuccessful attempts to bring the two poets and their families together (see McCracken, p. 68).

his domestic situation In 1804 STC had become estranged from his wife, Sara, a circumstance brought about partly by his love for Sara Hutchinson, MW's sister, and he had left the Lake District, more or less permanently, early in the year. But among other difficulties in the way of such a reunion were STC's addiction to opium and recurrent illnesses and the friction between Sara Coleridge and the Wordsworths.

down the side of Skiddaw   'Skiddaw's lofty height' rises to the north of Derwentwater and the town of Keswick. In *Select Views* (an early version of his *Guide*) WW wrote of Applethwaite, 'This is a hamlet of six or seven houses, hidden in a small recess at the foot of Skiddaw, and adorned by a little Brook, which, having descended from a great height in a silver line down the steep blue side of the Mountain, trickles past the doors of the Cottages' (*Prose*, II, 274). By 1814–15 WW had enlarged the property called Applethwaite by purchase and by accepting an allotment of enclosed common land.

130 *the mountains of Borrowdale & Newlands* South and west of Derwentwater.

not many years ago DQ's pencil note: 'Many years ago Sir—for it was given when she was a frail feeble Monthling—'; that is, within a year of his receiving the property from Beaumont.

Epistle to Sir George Howland Beaumont, Bart. From the South-west Coast of Cumberland.—1811 (in its printed form) ('Far from our home by Grasmere's quiet Lake'). Begun in late summer 1811, perhaps about 30 August, when WW and his family were vacationing at Bootle, and perhaps mainly completed by 6 September. Thirty-two lines-the opening 'paragraph'—were excerpted and published in 1827 as *Departure from the Vale of Grasmere. August, 1803* (see notebook p. 51). The remaining lines were taken up again in early 1842 and, after much revision, published in *Poems, Chiefly of Early and Late Years* later that year. For a discussion of the evolution of the poem, its sources and context, and a presentation of the early and late versions, see *Poems, 1807–1820*, pp. 78–95.

The head of Yewdale Yewdale is 'a branch of the Vale of Coniston' (*Select Views, Prose*, II, 262). James Marshall was the third son of John Marshall of Halsteads.

at Hackett See WW's note to the sonnet, 'The fairest brightest hues of ether fade', on notebook p. 37, and his note to *Excursion* on the 'Church' on notebook p. 165.

It was in front…as described in the Poem EQ noted in pencil, '?revise this sentence[;] here is some[thing *inserted*] awkward?' JC added, in *PW* (1857), 'This matron and her husband were then residing at Hackett. The house and its inmates are referred to in the fifth book of the "Excursion," in the passage beginning—

"You behold,
High on the breast of yon dark mountain, dark
With stony barrenness, a shining speck."' (*Excursion*, V, 670–3).

131 *M^r. Rowlandson*   Edward Rowlandson, who died in 1811 at age 77.

133 *Loughrigg Tarn*   The tarn is on the western flank of Loughrigg Fell (see Glossary); see also ll. 166–202 of the poem. WW described the Tarn, 'the most beautiful example' of the 'class of miniature lakes', in *Guide, Prose*, II, 186.
Old Brathay   On the south side of the river in the hamlet of Clappersgate, about a mile and a half from the tarn. EQ's pencil note queries the distance to "?the tarn?". Beaumont's antagonist was Sir Michael Le Fleming of Rydal Hall.

134 *Mr. Barber, Mr. Greenwood & myself*   See the discussion of 'Church and Churchyard' in the note to *The Excursion*, notebook p. 168.
"Green is the Church yard"   From *Excursion*, VI, ll. 605–10.

135 *A Night Thought* ('Lo! where the Moon along the sky'). Mrs Luff moved into Fox Ghyll in Rydal in the summer of 1825. The poem was first published as *Stanzas* in 1837 in *The Tribute: a Collection of Miscellaneous Unpublished Poems, by Various Authors*, (London), edited by Spenser Compton, 2nd Marquess of Northampton. WW included the poem under its present title in the volume of 1842.
The good woman...nor Cavaliers   EQ wrote 'gossip' in pencil beside this sentence.

136 *Farewell Lines* ('"High bliss is only for a higher state"'). The Lambs moved to Chase Side, Enfield, Hertfordshire, in September 1827, Charles having retired from India House in 1825. At the time of his retirement DW had hoped that 'this release from the necessity of remaining in, or near London would ever bring us the happiness of seeing them here—and, above all, of having them stationary near us for a few months—a whole winter—or a whole summer! This I fear can never be' (DW to HCR, 12 April 1825; *LY,* I, 337). WW visited the Lambs at Enfield Chase on 10 August 1828 (*LY,* I, 626) and probably composed the poem soon after.

Love Lies Bleeding (in its printed form) ('You call it, "Love lies bleeding,"—so you may'). Composed as a sonnet on or shortly before 20 February 1834. Both this poem, in an expanded form, and its 'companion' poem, were sent to EQ by Dora W in June 1835. The two poems were published for the first time in 1842.

137 *theories of political economy*   Adam Smith's *Wealth of Nations,* published in 1776, had built so strong a reputation in England's economic and political community by 1829 that WW was led to condemn the 'schools' it spawned in *Humanity* as 'heartless schools/that to an Idol, falsely called "the Wealth/Of Nations", sacrifice a People's health,/Body and mind and soul' (see also his attack on 'false philosophy' in the *Prelude,* XII, 75–81 [1805], and XIII, 70–9 [1838–9]).

Oh for the reign of justice   Cf. WW's poem *The Warning* for a similar expression of pessimism, there counterbalanced by the birth of a child.

Address to the Clouds ('Army of Clouds! ye winged Host in troops'). In editions of 1845 and 1849–50 titled *To the Clouds.* Composed in 1808 with other verse for *The Recluse,* it was revised and published as a separate poem in 1842. See Kishel, *Tuft of Primroses,* pp. 13–17.

the foot road   Along Loughrigg Terrace from Rydal Water to Red Bank, above Grasmere Lake.

Suggested by a Picture of the Bird of Paradise (in its printed form) ('The gentlest Poet, with free thoughts endowed'). See WW's note to *Upon Seeing a Coloured Drawing of the Bird of Paradise in an Album* on notebook p. 94, above.

138 *objects*   *PW* (1857) has 'objects'; in the notebook the 'u' of 'subjects' has been altered to an 'o' but the 's' was not deleted.

Maternal Grief ('Departed Child! I could forget thee once'). See *Excursion*, III, 636ff. The Wordsworths' two children died in 1812, Catherine on 4 June and Thomas on 1 Dec. The lines were probably composed as part of work on *Excursion* in early January 1813 (see *Poems, 1807–1820*, pp. 522–3; *MY*, II, 64; and *Exc*, pp. 451–3). It was published as an independent poem in 1842.

Memorials of a Tour in Italy. 1837 (in its printed form). For additional details see Hayden, *Europe II*, pp. 64–95; *HCR Books*, II, 515–33; and HCR's recollections of the tour after WW's death in *Memoirs, II*, 328–32. WW left London for Paris on 19 March and returned on 7 August 1837. He was accompanied by HCR, to whom the sequence of poems is dedicated, and by Edward Moxon as far as Paris. Only *Cuckoo at Laverna*, or part of it, was composed during the journey. All the sonnets in the sequence were composed between late November 1838 and 8 February 1842. For a history of composition of the series see *Sonn*, pp. 731–739.

M^r. *Moxon*   Edward Moxon (1801–58), poet, and publisher of Charles Lamb and WW (after 1835). He travelled to Paris in 1837 with WW and HCR after publishing a six-volume edition of WW's *Poetical Works* in 1836–7. Moxon was married to Lamb's adopted daughter, Isola.

139 *Pont de Degard*   Pont-du-Gard, east of Avignon on a tributary of the Rhone.

Petrarch   Francesco Petrarca (1304–74), Italian poet and humanist; Fontaine de Vaucluse was the site of his beloved retreat. WW refers below to his long series of love poems in praise of Laura.

seasons   EQ queried 'seasons', but WW seems to mean the rocks are impressive in all seasons.

140 *Aquapendente*   That is, *Musings Near Aquapendente. April, 1837* ('Ye Apennines! with all your fertile vales'). Composed in March 1841; perhaps completed in April. WW quotes ll. 60–1, 'Had his sunk eye …/That spake…minstrels'.

the lines "Places forsaken now"…he never forgot them   Ll. 50–2 of *Musings* were written in 1800 for the poem *Michael* though never included in the latter poem's published form.

"Old Helvellyn's brow…rejoicing'."   *Musings* (ll. 62–4). Humphrey Davy and Scott climbed Helvellyn with WW in August 1805. For Helvellyn see Glossary.

Striding Edge   A narrow spine of the ridge which falls away sharply on both sides of the track. Scott was lame from a childhood illness.

"When I am there….another Yarrow"   Ll. 55–6 of WW's *Yarrow Unvisited* (which read 'For when we're there …'). Scott quoted the lines on two occasions: in 1842 WW printed a note with the poem that reads, 'These words were quoted to me from "Yarrow Unvisited," by Sir Walter Scott when I visited him at Abbotsford, a day or two before his departure for Italy: and the affecting condition in which he was when he looked upon Rome from the Janicular Mount, was reported to me by a lady who had the honour of conducting him thither'. See WW's second note to *Yarrow Revisited* on notebook p. 99.

141 *A few short steps*   'A few short steps (painful they were)', *Musings*, l. 83.
   Miss Mackenzie of Seaforth   Frances Mackenzie (d. 1840), younger daughter of Francis Mackenzie, Lord Seaforth. HCR met her in Rome in 1830, where she was renowned as 'a woman of taste and sense, and the associate and friend of artists'; in 1837 he introduced her to WW, who became 'her constant visitor, and she was proud to be considered as his chief friend among the inhabitants of Rome' (*HCR Books,* I, 389; *LY,* III, 395 and note).
   the grave of Tasso   Torquato Tasso (1544–95), Italian poet, author of *Gerusalemme Liberata,* a copy of which in Hooke's translation WW, with three other students, presented to the Hawkshead School library upon their leaving school. WW read Tasso in Italian at Cambridge under his tutor Isola, and retained his interest in Italian renascence poetry throughout his life, translating poems or fragments from the works of Metastasio, Ariosto and Michelangelo.
   "*Over waves rough & deep*"   From *Musings*, l. 121.

142 *Shelley & Byron*   A likely source for WW's information was Leigh Hunt, whom he had met at Haydon's studio. Hunt included accounts of Byron's sailing in *Lord Byron and Some of His Contemporaries* in 1828.
   "*How lovely didst thou appear, Savona*"   An elision of *Musings*, ll. 205–7.

143 *'This flowering broom's dear neighbourhood"* Musings, l. 369.
The note at the close...Faber That is, the final note to *Musings Near Aquapendente*. Frederick Faber (1814–63) was a poet and hymn writer, a Tractarian (with Newman and Pusey) and, after converting to Catholicism in 1845, an Oratorian priest. Introduced to WW by IF in 1835, in 1837 Faber brought a 'reading party' from Oxford to Ambleside where he formed a lasting friendship with WW. He returned in 1841 and lived in Ambleside for nearly a year in 1842–3; when he published his account of a tour of the continent taken late in that year he dedicated the work to WW, 'in affectionate remembrance of much personal kindness, and many thoughtful conversations on the rites, prerogatives, and doctrines of The Holy Church' (*Sights and Thoughts in Foreign Churches and among Foreign Peoples,* London, 1842; see also some notes of CWjr on Faber and IF, WL 1/12/4, and *HCR Books,* II, 605 [December 1841] 628 [January 1843], and *Diary,* II, 237–8 [January 1843]). After Faber's conversion to the Catholic Church in 1845, WW expressed 'regret' to HCR that 'he had ever uttered a word favourable to Puseyism' and spoke 'strongly against Faber'; but, to HCR's displeasure, he did not alter the text of Faber's note in subsequent editions of his poems (*HCR Books,* II, 655, 19 December 1845). In the note composed by Faber WW praises the Oxford movement as one that 'takes, for its first principle, a devout deference to the voice of Christian antiquity' and draws 'cheerful auguries for the English Church from this movement, as likely to restore among us a tone of piety more earnest and real than that produced by the mere formalities of the understanding'. Faber's *Life of St. Bega* was published in *Lives of the English Saints* (edited by J. H. Newman) in 1844; in his *Life* of the saint for whom St. Bees' Heads was named, Faber included WW's *Stanzas suggested in a Steam-boat off Saint Bees' Heads* with a note praising the 'remarkable way' in which WW's poems anticipated 'the revival of catholic doctrines among us' and, in the St. Bees poem, his 'affectionate reverence for the catholic past, the humble consciousness of a loss sustained by ourselves, the readiness to put a good construction on what he cannot wholly receive'. See also WW's note on the *Ecclesiastical Sonnets,* notebook p. 70.

144 *The Pine of Monte Mario at Rome* (in its printed form) ('I saw far off the dark top of a Pine'). Composed between late November 1838 and 8 February 1842, perhaps in January 1839. WW printed the following note with the poem in 1842: 'Within a couple of hours of my arrival at Rome, I saw from Monte Pincio, the Pine tree as described in the sonnet; and, while expressing admiration at the beauty of its appearance, I was told by an acquaintance of my fellow-traveller, who happened to join us at the moment, that a price had been paid for it by the late Sir G. Beaumont, upon condition that the proprietor should not act upon his known intention of cutting it down'. In a letter to MW and Dora W, 6 May 1837, WW reported that he stood upon the Monte Mario 'under the pine redeemed by Sir. G. Beaumont …I touched the bark of the magnificent tree and could almost have kissed it out of love for his memory'.

Is this ye Gods At Rome ('Is this, ye Gods, the Capitolian Hill'). Composed in January 1839.

145 *to perceive as much as that of the* [.]   The blank left in transcription was never filled. EQ queried the gap in pencil but supplied no reading; *Memoirs* has 'imagination' but 'senses' or 'body' is more likely.

At Rome.b.   That is, the second *At Rome*, 'They—who have seen the noble Roman's scorn'; composed between 20 November 1838 and 29 January 1839.

Anna Ricketts   One of four daughters of Mrs Ricketts, who was a friend of IF. All four sisters accompanied WW, Dora W, and her cousin John Wordsworth on a three-day excursion to the Duddon Valley in October 1838 (*LY,* III, 759–65). Anna Ricketts was brought to Rydal Mount by IF in 1841 for an extended visit and Anna returned by herself in 1842; she became a special friend of the Wordsworths ('Our love of her encreases every day—and I cannot but feel she has been thoroughly happy with us—Then she is such a useful little thing! She is ready to help with her pen, her dear voice, and in every way'; MW and WW to IF, 28 July 1842 [*LY,* IV, 358]). WW enjoyed taking her to favourite places of his that she might like to sketch (ibid., p. 360).

Albano   That is, *At Albano* ('Days passed—and Monte Calvo would not clear'); composed between April and 24 December 1841.

The Cuckoo at Laverna. May 25th, 1837 (in its printed form) ('List 'twas the Cuckoo.—O with what delight'). Composed between 27 May and 10 August 1837. According to HCR, it contains the only verses composed during the tour; it was revised in July and again in the summer of the following year and completed 26 March 1840 (*HCR Books,* II, 528, 533; see also *LY, II,* 422–3, 616, and *Memoirs,* II, 330).

146 *At Vallombrosa* (in its printed form). On 2 December 1841 WW reported to IF that during a walk along the lake at Keswick he 'added a Stanza to the Vallombrosa Poem which I send you' (*LY,* IV, 267). The rest of the poem was possibly composed between April and 5 December 1841. WW's note printed with the poem in 1842 reads:

> The name of Milton is pleasingly connected with Vallombrosa in many ways. The pride with which the Monk, without any previous question from me, pointed out his residence, I shall not readily forget. It may be proper here to defend the Poet from a charge which has been brought against him; in respect to the passage in Paradise Lost, where this place is mentioned. It is said, that he has erred in speaking of the trees there being deciduous, whereas they are, in fact, pines. The fault-finders are themselves mistaken; the *natural* woods of the region of Vallombrosa *are* deciduous, and spread to a great extent; those near the convent are, indeed, mostly pines; but they are avenues of trees *planted* within a few steps of each other, and thus composing large tracts of wood; plots of which are periodically cut down. The appearance of those narrow avenues, upon steep slopes open to the sky, on account of the height which the trees attain by being *forced* to grow upwards, is often very impressive. My guide, a boy of about fourteen years old, pointed this out to me in several places.

To praise great & good men DQ left a one inch gap between this and the previous sentences, perhaps to indicate a new paragraph.

147 *Sonnet on the King of Sweden*   Called *The King of Sweden* ('The voice of song from distant lands shall call') when first published in 1807. In the note published with the poem in editions from 1836 WW asked to 'be understood as a Poet availing himself of the situation which the King of Sweden occupied, and of the principles AVOWED IN HIS MANIFESTOES; as laying hold of these advantages for the purpose of embodying moral truths'.

At Florence (in its printed form) ('Under the shadow of a stately Pile'). Composed between 20 November 1838 and 29 January 1839.

favorite seat   Of another of Dante's seats, HCR wrote to CW jr in October 1850, 'I recollect…the pleasure he expressed when I said to him "You are now sitting in Dante's chair". It faces the south transept of the cathedral at Florence' (*Memoirs,* II, 331).

I remember how…"Old Bachelor"   DQ left blank spaces where the place-names appear in brackets. In 1777 Samuel Johnson and James Boswell were shown a rocky recess at Ilam, on the River Manifold (near its confluence with the River Dove and the southern access to Dovedale), where Congreve often visited and, they were told, where he was supposed to have written his first comedy, *The Old Bachelor* (*Boswell's Life of Johnson,* ed. George Birkbeck Hill [6 vols; Oxford, 1887] III, 187). The *Topographer* for September 1789 (no. 6, vol. I), ed. by Samuel Egerton Brydges and Stebbing Shaw, includes 'Journal of a Tour from Oxford thro' the Peaks of Derbyshire, &c.' (the area of Dovedale) in which is mentioned the spot in the Porte house garden where Congreve 'is said to have written his old batchelor…in a seat that is still shewn' (p. 320). In the summer of 1788, shortly after WW made his own excursion along the River Dove, he wrote a brief prose account of it which survives in DC MS. 6 in the Wordsworth Library. Perhaps because he was attempting a formal description of Dovedale in this fragment, he does not mention the side-trip to Ilam and his visit to the Porte house, but it seems likely he was told the story during this early tour. See *Poems, 1785–1797,* pp. 672–5.

148 *The Baptist* The full title is *Before the Picture of the Baptist, by Raphael, in the Gallery at Florence* ('The Baptist might have been ordain'd to cry'); composed April 1840.

149 *Florence* WW refers to two translations, *At Florence.—From Michael Angelo,* 'Rapt above earth by power of one fair face' (composed 22 June 1839), and *At Florence.—From M. Angelo,* 'Eternal Lord! eased of a cumbrous load' (composed around November 1805 but before April 1807 and revised 19 January 1840).

w^t DQ's compression of 'what'.

Among the Ruins of a Convent in the Apennines ('Ye trees! whose slender roots entwine'). Composed between 18 January and 14 February 1842.

Sonnets 20 & 21st *At Bologna, in Remembrance of the Late Insurrections* ('Ah why deceive ourselves! by no mere fit') and *Continued* ('Hard task! exclaim the undisciplined, to lean'). Though not mentioned in the note, the conclusion to the sequence of three sonnets, 'As leaves are to the tree whereon they grow', likewise recommends 'thought' to 'teach the zealot to forego Rash schemes'. The poems were composed between 6 December 1838 and 29 January 1839.

150 *Carbonari* Members of a secret society organised in Naples early in the century to establish a republic in Italy. The 'proof WW speaks of may have derived from his own visit to Italy with HCR in 1837 or from Italian exiles in England whom he had met or knew of through others (see Alan G. Hill, 'Wordsworth and Italy' *Journal of Anglo-Italian Studies* I [1991] pp. 119-20).

"Fair Land" & the concluding Sonnet After Leaving Italy ('Fair Land! Thee all men greet with joy; how few') and *Continued* ('As indignation mastered grief, my tongue'). The first was composed between April and 24 December 1841, the second between 20 November and 6 December 1838.

Allmagna Spelled 'Allemagna' in *Memoirs*.

Sonnet with which this imperfect series concludes DQ left a one-inch vertical space in the notebook, perhaps to quote from the sestet of this final sonnet in the series:

> witness that unwelcome shock
> That followed the first sound of German speech,
> Caught the far-winding barrier Alps among.
> In that announcement, greeting seemed to mock
> Parting; the casual word had power to reach
> My heart, and filled that heart with conflict strong.

Composed by the Sea-shore ('What mischief cleaves to unsubdued regret'). Probably composed, with *On a High Part of the Coast of Cumberland* ('The Sun, that seemed so mildly to retire') and *(By the Seaside)* ('The Sun is couched, the sea-fowl gone to rest'), in early April 1833 while WW was visiting his son John at Moresby; he wrote to his family at Rydal Mount, 'I have walked and ridden a great deal…, and one day with another, I have scarcely walked less than 12 miles. The sea is a delightful companion and nothing can be more charming, especially for a sequestered Mountaineer, than to cast eyes over its boundless surface, and hear as I have done almost from the brow of the steep in the Church field at Moresby, the waves chafing and murmuring in a variety of tones below, as a kind of base of harmony to the shrill yet liquid music of the larks above' (*LY,* II, 600). However, when WW and MW spent a fortnight with John and his family at the end of March 1834, WW 'took a long and most delightful walk, following from Whitehaven, along the top of the Cliffs the indentings of the Coast, as far as the Monastry of St. Bees' (*LY,* II, 697). *Composed by the Seashore* was placed among the *Evening Voluntaries* in editions of 1845 and 1849–50. See WW's notes to the other 'Voluntaries' on notebook p. 110, above.

151 *Mr. Landor*   Walter Savage Landor (1775–1864), poet and prose writer. In 1836, despite his long-standing friendship with WW, he published *A Satire on Satirists, and admonition to detractors,* in which he attacked WW for not appreciating the work of his contemporaries (Southey and Talfourd, for example) and for lifting his lines about the sea-shell (*Excursion*, IV, 1132–47) from Landor's poem, *Gebir* (I, 170–7).

The Norman Boy…Mrs. Ogle   Miss Elizabeth Frances Ogle's letter making the request and WW's reply are in the Wordsworth Library. WW sent her a copy of the poem with his letter on 20 May 1840, and on the 28th she acknowledged the receipt of a second copy with 'additional stanzas' (*LY,* IV, 73–5). The sequel, *The Poet's Dream,* was composed about the same time; they were published together in the volume of 1842 with a note explaining 'The Chapel Oak of Allonville', which features in the second poem. In a round-about way it was Elizabeth's mother, Mrs Ogle, who provided the subject of the poem, for her daughter related to WW an experience of Mrs Ogle as a young woman.

152 *the poem on the growth of my own Mind*   See *Prelude*, V, 223–45, where he gives thanks that he was 'reared/Safe from an evil which these days have laid/Upon the children of the land, a pest/That might have dried me up, body and soul'; and ll. 491–533, where he praises the 'tales that charm away the wakeful night'. Maria Edgeworth and her father, Richard Lovell Edgeworth, published *Practical Education* in 1798, a widely influential work based on utilitarian principles. She also produced multi-volume works of moralistic fiction for children: *The Parent's Assistant* (1798, 1800), *Moral Tales* and *Early Lessons* (both 1800). In the Preface to *The Parent's Assistant* she warned against 'inflaming the imagination, or exciting restless spirit of adventure, by exhibiting false views of life, and creating hopes, which, in the ordinary course of things, cannot be realized' (quoted by Marilyn Gaull in *English Romanticism, The Human Context,* New York, 1988, p. 57).

152 *Poor Robin* Composed in March 1840. WW wrote to Charles Alexander Johns, 29 July 1841: 'There is a little plant the small common Geranium, called with us "Poor Robin", that is an especial favorite with me, so much so that I was tempted last March [1840] to describe its characteristics in verse and to moralize upon it in a way which perhaps will give you pleasure, when the Verses see the light, which they will probably next Spring' (*LY,* IV, 220).

Chatterton 'The marvellous boy' (l. 43 of *Resolution and Independence*) is Thomas Chatterton (1752–70); the line 'Upon her head wild weeds were spread' is recalled from his verse play, *Goddwyn. A Tragedie:*

> Whan Freedom dreste, yn blodde steyned veste,
> To everie Knighte her Warre Song sunge;
> Uponne her hedde, wylde Wedes were spredde,
> A gorie Anlace by her honge.
> (ll. 196–9)

153 *The Cuckoo-Clock* WW composed the first draft on 24 March 1840 and enclosed it in a letter to IF; a third stanza was added on 26 March and a fourth on 7 April (*LY,* IV, 53, 56; a Wordsworth Library manuscript in Dora W's hand bears the date 7 April 1840).

The Wishing-Gate Destroyed (in its printed form). WW refers to the note first printed with the poem in 1842: 'Having been told, upon what I thought good authority, that this gate had been destroyed, and the opening, where it hung, walled up, I gave vent immediately to my feelings in these stanzas. But going to the place some time after, I found, with much delight, my old favourite unmolested'. In a letter to IF on 30 August 1841, WW told her 'that we hear that the Wishing Gate is destroyed, which put me upon writing a Poem which will go to Dora tomorrow with a request that a transcript may be made of it for you' (*LY,* IV, 235–6). See WW's note to *The Wishing-Gate* on notebook p. 32.

The Widow on Windermere Side (in its printed form) ('How beautiful when up a lofty height'). Perhaps in dictation WW substituted the ancient name of the lake, his usage in *An Evening Walk* and *The Prelude*. Robert Perceval Graves (1810–93), of Trinity College, Dublin, met WW in the summer of 1833, and in 1835, through WW's influence, was assisted to a curacy at Bowness, a village lying between the town of Windermere and the Lake (*LY*, II, 637n.). Graves dated the poem 1837 (*PW*, II, 485).

Cenotaph Mentioned in the note to *Elegiac Stanzas* ('the Verses on Mrs. F') that is transcribed on notebook p. 115 (as EQ's pencil note on p. 153 indicates). Frances Fermor, Lady Beaumont's sister, died in December 1824. MW sent a copy of the poem to Lady Beaumont 25 February 1825 (*LY*, 1,324).

Epitaph in the Chapel-Yard of Langdale, Westmoreland (in its printed form). WW sent a copy of the *Epitaph* to his brother Christopher on 11 August 1841 and published it in *Poems, Chiefly of Early and Late Years* in 1842. In editions of 1845 and 1849–50 the poem was moved to 'Epitaphs and Elegiac Pieces'. Owen Lloyd (1803–41), who suffered throughout his life from epilepsy, took up the curacy in Langdale in 1829 and died in early summer 1841. His tombstone in the chapel-yard at Chapel Stile, Langdale, bears WW's epitaph as inscription.

Charles Lloyd (1775–1839), student and friend, for a time, of STC, lived in the hamlet of Clappersgate, near Ambleside, in the same house, 'Old Brathay', referred to in WW's note to the *Epistle to Sir G.B. Beaumont, Bart.* (notebook p. 133). Charles Lloyd published *Poems* jointly with STC and Charles Lamb in 1797. In 1835 Owen Lloyd (1803–41) contributed an epitaph on the death of Charles Lamb.

He was educated That is, Owen Lloyd was educated under Mr Dawes.

Mr. Dawes The Revd John Dawes also taught Hartley and Derwent Coleridge, Basil Montagu's second son Algernon, and WW's son John (*MY*, I, 282, 402 and notes; *MY*, II, 123, 246); The Revd Samuel Butler, D.D. (1774–1839) was a contemporary of STC at Cambridge and headmaster of the school at Shrewsbury from 1798–1836 (*LY*, I, 371n.); 'Trin: Col.' is Trinity College.

154 *Sonnet A Poet*   'A Poet!—He hath put his heart to school'; never given any title in print. For no obvious reason DQ or EQ marked this entry and the next with a square bracket. The sonnet appears in a manuscript of draft material prepared for the volume of 1842, in the same section (DC MS. 151/3) with a version of the sonnet 'Well worthy to be magnified are they', published as *Pilgrim Fathers*, which can be dated February 1842 by WW's letter to Henry Reed written on March 1st.

Sonnet "The most alluring clouds"   'The most alluring clouds that mount the sky'. Like a '*A Poet*', the sonnet appears in its earliest form only among manuscripts prepared for the 1842 volume.

along the Rotha   The River Rothay as it flows from Grasmere Lake to Rydal Water.

"Feel for the wrongs"   'Feel for the wrongs to universal ken'. Perhaps composed around the same time as the *Prelude* to the 1842 volume, late November 1841.

Anti Corn Law Leaguers   For the Anti-Corn Law League see the note to *Prelude* on notebook p. 126 above. Conspicuous among 'political economists' in this period were Adam Smith (see the note to *Love Lies Bleeding*, notebook p. 137) and Robert Owen (1771–1858). The latter published his *Lectures on an Entire New State of Society, comprehending an Analysis of British Society, relative to the Production and Distribution of Wealth; the Formation of Character, and Government, Domestic and Foreign* in 1830 (a collection of separately issued tracts) and *The Body of the New Moral World, Containing the Rational System of Society, Founded on Demonstrable Facts, Developing the Constitution and Laws of Human Nature and Society* in 1836.

Aspects of Christianity in America (in its printed form). The note in 1842 reads:

> This and the two following sonnets are intended to take their place in the Ecclesiastical Series which the reader may find in the fourth volume of my Poems [*PW* (1841)]. American episcopacy, in union with the church in England, strictly belongs to the general subject; and I here make my acknowledgments to my American friends, Bishop

Doane, and Mr. Henry Reed of Philadelphia, for having suggested to me the propriety of adverting to it, and pointed out the virtues and intellectual qualities of Bishop White, which so eminently fitted him for the great work he undertook. Bishop White was consecrated at Lambeth, Feb. 4, 1787, by Archbishop Moore; and before his long life was closed, twenty-six bishops had been consecrated in America, by himself. For his character and opinions, see his own numerous Works, and a "Sermon in commemoration of him, by George Washington Doane, Bishop of New Jersey".

The sonnets were transferred to 'Ecclesiastical Sonnets' in editions of 1845 and 1849–50. In WW's letter to Reed, 16 August 1841, he mentioned a visit to Rydal Mount by Bishop Doane (1799–1859), a warm supporter of the Oxford Movement, who then sent him a copy of his sermon on William White (1748–1836), first Bishop of Pennsylvania, 'to assist me in fulfilling a request which you first made to me, viz, that I would add a Sonnet to my ecclesiastical series, upon the union of the two episcopal churches of England and America' (*LY,* IV, 228, 230 and notes). He sent the three sonnets to Reed on 1 March 1842, informing him that they were now in the 'New Volume of Poems which I am carrying thro' the Press' (*LY,* IV, 297).

Duke of Wellington   The full title is *On a Portrait of the Duke of Wellington, Upon the Field of Waterloo, by Haydon.* Composed 31 August 1840. WW reported to HCR, 4 September 1840, that 'Haydon has just sent me a spirited Etching of his Portrait of the Duke of Wellington taken 20 years after the Battle of Waterloo, from the Life. He is represented in the field; but no more of the Picture—take my Sonnet which it suggested the other day. The lines were composed while I was climbing Helvellyn' (*LY,* IV, 106). WW sent Haydon a copy of the sonnet and undertook several revisions at his suggestion in September and October, and, after it was printed by Haydon in the newspapers, with many errors, WW further revised it before publishing it himself in the 1842 volume (*LY,* IV, 100, 101, 105, 107, 108, 110–12, 115, 117, 120–1, 126, 131, 133, 246n). See the Glossary entry for 'Wellington'.

155 *Portentous Change*   The opening words of *In Allusion to Various Recent Histories and Notices of the French Revolution*. No note was entered. This sequence of three sonnets, beginning with 'Portentous change when History can appear', was probably written between late January and March 1839. Among the 'Histories' referred to in the title WW seems to have had Thomas Carlyle's *History of the French Revolution* (1837) in mind (for a similar 'difference' and mention of other histories see WW's note to *Ode. The Morning of the Day Appointed for a General Thanksgiving, January* 18, 1816, notebook p. 58 and editor's note).

WW had met Carlyle at Henry Taylor's house in London in April 1836, an occasion when Carlyle was 'largely silent' (Henry Taylor to IF, May 24, 1836; quoted in *LY,* III, 210n.). In December 1838 IF had loaned WW her copy of Carlyle's *French Revolution,* portions of which HCR read to WW in December when he visited Rydal Mount, but WW had apparently not read it through by 19 February 1839. On 26 January 1839 HCR recorded in his diary that he had read the third volume of Carlyle, 'of whom Wordsworth pronounces a harsh judgment. It is not only his style that he condemns, but his *inhumanity.* He says there is a want of due sympathy with mankind. Scorn and irony are the feeling and tone throughout. There is too much truth in this, and it is too strongly confirmed by the opinion strongly expressed by Carlyle at table at Crawford's, in favour of the continuance of Negro slavery by the Americans, which he, one might hope in a spirit of paradox only, was led to profess, even at war with his innermost feelings' (WW to HCR, *LY,* III, 665–6 and note; *HRC Books,* II, 563, 566). WW was more blunt: of Carlyle's notion that the Terror was an instrument of divine will WW asked 'Hath it not long been said the wrath of Man/ Works not the righteousness of God?' (ll. 9–10 of the first sonnet).

Presence of the heading and absence of a recorded note may have arisen through discussion with IF, who, according to HCR, admired 'both Carlyle and his writings' (ibid., p. 560). HCR recorded in his diary for 29 January 1839 that 'Wordsworth read to me some twelve or more new Sonnets—for the greater part excellent' (ibid., 567); but it seems improbable that these three sonnets on 'Histories and Notices of the French Revolution' were among them. They were placed among 'Sonnets Dedicated to Liberty and Order' in editions of 1845 and 1849–50.

To a Painter   WW refers to two sonnets, 'All praise the Likeness by thy skill portrayed' and 'Though I beheld at first with blank surprise', both on MW's portrait. Margaret Gillies (1803–87) specialised in water-colour miniatures on ivory and earned her livelihood as a miniaturist and water-colourist. Raised in Edinburgh after her father lost his fortune, she became the friend of Scott, Francis Jeffrey and the Wordsworths; she painted miniatures of MW, WW, Dora W, and IF in October–December 1839 at Rydal Mount. For WW's earlier comment on Margaret Gillies see his note on the sonnet, 'From the dark chambers of dejection freed', notebook pp. 41–2. MW's portrait was completed before the end of the year. Prior to their departure from Rydal together in mid-February Dora W had given IF copies of the two sonnets on the portrait of MW, remarking that 'The Sonnets are most beautiful, most true, most affecting, and Father tells me they were composed almost extempore'; in April WW wrote to Dora W, 'your mother tells me she shrinks from Copies being spread of those Sonnets: she does not wish one, on any account, to be given to Miss Gillies, for that, without blame to Miss G., would be like advertising them. I assure you her modesty and humblemindedness were so much shocked that I doubt if she had more pleasure than pain from these compositions, though I never poured out anything more truly from the heart' (*LY*, III, 756 and note; IV, 59 and note). The two sonnets *To a Painter* and *On the Same Subject* were composed in December 1839–January 1840.

To a Redbreast—(In Sickness)   Sara Hutchinson was 'laid upon [her] bed by sickness for three weeks' in January 1826 (*SHL*, p. 313).

Floating Island   Probably composed in the late 1820s. The 'floating island' is in Rydal Water. DW fell dangerously ill in April 1829 and had a second attack at the end of December 1831; shortly after this relapse WW wrote to his nephew CWjr that 'her recovery from each attack is slower and slower' (Gill, *A Life*, p. 358; *LY*, II, 521). See also Levin, pp. 207–9.

If with old love   Composed on a May Morning, 1838 ('If with old love of you, dear Hills! I share'). Composed May 1, 1838. WW first published it, with its companion sonnet, in the volume of *Sonnets* in 1838 and included them again in the volume of 1842. In 1845 he separated them and assigned new titles: *Composed at Rydal on May Morning, 1838* ('If with old love') and *Composed on a May Morning, 1838* ('Life with yon Lambs').

the following Sonnet   That is, *Composed on the Same Morning* ('Life with yon Lambs, like day, is just begun').

At Dover ('From the Pier's Head, musing, and with increase'). Composed in February 1838 as 'a conclusion to the class of our Continental Tour in —20' (WW to HCR, *LY*, III, 522 and note); Dora visited IF at Dover in December 1837–February 1838. The poem was first published in the volume of *Sonnets* in 1838 and included in the volume of 1842. In the edition of 1845, and its stereotypes, and in 1849–50 WW moved it, much revised, to the concluding position of 'Memorials of a Tour on the Continent, 1820'.

"Oh what a Wreck" ('Oh what a Wreck! how changed in mien and speech'). Written shortly after Edith Southey's death on 16 November 1837 and titled in manuscript *To R.S.* WW revised it, omitting 'the personalities', in February–March 1838 (*LY*, III, 534). It was first published in the volume of *Sonnets* in 1838 and included in the volume of 1842.

156 *Intent on gathering Wool* ('Intent on gathering wool from hedge and brake'). 'Miss F—' is Isabella Fenwick. WW printed the date, 'March 8, 1842', beneath the sonnet in editions from 1842.

here alluded to. Below the conclusion of this note DQ left a one-inch vertical space in the notebook. Since "Intent on gathering wool" is the final sonnet in the volume, before the title page for *The Borders*, it seems likely she meant the space to mark the transition.

The Borderers. A Tragedy. (Composed 1795–6) (as published). The earliest reference to the play is dated 24 October 1796; by 27 February 1797 WW reported to Francis Wrangham that the 'first draught…is nearly finished'. A completed version was read to STC in June when he visited Racedown (*EY,* pp. 172, 177, 189). WW revised the play for publication in 1841–2. See *The Borderers,* ed. Robert Osborn (Ithaca: Cornell University Press, 1982), pp. 3–17, for a history of composition.

Dorset^{re} Dorsetshire

w^d would

157 *Ridpath's history of the Borders* George Ridpath, *The Border-History of England and Scotland deduced from the earliest times to the union of the two crowns* (rev. and publ. by the author's brother, Mr Philip Ridpath; London, 1776).

thro' one of the M^r. Pooles M^r. Knight the actor For Thomas Poole see Glossary; perhaps WW includes Poole's father, also Thomas, who owned and operated a tannery in Nether Stowey. Thomas Knight (d. 1820), actor, dramatist and theatre manager, appeared in plays at Bath and Bristol and at Covent Garden Theatre in London in the 1790s.

Mr. Harris Thomas Harris (d. 1820) was the proprietor and manager of Covent Garden Theatre, London, during this period. Through his married sister, Harris was connected to the publishing family of Longman, the firm that bought Cottle's rights to publish the London edition of *Lyrical Ballads* in 1798.

Mr. Sheridan Richard Brinsley Sheridan (1751–1816), statesman and dramatist, was manager and chief proprietor of Drury Lane Theatre in London through the 1790s until the theatre burned in 1809. STC's *Osorio* (1798) was produced as *Remorse* at a revived Drury Lane in 1813.

158 *The Excursion*   WW has now returned to the 1841 set of his *Poetical Works,* the sixth volume of which contained *The Excursion.* See *Exc,* pp. 426–476 for a detailed discussion of the poem's several stages of development. In brief, some parts of the poem date from 1797–1800 when WW was beginning composition of materials for *The Ruined Cottage, Home at Grasmere* and *The Prelude,* all finally conceived as parts of the long unfinished work, *The Recluse.* He worked on *The Ruined Cottage* (eventually a main component of Book I of *The Excursion*) through 1804, and *Home at Grasmere* in 1806; and between December 1809 and early 1814 he undertook more or less continuous composition toward what ultimately became *The Excursion.* He revised and added to the poem until its publication in late May 1814; the bulk of the poem was composed, as WW says, during his residence at Allan Bank, 1808–12, and completed during the first two years at Rydal Mount. See *Chronology: MY,* pp. 656–86; see also the Cornell editions of these poems, *H at G,* ed. Beth Darlington; *The Ruined Cottage and The Pedlar,* ed. James Butler (Ithaca: Cornell University Press, 1979), and *Exc,* ed. Sally Bushell, James A. Butler, with Michael C. Jaye (Ithaca: Cornell University Press, 2007). The last of these volumes bases its reading text on the poem as published in 1814 edition, not the one WW is holding while dictating the notes (*PW,* 1841). But the editors usefully provide in Appendix III, 'Fenwick Note to *The Excursion*', a transcription of the note and annotations that relate to the 1814 text.

especially to Her   Isabella Fenwick, as EQ's pencil note indicates.

/95   DQ's abbreviation for 1795. WW recalls the earliest composition of Margaret's story at Racedown; WW's and DW's residence there began in September 1795 but composition of the poem did not begin until the spring of 1797.

The long Poem on my own education   Never given a title by the poet; the title, *The Prelude, or Growth of a Poet's Mind,* was chosen by MW for publication of the poem after WW's death in 1850.

159 *a month after his decease* Southey died 21 March 1843.

my Pedlar The Wanderer. WW recalls the prototype of the Wanderer from *The Ruined Cottage*.

160 *Sarah was brought up from early Childhood* See the illustration of this page on p. 93 above [FN 57]. MW corrected 'Childhood' to 'her ninth year' and 'eye' to 'roof' in pencil and added two pencil notes on the facing page, the second written over part of the first, which has been partly erased: 'Sarah went to Kendal within 2 years after our Mother's death but Mʳ. P. died [?when she was 10 years old]' and 'Sarah went to Kendal on our Mother's death but Mʳ. P. died in the course of a year or two'. Gordon Wordsworth added 'Mʳˢ. Hutchinson d. March 31. 1783. James Patrick March 2 1787'. Patrick married Mary's cousin Margaret Robison; he had herded cattle in Perthshire before becoming a pedlar and in Kendal he worked as a draper; he died at age 71. In notes on the family made for her son William, MW later described Patrick as 'the intellectual Pedlar' and added that though Sara 'went to School in Kendal,...the most important part of her education was gathered from the stores of that good man's mind' (*PW,* V, 374). See Glossary entries for Sara Hutchinson and Kendal.

a note attached to it In the note to his portrait of the 'Pedlar' published with the poem WW is at pains to show 'how far a Character, employed for purposes of the imagination,' may be 'founded upon general fact' and quotes in illustration a passage on 'travelling merchants' from Herron's *Journey to Scotland* in which Herron reports that 'as they wander, each alone, through thinly-inhabited districts, they form habits of reflection and of sublime contemplation'.

161 *Regim^t*   Regiment

M^r. Fawcett   Joseph Fawcett (?1758–1804) was an extremely effective and popular orator who lectured regularly at the Old Jewry. He published *The Art of War, A Poem,* in 1795, and followed it with *The Art of Poetry... by Simon Swan* (1797) and *Poems* (1798).

M^r. Nicholson   Samuel Nicholson, a Unitarian, was known to WW through his cousin Elizabeth Threlkeld, who patronised Nicholson's London haberdashery shop in Cateaton Street in Holborn, not far off the Strand, and through her father, Samuel Threlkeld, who had been a Unitarian minister at Penrith and Halifax. For accounts of Fawcett and Nicholson and their probable influence on WW's social and political ideas see Nicholas Roe, *Wordsworth and Coleridge, The Radical Years* (Oxford: Clarendon Press, 1988) pp. 23–8.

163 *Furness Fells*   These hills and valleys make up the southern Lake District.

Blea Tarn   Across the vale of Langdale, on the eastern slope.

the rude Chapel   EQ has marked this portion of the sentence with an 'X' and a vertical line in pencil, and made similar marks (a double 'X' opposite lightly underscored 'Grasmere' and 'Parish Church') on the next page, perhaps to highlight the transformation.

164 *in words which I hope my readers will remember* EQ's pencil note reminds us: 'last book at the end' (*Excursion*, IX, 615–754).
"*She was a woman…a life of happiness*" From *Excursion,* I, 513–19.
I was born too late WW was six in 1776.
Poem on Guilt & Sorrow See WW's notes to *The Female Vagrant* and *Guilt and Sorrow,* notebook pp. 15 and 126 respectively.

165 *the close of the 2ᵈ Book* From *Excursion,* II, 730–895.
Boardale & Martindale The two valleys lie south and east of Ullswater, respectively.
my friend Mʳ. Luff Captain and Mrs Luff lived in Patterdale until 1812 when they emigrated to Mauritius where Captain Luff died. For Mrs Luff see WW's note to *The Contrast, The Parrot and the Wren*, notebook p. 22 above.
Mary That is, MW.
Hartshope Hall On the southern edge of Brothers Water, near Hartshope, or Hartsop.
picture given by the Wanderer of the Living JC revised to 'The Pastor and the Wanderer' in *PW* (1857). Both the Wanderer in Book II and the Pastor in Book V describe the region ministered to by the Pastor.
The Cottage was called Hackett Also described, with its occupants, in WW's note to *Epistle to Sir George Howland Beaumont, Bart. From the South-west Coast of Cumberland—1811,* notebook p. 130.

166 *children were ill*   EQ's note: '?Dora'.
   sit separate   That is on separate sides of the church (*Memoirs*).
   Lady Huntingdon's Chapels   Selena Hastings, Countess of Huntingdon (1707–91), was a vigorous promoter of Methodism. She founded chapels throughout England, building many with her own funds and, though she did not achieve her goal, intending by this means to bring about the reform of the Church of England. An associate of George Whitefield, she devoted her time and considerable fortune to the advancement of Methodism in Britain and America.

167 *Sepulture*   The word means 'burying, putting in the grave' (the correct spelling is written in ink in the notebook above 'Sepulchre' apparently as a replacement).
   "Many precious rites…stealing from us"   From *Excursion*, II, 550–3.

168 *Mr. Barber…Mr. Greenwood*   See the discussion of 'Loughrigg Tarn' in the note to *Epistle to Sir George Howland Beaumont, Bart. From the South-west Coast of Cumberland.—1811,* notebook p. 133.
   the Yew of Lorton   At High Lorton, north of Crummock Water.
   in grand assemblage   At Seathwaite in Borrowdale; see WW's poem, *Yew-trees,* his note to this poem above (notebook p. 25), and his description of the trees in *Select Views* (*Prose*, II, 275).
   persons…lying in the Church yard   See *Excursion*, VI, 'The Churchyard Among the Mountains'.

170 *this fortunate Teacher* EQ's pencil note: 'Mr. Pearson—': William Pearson (1767–47) of Whitbeck, Cumberland, was 'second Assistant' in Hawkshead School in 1790. He took orders and was Rector first of Perivale, Middlesex, 1810–12, and then of South Kilworth, Leicestershire, 1817–47. From 1812–21 he operated his large private school at Temple Grove, East Sheen, Surrey, where he established an observatory and became renowned as an astronomer.

now erecting a boat-house EQ's pencil note: 'This boat house, badly built, gave way & was rebuilt. It again tumbled, & was a third time reconstructed but in a better fashion than before. It is not now, per se, an ugly building, however obtrusive it may be.' The boat-house survives, with 'W.P. 1843' cut in a stone over the door. Among Wordsworth Library papers are two letters from Pearson to WW, in 1812 and 1813, in which he discusses terms for the sale of his Grasmere and Rydal estates. But WW moved to Rydal Mount in 1813 and Pearson held on to his properties. See *Wordsworth's Hawkshead*, pp. 358–60.

171 *the impertinent structure will not stand* EQ's pencil note: 'It has been rebuilt in somewhat better taste, & much as one wishes it away it is not now so very unsightly.—The structure is an emblem of the man—perseverance has conquered difficulties, and given something of form and polish to rudeness.'

the Solitary Miner EQ's pencil note: 'as an epithet interfering?—' (that is, conflicting with the character called 'The Solitary' in the poem).

172 *by name Dawson*   Several Dawsons lived in the valley; in his later note on George Dawson, on notebook p. 176, WW supposes that this Dawson was an older brother to George.

the dear old Dame   Ann Tyson (see Glossary). See also WW's note to *Peter Bell*, notebook p. 34, above. For discussion of the local context of these and other stories told by Ann Tyson see *Wordsworth's Hawkshead, pp.* xv–xvi, 65–9.

Drummond…Vandepat   Drummond was perhaps the John Drummond buried in Hawkshead 8 July 1747; he may have been connected to the titular Dukes of Perth or their relatives the Viscounts Strathallan, all Jacobites and bearing the family name of Drummond. EQ's pencil note identifies the second man as Sir George Vandeput (1729–84); Vandeput contested with Lord Trentham for the City of Westminster in 1750 (see Hawkshead parish register, Burke's *Extinct Baronetcies*, and *DNB*).

Old Brathay   The Hall in Clappersgate just west of Ambleside on the River Brathay. The Weston bothers have not otherwise been identified.

173 *"Tall was her stature…saturnine*   See *Excursion*, VI, 678–75.
As on a sunny bank   See *Excursion*, VI, 787–1052.

174 *affect^te* affectionate

The Clergyman & his family The Revd Joseph Sympson (1715–1807) was vicar of the small church at Wythburn for over fifty years; he remained active until his sudden death at age 92. DW's Grasmere journal records their close ties with this family during the Wordsworths' Dove Cottage years. The Sympsons, including Joseph's wife Mary, his son Bartholomew and his daughter Margaret, lived at High Broadraine, a farmhouse near Dunmail Raise on the road to Keswick (see *Journals*, II, pp. 437–8). In his poem *The Tuft of Primroses* WW described Joseph Sympson as he knew him during the Grasmere years. An elder son, also Joseph, is mentioned below on notebook pp. 174–5.

our very nearest neighbours The Ashburners (see WW's note to *Michael*, notebook p. 20 above, and *Journals*, 1,433–4).

my Notes to the Sonnets on the Duddon In his published note to *Flowers in The River Duddon* WW acknowledged his debt to the poem, *The Beauties of Spring, a Juvenile Poem*, by the younger Joseph Sympson, as the source for ll. 9–10. He wrote of him, 'he was a native of Cumberland, and was educated in the vale of Grasmere, and at Hawkshead school: his poems are little known, but they contain passages of splendid description; and the versification of his "Vision of Alfred" is harmonious and animated'. *Science Revived, or The Vision of Alfred*, by the Revd Joseph Sympson, B.D., was published in London in 1802. It was the son, not the father, with whom WW had the conversation about Pope. See *Journals*, 1,437–8. EQ underlined 'talent' and 'talents' in pencil, probably to show his disapproval of the repetition.

175 *Robert Walker*   In the published note to *The River Duddon,* WW memorialises Walker as a model Christian and leader of his flock.

John Gough (1757–1825) was a scientific writer, blind from the age of three. He published *The Systematic Arrangement of British Plants* in 1796. STC also mentioned Gough, describing him in his essay, 'The Soul and its Organs of Sense', as 'not only an excellent mathematician; but an infallible botanist and zoologist.…[T]he rapidity of his touch appears fully equal to that of sight; and the accuracy greater'; not content with measured praise he added, 'Good heavens!…Why, his face sees all over! Is all one eye!' (in Robert Southey's *Omniana, or Horae Otiosiores,* II, 17–18 [London, 1812]). De Selincourt pointed out that WW placed Gough in the churchyard well before his death.

176 *"A volley thrice repeated"*   See *Excursion,* VII, 698.

Volunteer…Dawson   George Dawson, 'the finest young Man in the vale', as DW described him, after his death, in a letter to Catherine Clarkson, 19 July 1807 (*MY,* I, 15). His father, John Dawson, lived with his family at Ben Place, between Forest Side and the Swan on the road to Keswick.

of literary education & [   ] *experience*   A blank space was left for an adjective. EQ filled the gap with 'of' and queried the omission. *Memoirs* has 'considerable'.

Iron Works at Bunaw   At Bonawe, in northwestern Scotland.

the cell…guarded the property   Beside this passage EQ noted 'not clear'; but, as JC explained in his revised note, the 'Iron-closet' was a safe built into the wall in 'the long room at Rydal Mount' for valuable property (*PW* [1857]). One of WW's predecessors as Stamp-Distributor had owned Rydal Mount in the eighteenth century; he was the grandfather of the Wordsworths' friend, Miss Knott of Grasmere (*MY,* II, 89).

"Tradition tells…House is gone"   From *Excursion,* VII, 923–75.

177 *Nott Houses* The Knott Houses, a mile north of Grasmere on the road to Keswick, are all that remain of the mansion and estate of the Knott family whose holdings in Grasmere and Rydal, from Elizabethan times through the eighteenth century, were extensive. See *MY,* I, p. 464 and note, and the editor's note to *The Blind Highland Boy,* notebook p. 53 above.

Knott DQ called attention to the spelling by underscoring the 'K'; it is difficult to tell the difference between her upper and lower case 'k' but the name is presumably capitalised.

the discourse of the Wanderer upon the changes See *Excursion,* VIII, 87ff.

Happily...such unnatural proceedings The use of waterwheels to drive mill machinery along many streams and rivers of the Lake District was common from early times. An Act of Parliament limiting night work was passed in 1842 (see the next two editor's notes).

Lord Ashley's labours Anthony Ashley Cooper, seventh Earl of Shaftesbury (1801–85), was a philanthropist and social reformer, and a member of parliament from 1826. The Factory Act of 1833 acknowledged the twelve hour work-day, already the standard in most industries, but always under pressure for extension. Though Cooper worked diligently for reform from the beginning of his parliamentary career, not until 1847 did parliament pass an act which limited the work-day to ten hours. Under Cooper's urging an act was passed in 1842 abolishing the abuse-ridden system of apprenticeship, and excluding women and boys under thirteen from working underground.

178 *Sir James Graham's attempt to establish* James Robert Graham (1792–1861) was a native of Cumberland and one of its members for parliament for many years. In 1843, as Home Secretary in Sir Robert Peel's administration, he introduced a factory act containing clauses which would have established religious instruction for children employed in the factories. But as he offered no concessions to Dissenters on the form such education would take, the clauses were abandoned.
manufactoring A word derived from 'manufactory', a usage still current in the 1840s.
"I spake…may destroy! From *Excursion*, IX, 195–9

179 *The Chartists* Radical reformers who advocated the formation of workers' unions to force improvement in working conditions by the owners of factories and to secure equal political rights from Parliament. When their petition ('Charter') was refused by Parliament in 1839, militants made an abortive attempt to seize the town of Newport. After 1842 Chartism, largely through the public quarrels of its leaders and what were perceived as ill-considered schemes, steadily lost its hold on the working class. However, beginning with the repeal of the Corn Laws in 1846, many of their recommended reforms were achieved by the turn of the half-century.
"While from…We gazed" From *Excursion*, IX, 609–10.
"But turned not…In wandering with us" From *Excursion*, IX, 775–8. In editions of 1845 and 1849–50 the text reads (ll. 777–8) 'not loth/ To wander with us …'.

180 *Mid the Wreck…utterly decayed* From the sonnet, *Malham Cove*, ll. 11–14.
finished at the Vicarage Brigham DQ writes from her brother John Wordsworth's home at Brigham.

Glossary of Selected Persons and Places

Alfoxden, or Alfoxden House or Alfoxden Park, now usually spelled Alfoxton. The house and grounds where William and Dorothy Wordsworth lived in Somerset near Coleridge's home at Nether Stowey, from June 1797 until June 1798.

Ambleside. 'Market-village' (*Select Views, Prose,* II, 268) situated at the head of Lake Windermere, four miles southeast of Grasmere.

Beaumont, Sir George Howland, 7th Baronet (1753–1827), and Lady Beaumont, his wife, of Coleorton Hall, Leicestershire, and Grosvenor Square, London. Sir George was a connoisseur, patron of art and landscape painter, he was a close friend of Sir Joshua Reynolds, and the friend of Haydon, Southey, Samuel Rogers, John Constable, Coleridge and Wordsworth. As patron he assisted the painters Constable, Haydon, John Jackson and J.R. Cozens, and he helped Coleridge to set up *The Friend* and to obtain a pension. Himself a collector, he helped to found a national gallery by contributing many pictures from his own collection. He had visited the lakes in 1798 to sketch the landscape and in July and August 1803 he and Lady Beaumont occupied part of Greta Hall while Coleridge was living there. His gift of land to Wordsworth for a farmstead at Applethwaite, made before Sir George left Greta Hall in August, was intended, he wrote, 'to bring you and Coleridge together' and thus to increase the 'enjoyment you would receive from the beauties of Nature, by being able to communicate more frequently your sensations to each other' (*EY,* p. 406n.) The Beaumonts, particularly Lady Beaumont, were keen practitioners of landscape gardening and found in the Wordsworths a happy source of both theoretical and practical advice and aid.

Burns, Robert (1759–96), poet. He published *Poems Chiefly in the Scottish Dialect* in Kilmarnock in 1786. Wordsworth read the volume within the next year (*EY,* p. 13 and note).

Calvert, Raisley (1770–95). Raisley was the younger brother of William Calvert (1771–1829), Wordsworth's classmate at Hawkshead School and the owner of the land and farm at Windy Brow, Keswick, where William and Dorothy Wordsworth stayed in the spring of 1794. Raisley entered Magdalene College, Cambridge, in 1793 but left soon after to undertake his own education by travel on the continent. He inherited several farms, including Ormathwaite, a mile north of Keswick, the income from which was held in trust until he reached his majority in 1794. In that year he offered 'a share of his income' to Wordsworth (*EY*, pp. 126–7 and note) and Wordsworth attended him at Windy Brow during the final stages of his illness. Upon Calvert's death from tuberculosis in January 1795 Wordsworth received a legacy from the estate.

Clarkson, Thomas (1760–1846) and wife Catherine (1772–1856), of Eusemere at Pooley Bridge on the eastern end of Ullswater. Thomas was educated at St Paul's School and St John's College, Cambridge. An antislavery agitator and associate of Wilberforce, he was appointed to the committee for the suppression of the slave trade and travelled extensively in its cause. Forced into retirement by ill health in 1794, he built Eusemere on Ullswater where he retired with his wife. He rejoined the committee in 1803, selling Eusemere to Lord Lonsdale and moving his family eventually to Playford Hall near Ipswich. The bill abolishing slavery was passed in 1807. Friends of the Wordsworths from 1800, they introduced him to Henry Crabb Robinson, a childhood friend of Catherine (Buck) Clarkson.

Cockermouth, situated at the confluence of the Rivers Derwent and Cocker, northwest of Keswick. Cockermouth Castle, the 'noble ruins' (*Guide, Prose*, II, 172) of a thirteenth-fourteenth century castle on the River Derwent in the center of Cockermouth.

Coleorton, in Leicestershire, fifteen miles northwest of Leicester, home of Sir George and Lady Beaumont (Coleorton Hall).

Coleridge, Samuel Taylor (1772–1834). Poet, philosopher and critic. Sometimes referred to in these notes as 'C'. A life-long friend of Charles Lamb (they were educated at Christ's Hospital together), Coleridge probably met Wordsworth in Bristol in August 1795 and first visited the Wordsworths at Racedown in June 1797. In July, on a visit to Coleridge at Nether Stowey,

William and Dorothy made arrangements to move to Alfoxden, nearby, and remained until their departure, with Coleridge, for Bristol, on their way to Germany, the following June. Separated from the Wordsworths in Germany, on his return Coleridge joined them to tour the Lake District in late October 1799, and took up residence at Greta Hall in Keswick in July 1800. In Malta and travelling in Italy from April 1804 to August 1806, he separated from his wife Sara on his return and stayed with the Wordsworths at Allan Bank from September 1808 to mid-October 1810. Relations between Coleridge and the Wordsworths were strained at this time, and, though restored to some extent by 1828 when he toured the Rhine with Wordsworth and his daughter Dora, the old intimacy did not survive. Struggling against his addiction to opium when he left Allan Bank, Coleridge stayed first with Basil Montagu in London and eventually, as patient and friend, with Dr James Gillman at Highgate from 1816 until his death.

Crabbe, George (1754–1832), published *The Village,* the first of his realistic poems and tales of country life, in 1783, and, after a long silence, a series of verse narratives in *Poems* (1807), *Tales in Verse* (1812), and *Tales of the Hall* (1819). As a young man he trained for and practiced medicine, then took orders and served for many years as vicar of Trowbridge, Wiltshire.

Davy, Sir Humphrey (1778–1829), natural philosopher, trained as a surgeon and wrote verses as a young man, became professor of chemistry at the Royal Institution in London and greatly advanced the knowledge of chemistry and galvanism. Wordsworth first met him in Somerset while living at Alfoxden, near Coleridge and Thomas Poole (at Nether Stowey). Davy twice visited Grasmere and walked and fished with Wordsworth. In 1806–7 Coleridge arranged for Davy to correct Wordsworth's 'punctuation' in copy for *Poems. in Two Volumes* which Wordsworth was sending to his Bristol publisher, Joseph Cottle.

Derwent, river rising in the Cumbrian mountains north of Scafell and flowing through Derwentwater and Bassenthwaite Lake, through the towns of Cockermouth and Workington to the the Irish Sea. In *An Unpublished*

Tour WW describes the Derwent as 'little discoloured by tempestuous seasons & at other times the most pellucid of all rivers' (*Prose,* II, 345; see II, 396, for a list of WW's descriptions in verse and prose of this river and the River Duddon).

Duddon, river flowing south through Donnerdale to Duddon Sands. WW described it as 'a copious stream winding among fields, rocks, and mountains, and terminating its course in the sands of Duddon' (*Guide, Prose,* II, 172). Linking the Duddon and the Derwent rivers and their surroundings, WW remarks that 'the number of torrents and smaller brooks is infinite, with their waterfalls and water-breaks' (*Guide, Prose,* II, 188). See also WW's note published with *The River Duddon*.

Dunmail-Raise, or Dunmail Raise, the pass leading to Thirlmere, north of Grasmere. In a manuscript passage intended for *Select Views* WW described this 'gap', approaching it from Grasmere, as 'an opening in the shape of a huge inverted arch, the sides of which are formed by Steel fell on the left & on the right by Seat Sandal' (*Prose,* II, 272n.).

Easedale, valley northwest of the village of Grasmere; a region of 'delightful walks' (*Guide, Prose,* II, 159n.) and the 'Black Quarter', DW's term for the path—and warning sign—of foul weather from the north, in her Grasmere journal.

Esthwaite Lake, and Vale of Esthwaite, located near Hawkshead, to the west of Lake Windermere. See WW's lengthy description of this vale in *Unpublished Tour, Prose,* II, 352–9.

Fenwick, Isabella. See Introduction, n. 1.

Fleming. See the entry for Le Fleming, below.

Goslar, the town on the edge of the Hartz Forest in Germany where William and Dorothy lived in the harsh winter of 1798–9.

Greenhead Ghyll, in northeastern Grasmere, under the prominence called Stone Arthur and beyond it Fairfield.

Hawkshead, or Hawkeshead, market town situated two miles west of Lake Windermere in the Vale of Esthwaite, where Hawkshead School is located. The town is described at length in *An Unpublished Tour, Prose,* II, 324–32.

Haydon, Benjamin Robert (1786–1846), historical painter and diarist. Sir George Beaumont was an early supporter. High principled and 'difficult' with patrons, Haydon was often in debt. Yet his studio was a focal point for those interested in art, including Wordsworth, Leigh Hunt, John Keats, Charles Lamb and many others. Haydon committed suicide in 1846 after the financial failure of an exhibition.

Helvellyn, peak to the east of Wythburn, five miles north of Grasmere.

Hemans, Felicia Dorothea (1793–1835), poet. She bore five sons to her husband, Captain Alfred Hemans, who left her in 1818 and went abroad. She maintained her young family through her writing, gaining a reputation both in Europe and in North America. She visited Wordsworth at Rydal Mount for a fortnight, during a tour of the English lakes, in July 1830.

Hogg, James (1770–1835), the Ettrick Shepherd. He first published his Scots dialect poems in 1801 and later contributed traditional ballads to Walter Scott's *Minstrelsy of the Scottish Border.* After repeated failures at farming, he moved to Edinburgh to make his living as a writer. Through John Wilson, an editor and contributor to the 'Edinburgh Magazine,' he came to know Wordsworth and Southey. He married and settled at St Mary's Lake in Yorkshire where he received many visitors and kept up his literary career while making a modest success of farming. Despite a wickedly amusing parody of Scott, Wordsworth, Southey and others, published in 1816, he retained the affection and support of his friends to the end of his life.

Hutchinson, George (1778–1864), Mary's younger brother; he farmed at Sockburn (q.v.) and Gallow Hill with his brother Thomas (q.v.), and at Middleham in Yorkshire.

Hutchinson, Joanna (1780–1843), Mary Wordsworth's younger sister; she travelled with Dorothy Wordsworth in Scotland in 1822 and the Isle of Man in 1828; unmarried, like her sister Sara, she went to live with her brother Henry on the Isle of Man.

Hutchinson, Sara (1775–1835), Mary Wordsworth's younger sister; she made her home with the Wordsworths, when she wasn't keeping house for one of her brothers, from 1802 until her death. She died at Rydal Mount following a brief illness in June 1835.

Hutchinson, Thomas (1773–1849), Mary Wordsworth's younger brother; he farmed in various places including Sockburn on the Tees and Gallow Hill near Scarborough, the house from which Mary Hutchinson married William Wordsworth. He was also at Park House near Penrith and at Hindwell in Radnorshire. He married his cousin Mary Monkhouse in 1812 and eventually took a farm at Brinsop Court.

Jewsbury, Maria Jane (1800–33), poet and friend of the Wordsworths, especially Dora; she dedicated her *Phantasmagoria, or Sketches of Life and Literature* (London, 1825) to Wordsworth ('O long unrecked, and unseen/ Hast thou my spirit's father been'). Wordsworth returned the favour in 1829 by dedicating the poem *Liberty* to her. See Wordsworth's published note to *Liberty*. She died in India a year after her marriage to Revd W.K. Fletcher, a chaplain in the East India Company.

Jones, Revd Robert (1769–1835). Wordsworth and this Welsh college friend toured the Alps together in 1790; Wordsworth's account of the tour in verse, *Descriptive Sketches* (1793), is dedicated to Jones. They maintained a life-long friendship and often visited one another in Grasmere, Rydal, Jones' family home at Plas-yn-Llan, Denbighshire, and Jones' Oxfordshire parsonage at Souldern.

Kendal, market town at the eastern edge of the Lake District, fourteen miles southeast of Grasmere.

Keswick, market town on Derwentwater, twelve miles north of Grasmere. The Vale of Keswick comprises Derwentwater and the encircling fells. It was described by WW in *Select Views* (*Prose*, II, 274–6), and before him, as he notes, by Dr. John Brown (*A Description of the Lake at Keswick (and the Adjacent Country) in Cumberland: Communicated in a Letter to a Friend, by a Late Popular Writer* [Kendal, 1770]) and by Thomas Gray (whose 'Journal' was transcribed as letters to Thomas Warton and later published in William Mason's *The Poems of Mr. Gray* [York, 1775] and Thomas West's Addendum to his *Guide to the Lakes* in the second edition of 1780).

Kirkstone Pass, mountain pass northeast of Ambleside, leading to Patterdale and Ullswater. See *Guide, Prose,* II, pp. 250–1.

Lamb, Charles (1775–1834), author of *Elia* and other essays praising life in London. Introduced to William and Dorothy Wordsworth by Coleridge at Alfoxden in July 1797, Lamb, and later his sister Mary, remained close friends with the Wordsworths through the following years.

Langdale, Langdale Pikes. The two Langdales, Little and Great, lie west of the northern tip of Lake Windermere. The Pikes (or 'peaks') form the northern side of Great Langdale, seven miles west of Ambleside. This area, along with Loughrigg Fell and Grasmere, provides the scene for much of *The Excursion,* books II–IX.

Le Fleming, Lady Anne Frederica (1785–1861). The daughter and heiress of Sir Michael Le Fleming of Rydal Hall where she lived with her mother, Lady Diana (d. 1816). Lady Anne purchased Rydal Mount in 1813 and leased it to the Wordsworths, with whom she and her mother were on good terms. Lady Anne built Rydal Chapel, just below Rydal Mount, in 1823–4. When Wordsworth's lease on Rydal Mount ran out in December 1825 she threatened to install a relation there in 1827, but as her relative was disinclined to move and as Wordsworth had purchased 'Dora's field', below Rydal Mount and beside the chapel, with the intention of building a house upon it, she renewed his lease on Rydal Mount

Loughrigg Fell, or simply Loughrigg, 'rises abruptly from the foot of the Lake of Grasmere' where the River Rothay 'steal[s] out of the lake at one corner' (*Select Views, Prose,* II, 271n.); Loughrigg Tarn lies on its southwest flank at the eastern extension of Great Langdale.

Luff, Captain, and Mrs Letitia Luff, friends of the Clarksons, lived at Patterdale, where they received the Wordsworths as house guests on several occasions (see Dorothy Wordsworth's 'Excursion on the Banks of Ullswater, November 1805' in *Journals,* 1,413–22). They moved to Mauritius in 1812, but when her husband died in 1815, Mrs Luff returned to the Lakes, settling finally in Grasmere.

Montagu, Basil (1770–1851). The brilliant but eccentric, illegitimate son of

John Montagu, 4th Earl of Sandwich, and the singer Martha Ray. He was acknowledge by his father but married in 1791 without his approval; his wife died in childbirth in 1793 and he then went to London to read for the Bar. He met Wordsworth in 1795, and Wordsworth and Dorothy looked after young Basil for several years at Racedown and Alfoxden. Moresby, the village north of Whitehaven on the west coast where Wordsworth's son John was Rector.

Nab-Scar, or Nab Scar, the fell west of Dove Cottage and north of Rydal Mount.

Nether Stowey, the village in Somerset, thirty miles southwest of Bristol, where Coleridge lived, near his friend Thomas Poole, while the Wordsworths were staying nearby, first at Racedown and then at Alfoxden.

Patterdale, or Paterdale, at the foot of Kirkstone Pass on the southwestern end of Ullswater.

Penrith, market town thirty miles northeast of Grasmere, home of Christopher Crackanthorpe (Cookson), Wordsworth's maternal grandfather and his guardian after the death of his father in 1783.

Poole, Thomas (1765–1837), of Nether Stowey. Friend and patron of Coleridge, and through Coleridge a friend of Wordsworth. He was largely self-educated and an active supporter of the poor laws.

Quantock Hills, the hills in Somerset lying north of Taunton and stretching to the Bristol Channel, including the Over Stowey region where the Coleridges and Wordsworths lived.

Quillinan, Dora. See the entry for Dora Wordsworth, below.

Quillinan, Edward (1791–1851). Half-pay officer and occasional writer, married William Wordsworth's daughter Dora as his second wife 11 May 1841, at Bath.

Race Down, or Racedown Lodge, the house owned by John Pinney senior, lying a few miles west of Crewkerne in North Dorset, where William and Dorothy Wordsworth lived rent-free from the end of September 1795 to the end of June 1797, through the agency of Pinney's sons, John Frederick and Azariah, who used the Lodge on occasional visits from Bristol.

Robinson, Henry Crabb (1775–1867), barrister, diarist and literary man; friend and correspondent of Goethe, Wieland, Wordsworth, Coleridge and Lamb, European traveller, war correspondent of the *Times* in Spain, one of the founders of London University. He travelled with the Wordsworths to Switzerland in 1820 and with William to the Isle of Man in 1833 and to Italy in 1837.

Rogers, Samuel (1763–1855), poet and art collector. His most popular poem was *The Pleasures of Memory* (1792), published while he was director of a City bank. He retired from the bank with a comfortable income in 1793 and established himself as an important figure in the arts in London, both as a poet and as a patron. He was a long-time friend of Wordsworth and assisted him by suggesting to Lord Lonsdale that Wordsworth be appointed to the distributorship of stamps in Lord Lonsdale's jurisdiction.

Rydal Hall, in the hamlet of Rydal, the residence of Lady Anne Le Fleming, Wordsworth's landlord. It had been fronted in classical style by her father, Michael Le Fleming, at the turn of the century. Rydal Beck runs through the grounds of Rydal Park, forming several waterfalls including Upper Rydal Falls. For WW's descriptions of the Park and falls see *Evening Walk*, ll. 57–69, 'Lyre! though such power do in thy magic live', and *Select Views* (*Prose*, II, 269).

Rydal Mount, Wordsworth's home from 1813 to his death in 1850, is in the hamlet of Rydal, a mile and a half east of Grasmere (its situation is described by WW in his note to *Prefatory lines* on notebook p. 72). See also the entry for Le Fleming, above.

Scott, Sir Walter (1771–1832), Scottish novelist, poet, and man of letters. Qualified as an advocate, Scott published a collection of Scottish ballads, *The Minstrelsy of the Scottish Border* in 1802–3 and his own narrative poem, *The Lay of the Last Minstrel* in 1805. The success of the latter enabled him to quit the law and devote himself entirely to a literary career. With a wide social circle, first in Edinburgh where he met Burns, and then in Selkirk and later in Abbotsford, he was friend and host to Wordsworth, Southey, Hogg and many other writers. His friendship with Wordsworth was formed early, while he was still chiefly known as a poet of romantic narratives. Never robust, having suffered from poliomyelitis as a child, he fell into debt in 1826 through the failure of publishing firms he partly owned and struggled heroically in his remaining years to repay his creditors, chiefly through producing historical novels and other popular works at a great rate. The importance to Scott of his family and friends was very great and the inclusion of the Wordsworths in this circle continued until Scott's death in 1832.

Sockburn, Sockburn-on-Tees, in Durham, about seven miles south-east of Darlington, on the north bank of the Tees; described by Dorothy Wordsworth to Jane Pollard (mid-April 1795) as 'a grazing estate, and most delightfully pleasant, washed nearly round by the Tees', where Mary Wordsworth's brother Thomas Hutchinson farmed, and where both Mary and Sara Hutchinson 'kept his house' (*EY,* p. 142). From the house at Sockburn Mary and William Wordsworth were married in 1802.

Southey, Robert (1774–1843). Poet, journalist and man of letters; Poet Laureate 1813–43. Originally from Bristol, he was friend and brother-in-law of Coleridge, and friend of Wordsworth; after 1800 he moved his family, with Coleridge's family (Edith Southey and Sara Coleridge were sisters), to Greta Hall, Keswick, where Southey took primary responsibility for the combined households.

Town-End, or Town End, the hamlet on the south-eastern side of Grasmere Lake where the Wordsworths lived from the end of 1799 to 1808 (the cottage they leased had been an inn, The Dove and Olive Branch, and was named Dove Cottage after they had left it).

Tyson, Ann (1713–96), of Hawkshead and later the nearby hamlet of Colthouse, provided room and board to the Wordsworth brothers while they attended school. The fullest account of her is in *Wordsworth's Hawkshead.* Wordsworth's own tribute in verse is in *Prelude,* IV, 19–28.

Ulswater, or Ullswater, about ten miles northeast of Grasmere, by road over Kirkstone Pass and by footpath through Grisedale.

Wellington, Arthur Wellesley, first Duke of (1769–1852). Field-marshal, principal figure in the war with Napoleon in Spain and in France, and instrumental in his defeat at Waterloo in 1815.

Windermere, the Lake itself, and the town above it on its eastern shore. Imagining himself standing on 'a cloud hanging midway between' Great Gavel and Scafell, two of the highest peaks in the center of the Lake District, WW described Windermere and its long valley as one of the 'spokes from the nave of a wheel' that included the other major lakes and vallies of the district (*Guide, Prose,* II,171).

Wordsworth, Dora, Wordsworth's second child, born 16 August 1804. She married Edward Quillinan 11 May 1841, at Bath. She died of tuberculosis 9 July 1847.

Wordsworth, Dorothy (1771–1855). Wordsworth's only sister. On her mother's death in 1778 she lived with her second cousin, Elizabeth (Cookson) Threlkeld in Halifax. At age sixteen she was first summoned to her mother's parents' home in Penrith and, on the death of her grandfather Cookson, went to live with his son, the Revd William Cookson, and his new wife at Forncett in Norfolk. In 1795 she joined her brother William at Racedown and remained a part of his household until her death in 1855. From 1835 she suffered from the advancing effects of what was probably Alzheimer's disease.

Wordsworth, John (1772–1805). Wordsworth's second brother; a sailor from his leaving Hawkshead School in 1787. He lived with William and Dorothy at Dove Cottage for eight months in 1800 before taking up as Master of the *Earl of Abergavenny* and was in command when the East India merchant ship sank in a storm in the English Channel on 5 February 1805.

Wordsworth, John (1803–75). Wordsworth's first child.

Wordsworth, Mary (Hutchinson) (1770–1855). The wife of William Wordsworth.

INDEX and recommended search terms

Part One: Names and Places

Entries in square brackets show alternative search terms, such as [Dora W / DQ] for Dora Wordsworth, née Wordsworth, the poet's daughter.

Abbotsford, 136, 138, 319, 320, 353, 392
Aders, Charles, 69, 254
Aeschylus, 302
Aikin, John, 40, 219, 223; *Monthly Magazine*, 40, 219, 223
Allan-Bank
Alexander III, 106, 294
Allan, Sir William, 136, 137, 319–20
Allsop, Thomas, 13, 14
Anderson, Dr Robert, 90, 280, 338
Anti-Corn Law League, 162, 340, 366
Archimedes, 161
Arnold, Matthew, 27
Arnold, Thomas, 264
Ashburner, Peggy, 54, 231, 238, 380
Ashburner, Thomas, 231, 380
Baillie, Joanna, 63, 245; *Poetic Miscellanies* (1823), 245
Ballad of Sir Patrick Spence, 336
Barbauld, Anna Letitia, 47, 219, 223
Barber, Mr, 170, 204, 349, 377
Bartram, William, *Travels through North and South Georgia* (1791), 246
Beaumont, Lady, 57, 81, 86, 201, 230, 266 270, 322, 334, 335, 365, 384, 385
Beaumont, Sir George, 64, 65, 74, 151, 169, 230, 237, 243, 247, 261, 266, 292, 333, 349, 356, 384; excursions with WW, 146, 201, 330; gift

of Applethwaite to WW, 165-6, 204, 346, 348, 384, 385; subject or audience for WW's poems, 68, 85, 87, 101, 180, 356
  PAINTINGS: *Bredon Hill and Cloud Hill*, 74; *Piel Castle in a Storm*, 151, 292, 333; *The Thorn*, 64, 247
Benson, John, 234, 236
Blackett, Christopher, 251
Blackett, Dorothy and Elizabeth, 67, 251
Boccaccio, Giovanni, *Genealogica Deorum Gentilium*, 303
Bonaparte, Joseph, 282
Bonaparte, Napoleon, 73, 87, 94, 184, 258, 283, 302, 394
Braithwaite, Revd William, 109, 296
Brown, Dr John, *A Description of the Lake at Keswick*, 389
Bruce, Peter Henry, *Memoirs*, 321
Bürger, Gottfried August, *Leonora*, 87, 276
Burgoyne, Montagu, 67, 251
Burke, Edmund, 115, 300
Burns, Robert, 87, 89–90, 136, 143, 165, 275, 319, 321, 326–7, 344–6, 384, 392
Butler, Lady Eleanor, 82–3, 268
Butler, Revd Samuel, 189, 365
Byron, George Gordon, Lord, 147, 178, 331, 345–6, 354
Calvert, Raisley, 78, 218, 255, 263, 342, 384–5
Calvert, William, 384–5
Campbell, Colonel and Mrs, 134, 316
Carbonari, 186, 361
Carleton, Mary, 151, 333
Carlyle, Thomas, 368; *History of the French Revolution*, 368; *On Heroes, Hero-Worship and The Heroic in History*, 283
Carr, Dr and Mrs Thomas, 129, 311
Carter, John [JC], 26–28, 32, 230, 253, 264, 307, 348, 376, 381
Catullus, *To Lesbia*, 269
Charles I, 294

Chartism, chartists, 214–5, 340, 383
Chatterton, Thomas, *Goddwyn. A Tragedie*, 188, 364
Chaucer, Geoffrey, 91, 238
Chiabrera, Gabriello, 151, 333
Clarkson, Catherine, 115, 247, 280, 290, 381, 385
Clarkson, Thomas, 37, 64, 115, 217, 247, 299, 385
Clifford, Henry Lord, 92, 249, 281
Clifford, Lady Anne, 249
Cockermouth, 52, 55, 147, 187, 322, 385
Coleorton, 57, 63, 66, 74, 81, 85, 92, 95, 107, 152, 230, 237, 243, 245, 266, 272, 284, 292–3, 384, 385
Coleridge, David Hartley, 53, 124, 228, 305
Coleridge, Derwent, 305, 365
Coleridge, Henry Nelson, 13, 14, 252
Coleridge, Samuel Taylor [STC], 12–18, 39, 41–5, 47, 72, 149–50, 154–5, 178, 218–23, 228–30, 246, 250, 269, 276, 280, 338, 365, 381, 384, 385, 390, 392, 393; at Christ's Hospital, 154, 338, 385; death, 154, 338; domestic situation, 165, 346–7; at Grasmere, 53, 72, 87, 227, 236–7, 256; at Greta Hall, 165, 386; influence on WW, 38, 110, 162–3, 218, 297, 339; subject or audience for WW's poems, 52, 72, 217, 230, 241, 243, 257, 297, 371; in Somerset and Dorset, 39–45, 110, 297, 371, 384–6, 391; tours with WW, 12, 39–40, 68–9, 87, 126–7, 133, 218, 253–4
   WRITINGS: *The Friend*, 66, 151, 333, 384; *Ode to Georgiana, Duchess of Devonshire*, 328; *Osorio* (*Remorse*), 193, 372; *The Rime of the Ancient Mariner*, 9, 40–2, 218
Coleridge, Sara, 68, 229, 252
Coleridge, Sara (Fricker), 229, 256, 347, 386, 393
Coleridge, Sir John Taylor, 227
Collins, William, 110; *Ode on the Death of Mr. Thomson*, 296
Congreve, William, *The Old Bachelor*, 184, 359
Constable, John, 384

Cookson, Thomas, 141, 324–5
Cooper, Anthony Ashley, Earl of Shaftesbury, 213, 382
Cottle, Joseph, 13, 14, 66, 220, 226, 248, 250, 372, 386; *Early Recollections: Chiefly Relating to the Late S.T. Coleridge, During His Long Residence in Bristol*, 17
Cowper, William, 345
Cowperthwaite, Thomas, 299
Cozens, J.R., 384
Crabbe, George, 17, 38, 155-7, 338, 386
Crackanthorpe, Christopher, 145, 329, 391
Crackanthorpe, William, 238
Cruikshank, John, 40, 219
Cunningham, Allan, 326, 327
Curwen, John Christian, 50, 109, 225, 296, 310
Dampier, William, 278
Daniel, Samuel, 91, 281; *Defence of Rhyme*, 281
Dante, 183–4, 359
Darwin, Erasmus, 248, 345–6; *Zoonomia, or the Laws of Organic Life*, 65, 248, 345–6
Davy, Sir Humphrey, 150, 176, 332, 353, 386
Dawes, Revd John, 189, 365
Dawson, George, 208, 212, 379, 381
De Quincey, Thomas, 13, 14, 289
De Selincourt, Ernest, 229, 233, 263, 339, 381
Devonshire, Duchess of (Georgiana Spenser Cavendish), 144, 328; *Lines by Georgiana, Duchess of Devonshire*, 328
Digby, Kenelm Henry, *Orlandus, book four of The Broad Stone of Honour*, 234–5
Doane, George Washington, Bishop of New Jersey, 366–7
Douglas, Sir William, Duke of Queensbury, 278
Drayton, Michael, 91, 281
Drummond, John, 208, 379

Duddon, 13, 98, 288, 357, 387
Dunmail, 49, 58, 282, 380, 387
Duppa, Richard, 76, 261
Easedale, 71, 147, 255, 264, 387
Edgeworth, Maria, *Early Lessons, Moral Tales,* and *The Parent's Assistant,* 363
Edgeworth, Maria, and Richard Lovell Edgeworth, *Practical Education,* 363
    Edward VI, 338
Esthwaite
Estlin, Mrs John, 57, 236
Euripides, 251
Faber, Frederick, 106, 179, 294, 355; *Life of St. Bega,* 355; *Sights and Thoughts in Foreign Churches and among Foreign Peoples,* 355
Fawcett, Joseph, 197–8, 375; *The Art of Poetry,* 375; *The Art of War, A Poem,* 197, 375
Fenwick, Isabella [IF, Miss F, or Miss Fenwick], 12–13, 17–19, 22–4, 29–33, 192, 298, 355, 357–8, 364, 368–71, 373; criticism of WW's sonnet, 77, 262; role in producing Notes, 22–33, 128, 189, 192, 216, 226, 229–30, 258, 306, 315; source for WW's poetry, 192, 371; tours with WW, 12–13, 17–19, 21, 99–100, 237, 288, 297
Fermor, Frances, 151, 189, 334, 365
Field, Barron, 15–16, 251; *Memoirs of the Life and Poetry of William Wordsworth, with Extracts from his Letters to the Author,* 15
Fitzgerald, Lady Maria, 84, 270
Fitzgerald, Sir Maurice, 270
Fleming (see Le Fleming)
Fletcher, Elizabeth, 79, 264; *Autobiography of Mrs. Fletcher, of Edinburgh* (1871), 264
Fox, Charles James, 227, 234, 260, 327–8
Fox-Ghyll (or Fox Ghyll)
Fox How
Frederick I, Emperor (Barbarossa), 106, 294
Geoffrey of Monmouth, *History of the Kings of Britain,* 227

George III, 327
Gibson, John, 114, 299
Gillies, Adam, 78, 263
Gillies, John, 263
Gillies, Margaret, 78, 191, 263, 369
Gillies, Robert Pearce, 77–8, 262
Gillman, James, 386; *Life of Samuel Coleridge*, 13–15
Glover, John, 146, 330
Goldsmith, Oliver, 327
Goslar, 38, 112, 165, 223, 237, 243–6, 276, 332, 344, 387
Gough, Charles, 116, 301
Gough, John, 211, 381
Graham, Sir James, 214, 383
Grahame, James, 37, 217
Grahame, Robert, 37, 217
Graves, Robert Perceval, 17, 189, 365
Gray, Thomas, 117, 302, 389
Green, Joseph Henry, 14
Greenhead Ghyll
Greenwood, Mr., 170, 204, 349, 377
Gregory VII (Hildebrand), 106, 294
Grosart, Alexander, *The Prose Works of William Wordsworth* (1876), 26–7
Hamilton, William Rowan, 311, 316
Hardy, Thomas, of the London Corresponding Society, 221
Harris, Thomas, 193, 372
Harrison, John, 299
Hawkshead, 13, 48, 49, 98, 108, 109, 114, 225, 241, 243, 252, 299, 302, 332, 354, 378, 379, 380, 384, 387, 393
Haydon, Benjamin Robert, 247, 259, 265, 266, 274, 354, 367, 384, 388; portraits: *Napoleon*, 86–7, 274; *Wellington*, 190, 367
Hazlitt, William, 15–16, 255, 295

Hearne, Samuel, *A Journey from Prince of Wale's Fort in Hudson's Bay to the Northern Ocean*, 54, 231
Heath, Charles, 307
Helvellyn, 47, 67, 116, 165, 176, 190, 301, 346, 353, 367, 388
Hemans, Felicia, 157–8, 338–9, 388; *Scenes and Hymns of Life*, 339; *Works of Mrs Hemans*, 339
Henry IV, Emperor of Germany, 106, 294
Hernaman, John, 154, 338
Hoare, Mr and Mrs Samuel, 155, 338
Hogg, James (Ettrick Shepherd), 90, 154, 262, 280, 319, 338, 388, 392
Holmes, James, 125, 307
Homer, 121
Horace (Quintus Horatius Flaccus), 117, 302
Horrocks, Miss, 104, 290
Howard, Mrs, 144, 327
Hunt, Leigh, 354, 388; *Lord Byron and Some of His Contemporaries*, 354
Huntingdon, Selena Hastings Countess of, 202, 377
Hutchinson, George, 228, 233
Hutchinson, Henry, 141, 228, 324; *By a Retired Mariner. (A Friend of the Author.)*, 141, 324; *The Retrospect of a Retired Mariner*, 324
Hutchinson, Henry (WW's nephew), 97, 287
Hutchinson, Joanna, 72, 222, 256, 324, 388
Hutchinson, John, 287, 289
Hutchinson, Sara [S.H.], 19, 66, 76, 130, 191, 246, 250, 261, 278, 302, 313, 346–7, 369, 388–9, 393; death, 76, 130, 261, 313; early life, 374; source for WW's poetry, 67, 196; on tour with WW, 77, 89, 262, 278; *To a Redbreast (In Sickness)*, 191, 369
Hutchinson, Thomas, 116, 228, 230, 266, 333, 389, 393
Jackson, John, 384
Jackson, Ruth, 201
Jackson, William, 236
Jeffrey, Francis, 369

Jewsbury, Maria Jane (later Mrs Fletcher), 59, 83, 125, 240, 269, 307–8, 389
Johnson, Samuel, 305, 327, 328, 359
Jones, Revd Robert, 39, 59, 82, 111, 218, 240, 255, 268, 297, 324, 342, 389
Keats, John, 303, 388
Keble, John, 294
Ken, Thomas, 128, 310
Keswick, 94, 165, 258, 347, 348, 358, 385, 386, 389, 393
Kirkstone, 67, 122, 251, 390
Knight, Thomas, 193, 372
Knott family, 212–3, 278, 381, 382
Laidlaw, William, 136, 319
Lamb, Charles, 13–14, 16, 59, 153–5, 172, 220, 236, 240, 245, 254, 336–8, 344, 350, 352, 365, 385, 388, 390, 392; at Christ's Hospital, 154, 338; death, 10–11, 154, 336, 365; retirement to Enfield, 172, 350; visits from WW, 59, 236, 350
Lamb, Mary, 153–4, 336, 390
Landor, Walter Savage, 187, 363; *A Satire on Satirists*, 363; *Gebir*, 363
Langdale, 72, 73, 81, 167, 189, 190, 199, 201, 365, 375, 390
Laud, William, 106, 294
Le Fleming, Lady Anne, 124, 241, 285, 306, 390, 392; family seat, 48, 223–4
Le Fleming, Sir Michael, 99, 169, 224, 349, 390, 392; family seat, 48, 223–4
Lewthwaite, Barbara, 46, 222
Liddell, Henry, 136–7, 319–20
Liddle, Thomas, 136–7, 319–20
Lloyd, Charles, 189, 250, 256, 365
Lloyd, Owen, 189, 365
Lloyd, Priscilla, 256
Lockhart, John Gibson, 136–7, 139, 319; *Life of Scott*, 154–5, 319, 338

Long Meg, 116, 301, 318
Lonsdale, Lady Augusta, 97, 115, 287, 300
Lonsdale, William Lowther, Earl of, 115, 287, 299-300, 322, 329, 385, 392
Lonsdale, James Lowther, Earl of, 287
Loughrigg, 59, 66, 75, 78, 169, 190, 200, 204, 215, 239, 295, 349, 351, 377, 390,
Luff, Captain and Mrs. Letitia, 58, 171
Mackenzie, Frances, 177, 354
Mackenzie, Francis, Lord Seaforth, 354
Mackereth, George M, 89, 278
Mackreth, Daniel, 150, 332
Mackreth, Elizabeth, 332
Macpherson, James, 124, 305
Marshall, James, 134, 166, 208, 316, 348
Marshall, Jane (Pollard), 235, 254, 302, 393
Marshall, John, 69, 134, 254, 316, 348
Mary Queen of Scots, 53–4, 80, 140, 230, 323
Mason, William, 389
Meyrick, Sir Samuel Rush, 44, 221
Michelangelo [and Michael Angelo], 76, 185, 261, 354, 360
Mickle, William Julius, *Sir Martyn, a Poem in the Manner of Spenser*, 131, 314
Milton, John, 52, 73, 358; *The History of Britain*, 52, 120, 227, 303; *Lycidas*, 121–2; *Paradise Lost*, 183, 358; sonnets, 73, 258
Monkhouse, Jane (Horrocks), 104, 270, 290
Monkhouse, Mary, 84, 270, 389
Monkhouse, Thomas, 84, 104, 230, 270, 290
Montagu, Algernon, 111, 365
Montagu, Basil, 44, 111, 221, 365, 386, 390–1
Morning Post, The, 14–15, 269, 332
Morris, Thomas, 84, 270

Moxon, Edward, 14–15, 26–7, 32, 174, 352
Murray, Lindley, *Introduction to the English Reader*, 46, 222
Nelson, Viscount Horatio, 118, 302
Newman, John Henry, and Oxford Tractarian Movement, 106, 294; *Lives of the English Saints*, 355
Nicholson, Samuel, 197, 375
Nollekens, Joseph, RA, 144, 327–8
Ogle, Elizabeth Frances, 187, 363
Ossian, 124, 228, 305
Ovid, Metamorphoses, 121
Owen, Robert, *The Body of the New Moral World,* and *Lectures on an Entire New State of Society*, 366
Oxford Movement, 106, 294
Patrick, James, 196, 374
Patterdale, 116, 254, 270, 287, 300, 346, 376, 390, 391
Pearson, William, 206, 378
Pedlar, The, 195, 196, 199, 374
Peel, Sir Robert, 222, 383
Penrith, 54, 78, 135, 245, 248, 249, 299, 318, 329, 375, 389, 391, 394
Percy, Thomas, *Reliques of Ancient English Poetry*, 336, 346
Petrarca, Francesco, 175, 352
Phillips, Richard, *Monthly Magazine*, 40, 219
Pickersgill, Henry William, 274
Pinney, Azariah, 220, 391
Pinney, John Frederick, 220, 391
Pitt, William, 144–5, 328–9
Plato, Platonism, 161, 185, 303
Pliny the Elder (Gaius Plinius Secundus), 282; *Historia Naturalis*, 251
Plutarch, 303
Ponsonby, Miss, 82–3, 268
Poole, Thomas, 55, 149, 193, 231, 234, 332, 372, 386, 391
Pope, Alexander, 151, 211, 334; *The Rape of the Lock*, 151

Price, Sir Uvedale, 105, 151, 292, 333
Priestley, Joseph, 219
Pusey, Edward, and Oxford Tractarian Movement, 106, 294, 355
Quantock Hills, 13, 16, 40, 64, 391
Quillinan, Dora [DQ] (see Dora Wordsworth [Dora W])
Quillinan, Edward [EQ], 12–13, 84, 270, 312, 391, 394; additions to and corrections of Notes, *passim* 36ff; his intended use of notes, 24–26; marriage to Dora W, 19, 237, 297, 394; role in producing Notes, 12, 22–26, 29–33, 38, 218; tours with WW, 100, 136, 216, 237, 297
Quillinan, Jemima (first wife of EQ), 270, 286, 312
Quillinan, Jemima (daughter of EQ), 12, 26, 129, 136, 312
Quillinan, Rotha, 26, 84, 96, 270, 286, 288
Racedown, 221, 295, 331, 371, 373, 385, 391, 394
Raincock, Fletcher, 241
Raincock, William, 60, 241
Rawnsley, H.D., 304
Ray, Martha, 391
Reed, Henry, 345, 366–7
Reynolds, Frederick Mansel, 307
Reynolds, Sir Joshua, 384
Ricketts, Anna, 181, 357
Ridpath, George, *The Border-History of England and Scotland*, 193, 372
Robinson, Henry Crabb [HCR], 14, 25, 242, 245, 254, 292, 306, 367–9; anecdote concerning Titian's Last Supper, 313, tours with WW, 104, 140–1, 174, 182, 290, 321, 352, 354–5, 357, 359, 361, 385, 392
Rogers, Samuel, *passim*; 119–20, 130, 146, 155–7, 270–1, 313, 330, 351, 353, 384, 392; *The Boy of Egremond*, 119, 302; *Italy*, 130, 313; *The Pleasures of Memory*, 392
Rowlandson, Edward, 167, 349
Rydal, Rydal Hall, Rydal Mount, *passim*
Sandys, Edwin, 62, 243
Satterthwaite, James, 95, 284

Scarisbrick, James and Thomas, 272–3
Schiller, Johann Christoph Friedrich von, 345–6
Scott, Anne, 136–7, 177
Scott, Major, 136–7
Scott, Sir Walter, 89, 116, 176–8, 193, 245, 314, 319, 338, 353, 369, 392–3; journey to Italy, 133, 136–7, 177, 315; style compared to WW's style, 102–3; visited by WW, 131, 133, 136–7, 154–5, 314, 319, 353; visit to WW, 176, 319, 353
  WRITINGS: *Helvellyn*, 116, 301; *The Lay of the Last Minstrel*, 392; *Life of Napoleon Buonaparte, Emperor of the French*, 283; *The Minstrelsy of the Scottish Border*, 319, 388, 392–3
Scrope, William, 80, 265
Shakespeare, William, 73, 135
Shelley, Percy Bysshe, 178, 303, 354
Shelvocke, George, *Voyage round the World, by the Way of the Great South Sea*, 40, 219
Shenstone, William, 115, 300
Sheridan, Richard Brinsley, 193, 372
Smith, Adam, 351; Wealth of Nations, 173, 351, 366
Smith, Elizabeth, 115, 300
Smith, Mary Wordsworth, 99, 288
Sockburn, 55, 65, 116, 248, 388, 389, 393
Southey, Edith (Fricker), 191, 370, 393
Southey, Edith May, 68, 238, 252, 272
Southey, Robert, 47, 76, 130, 150, 195, 219, 229, 236, 238, 250, 261, 282–3, 292–3, 305, 336, 363, 374, 384, 388, 392, 393; *Ominiana, or Horae Otiosiores* (1812), 381
Stone, Frank, RA., 129, 311–12
Stuart, Daniel, 14
Sympson, Joseph (the younger), *Science Revived, or The Vision of Alfred*, 210, 380
Sympson, Mary, 380

Sympson, Revd Joseph, 210, 380
Tait's Magazine, 14
Talfourd, Sir Thomas Noon, 13–14, 153, 336–7, 363
Tasso, Torquato 177, 283, 354; *Gerusalemme Liberata*, 283, 354
Taylor, Henry, 12–13, 18, 368
Taylor, William (Hawkshead schoolmaster), 299
Taylor, William (poet and translator), 276
Thelwall, John, 44, 45, 221, 222, 228
Thomson, James, 296
Threlkeld, Elizabeth, 375, 394
Tilbrooke, Samuel, 74, 259
Tobin, James Webbe, 42, 220
Tobin, John, 43, 220
Tooke, John Horne, 221
Town End [and Town-End], *passim*
Tractarian, *see* Oxford Movement
Tyson, Ann, 71, 379, 393
Ullswater [and Ulswater], 247, 254, 316, 321, 330, 376, 385, 393
Vandeput, Sir George, 208, 379
Virgil, 121, 283; Aeneid, 251
Walker, Adam, 84, 270–1
Walker, Adam John, 84, 271
Walker, Ellen Loveday, 83–4, 269
Walker, Robert, 211, 381
Warter, Revd J.W., 252
Watson, John, 236
Wellington, Arthur Wellesley, first Duke of [Wellesley], 190, 282, 327, 367, 393–4
West, Thomas, *Guide to the Lakes in Cumberland, Westmorland and Lancashire*, 199, 224, 296
Weston brothers, 208, 379
Whewell, Revd William, 234

Whitaker, Thomas Dunham, *The History and Antiquities of the Deanery of Craven*, 119, 302
White, William, Bishop of Pennsylvania, 367
Whitefield, George, 377
Wilkie, David, 64, 130, 247, 313
Wilkinson, Thomas, 114–6, 299, 301
Wilson, John (landscape painter), 64, 247
Wilson, John (Chistopher North), 247, 388
Wolcot, John, 219
Wordsworth, Ann (WW's mother), 37
Wordsworth, Catherine, 37, 74, 76, 174, 217, 259, 261, 352
Wordsworth, Christopher (Wordsworth's brother), 85, 272, 293, 297, 365
Wordsworth, Christopher Jr [CWJr], 17, 62, 274; Memoirs of William Wordsworth (1851), 24–26, 32, 297
Wordsworth, Dora [Dora W](later Dora Quillinan [DQ]), 18, 22, 29–33, 222–3, 229–30, 238–41, 274, 297, 364, 369–370, 389, 391, 394; additions and corrections to Notes, 30, *passim* 37–216 *in manuscript notes*, 304, 315, 320, 335; death, 23, 25, 30, 394; 'Dora's field', 60, 241, 390; health, 238, 265, 311, 377; marriage, 13, 19, 394; subject or audience for WW's poems, 17, 20, 48, 60, 68, 88, 107, 222, 238–40, 265, 294, 304, 307, 322, 350; excursions with WW, 12–13, 18, 82, 86, 99, 126, 136–7, 229, 254, 268, 288, 286, 297, 311, 319, 357, 386
Wordsworth, Dorothy [DW], 12–14, 19–21, 34, 37, 38, 52, 54, 72, 77, 91, 95, 101, 117, 209, 253, 256, 290, 300, 350, 394; affected by sounds, 66, 147; at Alfoxden, 12, 39, 42, 111, 297, 384, 386, 390–1; childhood, 37, 147; at Coleorton, 81, 95, 152, 230, 237, 266; in Goslar, 112, 116, 220, 243, 298, 386–7; in Grasmere, 52, 73, 222, 231, 237, 257, 346, 387, 394; illness, 56, 191, 241, 369–70, 394; at Racedown, 44, 221, 295, 331, 373, 391, 394; at Sockburn (Yorkshire), 65, 116, 248, 265, 393: at Windy Brow, 385; reading Shakespeare's sonnets, 73, 258; subject or audience for WW's poetry, 42, 49, 63, 111, 148, 235, 250, 252, 255, 272; tours and visits: Continent (1820), 104, 290,

France, 228, 265, 267, Gallow Hill, 228, Germany, 74, 110, 243, 276, Isle of Man, 324, Rampside (Cumberland), 288, 333, Scotland (1803), 87, 126, 131, 165, 279–80, 284, Scotland (1822), 388, Valley of Stones, 39–40, 218, visit to Thelwall, 44, Wye Valley, 66, 250

WRITINGS:

Address to a Child, During a Boisterous Winter Evening. By a Female Friend of the Author, 37, 217; *The Cottager to her Infant. By a Female Friend*, 54, 231–2; *Excursion on the Banks of Ullswater*, November 1805, 390; *Floating Island*, 191, 369; *Journals*, 34, 87, 88, 105, 131, 133, 225, 231, 235, 237, 244, 245–6, 253, 254, 256, 258, 290, 297, 309, 380; *Journal of a Tour of Continent*, 1820, 104, 290–2; *Loving and Liking: Irregular Verses, Addressed to a Child*, 56, 235; *The Mother's Return. By the Same*, 37, 217; *Recollections of a Tour Made in Scotland* A.D. 1803, 18, 87, 275, 277, 315, 317, 345

Wordsworth, Gordon Graham, 231, 374

Wordsworth, Isabella (Curwen), 128, 310

Wordsworth, Jane Stanley, 128, 310

Wordsworth, John (Wordsworth's brother), 222, 346; his books, 91; death at sea, 118, 257, 302; in Grasmere, 46, 72, 257; subject of WW's poems, 118, 165, 227, 298, 302, 346

Wordsworth, John (Wordsworth's nephew), 310, 357

Wordsworth, John (Wordsworth's son), 122, 140, 141, 146, 241, 304, 321, 322, 324, 330, 361–2, 365, 383

Wordsworth, John (WW's father), 287

Wordsworth, Mary (Hutchinson) [MW], *passim*, 394; additions and corrections to Notes, 37–217 *passim* in manuscript notes, 230, 243; planning garden at Coleorton, 81, 95, 266, 284; role in producing Notes, 20, 24, 29–30; source for or contributor to WW's poems, 20, 54, 56, 62, 105, 174, 244; subject or audience, 52, 62, 67, 243, 244, 369; tours with WW, 12–13, 77, 82, 89, 99, 104–5, 111, 136, 278, 290, 327

Wordsworth, Thomas, 66–7, 74, 250, 259

Wordsworth, William
- ART AND ARTISTS; Beaumont's paintings of Bredon Hill and Cloud Hill, 74, *The Thorn*, 64, and *Piel Castle in a Storm*, 151, 333; comparative gifts of painter and poet, 133; Margaret Gillies's portraits, 78, 191, 369; James Holmes's *The Gleaner*, 125, 307; Nollekin's sculpted busts, 144, 327–8; Pickersgill, 274; Raphael's *The Baptist*, 184; anecdote concerning Titian's painting of *Last Supper*, 130, 313
- CURRENT AFFAIRS AND POLITICS; alms-giving and the poor law, 148–9; child labour and Chartism, 213–6; corrupting influence of power, 94–5; enclosure of Inglewood Forest, 135; French Revolution, 55, 66, 94, 117–8, 193–4, 197, 283, 300, 341, 368; Italian independence movement, 185–6; manufacturing in Lake District, 213; Oxford Tractarian Movement, 106, 179, 294, 355; reform bill (1832), 128, 140, 310, 322, 329; social and political reform, 128, 162–3; Spanish resistance to Napoleon, 94–5
- FAMILY; death of daughter Catherine, 37, 74, 259, 261, 352; death of his son Thomas, 67, 74, 259, 352; death of SH, 76, 130; DW's childhood, 37, 147; DW's illness, 56, 191, 261, 369–70; his children, 48, 60, 68; his brother John's character, 118–19
- FRIENDS (*see also entries for each*); deaths of Coleridge and Lamb, 153–4; Crabbe, 155–6; Joseph Fawcett, 197–8; Mrs Fermor, 151–2; Mrs Hemans, 157–8; Mary Lamb, 154; Owen Lloyd, 189–90; William Pearson, 205–6, 378; Thomas Poole, 55, 149–50, 234, 332; Edward Rowlandson, 167–8; Scott's illness and misfortunes, 137–8, 176–7; Thomas Wilkinson, 114–6
- INTERESTS AND OPINIONS; ancient monuments, 43–4, 48, 84, 115–6; Church history and practices, 46, 76, 89–90, 105–6, 128–9, 132, 198, 202–3, 214, 292, 294; coach travel and coachmen, 82, 85–6, 143; cottage industry (wool and flax), 75–6, 119–20; sound and echoes, 66, 72, 147, 181–2; education of children, 187–8, 213–4; effects of sudden wealth, 207; gardens and gardening, 57, 81, 126–7, 172–8, 188; inadequacies of Rydal Chapel, 124–5; local customs, 55–6, 61–2, 65,

81–2, 128–9, 202; London life, 59, 63; military character, 117–8; natural beauty, appreciation of, 50–1, 126–7, 142–3; natural beauty, human destruction of, 52, 72, 104–5, 172–3, 206–7; praise of great and good men, 182–3; removal of swans from Lake Windermere, 50

LITERATURE; *Anderson's British Poets*, importance of, 90–1; Byron's character as a poet, 147, 178, 345–6; classical imagery and myth, 87–8, 121–2; classification of his poems, 162; close observation, value of, 49–50, 127; criticism by others, 38, 43, 59, 102, 120; criticism, language of, 190; imaginative versus matter-of-fact style, 38; Milton's sonnets, 73; morning voluntaries, 148; narrative, general rule of, 163; natural appearances in poetry, 51, 142, 164; philosophy in literature, use of, 159–60; poetic composition, habits and hazards of, 38–42, 48–50, 81–2, 101–2, 123; poet versus painter, their comparative gifts, 133; poetic names of flowers, 182; Pope, versification in, 210–11, *Rime of Ancient Mariner*, contributions to, 40–1; Scott's narrative style compared with his, 102–3; stanza form, experiments with, 87–8, 97, 189; tyranny of the object, 173–4, 180–1;

ON HIS OWN LIFE; arrival in Cumberland (1799), 73; Cambridge years, 109–10; childhood and school days, 37, 52, 55, 60, 62, 98–9, 108–9, 121, 145, 147, 150, 159–60, 186–7, 204–5; condition of his eyes, 122, 136; experiences 'abyss of idealism', 159–60; loss of hearing, 181–2; marriage, 52, 80; passion for wandering, 195; planting yews in Grasmere churchyard, 170–1, 204; resolution to write poetry, 49–50

VISITS AND JOURNEYS; Thelwall's visit to Nether Stowey (1797), 45; Alfoxden (1841), 13, 16–17, 39–42, 44–5, 54–5, 57, 61, 64–5, 70–1, 108, 110–12, 148–9, 194; Black Comb, 68, 252, 284; Bootle and southwest coast of Cumberland (1811), 95, 166, 275, 348; Cambridge on Dora's pony, 85; Coleorton, 57, 63, 65, 81–2, 85, 92, 95, 107, 152, 230, 236–7, 243, 266, 272, 284, 292–3; Continent (1820), 104–5; Duddon Valley (1789), 98–9; Duddon Valley (1840), 98–102; France (1790), 59, 240; France (1791–2), 51, 226; France (1802), 82, 92; Germany (1799), 112–3, 165, 243–4; Holland and the Rhine val-

ley (1828), 68–9, 126, 253–4; Ilam and Dovedale (1788), 183–4, 359; Ireland (1828), 69–70, 134; Isle of Wight, Salisbury Plain, Wye valley (1793), 39, 70, 163; Italy (1837), 174–86; River Eden (1833), 144; Scotland (1803), 87–9, 131; Scotland (1814), 77–8, 89–90; Scotland (1831), 131–39; Scotland (1833), 140–4, 321; Sockburn, 55, 65, 116; Stockton-on-Tees (1807), 101; Ullswater and Lyulph's Tower (1826), 146; Vale of Newlands (1826), 129; Valley of Stones (1798), 39; Wales (1824), 82–3; Wensleydale (1802), 80; Wye valley (1798), 66; Yorkshire, 80, 119, 228, 248, 265
Wordsworth, William Jr, 141, 230, 237, 287, 324
Yewdale, Jonathan and Betty, 201

Index, Part Two: Wordsworth's Writings

[Please note: page numbers are not provided, as these titles are searchable in the electronic edition of which this is a print-out]

A fairer face of evening cannot be
A little onward lend thy guiding hand
A narrow girdle of rough stones and crags
A Poet!—He hath put his heart to school
A slumber did my spirit seal
A volant Tribe of Bards on earth are found
A whirl-blast from behind the hill
A Youth too certain of his power to wade
Address to Kilchurn-Castle, Upon Loch Awe
Address to the Clouds
Address to the Scholars of the Village School of ——
Addressed To My Daughter, Dora (see *The Longest Day*)
Adventures an Salisbury Plain
Aerial Rock—whose solitary brow
Affliction of Margaret, The
After Leaving Italy
Ah why deceive ourselves! by no mere fit
Alice Fell; Or, Poverty
All praise the Likeness by thy skill portrayed
Among the Ruins of a Convent in the Apennines
Anecdote for Fathers, Showing How the Practice of Lying May be Taught
Animal Tranquillity and Decay. A Sketch
Armenian Lady's Love, The
Army of Clouds! ye winged Host in troops
Artegal and Elidure
As indignation mastered grief, my tongue
As leaves are to the tree whereon they grow

Aspects of Christianity in America
At Albano ('Days passed—and Monte Calvo would not clear')
At Applethwaite. Near Keswick. 1804
At Bala-Sala, Isle of Man. (Supposed to be Written by a Friend of the Author.)
At Bologna. in Remembrance of the Late Insurrections ('Ah why deceive ourselves! by no mere fit')
At Dover ('From the Pier's Head, musing, and with increase')
At Florence ('Under the shadow of a stately Pile')
At Florence.—From M. Angelo ('Eternal Lord! eased of a cumbrous load'), 149
At Florence.—From Michael Angelo ('Rapt above earth by power of one fair face')
At Rome ('Is this, ye Gods, the Capitolian Hill')
At Rome ('They-who have seen the noble Roman's scorn')
At the Grave of Burns. 1803
At Vallombrosa
The Avon. (A Feeder of the Annan.) ('Avon—a precious, an imm:n1al name!')
Beaumont! it was thy wish that I should rear
Before the Picture of the Baptist, by Raphael, in the Gallery at Florence
Beggars, The
Behold an emblem of our human mind
Between Namur and Liege ('What lovelier home could gentle Fancy choose')
Black Demons hovering o'er his mitred head
Blind Highland Boy, The
Borderers, The. A Tragedy. (Composed 1795–6)
Bothwell Castle. (Passed Unseen, on Account of Stormy Weather.)
Brothers, The
Brownie, The

By a Blest Husband guided, Mary came
By a Retired Mariner. (A Friend of the Author.)
(By the Seaside)
By the Side of the Grave Some Years After
By vain affections unenthralled
Cave of Staffa ('Thanks for the lessons of this Spot-fit school')
Cenotaph
Character of the Happy Warrior
A Character
Characteristics of a Child Three Years Old
Chatsworth! thy stately mansion, and the pride
Childless Father, The
Church to be Erected
Complaint, A
Complaint of a Forsaken Indian Woman, The
Composed after a Journey Across the Hambleton Hills, Yorkshire
Composed After Reading a Newspaper of the Day
Composed at Cora Linn, In Sight of Wallace's Tower
Composed at Rydal on May Morning, 1838
Composed by the Sea-shore
Composed During a Storm
Composed in Roslin Chapel, During a Storm
Composed in the Glen of Loch Etive
Composed on a May Morning, 1838
Composed on the Banks of a Rocky Stream
Composed on the Same Morning
Composed Upon an Evening of Extraordinary Splendour and Beauty
Composed upon Westminster Bridge, Sept. 3
Composed when a probability existed of our being obliged to quit Rydal Mount as a Residence
Concerning the Relations of Great Britain, Spain, and Portugal...as Affected by the Convention of Cintra

Continued (After Leaving Italy)
Continued (At Bologna, in Remembrance of the Late Insurrections) ('Hard task! exclaim the undisciplined, to lean')
Continued (Church to be Erected)
Contrast, The, The Parrot and the Wren
Convict, The
Could I the priest's consent have gained
Countess' Pillar
Cuckoo at Laverna, The. May 25th, 1837
Cuckoo-Clock, The
Daffodils, The (see 'I wandered lonely as a cloud')
Danish Boy, The. A Fragment
Dear Child of Nature, let them rail
Dear to the Loves, and to the Graces vowed
Decay of Piety
Departed Child! I could forget thee once
Departure from the Vale of Grasmere. August, 1803
Description of the Scenery of the Lakes in the North of England, A
Descriptive Sketches Taken During a Pedestrian Tour Among the Alps
Devotional Incitements
Dion. (See Plutarch)
Dirge
Dishonoured Rock and Ruin! that, by law
Dogmatic Teachers, of the snow-white fur
Eagles. Composed at Dunollie Castle in the Bay of Oban
Earth has not anything to show more fair
Ecclesiastical Sonnets. In Series
Eden! till now thy beauty had I viewed
Effusion, In the Pleasure-Ground on the Banks of the Bran, near Dunkeld
Egyptian Maid, The: Or, The Romance of the Water Lily
1830 ('Chatsworth! thy stately mansion, and the pride')
Ejaculation at the Grave of Burns

Elegiac Musings in the Grounds of Coleorton Hall, the Seat of the Late Sir G. H. Beaumont, Bart.
Elegiac Stanzas, Suggested by a Picture of Peele Castle, in a Storm, Painted by Sir George Beaumont
Elegiac Stanzas. (Addressed to Sir G.H.B. Upon the Death of His Sister–in–Law.)
Elegiac Verses in Memory of My Brother, John Wordsworth
Ellen Irwin: Or, The Braes of Kirtle
Emigrant Mother, The
Epistle to Sir George Howland Beaumont, Bart. From the South-west Coast of Cumberland—1811
Epitaph in the Chapel-Yard of Langdale, Westmoreland
Epitaphs and Elegiac Pieces
Epitaphs Translated from Chiabrera
Ere with cold beads of midnight dew
Ethereal Minstrel! pilgrim of the sky
Even so for me a Vision sanctified
Evening Voluntaries
An Evening Walk, Addressed to a Young Lady
The Excursion
Expostulation and Reply
Extempore Effusion Upon the Death of James Hogg
Extract from the Conclusion of a Poems, Composed in Anticipation of Leaving School ('Dear native regions')
Fact, and an Imagination, A; Or, Canute and Alfred. on the Sea-Shore
Fair Land! Thee all men greet with joy; how few
Fair Prime of life! were it enough to gild
Fallen, and diffused into a shapeless heap
Farewell Lines
Farewell, A
Farmer of Tilsbury Vale, The
Feel for the wrongs to universal ken

Female Vagrant, The
Fidelity
Filial Piety. (On the Way-side between Preston and Liverpool.)
A Flower-Garden, At Coleorton Hall, Leicestershire
Flowers
Fly, some kind Harbinger, to Grasmere-dale
For a Seat in the Groves of Coleorton
Force of Prayer, The: Or, The Founding of Bolton Priory. A Tradition
The Foregoing Subject Resumed (Lines Suggested by a Portrait from the Pencil of F. Stone)
Foresight
Forsaken, The
Fountain, The. A Conversation
Four fiery steeds impatient of the rein
French Revolution, As It Appeared to Enthusiasts at its Commencement. Reprinted from The Friend
From the dark chambers of dejection freed
From the Pier's Head, musing, and with increase
From the Italian of Michael Angelo
From the Restoration to the Present Times ('I saw the figure of a lovely Maid')
From the Same (From the Italian of Michael Angelo) ('No mortal object did these eyes behold')
Gipsies
The Gleaner. (Suggested by a Picture.)
Gold and Silver Fishes in a Vase
Goody Blake and Harry Gill. A True Story
Grave-Stone Upon the Floor in the Cloisters of Worcester Cathedral, A
The Green Linnet
Grief, thou hast lost an ever ready friend
A Guide Through the District of the Lakes
Guilt and Sorrow: or, Incidents upon Salisbury Plain

Hard was thy Durance, Queen, compared with ours
Hart-Leap Well
Hart's-horn Tree, Near Penrith
Hast thou seen, with flash incessant
Haunted Tree, The. To ——
Her Eyes are Wild (The Mad Mother)
Here stood an Oak, that long had borne affixed
High bliss is only for a higher state
Highland Broach, The
Highland Hut
Hint from the Mountains For Certain Political Pretenders
Home at Grasmere
Horn of Egremont Castle, The
How clear, how keen, how marvellously bright
How rich that forehead's calm expanse
Humanity, xx
I come, ye little noisy Crew
I grieved for Buonaparte, with a vain
I met Louisa in the shade
I saw the figure of a lovely Maid
I shiver, Spirit fierce and bold
I travelled among unknown men
I wandered lonely as a cloud
I watch, and long have watched, with calm regret
Idiot Boy, The
Idle Shepherd Boys, The: Or, Dungeon-Ghyll Force
If Nature, for a favourite child
If the whole weight of what we think and feel
If thou indeed derive thy light from Heaven
If to Tradition faith be due
If with old love of you, dear Hills! I share
Immured in Bothwell's towers, at times the Brave

In a Garden of the Same ('Oft is the medal faithful to its trust')
In Allusion to Various Recent Histories and Notices of the French Revolution ('Portentous change when History can appear')
In desultory walk through orchard grounds
In the Frith of Clyde, Ailsa Crag. (July 17.)
In the Grounds of Coleorton, the Seat of Sir George Beaumont, Bart., Leicestershire. 1808 ('The embowering rose, the acacia, and the pine')
In the Sound of Mull
In the Woods of Rydal ('Wild Redbreast! hadst thou at Jimima's lip')
In these fair vales hath many a Tree
In youth from rock to rock I went
Incident at Brugés
Incident Characteristic of a Favourite Dog
Infant M—— M——, The
Influence of Natural Objects in Calling Forth and Strengthening the Imagination in Boyhood and Early Youth. From an Unpublished Poem
Inscribed Upon a Rock ('Pause, Traveller! whosoe'er thou be')
Inscriptions Supposed to be Found in and Near a Hermit's Cell, 235
Intended for a Stone in the Grounds of Rydal Mount ('In these fair vales hath many a Tree')
Intent on gathering wool from hedge and brake
Invocation to the Earth. February, 1816
Is this, ye Gods, the Capitdian Hill
Isle of Man ('A Youth too certain of his power to wade')
It is a beauteous Evening, calm and free
It is no Spirit who from heaven hath flown
It was an April morning: fresh and clear
I've watched you now a short half-hour
Itinerary Sonnets. Composed or Suggested During a Tour in Scotland, in the Summer of 1833
A Jewish Family

The King of Sweden
The Kitten and Falling Leaves
The Labourer's Noon-day Hymn
Lady! the songs of Spring were in the grove
Lament of Mary Queen of Scots. On the Eve of a New Year
The Last of the Flock
Let other Bards of angels sing
Liberty. (Sequel to the Above.) [Addressed to a Friend: The Gold and Silver Fishes having been Removed to a Pool in the Pleasure-Ground of Rydal Mount.]
Life with yon Lamb, like day, is just begun
Lines Left upon a Seat in a Yew-tree, which stands near the lake of Esthwaite, on a desolate part of the shore, commanding a beautiful prospect
Lines on the Expected Invasion. 1803
Lines Suggested by a Portrait from the Pencil of F. Stone
Lines Written in Early Spring
Lines Written in the Album of the Countess of Lonsdale. Nov. 5, 1834
Lines Written While Sailing in a Boat at Evening
Lines, Composed a Few Miles Above Tintern Abbey, on Revisiting the Banks of the Wye During a Tour. July 13, 1798
Lo! where the Moon along the sky
Long time his pulse hath ceased to beat
Longest Day, The. Addressed to ——— (The Longest Day. Addressed to My Daughter Dora [1850])
Look at the fate of summer flowers
Louisa. After Accompanying Her On a Mountain Excursion
Love Lies Bleeding
Lowther ('Lowther! in thy majestic Pile are seen')
Lucy Gray: Or, Solitude
Lyre! though such power do in thy magic live
Lyrical Ballads
Mad Mother, The (see *Her Eyes are Wild*)

Malham Cove
Mark the concentred hazels that enclose
Mary Queen of Scots. (Landing at the Mouth of the Derwent, Workington.)
Maternal Grief
Matthew ('If Nature, for a favourite child')
Memorials of a Tour in Italy. 1837
Memorials of a Tour in Scotland, 1803
Memorials of a Tour in Scotland. 1814
Memorials of a Tour in Scotland in 1833 (see *Itinerary Sonnets*)
Memorials of a Tour on the Continent, 1820
Memory ('A pen—to register; a key')
Methought I saw the footsteps of a throne
Michael. A Pastoral Poem
Miscellaneous Poems (1820)
Miscellaneous Sonnets
Monument Commonly Called Long Meg and Her Daughters, The, Near the River Eden
Monument of Mrs. Howard, (by Nollekens,) In Wetheral Church, Near Corby, on the Banks of the Eden
Morning Exercise, A
Mourn, Shepherd, near thy old grey stone
Musings Near Aquapendente. April, 1837
My heart leaps up when I behold
New Church-Yard
Night Thought, A
Nightingale, The
Night-piece, A
No mortal object did these eyes behold
Norman Boy, The
Not in the lucid intervals of life
Not Love, not War, nor the tumultuous swell
November 1 ('How clear, how keen, how marvellously bright')

November, 1836 ('Even so for me a Vision sanctified')
Nunnery
Nun's Well, Brigham
Nutting
O Friend! I know not which way I must look
Oak and the Broom. A Pastoral, The
Ode to Duty
Ode to Lycoris. May, 1817
Ode, Composed on May Morning
Ode. Intimations of Immortality from Recollections of Early Childhood
Ode. The Morning of the Day Appointed for a General Thanksgiving. January 18, 1816
Oft is the medal faithful to its trust
Oh dearer far than light and life are dear
Oh what a Wreck! how changed in mien and speech
Old Cumberland Beggar, The
On a High Part of the Coast of Cumberland Easter Sunday, April 7. The Author's Sixty-third Birth-day
On a Portrait of the Duke of Wellington, Upon the Field of Waterloo, by Haydon
On Man, on Nature, and on Human Life
On Seeing a Needlecase in the Fonn of a Harp, The Work of E.M.S.
On the Banks of a Rocky Stream
On the Departure of Sir Walter Scott from Abbotsford, for Naples
On the Frith of Clyde. (In a Steam-Boat.)
On the Power of Sound
On the Same Subject (To a Painter)
On the Sight of a Manse in the South of Scotland
Once I could hail (howe'er serene the sky)
Once on the top of Tynwald's formal mound
Pansies, lilies, kingcups, daisies
Parsonage in Oxfordshire, A

Pass of Kirkstone, The
Pastor and Patriot!–at whose bidding rise
Pause, Traveller! whosoe'er thou be
'People! your chains are severing link by link
Personal Talk
Pet Lamb, The
Peter Bell. A Tale
Pilgrim Fathers
Pilgrim's Dream, The: Or, the Star and the Glow-worm
Pillar of Trajan, The
Pine of Monte Mario at Rome, The
Place of Burial in the South of Scotland, A
Pleasures newly found are sweet
Poems (1815) [search on Poems (1815) or the date alone]
Poems Dedicated to National Independence and Liberty
Poems Founded on the Affections
Poems on the Naming of Places
Poems, Chiefly of Early and Late Years (1842)[search on Poems (1842) or the date alone]
Poems, in Two Volumes (1807) [search on the bracketed date]
Poet and the Caged Turtledove, The
Poetical Works (1827) [search on the bracketed date]
Poetical Works (1836–7) [as above]
Poetical Works (1841) [as above]
Poetical Works (1849–50) [as above]
Poetical Works (1857) [as above]
Poet's Dream, The, Sequel to The Norman Boy
Poet's Epitaph, A
Point Rash Judgement (see 'A narrow girdle of rough stones and crags')
Poor Robin
Portentous change when History can appear'
Power of Music

Preface to *Poems* (1815)
Prelude, The, Or Growth of a Poets Mind
Prelude Prefixed to the Volume entitled Poems Chiefly of Early and Late Years
Presentiments
Primrose of the Rock, The
Prospectus to *The Recluse*
Rapt above earth by power of one fair face
Recluse, The
Redbreast chasing the Butterfly, The
Redbreast, The. (Suggested in a Westmoreland Cottage.)
Remembering how thou didst beguile
Remembrance of Collins, Composed on the Thames Near Richmond
Repentance. A Pastoral Ballad
Resolution and Independence
Retirement
Reverie of Poor Susan, The
River Duddon, The. A Series of Sonnets
River Eden, The, Cumberland
Rob Roy's Grave
Roman Antiquities Discovered at Bishopstone, Herefordshire
Rural Architecture
Rural Illusions
Russian Fugitive, The
Ruth
Sailor's Mother, The
Salisbury Plain
Say, ye far-travelled clouds, far-seeing hills
Scene in Venice ('Black Demons hovering o'er his mitred head')
Scorn not the Sonnet; Critic, you have frowned
Select Views
September, 1815 ('While not a leaf seems faded; while the fields')

September, 1819 ('The sylvan slopes with corn-clad fields')
Sequel to the Nonnan Boy, (see *The Poet's Dream*)
She dwelt among the untrodden ways
She was a Phantom of delight
Simon Lee, The Old Huntsman With an Incident in Which He Was Concerned
Since risen from ocean, ocean to defy
Somnambulist, The
Song at the Feast of Brougham Castle, Upon the Restoration of Lord Clifford, the Shepherd, to the Estates and Honours of His Ancestors
Song for the Spinning Wheel. Founded Upon a Belief Prevalent Among the Pastoral Vales of Westmoreland
Song for the Wandering Jew
Sonnet, on seeing Miss HELEN MARIA WILLIAMS weep at a Tale of Distress
Sonnet. Composed at —— Castle
Sonnets Dedicated to Liberty
Sparrow's Nest, The
St. Catherine of Ledbury
Stanzas suggested in a Steam-Boat off St. Bees' Heads, on the Coast of Cumberland
Stanzas Written In My Pocket-copy of Thomson's Castle of Indolence
Star-gazers
Stay, bold Adventurer; rest awhile thy limbs
Stay near me—do not take thy flight
Strange fits of passion have I known
Stray Pleasures
Stretched on the dying Mother's lap, lies dead
Sweet Flower! belike one day to have
Suggested by a Beautiful Ruin upon one of the Islands of Loch Lomond, a Place Chosen for the Retreat of a Solitary Individual, from whom this Habitation Acquired the name of The Brownie's Cell

Suggested by a Picture of the Bird of Paradise
Suggested by a View from an Eminence in Inglewood Forest
Surprised by joy—impatient as the Wind
Tables Turned, The: An Evening Scene on the Same Subject
The Baptist might have been ordain'd to cry
The cock is crowing
The embowering rose, the acacia, and the pine
The fairest, brightest hues of either fade
The floods are roused, and will not soon be weary
The forest huge of ancient Caledon
The gentlest Poet, with free thoughts endowed
The leaves that rustled on this oak-crowned hill
The massy Ways, carried across these heights
The most alluring clouds that mount the sky
The prayers I make will then be sweet indeed
The sun has long been set
The Sun is couched, the sea-fowl gone to rest
The Sun, that seemed so mildly to retire
The voice of song from distant lands shall call
The wind is now thy organist;—a clank
There is a change, and I am poor
There is a little unpretending Rill
There is an Eminence,—of these our hills
'There!' said a Stripling, pointing with meet pride
There was a Boy
There's not a nook within this solemn Pass
This Land of Rainbows (spanning glens whose walls
This lawn, a carpet all alive
Thorn, The
Though I beheld at first with blank surprise
Though narrow be that old Man's cares, and near
Thought of a Briton on the Subjugation of Switzerland

Thought on the Seasons (Thoughts on the Seasons)
Thoughts Suggested the Day Following on the Banks of Nith, Near the Poet's Residence
Three years she grew in sun and shower
Three Cottage Girls, The
Through Cumbrian Wilds, in many a Mountain cove
'Tis He whose yester evening's high disdain
'Tis said, that some have died for love
To —— ('Let other Bards of angels sing')
To —— ('Look at the fate of summer flowers')
To —— ('Oh dearer far than light and life are dear')
To —— ('"Wait, prithee, wait!" this answer Lesbia threw')
To ——, *In Her Seventieth Year*
To ——, *On Her First Ascent to the Summit of Helvellyn*
To ——. *Upon the Birth of Her First-born Child, March, 1833*
To a Butterfly ('I've watched you now a short half-hour')
To a Butterfly ('Stay near me—do not take thy flight')
To a Child, Written in Her Album
To a Friend. (On the Banks of the Derwent.)
To a good Man of most dear memory
To a Highland Girl. (At Inversneyde, Upon Loch Lomond.)
To a Painter
To a Sexton
To a Sky-Lark ('Ethereal Minstrel! pilgrim of the sky')
To a Young Lady, Who had been Reproached for Taking Long Walks in the Country
To B.R. Haydon, on Seeing his Picture of Napoleon Buonaparte on the Island of St. Helena
To H.C. Six Years Old
To Joanna
To M.H.

To May

To My Sister. Written at a Small Distance From My House, and Sent By My Little Boy

To Rotha Q——

To the Author's Portrait

To the Clouds, (see *Address to the Clouds*)

To the Cuckoo ('O blithe New-comer! I have heard')

To the Daisy ('Bright Flower! whose home is everywhere')

To the Daisy ('In youth from rock to rock I went')

To the Daisy ('Sweet Flower! belike one day to have')

To the Daisy ('With little here to do or see')

To the Lady Beaumont ('Lady! the songs of Spring were in the grove')

To the Lady E.B. and the Hon. Miss P. Composed in the Grounds of Plass Newidd, near Llangolen, 1824

To the Lady Fleming, On Seeing the Foundation Preparing for the Erection of Rydal Chapel, Westmoreland

To the Memory of Raisley Calvert

To the Moon

To the same flower (To the Small Celandine) ('Pleasures newly found are sweet')

To the Same (Ode to Lycoris)

To the Small Celandine ('Pansies, lilies, kingcups, daisies')

To the Sons of Burns, After Visiting the Grave of Their Father

To the Spade of a Friend. (An Agriculturist.) Composed While We Were Labouring Together in his Pleasure-Ground

To the Supreme Being

Too frail to keep the lofty vow

Tradition, be thou mute! Oblivion, throw

Tradition of Oken [Oker] Hill in Darley Dale, Derbyshire, A

Triad, The

Trosachs, The ('There's not a nook within this solemn Pass')

Tuft of Primroses, The

Two April Mornings, The
Two Thieves, The: Or, The Last Stage of Avarice
Tynwald Hill
Unpublished Tour, An
Upon Seeing a Coloured Drawing of the Bird of Paradise in an Album
Upon the Same Occasion (September, 1819)
Upon the Sight of a Beautiful Picture, Painted by Sir GR. Beaumont, Bart.
Vale of Esthwaite, The
Vaudracour and Julia
Vernal Ode
View from the Top of Black Comb
The Waggoner
'Wait, prithee, wait!' this answer Lesbia threw
The Warning, A Sequel to the Foregoing (To ——. Upon the Birth of Her First-born Child, March, 1833)
The Waterfall and the Eglantine
Water-Fowl
We are Seven
Well worthy to be magnified are they
What lovelier home could gentle Fancy choose
What mischief cleaves to unsubdued regret
When first, descending from the moorlands
When, to the attIactions of the busy world
Whence that low voice?—A whisper from the heart
While Anna's peers and early Jiaymates tread
While beams of orient light shoot wide and high
While not a leaf seems faded; while the fields
While the poor gather round till the end of time
The White Doe of Rylstone: Or, The Fate of the Nortons
Who swerves from innocence, who makes divorce
Why art thou silent! Is thy love a plant
The Widow on Windermere Side

The Wild Duck's Nest
Wild Redbreast! hadst thou at Jemima's lip
Wisdom and Spirit of the universe
The Wishing-Gate
The Wishing-Gate Destroyed
With little here to do or see
A Wren's Nest
Written after the Death of Charles Lamb
Written at the Request of Sir George Beaumont, Bart., and in his Name, for an Urn, Placed by Him at the Termination of a Newly-Planted Avenue, in the Same Grounds
Written in a Blank Leaf of Macpherson's Ossian
Written in Germany, On One of the Coldest Days of the Century
Written in London, September, 1802 ('O Friend! I know not which way I must look')
Written in March, While Resting on the Bridge at the Foot of Brother's Water
Written in the Album of a Child
Written with a Slate Pencil on a Stone, on the Side of the Mountain of Black Comb ('Stay, bold Adventurer; rest awhile thy limbs')
Yarrow Revisited and Other Poems (1835)
Yarrow Revisited, and Other Poems, Composed (Two Excepted) During a Tour in Scotland, and on the English Border, in the Autumn of 1831 (the sequence)
Yarrow Revisited (the poem)
Yarrow Unvisited
Yarrow Visited, September, 1814
Ye trees! whose slender roots entwine
Yes! hope may with my strong desire keep pace
Yes, it was the Mountain Echo
Yew-trees

Also from Humanities-Ebooks

John Beer, *Blake's Humanism*
John Beer, *The Achievement of E M Forster*
John Beer, *Coleridge the Visionary*
Jared Curtis, ed., *The Fenwick Notes of William Wordsworth*
Steven Duncan, *Analytic Philosophy of Religion: its History since 1955*
Richard Gravil, ed., *Master Narratives: Tellers and Telling in the English Novel*
Richard Gravil and Molly Lefebure, eds., *The Coleridge Connection: Essays for Thomas McFarland*
John K. Hale, *Milton as Multilingual: Selected Essays 1982–2004*
John Lennard, *Of Modern Dragons and other essays on Genre Fiction*
Colin Nicholson, *Fivefathers: Interviews with Twentieth-Century Scottish Poets*
W J B Owen, *Understanding 'The Prelude'*
Keith Sagar, *D. H. Lawrence: Poet*
William Wordsworth, *The Convention of Cintra*